Thy Will Be Done

THE CHERUBIM

JACQUELINE BELL

authorHOUSE®

AuthorHouse™
1663 Liberty Drive
Bloomington, IN 47403
www.authorhouse.com
Phone: 1-800-839-8640

Published by AuthorHouse   9/12/2012

ISBN: 978-1-4772-3015-2 (sc)
ISBN: 978-1-4772-3014-5 (hc)
ISBN: 978-1-4772-3016-9 (e)

Chapter 1

November 2005

He had said good-bye to the other, waving a fond farewell from the doorstep. They had shook hands and one of them had smiled bravely, but each knew they would never meet again. Quickly closing the door on the crisp night air, he hurried along the now chilly corridor of the dim old house. He didn't have time for any modern conveniences like central heating, preferring the old-fashioned coal fires much to the exasperation of his now deceased wife; she hated coal fires with a passion – hated the mess and the inconvenience of it all. He allowed himself a small smile in remembrance of how she used to complain at this time of year when the weather changed and the cold used to seep through the house like an unwelcome visitor. Now that he was on his own, he found it a nuisance to maintain any sort of warmth around the place, preferring to huddle in layers of jumpers.

Over the years since his wife's death he had removed himself from the vast rambling house to locate himself in one corner of it … the library. This was where he felt happiest, surrounded by his books and where he kept the vast majority of his work.

He paid a lady from the village to come in three days a week to maintain some semblance of order about the place. Mrs Evans always left him ready cooked meals in the freezer and numerous Post-it notes to remind him to eat them.

He had found one only this morning stuck to the kettle.

She had told him time and time again that she didn't mind coming in every day to check on him, but he cherished his privacy above all else and so he had to be firm with her.

He told her he could perfectly manage the rest of the time, but to hear Mrs Evans talk you would think he was some doddery old pensioner who couldn't look after himself.

He hurried on; there was little time and he wanted to be prepared. Shadows sprang out at him as he reached the dimly lit library. The roaring fire he had made for his guest was dying now and cast a dull red glow around the room, but he was heedless of any warmth that remained within it.

He nudged the remnants of some paper that had spilled out of the grate with his foot, setting them alight in the glowing embers.

Nothing now remained and he smiled to himself as he remembered the blaze.

He turned away from the fire and slowly walked round his desk, feeling every one of his years. His mop of white hair flopped into his eyes, which were useless now without his glasses and his back, now slightly bent, ached especially in this cold weather.

He felt old and tired.

He had actually boasted that his tall thin frame had never carried an extra pound and many of his colleagues remarked that he looked the same as he did in his youth.

He felt old and tired.

He knew they were just flattering him; he saw it when he looked in the mirror only too well. His frame might be the same, but the eyes held the key, and they looked more haunted the older he got.

He should be enjoying his retirement, but this was not to be; his work was too important. A large sigh escaped him as he eased himself down into his large leather chair and he pulled his thick cardigan around him, needing its warmth. Had they made the right decision?

They had talked for a long time, the two of them planned every action, but he knew it would do no good.

It had found them and it wanted what they knew and now nothing would stop it. He gathered all the papers on his desk into a neat pile and straightened the now empty box his guest had brought and waited. Sitting there in the dying fire's glow, his mind drifted back over time, back to the time when they were young men with the entire world and all that it offered in front of them.

2

He eased his back into a better position in the chair and reaching over; he saw that his hand was trembling as he lifted the glass of whiskey he had placed on the table earlier. The liquid was smooth and well blended, his favourite and he felt it slide down with an ease of long use, dulling a little the fear he had kept locked away in the far reaches of his mind.

Now it was back with him, stronger than before!

Feeling the liquid warm him as it reached his stomach, he smiled to himself, savouring each mouthful; another few of these, he thought, and even his courage might return.

Still he waited.

His head tilted back and he let his eyes close, bringing the memories closer. Once again he could hear their happy banter and for a moment the bittersweet feeling of nostalgia for all the innocence they had started out with and lost, brought a fragile smile to his trembling lips.

1955

"What have you found now?" Jonathan called over in response to Davy's cry of "Eureka!" He stopped momentarily in his exploration of the many books he had found to brush the mop of unruly hair out of his eyes.

He choked a little on the dust that was flying around with his endeavours.

"Well, wouldn't you like to know, Mr 'Top Grades I'm an Expert Hawker,'" responded Davy, hugging the manuscript to his chest.

He was the youngest of the four and many a time Henry had likened him to the red setter he used to own, he was bouncy, enthusiastic and fun to have around.

David's red hair looked aureate in the glow of the flickering candlelight and his slender frame was bent nearly double under the weight of the book he was carrying.

"Please yourself, you'll only come to me later to authenticate it," Jonathan replied with more than a little pomposity.

After all he was head of the student Archaeology Department at Oxford and had arranged this particular foray into York's church antiquity as an aid to his thesis; he was hoping that it would turn out to be the highlight of his final year. When the others heard where he was going, they were more than eager to tag along.

It had not been easy getting the permission to work down here, but they had begged and bribed numerous relatives to vouch for them; even young David's father, being only too glad he was interested in something, allotted to the church a large undisclosed amount for his son to work during the university's summer term, preferring him there than lounging in the ancestral home.

The Right Honourable Horatio David Franklin Penn-Wright, or just plain Davy to his friends, scurried over to the array of candles they had burning on the central table, brushing the dust from the volume as he went.

They were all heedless of the old and dried smell of antiquity down in this remote part of the cathedral, too excited at being allowed down here in the first place. The room had been kept locked and sealed for more years than anyone cared to remember and it was only by chance that Jonathan had found it towards the end of their uneventful field trip.

They had just entered the vault when Henry tripped and dropped his flask, and the liquid had spilled from the broken canister all over the flagstone floor, but instead of lying there, it disappeared through the cracks of the floor. Jonathan's excitement grew as he watched the liquid seep away and not wanting to wait for permission, Jonathan had lifted one of the stones. There before them was a flight of steps leading down into the bowels of the church.

The wardens had flapped around them, not wanting them to venture down, but could not give a good enough reason to stop them. So with infinite glee the troupe scurried down the steps until they came to a door that barred their way.

They jostled each other on the steps, laughing and cracking jokes about Dracula and ghosts. In a vain attempt to see more clearly, practical Henry scrabbled around in his satchel, got out his torch, and shone the thin beam down, illuminating the strands of cobwebs that had stretched across the fascia of the door. As Jonathan wiped his hand across the door, he uncovered a large brass ring, and as he turned it, he felt it move ever so slightly, but it was not until Adam had put his shoulder to it that it really moved.

They all gave a whoop when, after a rather successful shove from Adam, who found himself flying through the now open doorway, they all piled in after him, laughing. Davy scampered back up the stairs and came back with an armful of candles and they all set about lighting them with Adam's matches, as he was the only one of them that smoked. As the candles caught, the room was gradually brought into view and they stood and looked in amazement at all the old books, manuscripts, and parchments that were stacked around the room.

Jonathan and Henry exchanged a look of excitement and then, slapping each other on the back, set about searching meticulously through the old documents.

Some were too far gone to be saved, for as soon as Jonathan touched them they disintegrated between his fingers and others had been eaten by mice, but the majority looked in quite good condition.

Jonathan stopped more than once in what he was doing because he could not help but feel empathy towards the people who had built this magnificent cathedral, carving out with precision each marvellous block of stone.

He knew that most religious places were built on original pagan sites where the missionary priests of the day wanted to eradicate, or sometimes incorporate, the local religion into the fast expanding religion of the time, Catholicism. So the deeper he went into any church, the further back in time he went, until, if he was right, he would come to the very place where the pagan religions began. But not today, though. This was more than enough for him to take in; it was a wonderful find. They laughed and joked together in their excitement, their mood light.

They had been working a good part of the day and it was getting towards the time when the Minster would be shutting down. The conditions were not conducive to the work they were undertaking, but at least it was not damp down there – cold maybe, but not damp.

"I think we could do with a little more light down here; it's like working in a mine," said Davy as he flopped the tome onto the table.

Millions of little dust mites floated into the air, dancing in the candlelight. None of the four seemed to care about the drop in temperature in this unused part of the Minster. In fact, it was what had kept everything in near perfect condition. Only Henry seemed to feel the cold and he made allowances by wearing one of the myriad scarves his mother had knitted for him. Sitting on the ground with his head bent over a multitude of rolled papyrus scrolls, he was oblivious to what was going on around him.

If it wasn't for the habit he had of continually adjusting his glasses, the others would have sworn he had nodded off. He had the unkempt scruffy appearance of a born academic, taking more pride in his work than in his looks.

Adam sauntered over from his corner of the crypt, already bored with what they were doing. Of the four of them, he did not seem to take the find very seriously; he was a mathematician and an extremely good one, but he preferred to cruise through his courses with the minimal of effort needed to obtain good grades. He had a mind like a razor, as was shown often enough in his last minute assignments, but he lacked drive and commitment as Jonathan often pointed out to him.

They all had their reasons for not wanting to go home for the holidays; Jonathan and Henry preferred going on digs together and had done so since they met in their first year. So long as Henry went home for Easter and Christmas, his doting mother made allowances for him to do what he wanted during the summer vacation. Jonathan's parents, both being teachers, were more than happy to see him follow his dream of becoming an historian.

Davy, as they knew, never went home; he found the large rambling ancestral mansion too lonely, as his parents were usually away at Monte Carlo or some other place where the rich and famous gathered, leaving only a small staff to cater to him. Davy was never really interested in all the trappings of society, preferring to go wherever Jonathan had picked for their next site.

It was not as if Davy did not use the money his father threw at him, though, for many a time it opened doors where usual persuasion failed. It also provided much needed equipment that the others could not afford, and, as in this case, he paid for the accommodations for everyone while they stayed in York for the summer.

Adam seemed to join their group suddenly, having first made friends with Davy, but he provided much needed entertainment when the three of them started to get too stuffy. He cajoled and sometimes forced Henry and Jonathan out for much needed drinking sessions; Davy never needed much persuasion and he was always ready to follow where Adam led.

So between the four of them, they made up quite a party, each one a foil for the others and each one knowledgeable about something. So when they came together it was like bringing together the four quarters to make a whole. Always at the end of the holidays, like now, they all felt the loss of the imminent breakup of the group, because they would be far too busy to socialise much when they got back to Oxford, especially as it was their last year and they had to work harder than ever to achieve their own personal goals.

Adam lazily flicked specs of dirt from the sleeve of his linen jacket and sauntered over to the table as the exchange with Davy and Jonathan had sparked his interest.

"What have you found, buddy?" he enquired upon reaching Davy, using the American colloquialism he had picked up from the US teammates on the rowing crew. He slipped his arm across his friends' shoulders and together they leant forward to gaze at the book's front inscription.

"Can you make that out?" Davy enquired of Adam as they both leant nearer to the faded gold writing on the cover. Davy felt Adam's body slightly stiffen and his arm closed a little tighter round his shoulder. But Adam spoke these words in the same bored tone: "It's a mystery to me, Davy. I'm just a maths buff, not really into this mumbo jumbo. Just go for it. Open the thing."

David glanced sideways at him, his brown eyes trying to see beyond Adam's green ones. They looked cold and distant, and for a moment Davy was confused, but instead he laughed nervously at what he thought was just mock severity on Adam's face.

"Then why did you join us if you don't like being here?" Davy bravely replied, still staring into Adam's hard green eyes. Adam's mood suddenly changed, like the sun coming out from behind a dark cloud and once again he was the handsome athletic friend that Davy knew best.

"So that I can be with you guys; what on earth would I have done all summer? You didn't want to come to France with me, Davy, so I had to come with you here. We have to impress the girls when we all go out, I can't have you boasting about grand finds when we get back to Oxford and me just sitting there twiddling my thumbs. Anyway, how would you meet any girls if it wasn't for me?" said Adam as he gave Davy a playful hug.

This was perfectly true in Davy's eyes, as more than enough girls seemed to throw themselves at Adam's feet and he was just grateful he was his friend and could share in his bounty, otherwise he would never meet any girls.

For a moment Davy forgot about Adam and thought about one particular girl he had seen just before they left for the summer break.

Adam's voice cut through his thoughts as he whispered softly into his ear, "I bet I know who you're thinking about."

Davy flushed a deep shade of red at being found out. Adam, it seemed, always had an uncomfortable way of reading his thoughts. He gave his full attention back to the book and ran his fingers, gently and lovingly, across the front cover; turning to face Adam, he said in a hushed voice, "It's extremely old, even I can tell that; what do you think it's on, land usage, or a tax book?" His eyes had taken on the look of the true academic and he was practically shaking with excitement.

Adam laughed to behold such fervour; he was always amazed that Davy wanted so much to be an academic. With his looks and money he seemed more suited to being a playboy; patting him gently on the shoulder, he said, "Go for it, Davy, you never know: your name might be up there in lights along with old Jonathan over there. The most important tax book ever found." On a laugh, he turned and walked towards Jonathan.

Davy took hold of the corner of the book and gently turned the large leather bound front cover. With the turning of the page, it seemed like a hush had descended on the crypt; the far off voices of the choir that they could still hear, even this far down had fallen silent, and not a thing could be heard from the customary movement of the church or the people therein.

For some reason Jonathan recalled to mind his granny, who towards the end of her life always sat in a chair in the kitchen near the big open range in his parents' house. Once when he was little, stillness had come like the one that was happening now; it had made him stop playing and feeling confused, he had looked to his granny for consolation. Pulling his young frame onto her knee, she gently explained it was nothing to be frightened of; it was just the angels passing overheard on a mission for God.

He remembered how she had stroked his hair and hugged him to her and how he had laughed at her and at her strange old ways, but suddenly it didn't seem so funny.

They all seemed to stop what they were doing at once.

The silence seemed palpable, almost physical and then everything seemed to go in slow motion; as Jonathan started to rise from his knees, his legs suddenly felt shaky. He placed his hand against the rough wall to steady him and glanced over to Henry to see if he had been affected.

He could see that Henry too was feeling the effect of the silence, as the look on his face was one of disbelief, his eyes dancing round and round the room, looking for an explanation.

The smile had left Adam's face and he turned back to face Davy; Adam reached out a hand to steady himself against the side of the table.

The ringing of what seemed like a thousand bells had each of them clasping their hands over their ears in a vain attempt to cut out the noise. Confused by the noise and disoriented in the dim light, Jonathan tried his best to open his mouth to speak to his friends.

His tongue felt twice the size as if he had not drunk for a week.

Following on the heels of the violent noise, there came the beating of a million wings which seemed to rush into the crypt on a never ending journey. They beat against their faces, smothering and blinding them.

Davy was struggling to breathe under the deluge, and Adam dropped to his knees, shielding his face with his arms. Jonathan turned his face to the wall, but he could feel whatever it was beating against his back with the utmost ferocity. They tore and bit at him and he suddenly feared for his life and that of his friends.

The crypt plunged into darkness as the candles were snuffed out all at once; Jonathan could hear Henry calling above the din, shouting for help. As quickly as the winged creatures came, they went, and in the darkness the eerie calm left them all shaken and confused.

Adam was the first to find his voice. "What the hell was that?" he said as he got unsteadily to his feet in the darkness.

"It must have been bats," Jonathan weakly replied as he lay huddled in the corner of the room.

"Bats, I don't think so," replied Henry, shaking his head sagely in the dark. "I've studied bats during term breaks and trust me, they weren't bats."

"Well, if it wasn't bats, birds, or whatever, then what was it? Tell me, 'cause I would really like to know." Adam's voice had taken on an angry tone and like all of them he looked severely shocked at what had just happened.

Davy spoke quite softly, but his shaky words cut through the room like a hot knife through butter.

"It ... it ... was me, I did it, I opened the book and it just happened."

Davy had gotten back on his feet and was leaning over the table; the other three carefully made their way through the scattered books to where he was standing. Adam had relit the candles and watched as the others patted down their clothes, trying to remove the layers of dust which had settled onto all of them. As they all stood there drawn to the comfort of the small candles they noticed their skin was covered in tiny claw-like scratches, but Jonathan seemed to have come off the worst.

Blood flowed quite freely down the side of his left arm and dripped slowly onto the floor where he stood, for whatever it was had sliced through his coat and clothes with ease.

Still dazed Jonathan finally joined Adam and Davy, stumbling his way across the damaged room and trying to stem the blood by holding his arm with his right hand. They could see Henry making a similar journey and his voice floated over to them in the semi darkness.

"Will one of you kindly light some more of those candles, so that I don't do myself any more damage? How are you lot, anyway? I think my back is cut."

"Stop your moaning and get yourself over here," announced Adam, trying to lighten the mood of the small party.

They could see Henry wincing in pain at the wounds that had been inflicted on him. Standing there in the soft glow of the candlelight, Jonathan stepped aside as Adam made a move forward to help Henry. They would see to their injuries later, but for now he was concerned about Davy and the words he had just spoken.

As Jonathan moved closer to Davy he could see tiny beads of sweat glistening on his forehead. He watched in fascination as Davy's trembling hand went to turn another page.

They did not see or hear Adam, who, seeing the move Davy was about to make, leant over and wrapped an iron grip around Davy's hand, stopping him before his fingers could reach the page.

"Have you any idea what you are doing?" Adam hissed.

"Let him go, Adam, can't you see we have to do this?" replied Jonathan calmly, placing his own hand over Adam's.

"Are you mad? Didn't you see what just happened? Weren't you in the same room as us, will you not think about this before you do this crazy thing." Said Adam angrily, then he half turned to face Henry, his hand still clutching Davy's and said, "You're in this as well. You've got a say; are you with me or Jonathan?"

Henry lowered his head, thinking. It was his nature to be cautious, he did not make his decision lightly and he knew this was a big decision.

Finally he answered, "I have spent the time at university studying what I love best, theology and I have worked with you chaps at what I deem a privilege … antiquity." He paused to take a small shuddering intake of breath before he continued, "It is now our duty to find out whatever it is that awaits us in that book." He nodded his head towards the book and continued, "It seems to me that perhaps we have been chosen to do something. We are after all in God's house, reading a book written by men of God – we think, I hasten to add." He looked round at each of them and said, "Somehow I feel we are being tested, because it's all too much of a coincidence us being here and finding it, the locked door and everything."

With the ending of his speech he gently reached over and removed both Jonathan's and Adam's grip from Davy's hand. Angry now at being outnumbered, Adam slammed his hand onto the table and cried, "This is not happening!" In exasperation, he glared at each of them in turn and said, "Miracles just don't happen, there is always a logical explanation to all this. We are not God's chosen! If he even exists! Why would he want four lads in the backwater of York to run his errands? They were bats, for fuck sake. You are always looking for your Holy Grail, Henry." Turning angrily to Jonathan, he continued, "And you are as bad as any tomb robber, you just want the glory. And as for poor ol' Davy, well, we all know how impressionable he is, the Salem trials have nothing on our Davy."

"Have you quite finished?" Jonathan replied, his own anger rising at Adam's words. "We all heard and saw whatever it was; it was not a figment of our joint imagination."

"No? Okay, maybe it wasn't." Here Adam stopped to run a hand over his face before he continued, taking time, it seemed, to gather his thoughts. "But let's be realistic; this is 1955, not the Dark Ages; half of us don't believe in this superstition any more. It's just a book and this is just another little northern church of no particular significance."

"I'm sorry, Adam, but York was the second largest city in England," Davy said, his voice cutting like a sword through the argument. As he continued talking his voice became stronger. "Even the sovereign's second son bears the title of the Duke of York. Richard II gave the city its first Sword of State and created York as a county in its own right. It's not some little backwater, Adam; York was an established religious centre for generations. People came from all over the known world to worship in the great Minster."

"Please spare me the history lesson," replied Adam, taken slightly aback by Davy's defence of the book.

"Ah, but in history lies the answer," Jonathan replied, leaning avidly forward across the table, carrying on where David left off, his face now alight with enthusiasm. His blue eyes sparkled and he brushed the mop of dark hair from his face before he continued, "When Henry VIII broke with Rome and set himself up as the head of the church, York suffered very badly. With the dissolution of the monasteries in 1536 York lost all its abbeys, priories, friaries and great religious hospitals. Their sacred treasures were stolen or destroyed and although the minister survived ..." Jonathan swept his arm all around to encompass the whole domain, "many of its priceless treasures were lost."

"So what are you trying to say to me?" replied Adam, still not convinced.

"He's trying to say, Adam, that perhaps we may have stumbled on something that has been hidden away from greedy hands and prying eyes for a very, very long time," answered Henry, close to his ear.

Adam leant forward and the candlelight flickered and played with the contours of his face, making him at once angelic and demonic.

A shiver ran the length of Jonathan's spine as he watched him and he wondered if this was indeed a good thing to do in front of Adam. He had never had any reason to doubt him before, but for some reason Jonathan started to feel uneasy.

It was too late now, as Davy, egged on by Henry, had started to turn the next page. They braced themselves, their eyes darting round the room, expecting the worst to happen. A collective sigh escaped them when nothing happened as the heavy paper turned and gently floated down, revealing on the next page some Latin script.

There in the middle of the page were just four lines.

Davy translated for them: "QUI SUMUS, well, that means 'who are we?' and E PLURIBUS UNUM translates as 'out of many one'; well, that's strange to start with. ANNUIT COEPTIS is 'he has favoured our undertakings.'"

At this point he stopped and glanced round the group; they all looked as puzzled as he did. Continuing he said, "NOVUS ORDO SECLORUM means 'a new order of the ages.' Come on, Henry, help me out here; you're the one studying theology."

Davy turned the next page and Henry edged nearer. "Well," said Henry, leaning closer to read the fine hand, adjusting his glasses as he did so, "I think it is taken from Revelation chapter 1."

And following the words with his finger, he deciphered the script as he went along: "Beatus qui legit et qui audiunt verba prophetiae et servant ea quae in ea scripta sunt tempus enim prope est. Basically it says, 'Blessed is he that readeth and they that hear the words of this prophecy and keep those things which are written therein, for the time is at hand.' It then goes on to say a lot of other things about dire consequences and such like."

Jonathan interrupted him. "Thanks, Henry, but I think we shall have to leave all this for another day," he said, trying to sound nonchalant about it all so as not to arouse suspicion. They all seemed to fidget round the table, reluctant to leave their find. They each seemed disappointed that it was not more revealing.

"Yes okay, let's put it somewhere safe so we can read what else it says and hopefully if the church warden doesn't catch us looking like this, we can come back tomorrow," added Henry as he adjusted his glasses again.

"Actually I am feeling rather drained and we do need to get these cuts sorted out," returned Davy as he straightened his torn coat.

"What about you, Adam? What do you say?" asked Jonathan, looking at Adam, who had moved round the table to stand opposite to him. They looked each other straight in the eye.

Their glance met and clashed, green eyes meeting blue.

For a millisecond Jonathan saw something in his friend's eyes; was it just the reflection of the candle flame? Whatever it was, it left him very worried. Adam's face broke into a smile and Jonathan was left wondering if he had just imagined it.

"Yes, let's get out of this dungeon and have a drink in the pub down the road," Adam answered with a smile. "Then perhaps we will all feel a little better," he added.

With that Adam walked over to where Davy was standing and swung his arm round his shoulder, adding as he did so, "I'm sorry I had a go at you. It was just the stress of the moment, and those damn bats had us all spooked. Come on then, chum," he added as he pulled Davy away from the table, "let's go and assail the girls with tales of good deeds and fiery dragons."

Davy, although covered in fine dust, smiled at the easing of the tension between them all and joined in the easy banter and together the two of them, their arms round each other's shoulders, made their way over to the stone staircase. Their laughter could be heard as they ascended the steep stairs.

Jonathan held onto Henry's arm, forcing him to stay a little longer in the room. With a worried expression on his face, Henry turned to face Jonathan.

"What's the matter, Jon? I could see you were worried earlier; why did you stop me from continuing?"

Jonathan turned back to the table and drew the heavy book towards him. His fingers absentmindedly caressed the front cover. "Nothing really escapes you, does it, Henry?" he replied, smiling.

"Well, actually it must do, because I don't know what's worrying you, other than the fact we have just had the most peculiar experience, been in total fear of our lives, unearthed a book that we think is totally unknown to anyone and got ourselves covered in cuts and scratches. Oh, and we have to decipher a long lost prophecy. So tell me, Jon, what is worrying you."

Suddenly feeling very tired, Henry straightened an overturned stool and unceremoniously flopped down onto it. Leaning against the table with his arm resting on the top, he turned his full attention to Jonathan, who was standing slightly in the shadows.

"Come on then, tell me, because to be quite honest, I've had about enough excitement for one day." Henry smiled to ease the retort.

"Did you notice the way Adam behaved when we found the book?" Jonathan finally answered him.

"Not really," replied Henry as he tried to read Jonathan's expression, but he was just outside the candles' glow.

"Well, I did and I didn't like what I saw; it was as if he didn't want us to find the book and when we did, he certainly didn't want us to read it."

"I think you're being a bit paranoid, Jon; let's face it, Adam is not really into archaeology, or church antiquity, he's a science person, everything has to have a reason; there are no myths or miracles in mathematics."

"That may be so," replied Jonathan, "but there was a look in his eye, I know it was only fleeting but it made me shudder."

"For God sake," and realising he had blasphemed, Henry quickly crossed himself and added, "You've known him for years; this is Adam we are talking about."

Jonathan had to smile when he saw Henry cross himself, but his mood remained sober and leaning across the desk so that his face was visible once again, he said to Henry, who was looking at him in amazement, "I'm going to take the book with me, and if anyone asks, say you don't know where it is."

"Is that wise? I mean, Davy did find it," answered Henry, somewhat perturbed by Jonathan's announcement.

"Can you keep a secret, Henry?" said Jonathan, his voice coming once more from the gloomy shadows of the crypt.

"Of course I can, what do you take me for? I'm a theology student; that should count for something," said Henry, somewhat annoyed.

Jonathan stepped fully into the light cast by the candles on the table and turning to his left, he pulled up the material on his sleeve; there should have been a long bloody gash down the length of his arm, but instead there was nothing there.

His arm was as perfect as it was before. His coat was still torn and the shirt he was wearing was shredded, but no wound could be seen through the material.

"Now do you believe me that this book holds some significance for me? You yourself saw the gash on my arm and the blood drip on the floor." Jonathan ran his fingers up and down the spot where the injury should have been, his blue eyes welling with unshed tears.

"I don't know what to say," Henry replied, crossing himself repeatedly, "only that whatever you decide I will help you to the best of my ability, and if you think Adam is dangerous, then you have my wholehearted support in keeping this book away from him."

"Thank you, Henry, between the two of us I'm sure we will be able to decipher what it all means." Jonathan leant forward and grasped Henry's hand as it lay on the table and as the tears started to spill onto his cheeks, he once again thanked him.

Neither of them knew what lay ahead. Jonathan felt relief flood through him like water on a parched desert floor, renewing everything with its bounty. He drew the book to him, feeling more certain as he felt the strong bindings in his hands. He knew he was meant to look after it, knew he had to protect it, because it held the key to something very important in his life.

Chapter 2

November 2011

In the semi darkness where he sat he could hear all the creaks and groans his old house made. He had sat listening for a while, in sad contemplation, going over all the years since that strange beginning. His thoughts eventually turned to the untimely death of his long term friend and colleague Davy Penn-Wright, fourteenth Lord and Baron. He had eventually attained the title after his father died in a skiing accident in Switzerland.

Sir David, as he liked to be known, having always hated the name of Horatio, had been in touch only a few times since university, preferring to spend his time haunting the auction rooms of the world for rare and precious objects, books mainly. He had shown Jonathan a few of his purchases, looking for his approval, but it seemed the light in his eyes never quite shone like it did when he first beheld "the Book."

1955

He remembered vividly the conversation he had with him in his room the day after the discovery of the Book. Like most bed sit rooms around York, Jonathan's was crammed full of books and papers he had been working on for the whole of the summer and Davy had a hard job to find somewhere to sit.

He scooped a load of papers up off of Jonathan's lone chair and placed them on the floor before sitting down. They all preferred to have their own rooms, which were scattered around the town, giving them the privacy they so needed after being surrounded by so many students during term time. This came as a relief to everyone and was part of the conditions when they all went away (unless, of course, it could not be helped and they had to share a room like the time they all went to Egypt).

Jonathan could see by Davy's clothes that he had not been home to change since cleaning up after their trip to the crypt. He was wearing the same outfit for his night on the town with Adam, having earlier discarded the torn and bloody clothes he was wearing in the crypt in favour of more casual attire that was now all creased and had the occasional beer stains down the leg of his trousers.

Jonathan had already heard from Henry, who had come by earlier, that the word round the town was that Adam and Davy had been barred from at least three public houses for loud and disruptive behaviour and it was Davy's money again that had allowed them to stay after hours in one of the back street pubs, where they could carry on drinking.

Henry had told Jonathan that it was when he was on his way to collect some milk from the local shop that he had bumped into Davy, whom he had found staggering home to his room after leaving Adam around six o'clock that very morning. Hearing from Henry that they were not allowed back down in the Minster had spurred Davy to visit Jonathan.

Henry had only just managed to impart his news to Jonathan before Davy turned up and not wanting Davy to see them together, Henry had made his escape down the back stairs.

As he sat there before him, Jonathan could see how much Davy was suffering and it was not just the alcohol. Davy's eyes were red and bloodshot and he swayed slightly as he sat on the chair. His words, when he finally spoke, were slightly slurred, "What are we g … going to do, Jonathan?" as he continued speaking his voice became stronger as the passion in him took hold again. "How are we going to get back down there? Henry told me the church warden said the area … the area down there was unsafe, and that we weren't allowed back down there." Davy slumped forward in his chair, pressing the palms of his hands into his eyes, trying to relieve some of the pressure there.

Jonathan stepped over a pile of books to where he was sitting and patted Davy gently on the back, saying in a fatherly tone, "Sorry Davy, it's just one of those things; they're within their rights to close it off if they think it is unsafe."

"But the Book, Jon, the Book …" And as Jonathan looked at him he saw the tears well up in Davy's eyes and splash down onto his freckled cheeks.

To cover his feelings Jonathan carried on, in a more pragmatic tone, "It's no good. I went to see the warden first thing this morning and he gave me short shrift, I can tell you. Quite adamant he was as well, said we were causing more problems down there than it was worth. It was not as if we had permission in the first place. He gave me quite a lecture on destroying church property; I thought it better to just pack up now and go home. There are only a few days left for us here anyway and I just telephoned my parents and told them I would pop down and see them before I start the new term."

Davy sat up squarely in his chair and faced Jonathan with an animated look on his face, all vestige of his earlier anxiety gone. Jonathan started to have a queasy feeling in the pit of his stomach, and fearing the worst he crossed over to the window to buy a little time.

"Let me ring my father, I'm sure he can call a few people," said Davy with enthusiasm, "or why not break into the Minster and steal the Book?"

Gazing out onto the view below, Jonathan listened as Davy rambled on and closing his eyes, he heaved a sigh as he turned to face Davy. Resting his back against the window sill, Jonathan said, "Do you remember the last time you disturbed your father? If not, I do and he was not pleased I can tell you and if I remember rightly he threatened to cut your next term's allowance if you did it again. Secondly, we shall not break into the Minster; what are you thinking of? That goes against everything we have worked towards. The research we have done all summer will be as nothing if the church were ever to find us doing such an illegal thing and as for Henry, well, he could hardly go on to theological college with a police record."

Taking on the role of mentor, Jonathan turned to face Davy, whose face was now sad and crestfallen. He stood before him; his arms folded across his chest, looking every inch the master he would eventually become.

Seeing Davy at once so animated and now cast into a pit of despair, Jonathan silently asked his forgiveness. Brushing the remainder of his tears away with the back of his hand, Davy looked to Jonathan for an answer and was disappointed to see him standing before him, sadly shaking his head.

"It's no good, Davy, we've all got too much to lose; it may sound cruel but we haven't got a peerage to fall back on. Henry has been promised a position at Oxford, the youngest ever I hear and well, my future is pretty much mapped out." He paused to see the effect his words were having.

"Also are we sure what really happened down there? I mean, it could have been like Adam said or a bit of movement in the Minster, it did survive the war, after all, and we don't really know what damage it sustained and maybe … just maybe we read into the Book the interpretation we wanted to see, we were all pretty geared up to find something."

Jonathan looked at Davy to see how much of this he was actually taking in and to his surprise he could see Davy nodding his head in agreement. Good, honest Davy, never expecting anyone to lie to him, looked at Jonathan with his big brown eyes and again nodded in sad agreement.

"Yes, you're right of course; I am being a bit selfish, taken away by the moment, so to speak. Adam was all up for it, you know." The mention of Adam sent alarm bells ringing through Jonathan's head, the last thing he wanted was him poking about and if he had to be honest, Adam was the one who could break in and not be caught.

"Tell Adam from us that it's not going to happen and if he or you continue in this hare-brained scheme, I … I shall have to inform the authorities. I have a duty to the department and the Minster."

Davy was taken aback by the threat; jumping to his feet, he swiftly closed the gap between them. "Gosh I'm sorry, Jonathan, I didn't mean anything by it. I'll tell Adam that it's all under control and Jonathan …"

"Yes Davy?" replied Jonathan, getting his breathing under control along with the beating of his heart which had finally slowed to its normal pace. The relief at Davy's capitulation so easily brought an unsteady smile to Jonathan's lips.

"It was a beautiful book, wasn't it?" Davy smiled and held out his hand for Jonathan to shake. Taking his friend's hand, Jonathan found himself overcome with emotion, and so that Davy would not see through the mask he felt slipping, he pulled his friend into his arms and gave him a hug, making sure his face was out of view until he could compose himself.

Fearing his voice would give him away, all he could do was nod.

2011

Jonathan had felt ashamed that he had to keep the truth from Davy; even to this day it still rankled. He thought he was doing the right thing and in time he thought Davy would thank him for it. They had met from time to time when his research allowed him to take time off and he would have liked nothing more than to talk things over with his old friend, but it seemed after their foray into York's dim and dark religious past, Davy lost all interest in his work. He dropped out of college halfway through his final year and Jonathan felt the blame for it as keenly as if he had him thrown out. He saw his face in the occasional paper his wife left lying about and several members of the governing faculty at the college were always asking him if Sir David would contribute to the college, seeing as he was a friend of his, but Jonathan never had the heart to ask him which did not put him in good favour with the vice chancellor of his college.

The fire spluttered, sending a shower of sparks into the hearth and he eased his stiff and tired joints into a better position.

"I'm here," the voice said near to him.

Jonathan felt his insides turn to water, and the fear he had kept at bay flooded over him. In his old man's terror he forgot his mission and the unspoken words of mercy sprang readily to his lips.

"Did you think I wouldn't come?" he enquired.

Jonathan fought to get a little moisture into his mouth, fearing the words would stick in his throat and he would die with his questions unanswered.

"How did you know it was me?" he finally managed to ask, turning in his chair to finally put a face to the voice, but he remained in the shadows.

"It wasn't easy; you fooled me for a long time. I had to get as much information as I could from your little friend, David. He put up quite a struggle, I can tell you."

Jonathan's head sank forward onto his chest in sorrow and now with a stronger tone, he asked the question that had bothered him for a long time about the circumstances of his friend's death.

"I was under the impression he died in a car crash," he said.

"Oh, is that the official view? Very clever of the police; well, never mind, I'll tell you, seeing as how we have become so close and indeed are going to get closer."

Jonathan could sense him smiling at his own words and it made his flesh creep to listen to him. "Tell me then, what did you do to him?" he said, bracing himself for the reply.

"Well, I was quite surprised how much he held out, but you tend to get a lot of information – some very useless, I might add – when someone, well … me actually, removes your eyes and then makes a little incision in the base of your spine and severs your spinal cord. You can talk but you just can't walk. In the end he didn't know anything and so I put him in his car and made it look like an accident."

Hearing these words spoken in such a mundane way doubled the horror of what he was hearing. Tears sprang to his eyes in remembrance of his dear friend. Tears for Davy and for himself, because he knew his turn was coming. His tears fell in rivulets down the furrows of his face, because he finally admitted to himself after all the years that it was his fault that Davy had died, because it was his lies that had caused his death. This thing … this abomination that had stalked him all his life had sucked the life from his friend and he had helped it … albeit unwittingly.

They had both used Davy for their own ends and he had become a pawn in this deadly game of chess. Anger coursed through his veins, hardening his heart, making him, if only for a moment, a warrior instead of a mere academic.

"Don't let us play any more games; where is the Book?" he heard him say, his voice rumbling with its undertones of anger.

With more strength than he knew he had, he purposefully wiped the tears from his face and replied courageously, "I don't have it any more, I destroyed it, in fact you are too late and its remains lie within that lovely fire that is slowly dying in front of you."

"Just like you will if you speak the truth," his words were clipped now with his anger and he could hear him moving slowly towards him, feel the cold exuding from his body, chilling the room as he drew nearer.

Fear tugged at Jonathan's insides, but he was unable to tear his eyes away from the place in the shadows where the words originated from. Nearer and nearer he came through the gloom and shadows of the room. Until the glow from the dying fire cast an unholy red glow over this would-be assassin.

"Adam!" The word was wrung from his throat, so shocked was he, but he didn't look like him, old and bent; it was the Adam of his youth, young and vibrant, his green eyes blazing. His fear suddenly turned to anger, fuelling his body and with strength he didn't know was in him, he raised his tired, aging body from his chair and steadied himself to meet his foe.

On reaching his desk, Adam leant forward and swiftly grabbed him by the throat. Jonathan could feel the blood trickling down his skin where Adam's nails, like claws, were cutting into his neck. His breath was becoming shallow and he feared his time was not far off. He was startled to hear Adam's voice above the echo of his own heart beating in his ears. His words came softly to him, as if Adam was afraid he had finished him off too quickly.

"Tell me, old man, what the secret of the book really is and I will end you quicker than you deserve."

Jonathan laughed in spite of the terrible pain he was going through; he could feel the claws sinking further into his neck, aiming for his jugular.

"You think to annoy me so much that I will end you now? No … my friend, my Master does not like to be defeated and neither do I." With that he released Jonathan, who gratefully sank back into his chair.

"I will give you one last chance to help yourself and I really do promise you your end will be quick."

Jonathan, although slumped in his chair, managed to stem the flow of blood by tying his handkerchief round his neck. He sat there and watched Adam, if it really was him, and he had no reason to doubt him. He looked the same as on the day they parted at university. His frame was still tall and athletic. The muscles he had acquired in the college's rowing team still bulged under the thin jacket he was wearing.

He was interrupted in his appraisal by Adam's voice, saying, "I suppose you are wondering why I look so young."

Jonathan felt sick to see that he was even smiling at him. "Yes, it did cross my mind," he said, his voice cracking under the pain.

"Well, I'm all things to all people, to you I am Adam, because that is how I want you to remember me; I take on the mantle of many and in fact I speak in forked tongues."

He stopped talking and wagged his tongue at Jonathan, the gesture lewd and obscene. He continued, "There are quite a few of us; we want only what is good for you." With this Adam sat himself on the corner of the desk and leant towards Jonathan.

"So tell me what you managed to decipher from the book, because I recognised it straight away, I just prayed to …" At this point he actually winked at Jonathan, adding, "my Master." The way he said "Master" sounded salacious.

"I deciphered a lot of things," replied Jonathan wearily.

"It has not gone unnoticed that you said 'I' instead of 'we.' Are you trying to tell me that you did all this on your own?" said Adam with some amusement.

"Of course," replied Jonathan with a hint of pride in his voice.

"Oh well, what does it matter?" Adam said. "It won't take me long to find who else is involved." He stopped and tapped his finger to his lips in a gesture Jonathan always found disturbing, even when they were young men.

"Come now, stop teasing me, you know I like a joke along with the rest of you snivelling mankind, but you try my patience." He leant nearer, reducing the space between them.

Jonathan could smell the aroma of decaying things and the bile rose involuntarily to his mouth, the bitterness matching his feeling of loss.

He hoped he would last to the end, that his courage would not fail him. There was only a little time to go, but the seconds dragged by like eons. He closed his eyes briefly and the words came unbidden, almost as if waiting to be called, waiting to give him comfort:

The lord is my shepherd,

"I'm sorry for you, Adam and I forgive you," he said softly.

I shall not want,

"Forgive me?" On hearing this, Adam threw back his head and laughed, shattering the silence.

He maketh me to lie in green pastures.

"Tell me what I want to know, what the prophecy was." His lips pulled back over his large sharp teeth, Adam looked to Jonathan every inch the evil nemesis of his nightmares.

He leadeth me besides still waters.

"I told you I have burnt the book and the prophecy went up in flames with it before I could decipher it.." The effort of getting the words out left Jonathan feeling weak and light headed.

He restoreth my soul.

"Well, if the book's destroyed, that's half the battle, but I don't for one minute believe you. You always were a sneaky little devil, look how you hoodwinked me at university. Even I didn't think you could be that devious; you could almost be me." Laughing at his own joke, Adam slid off the table and started to stroll round the desk, coming to a halt behind Jonathan's chair.

> He leadeth me in the paths of
> righteousness for his name's sake.

Jonathan closed his eyes; waiting for the death blow he knew was coming.

> Yet though I walk through the valley
> of death I will fear no evil.

The words brought a smile to Jonathan's lips at the thought of the evil that was present. He felt Adam's hand stroking his hair.

"Haven't you got old? Old and lonely and your hair's so white."

Jonathan kept his peace; no need for Adam to know anything about him.

> For your rod and staff do comfort me.

"Tell me before I go, was there ever a Mrs Hawker to ease your loneliness and bring you succour?" enquired Adam, his voice filling with concern as if he was genuinely interested.

> You prepareth a table before me in the
> presence of mine enemies.

Jonathan prepared himself mentally for this answer, because this was the key, this was the reason for Adam being here in the first place. He gave himself time before he answered, not wanting to give anything away by tone or inflection.

> You annointeth my head with oil, my cup overfloweth.

"No. I remained a bachelor all my life. The life of an academic is not always suited to married life. It's hard on a woman, having to put up with losing her husband for months at a time if they are engrossed in their work like I have been all my life." He prayed his answer was good enough and the frown that passed over Adam's brow gave credence to his worries.

> Surely goodness and mercy will follow
> me all the days of my life.

Adam spun the chair round with a violence that nearly sent Jonathan flying from his seat. It was only the strong vibrant hand placed on his chest by his assailant that stopped him from dropping to the floor.

"Do you honestly expect me to believe anything you say?" Adam said, pressing his twisted face of fury into Jonathan's.

And I will dwell in the House of the Lord forever.

Like a thing possessed, his anger finally unleashing, he plunged his hand into Jonathan's chest, seeking his pumping heart.

Adam could see Jonathan's lips moving and bending forward to hear his final words; his anger knew no bounds when he heard Jonathan's words spoken through the blood and froth: "Now it is done … with my death the prophecy is complete. I was waiting for you to come …Bless you; Adam … you have fulfilled … my destiny."

With that, Jonathan's lifeless body sank to the ground.

Adam, his intense rage needing an outlet, ripped Jonathan's bleeding heart from his body. He turned to the window and pulled back the curtain. As he stood there with Jonathan's heart in his hand he raised his face to the heavens and screamed his rage and his fury.

Chapter 3

Gemini hurried along the hot, dusty pavements of York; she had already made her way down the Shambles, York's most famous street and the only one mentioned in the Doomsday Book of 1086. The street was so narrow that, from the upper storeys of its timber-framed medieval buildings, people could shake hands across the divide and for centuries butchers and slaughterhouses occupied the very same street. In fact it was a little over a hundred years ago that there were still thirty-one butchers in the Shambles. They laid out their meat on low, wide shelves, or shammels, in front of their open windows, but today gift shops have taken over the street and the last remaining butcher in Little Shambles displayed his meat more hygienically. She learned this the other day when she went to buy her and Bethany's tea.

She had come to love the feel and age of the city. It was hard to believe that over a million people a year came to walk through nineteen hundred years of history.

Gem walked past the famous Golden Fleece as she turned into the road called the Pavement, which itself dated back to 1329 and was probably one of the first streets in York to be paved; even the half-timbered house next door to the Fleece was dated back to 1620 and belonged to a friend of Charles I, Sir Thomas Herbert, who kept the king company the night before his execution.

The heat of the day was finally abating as Gem walked down into Coppergate; it was hard to believe that beneath her feet York's past had been excavated and reconstructed into the Viking street in Jorvik, the Viking City.

The pleasant and balmy evening, if the forecast was right, would be broken by a storm later on during the night, but for now the air, what there was of it, still laid full and heavy. Gem could feel the sweat beneath her thin blouse beginning to trickle down between her breasts.

She was late as usual and knew the longer she took, the more anxious Beth would be. People streamed in front of her, oblivious to her own haste. Earlier she had sat on the window seat in her office and leant her hot forehead against the cool of the glass. The glasses that she wore for reading had been pushed up into her hair and she rubbed the bridge of her nose to ease the small throb in her temple that was beginning to plague her. She had been studying the typewritten papers of her forthcoming court case all day and she still felt unprepared. Her mind would not concentrate and she was glad it was Friday, that would give her the weekend to get things sorted out. She might even relax a bit after her meal that she had planned with Beth later on this evening.

She had watched with idle curiosity as the majority of the shoppers began to retreat back to their homes, listless and laden with parcels after having made good use of some of the late summer bargains still to be found in the town. She had felt out of sorts all day and realising she was getting nowhere, she bundled all the papers together and put them back into the files of her desk drawer.

Now as she hurried along Gem noticed that like her, the few office workers left in the city at this time of night were all wanting to get home as quickly as possible, each seeming to find new volition and purpose in their quest for the nearest bus stop or railway station, oblivious to the heat, but unlike them, she headed off in the direction of her and Beth's favourite wine bar.

Gem had left her St Andrew Gate office with a slight skip in her step twenty minutes ago and was now, like a salmon, swimming against the tide as she fought her way to her destination. What she wouldn't give to be able to shove a few pedestrians out of the way. She suffered in silence though and her innate sense of good manners had her excusing herself all along the road until she turned left down into High Ousegate.

The city was starting to turn over to its wonderful night life, lights were beginning to be turned on and York had started to put on her party dress. It still amazed her that the city seemed to have a different pub for every night of the year. Some of the more historic pubs were tucked away in the city's ancient snickleways and she had promised Beth that in time they would explore some of them.

The scent of flowers came to her from the hanging baskets and she already felt better; it was good to be out in the fresh air, to be young and single and if she was not so worried about being late to meet Beth, Gem would have noticed the many admiring stares she got as she strode down through the city. As it was she was just happy to have finished work for the weekend and she found herself smiling broadly at the thought of putting the numerous difficult court cases behind her, if only for a few hours. For now, though, she was heading for one of the trendy wine bars found along the riverside and a large glass of alcohol with her name on it.

Finally she reached her destination like some lost and lonely traveller finding a desert oasis. As she stumbled through the doors of the wine bar, the air conditioning hit her like a slap in the face and she stood there for a minute in the machine's downdraft, relishing the coolness that caressed her body. With a gentle sigh she moved further into the restaurant; catching sight of Beth, she hesitated a moment to take in the view of her friend, sitting there on her own.

Bethany's face was in profile to her, but even at this distance she could see the beauty that it held. Her long dark hair fell over part of her face and as if on cue Beth reached up a small slender hand to sweep the mass from her face where it had fallen; with her fingers running through her hair, she slowly swept it over her shoulder. It was a seductive and very feminine gesture, one Gem had seen many times before, but one that left many a male weak at the knees. The gesture had fully revealed her face and the soft light lessened the sadness that was ever present in her eyes, making her beautiful features mellow and easing out the worry lines that were etched between her eyes.

She could see that Beth was wearing her office clothes as well, although for a long time since they had moved away from London, she noticed that Beth had a tendency to wear clothes that covered more and more of her body. Gone were the low cut blouses and designer jeans, big belts and off the shoulder jumpers of ten months ago and in were the classy suits and long skirts, nice but not quite Beth.

As always her thoughts drifted back to that January night eight months ago and the frantic phone call she had received. Only half awake, she felt around under her pillow for her mobile phone and with her eyes still shut she automatically flipped the case of her phone to answer. "This had better be important," she had mumbled, "I've got court in the morning."

Silence had followed and for some reason she started to feel very nervous. She suddenly sat up; gone was the sleepy eyed somnolent and in its place was someone who gripped the phone like her life depended on it. She knew instantly that it was her friend on the other end of the line.

"Talk to me, please Beth, I know it's you," she said, with a whimper that travelled down the phone until, like an arrow finding its mark, it pierced her heart with a sadness she didn't know could exist. Ignoring the tears coursing down her face, she closed her eyes and tried not to let her voice tremble as she gently asked Beth where she was.

"I think I'm in a park somewhere, I don't really know it is so dark; Gem, come and get me. I'm so frightened."

Gem could hear the gentle sobbing of her friend and it pierced her heart anew, but she didn't really have a lot to go on. Scrabbling from her comfortable bed, she searched around for some warm clothes and retrieved her trainers from under the bed where she had kicked them.

"Beth, darling, please hold on. I'm coming, but you must help me, are there any street lights or signs or anything?" She waited tensely and with her heart throbbing in her chest she clutched the phone tighter to her ear. She could hear the wind whistling into the phone as Beth started to move from where she was. Then her trembling voice came down the line once more: "I ... I ... think I can see something, yes it says West London and Westminster Cemetery, oh God, Gem, oh God, I'm in old Brompton Cemetery, please hurry."

Listening to Beth's voice rising with panic, Gem tried to keep her calm, saying, "I'm coming, sweetie, I'm coming now; you know I'm not far away, I'll be with you in about ten minutes, but Beth darling, listen to me: I have to close the line down now."

Instantly she could hear Beth sobbing on the other end and she was starting to babble now, as the shock was starting to set in.

"Okay, okay, I'll tell you what we'll do, I'll keep the line open but please Beth, get yourself near the gate, so that I can find you when I arrive; can you do that for me, sweetie?"

She felt rather than heard Beth nodding her agreement and with that she set about pushing her long legs into her jeans and she enveloped her body in the thick jumper she had found. She pulled on her Nike trainers, not bothering with her socks and grabbed a large woollen jumper for Beth, along with a blanket she had hastily pulled off her bed. She grabbed her keys from the hall table and dashed out of the flat with the bundle under her arm. With her mobile still pressed to her ear, she kept up a steady stream of comforting words to her distraught friend.

Gem threw the bundle into the boot of her Triumph Stag convertible. She then hurried to the driver's door and leapt in and with all the will power she could muster she gently said to Beth, "How you doing, Beth? Have you got yourself to the gate?"

She could just make out a feeble yes.

"Then listen carefully, Beth, please be extra brave, I know you can do it."

"Do what?" Came her reply in a quiet voice.

At least her sobbing had ceased, but Gem was aware of her trauma and could feel her suffering.

"I want you to crouch down where you are into a little ball and cover your ears with your hands; shut your eyes and count to one hundred, slowly. Can you do that for me, sweetie? I have to make a very important phone call to someone so that they can meet me at the cemetery; then when you have done counting, I shall be with you. Do you think you can do that, just for me?"

"I'll try, but please hurry, Gem. I don't know how much more I can stand and I'm so cold," Beth said as she sobbed on the line.

With that Gem broke the connection and quickly dialled the police and told them as much as she knew about the situation. She reversed the Stag out of the garage and pulled out onto Parsons Green Lane, heading for the Fulham Road and the Brompton Cemetery. It didn't take her very long to reach it at that time of night, flooring the accelerator and oblivious to any speed cameras. She could see the blue flashing lights up ahead.

Although she knew there was always a police presence around London late at night, it was a sign of the times as she marvelled at the speed the police had taken to react. As she pulled up alongside the police cars, an ambulance arrived from the nearby Chelsea and Westminster Hospital, its name emblazoned down the side of the vehicle. Its siren broke off in mid-squawk as it pulled into the kerb, giving back to the area the silent and eerie feel it had before the ambulance had arrived.

A police officer came straight over to Gem's car to enquire why she was there. After informing him that it was she that had phoned, he directed her over to the gates, where a small group of officers were gathered. He also stressed that the matter was in their hands now and any interference from her would not be tolerated.

She parked the Stag and hurried over to the group.

The air was so cold that the exhaust fumes hung in the air like a conjurer's trick and the breath from her body floated lazily in front of her, oblivious to her frantic need to be with her friend.

As she neared the group they looked to her in the cold, clear air like nicotine addicts frantically drawing on their last cigarette as their breaths all mingled as one. A few of them were stamping their feet to get the circulation going, some were checking the batteries on their torches, all were poised and ready for what awaited them behind the large gates.

A tall plain clothed police officer, whom she assumed was in charge, gathered the group around him, and even though she was on the outer rim his voice came over to her firm and strong.

"Now listen, lads, when the gates open I want you all to spread out, it's a large area we have to cover and the vic could be anywhere and as for the perp, well, what can I say, just remember your training and don't destroy any evidence with those large size eleven feet." Turning slightly to his left he made a small bow and aimed his next words to an officer whose back was to Gem. "With apologies to WPC Robins, who I am sure only has a size five."

A small ripple of laughter ran through the group, easing the tension slightly.

She suddenly realised how difficult it was for these young officers to go out night after night, not knowing what they might find and like the rest of the public she took them all for granted. They streamed through the gates with the enthusiasm of youth, leaving her momentarily alone.

She decided to head back to her car and get out the jumper she had bought for Beth, as the weather was freezing at this time of the morning. Reaching the car she leant against the boot lid before raising it and lowering her head in sorrow she closed her eyes and found herself silently praying that they would find Beth quickly. Her hand reached around to her back pocket for her mobile; surely it wouldn't hurt to give Beth one more ring when suddenly she felt a strange presence beside her, felt it in the very core of her, felt the bile rise in her throat at the very thought of it. The hairs on the nape of her neck started to raise, her body giving her a warning long before her brain could register it and the feeling of panic that she had felt when she first picked up the phone returned with an even stronger force.

She thought she felt a breath on her lowered face, a timeless breath, an old breath, of things rotten and used and what was it … not warmth but a coldness of somebody close to her. She wanted to open her eyes, but for a brief instant the thing held her enthralled. *Open your eyes*, her mind screamed, *open your eyes*; it began to sound like a mantra.

She tensed her body, felt the blood rushing to her limbs, felt the suddenly flood of adrenalin, her body now ready to fight whatever it was that was so close to her. With all the strength she could muster she prepared her mind, as well as her body and letting go of the car boot lid, she turned with a swiftness that surprised even her. To her utter amazement she found she was alone, there was nobody around, even the ambulance men had gone into the cemetery to look for Beth.

She twisted her body all ways, searching, her eyes piecing the darkness; searching. She raised her hand to where she had felt the breath, but nothing remained, only the cold numbness of the weather. A small ragged laugh escaped her lips and she tasted the saltiness of her own blood where she had bitten down hard on her lip in her fear.

Her practical and analytical mind refused to accept the anathema and she found herself mentally putting forth explanations for what had just occurred, as the truth, if such a truth existed, was just too horrible to contemplate.

With her breathing now under control, Gem leant against the boot of her car again, feeling suddenly drained of all energy, but seconds later she was spurred into action once again by a sudden cry from inside the gates. They must have found Beth and the discovery made Gem sink slowly to her knees in thankfulness. Her thoughts came swiftly back to Beth and what had transpired a few minutes ago was immediately forgotten in her relief. She felt neither the cold nor the damp as it soaked through her jeans. Her emotions had gone through a helter-skelter ride and she felt physically drained.

Officers were now streaming back out through the gates, regrouping around their superior, who was now taking charge of the crime scene. She could hear him throwing orders to one officer after another.

The gurney on which Beth's small motionless body lay rushed past her and she momentarily caught a glimpse of her friend's face drained a deathly white in the glow from the streetlights. She looked to the world as though she was dead and Gem's heart skipped a beat in trepidation.

Scrambling to her feet, she rushed over to where the ambulance was parked and just before they lifted Beth into the back, she took hold of her cold and stiff hand. Unable to utter the words that would confirm her friend's status, she turned pleading eyes towards the ambulance crew for confirmation of her condition. Silent tears of gratitude dripped from her eyes when they told her she was alive – but barely.

"I'm sorry, miss, we have to get going; she has hypothermia, she's lost blood from several bad cuts and the damage to her back is going to need specialist treatment," said one of the crew, his strong lean body poised ready to take the weight as they positioned themselves to lift Beth into the back of the ambulance. As they were explaining the extent of her injuries, Gem raised Beth's hand to her lips and kissed her frozen fingers, trying to pour a little warmth back into her body.

Still in a daze she felt two strong hands gently take her by the shoulders and ease her away from the gurney as a soft but commanding voice told the crew to take Beth straight to the A & E Department, where a team of medical consultants were waiting for her.

"Come with me, I think you need a cup of coffee," she heard someone say, "or would you like something stronger? Your clothes are all wet, you'll have to get them changed and quickly, or else you'll be in hospital as well."

Turning, she came face to face with the senior detective and was amazed at his consideration. Scraping her long blonde hair out of her face, where the dampness of the evening had plastered it, she tilted her head back a little to get in the full height of him; needless to say, it was a pleasant sight even so.

"No, but thank you, officer," she said as she rearranged her hair. "I ..."

Before she could continue, he interrupted her, saying, "DI Grantly, in charge of the investigation, and you are ..." He waited patiently for her reply.

"Gemini M. Hawker and that is my best friend they put in the back of that ambulance." She lifted her hand to point at the now retreating ambulance, its siren slicing through the night air.

"Is that Miss, Mrs, or Ms Hawker?" he asked softly.

"Sorry, DI Grantly, it's Miss and although I would love to stay and chat I must get to the hospital and be with Beth."

"I'm sorry too, but I have to ask these questions; if you won't answer them now, I'll have to ask you to come to the station later on today to fill in all the blanks for me."

Gem looked at him askew and, relenting, replied, "I don't really know much, I had a phone call from Beth about an hour ago, and then I phoned you, and you know all the rest."

"When did she phone you?" he asked. "At what time was that precisely?"

Gem looked at him with new interest, wondering why he was questioning her about the phone call. The cold of the evening was beginning to seep into her bones, and the longer she stood there, the more uncomfortable she started to feel. "Why are you so concerned about the phone call, DI Grantly? Isn't it more important that we found her?"

"Not really," he replied softly.

Gem's voice started to take on an edge of irritation; who was this officer and who did he think he was, questioning her about the phone call?

"What do you mean, not really? For God sake she could have died, and you're wasting time talking to me about the phone call! You should be out there looking for whoever did this."

Drawing herself to her full height, she stood there in front of him, a picture of righteous indignation, her hands balanced on each hip; her chin was thrust out and she looked as though she wanted to punch his lights out.

He was impressed in spite of himself.

"Yes, Miss Hawker, we are, but there are just a few things that need clearing up here first. Rest assured we will do everything possible to find whoever did this." For some reason he felt drawn to this tall young girl, felt her passion and admired her defence of her friend. Looking at her, he knew instinctively how loyal she was, but how brave remained to be seen and she was going to be tested now.

With his next words, he took hold of Gem's shoulders and braced her, knowing what the full force of his words would do to her. Taken by surprise by his action, Gem struggled to release herself, but she could hear his words dropping like icicles into her heart:

"Gemini, there was no phone; she had no phone, do you hear me?" With the ending of his sentence, the world just seemed to fold in upon her as she sank into his arms and total oblivion.

Beth remained in hospital for several weeks; the extent of her injuries were documented and photographed, and with each picture Gem saw a little more of her being eroded away. Beth had suffered severe lacerations to her shoulder blades; someone had cut away the skin in a ritualistic fashion, or as if they were looking for something, only the perpetrator knew what! Beth's hands and feet were also cut in the same fashion, but the doctors seemed confident that they could patch her up as good as new. But it was the damage to her inner self that Gem was worried about; she had not mentioned to her what DI Grantly had said that fateful night, not wanting to believe it herself. So with a confidence she hardly felt, she put a proposal to Beth that was to change both their lives.

"You know I own my flat in Parsons Green, well, I was thinking of selling up." Gem was perched on the bottom of Beth's hospital bed, flicking through a magazine, but not really looking at it, more concerned at how well her proposal would go down. Beth had been looking out of the window at a not very inspiring sight and was a little taken aback by Gem's news.

"Selling up? But you can't; where would you go? Your work is here, your career, your, your …" Suddenly unable to carry on Beth's eyes brimmed over with tears, and in a little jerky voice she said, "I'm here."

"Exactly!" shouted Gem.

Now quite excited she had gotten a reaction out of her friend, she couldn't stop, and swinging her legs round so that she was face to face with Beth, she played her trump card.

"It's all arranged, I've sold my flat and you only rent anyway. Well, the two of us are moving to York, back to my parents' house. Mummy and Daddy have decided to stay in the country house, so they said if I moved back I could have the one in York. " Pausing for a quick breath, she rushed on, "Daddy had to pull a few strings about getting me into a legal practice up there at such short notice, but what the heck; he didn't want me to work in the big, bad Smoke anyway. So I'm going home and my darling, you are coming with me."

Taken aback by the suddenness of the proposal, Beth was at a total loss for words. She laid her head back on the pillows and in a soft voice she said, "I know why you are doing this, Gem and thank you, I really don't think I could have continued living here."

Her words caught on a sob and before the tears could run down her cheeks, Gem had thrown herself forward and gathered the broken girl into her arms.

"From now on it's the two of us, nobody is going to hurt you again, I promise you, Beth."

"Do you, Gem? That's an awful big promise came the muffled reply against her shoulder. "Sometimes I think I remember what happened and then it all goes like a dream; the thing I do remember, though, is this terrible fear. Like an unknown fear of the dark or something you can't quite see. I don't think it will ever go away, Gem."

Gem stroked the damp hair away from her friend's cheek and looking into her eyes, she knew Beth was right, but bravely Gem answered her, saying, "Yes it will, in time. I'll take you to my family home in the country and you will be able to smell the heather on the moors, you will get strong there, Beth; my mum will do her mother hen bit and if you're lucky my father will take you fly fishing." Both girls grimaced at this.

"Yuk! Well, forget about that; a bit of peace and quiet is what we both need. You'll get well and I will conquer the legal world of York and Leeds."

Letting go of Beth she grabbed the front of her own blouse in imitation of a barrister in full flood.

"Okay, let's do it," Beth said with more strength in her voice than Gem had heard for a long time.

With that the two girls' foreheads came together and as they looked into each other's eyes Gem had the uneasy feeling that her promise was indeed going to be very hard to keep.

Chapter 4

The slight touch on her arm brought her swiftly back to the present and turning, she noticed a young waitress with a slightly concerned look on her face, wondering why she wasn't moving to her table.

"Sorry, I know where I am sitting, just over there, look," and with a little wave she attracted Beth's attention.

Beth fluffed herself up in her seat; straightening her back and giving a half-hearted scowl, she said, "You finally made it then, not bad for you, only half an hour late."

The words were issued through slightly clenched teeth and Gem realised that she had a bit of making up to do. Tired, dusty, and definitely in need of a shower, Gem turned her full attention to her friend's bruised feelings.

"I'm so sorry, Beth, please forgive me. I was caught up with a client's notes and it just dragged on and on." She smiled her best "please forgive me smile," and Beth immediately thawed.

"You are a pest, though, Gem; you could have phoned me or texted me or anything; you know I hate waiting." With a quick look over her shoulder, Beth leant forward towards her friend and added in a low whisper, "I look so desperate, as if I haven't got a date or anything."

"Well, you haven't," replied Gem, "and you haven't had for a long time." She leant forward and whispered also, imitating her friend. "And you never will until you come to terms with what happened to you."

Beth's head sagged towards the table, but not before Gem had seen her eyes fill with the tears that were always threatening.

"Oh God, I'm so sorry," said Gem. She leant forward to put a comforting arm around her friend's shoulder. "Sorry, sorry, sorry. I didn't mean to sound so harsh, it is just that I care about you and I hate to see you like this. You always used to be so strong and dare I say it, you were the one to always look after me."

A discreet cough sounded next to Gem's chair and as she turned in surprise at the sound, a waiter stood beside her; to her amazement, he had a smirk across his face. He proceeded to ask her if she would like to order now, but his eyes were looking at her arm resting on her friend's shoulder.

"Yes thank you, we'll have two tequila sunrises and the menu," replied Gem in her best solicitor's voice.

When the waiter had left them, Gem turned her head and followed his departure.

"What's wrong now?" asked Beth as she studied the back of Gem's head.

"Oh nothing really, it's just that I'm sure that waiter thinks we are gay," laughed Gem. Her infectious laugh brought the smile back to Beth's face and their serious conversation of a moment ago was temporarily forgotten, but Gem knew deep down that the moment of confrontation to her friend's problems were not so far in the future.

"Now then," said Gem, wriggling with anticipation, "what are you going to eat? I'm starving; I only caught a quick sarnie at lunch-time. Dad was going to help me run through a few things at work but he's not feeling too well and Mum has made him stay in the country for a few days' rest. He's taken it hard since Grandpa's death and the police gave us so few details about what happened, even I can't prise anything out of them."

Gems face registered concern, and Beth, now that the subject was raised, asked the question that had been bothering her for a long time:

"Gem … do you … think, well. Do you … think that the two could be related, you know, my attack and his death?" She finished her words in a rush.

Beth suddenly looked concerned and her brown eyes filled with fear, but she caught the edge to Gem's voice.

"No, honey, I don't think they are connected; besides, they happened at different ends of the country. Also we still don't really know what happened to Grandpa, and well, yours is still being investigated."

She reached over and laid a comforting hand across her friend's and at that moment the waiter returned with their drinks and his smirk turned to a leer when he saw the gesture.

Beth quickly withdrew her hand and tucked it away under the table. Gem was not so easily intimidated and boldly stared at him, waiting for him to finish laying the table for their meal.

That's it, thought Gem and her eyes took on a steely determination.

"Have you got a problem?" she hissed her anger for some reason leaping up to a boiling point.

The waiter straightened up and looked slightly taken aback at her question. "I don't know what you mean, madam," he answered.

"I'm sure you don't," Gem replied. "I would appreciate less of the unspoken social commentary and more of the service you should be providing." With that, she turned her attention to the menu in front of her. After giving him their order, she watched as he stalked off.

"I think you hurt his feelings," Beth said with an almighty grin on her face.

"Well, I'm not having that jumped up little sod casting aspersions on our characters; straight or gay, it's nothing to do with him," Gem replied with the same gusto that had won her more than one argument with her father.

With her left hand, she reached up and patted a few strands of hair that had come loose in her chignon and with the right, she reached out, picked up her glass and took a well-earned drink of her cocktail.

She couldn't help feeling annoyed about the waiter, silly she knew, childish even and for a moment her thoughts lingered on revenge. The crash that followed had all the heads spinning in the direction of the kitchen and out through the door came their waiter, covered in sauce.

His white shirt was stained a very colourful red.

The patrons that he passed found it hard to conceal their amusement and the laughter went like a Mexican wave around the restaurant.

"Well, look at him," said Beth in amusement, and turning back to Gem she leant forward; half closing her eyes in concentration, she said softly, so as not to be overheard from the next table, "Was that you, Gem?"

"Was that me, what? I don't know what you mean. I'm sitting here waiting for my dinner and you blame me for some stupid klutz."

"Don't play the innocent with me, I've seen this happen more and more since … well … you know, since London."

"London shmundon, what has that got to do with anything? I'm telling you the boy must be accident prone." Gem took a sip of her drink and eyed her friend over the rim of the glass, looking like the cat who had just got hold of the great big cream pot.

It had worried her at first, when things like this had started to happen; it wasn't as if she wanted them to, it was more her subconscious making them happen. But now she was getting used to it, and she could feel her power growing like a small seed on a dry and dusty patch. She watered it with her mind, tended it with her subconscious and knew she was lovingly bringing it to fruition with her rage.

Rage that left Beth's attacker to roam free.

Rage that he had done the things he had to her. How he had slashed and cut into her lovely young back, leaving her scared and brutalised.

Rage that she carefully covered over with the polished veneer of a private education and a degree in law.

The most bitter pill to swallow and the one that hurt her the most, was the feeling of impotency, that nobody could do anything to help, not the police and especially not her.

She reached over and patted Beth's arm. "Don't worry so much about things, we're here to enjoy our meal; well, look at that, it's arrived."

Another waitress placed the small tapas bowls on the table before them and with the incident forgotten in Beth's mind, Gem was free to breathe a small sigh of relief and promised that she would take more care in the future.

The rest of the meal passed in comfortable conversation made even more enjoyable with a few more cocktails.

"Well, I appreciated that," remarked Beth as she dabbed at her full lips with her serviette. "It might have got off to a bit of a shaky start, what with the waiter and all, but I feel stuffed now. I couldn't eat another thing."

She leant back in her chair and eyed her friend through a happy plethora of good food and drink.

She had always liked Gem.

Gem of the unusual name, her friend since as far back as she could remember. They had liked each other straight away, recognising the bond that had been struck the moment they had seen each other at Oxford.

They couldn't have been more different in looks if they had tried, what with Gem's long blonde hair and blue eyes and an awesome five feet eleven, and herself with dark brown tresses, dark eyes, and a mere five-five.

Not only did they share rooms at university, they shared their lives as well.

Beth had told Gem that she was only sent there by the generosity of her uncle, as both her parents had died several years before. He was her father's brother and having never married he made it his job to oversee her education and her well-being. Beth explained that although he had opened his house to her, he had not wanted to get too involved in the life of a young teenager; being a retired Oxford don he preferred his books and so left her upbringing to Mrs Vera Dunn, a very worthy and well upholstered housekeeper.

This wonderful woman, Beth mused, had made it her mission in life never to let a term go by without sending several large hampers of her best food, food that Fortnum & Mason would have been proud of.

Even now Beth remembered it as though it was yesterday, that all through their ups and downs of college life, they were always assured of never going hungry and their room became the place to be for all the other perennially hungry students; many a glass was raised to the excellent Mrs Dunn.

She sat there for a moment, mentally raising a glass to her now, that wonderful, thoughtful woman whose death two years ago had left her feeling alone and bereft.

Her uncle had retreated further into himself and shut himself completely away from society. The death of the only woman in his life must, Beth felt, have hit him harder than he would have liked to admit.

Beth was eternally grateful that Mrs Dunn had died before the attack, as she was sure the horror of it would have finished the poor woman off completely.

As for her uncle, she was spared the telling of her ordeal to him, as he never read the papers and he certainly did not have a telephone or any of the modern day conveniences. So she thought it best that he remained ignorant of the extent of her injuries.

Not wishing to recall any part of her attack, she pushed it to the back of her mind. It was better to get on with one's life; everyone told her so, everyone except Gem. She continued to pick away at it like some old sore, but it was her life and her attack; she would deal with it as best she could.

Gem saw the myriad of emotions crossing Beth's face and knew her thoughts were dwelling on things past. She leant across, smiling to alleviate the sudden look of fear she saw etched on Beth's face.

"If you are so comfortable now, how are you going to move yourself to go and meet Cybil? We promised her we would go round and view her new flat," remarked Gem in a mock tone of surfeit indulgence as she drained the last of her cocktail.

"Oh please, look who's talking, it was you who ordered those last two drinks, I am just a patsy in your hands," replied Beth, adding, "and not only that it was you who arranged to meet Cybil, I don't think she likes me very much."

An untimely hiccup put paid to what she was going to say next and Gem took advantage of her friend's sudden incapacity to call for the bill.

They split the bill as usual and then made their slightly unsteady way to the exit. It had grown a little darker outside, but the light gave enough illumination for them to look for a passing taxi. People were still strolling up and down, taking advantage of the general cooling of the weather after such a hot and humid day. Young girls in skimpy tops and tight skirts were heading off to the nearest available hot spots, and young men with their trousers practically falling off their bums were not far behind them. Gem had to smile at the fashion of the day; her father she knew would just call them scruffy or even licentious, if she knew his more scurrilous remarks, but kids would always follow what they wanted to follow, and no amount of verbal aberration from parents or adults were likely to change them.

Gem grabbed hold of Beth's arm and pulled her to the edge of the kerb, where she unceremoniously placed two fingers in her mouth and blew a very fine whistle, practically stopping a passing taxi in its tracks.

Beth looked at her in amazement and said, "How do you do that? It's always fascinated me."

"No times for lessons now, just get in the taxi," replied Gem as she gently shoved Beth into the back seat.

"22 Micklegate, please, Mr Taxi Driver and don't spare the horses," said Gem as she plonked herself down next to Beth. Beth started to giggle and Gem was glad that the evening had taken some of the tension away from her friend. It only remained to be seen if the rest of the night would go so well; for some reason, she had her doubts.

The taxi pulled up to the kerb and while Beth paid the driver, Gem made her way up the steps that were festooned with pots of geraniums. The front door had numerous baskets hanging from its lintel. When Beth finally made her way there she found Gem leaning on the buzzer.

"I take it you have arrived then," said a disembodied voice emanating from the speaker-phone. "Go to the lift when you're in and press number three; see you in a mo."

Gem and Beth did as instructed and made their way over the black and white marble tiles. The sound of their high heels resonating in the empty lobby caused them both to stop in mid step and look at each other.

Gem as usual broke the spell with a sudden burst of giggling, saying, "Well, I'll tiptoe if you do."

"Don't start please," Beth giggled in response. "It's bad enough as it is; this is all a bit, you know ... a bit ..." Beth suddenly flushed a light pink as her words stumbled to a halt.

"Oh, you mean it should be a bit more down market?" replied Gem with mock disapproval, eyeing her with more than a little scepticism as they entered the lift.

"No, oh God, I didn't mean that, it's just that, well, you know," said Beth, blushing even more.

"Actually, I do know, and Cybil would be the first to admit it; look Beth, it's true we haven't known her long and you can blame Rupert for us knowing her at all. Well, it's that, just because she doesn't come from a privileged background like us doesn't mean she can't enjoy the better things in life, good God, she's worked hard enough for it, or so she says. What number did she say? Oh yes, three."

Beth looked across at her with mild curiosity. "Well, don't leave it there," Beth said eagerly.

"To be truthful, I'm not breaking any client confidentiality by adding her rise to the top came a little quick to be purely her own doing." Gem hemmed and hawed, with a little knowing nod and a wink.

"Oh, you are awful, Gem, preaching to me when all the time you've got some inside information on her," Beth answered with a laugh.

"No, not really, she says she comes from Manchester, but I made a few discreet inquiries, and they all came back a blank." She lifted her hand to silence the questions she could see rising on Beth's lips and added, "Which is not so unusual, you don't know for what reason people hide their identity, perhaps there is a bully of a husband out there that she does not want to see again. It could be any number of reasons and I for one am not going to ask her. Anyway, how would you like it if someone started digging around in your past?"

As Gem pressed the button Beth leant against the side of the lift and fiddled with the strap of her handbag; after a pause she said, sounding somewhat chastened, "Anyway I'm sorry about what I said. I didn't mean anything by it; actually I'm a bit taken back by how good her taste actually is."

Gem looked across at her friend and smiled and as the lift finally slid to a halt at the third floor, Gem automatically picked up her good mood again.

Grinning now with enthusiasm as the doors slid open, she said, "This is nothing, I can't wait to see the inside and from what I have heard it's something else." With that Gem pulled Beth out of the lift with her and linking arms they made their way along the corridor.

The door was on the latch and so they were able to enter the apartment. They walked inside and Gem was the first to see Cybil as she made her way round the room, plumping up cushions and straightening chairs, unaware of their presence.

Cybil's red hair fell over her shoulders; it was the hair colour made famous by the Duchess of York: Titian.

No common red for Cybil and only her and her hairdresser knew if it was natural or not.

Cybil worked out and it showed in the lithe contours of her body, wrapped in her designer cat suit. The long flowing lines of the trousers sinuously wrapped around her legs as she walked. Cybil eventually spied them standing there in the doorway and motioned them to come in and both Gem and Beth moved as one into the room.

"Thank goodness you're here, I'd about given you up for lost," she said, waving her arms in the air. "And then all my goodies and pastry things would have gone to waste. I've been slaving away over a hot oven for the past two days and I just know you'll both do justice to everything ..."

Cybil let her voice trail away as she eyed the two women.

"Have I said something wrong, darlings? You look a bit upset."

Gem felt Beth squeeze her arm and she herself felt a moment of panic as she thought of all the food waiting to be consumed.

"No, we're fine," Gem said on a swallow and without looking at her, she knew that Beth was nodding her head in agreement. Cybil watched them as they crossed the large open plan living room, looking for the entire world like a pair of condemned criminals than guests at a house-warming.

"Please, please, pleeeease, the pair of you," she said, starting to laugh. "Just look at you, I'm sorry, I was only joking. I haven't been baking till God knows when." Pointing towards the kitchen area, she said, "I don't know how to use anything yet and besides, Rupert saw you at that restaurant tonight stuffing your faces, both of you. So I thought what the hell, let's have a little bit of fun."

Cybil had followed them into the room and now after taking centre stage, she collapsed into a large comfy armchair; her peals of laughter bounced around the room.

Kicking off her shoes and tucking them under her, Gem instantly saw the funny side and, turning to Beth, who was at the other side of the settee, gave her a quick wink.

"See, I told you, Beth, don't worry so much," she mouthed, and Beth, who was prepared to be seriously mortified, gave a nervous little giggle.

At that moment Rupert entered the room and said, "Hi pals of mine, has Cybil done her little bit yet?" He looked around the room and noticed Gem and their hostess in various stages of hilarity, while Beth was subdued as usual.

"Yep, well, that's out of the way, who wants a drink?" Rupert said. "Cyb, can I get you anything, seeing as how you are the hostess with the mostest."

Cybil raised her full glass and shook her head, still laughing until her abundant head of hair flopped over her face and rather irritated, she flicked it to one side.

"No? Right, how about you, Gem? What would you like? I'm official barman tonight, name your poison."

Rupert made his way over to the kitchen and amongst the clattering and chinking, Gem assumed he was setting up some sort of bar.

"I'll have a white wine, thanks Rupert."

Gem looked at Beth, who seemed to have recovered a bit. "What are you having, B?" she asked.

"I'll have the same as Gem, thanks Rupert," she called out over Rupert's noisy preparations.

While Rupert attended to the drinks, Gem watched him work, which was always a pleasure in her opinion. He was just over six feet, with blond hair and looked kind of "film star"-ish in a normal guy sort of way, no Hollywood veneer for our Rupert. Rupert was too much a man of the moment; he was a GP with hobbies that an SAS man would find hard to keep up with.

Gem had been on one of his outward bound adventures and found herself up to her neck in freezing water, miles underground, in a series of pot-holes.

After that, she always politely refused his offers to join in on the next adventure. She admitted to herself that she wished there had been more between them, but the moment had never seemed right.

"Penny for your thoughts, Gem," said Cybil as she leant forward to grab a handful of cashews from a bowl on the coffee table.

"Oh nothing, really, I was just daydreaming; it's been one of those days, what with the heat and everything. I shall be glad to get into bed tonight, not that I shall get much sleep. I never do when the weather is hot like this."

"Well, that's okay then because I've got a special guest coming this evening. I'm sure you will all find her fun."

"Fun, oh do tell whatever do you mean, Cyb?" replied Beth with a nervous little laugh.

"Just fun, fun, fun, darling, don't be so uptight, you'll enjoy yourself, I promise." As Cybil spoke her last word the doorbell rang.

"I'm there," replied Rupert as he hurried over to the door to let the mystery guest in. Beth and Gem exchanged glances and with a slight shrug of her shoulders Gem looked towards the lounge door, waiting with an unexpected feeling of nervousness to see who would enter.

Chapter 5

The visitor was not what Gem was expecting and because of this her nervousness increased. There before her stood a woman nearly six feet tall, her hair in long fine braids, tied together with myriad ribbons. She had features like a Greek goddess and in her nose was a ruby stud, which matched the numerous earrings dotted around her ear. Her clothes were pure hippy, long and flowing and on her feet were small beaded mules.

Her hands were long and delicate and on her fingers Gem could see a multitude of rings.

She carried a large leather bag, which she had draped over her shoulder and she just stood there in the middle of the room, waiting for everyone to take their fill of her. Gem had never seen such a confident young woman and it took all her self-control not to gawp with her mouth open.

She managed to steal a glance at Beth and could see she was also enthralled; as she looked around the room it felt as if they were all under this woman's spell, waiting for her to bring them each to life again.

The spell was broken when the woman turned to Cybil and finally spoke, but even her voice held a sort of enchantment; it was soft and genteel, a voice that you could listen to and never tire of … a siren's voice.

"Good grief, whatever made me think of that?" muttered Gem and she mentally shook herself. Everyone began to move at once as if embarrassed by the effect this woman had on them.

Rupert jumped forward to introduce the others, saying, "Hello, so nice to meet you, my name is Rupert we met at the door." He held out his hand

and as they shook hands, he continued, "and this is Cybil, who I imagine you spoke to on the phone when she arranged this little soiree."

When he saw the woman nod her head in agreement, he carried on round the room, taking the woman by the elbow and guiding her as he went over to the settee, saying, "This is the lovely Beth."

Beth's face glowed with embarrassment at Rupert's words, but she managed to smile back at the woman, who gazed down at her intently.

"And last but not least," Rupert said, "is the luscious Gemini."

"Oh, do behave," said Gemini, laughing at Rupert and turning her head to examine the woman more closely; she was disappointed to see her turn away.

Rupert walked after her and gallantly offered the guest a drink, in a soft tone she asked for a mineral water.

She took a seat opposite everyone, a seat that positioned her with her back to the window, so the evening light cast her in a slight shadow.

"It's getting quite dark now, shall I put the lights on?" asked Cybil.

"No thank you," the woman instantly replied, adding, in her soft tones, "If you don't mind, can we just have the table light on? I find a softer light more conducive to what I have to do."

"What's going on?" whispered Beth, and Gem could hear the nervousness in her voice. She reached over and gently squeezed her friend's hand; as Beth slowly turned her head away from the figure sitting in front of her the look on her face started to worry Gem, and for a moment the strange woman was forgotten.

Words of comfort were on her lips, but before she could utter anything Rupert came bounding over with the glass of water the woman had asked for.

"Here you go, water au natural," he said, laughing at his own joke and handing the glass to the woman. She reached out her long slender arm and the soft folds on the sleeve of her dress gently slid back towards her shoulder; for a moment, Gem caught sight of what was either a strange birthmark or a tattoo on the inside of the upper part of her arm.

Suddenly she felt the woman watching her and as their eyes met, the world was thrown a little off kilter; she could feel the hairs on her arm rising and a large knot of panic started to form in her stomach.

The woman's features swam in front of her and she felt as if she was falling through time and space, losing all sense and identity.

Her breathing grew shallow and the woman still held her in her intense green gaze, her eyes burning holes into her.

Just as suddenly as it started it came to an abrupt halt and Gem found herself back in the room, surrounded by her friends, who were all talking and laughing together. The last of the evening light was still falling into the room, but the skies were darkening fast with the night clouds that were tumbling in over the moors. They marched steadily westwards towards the setting sun, cloaking everything with their darkness.

Gem was not given to sudden premonitions, but as she looked out of the window she felt suddenly scared, as if the darkening of the room heralded something similar in her own life.

Not wanting to give credence to these feelings, she turned her attention back to the others. Beth was smiling into her second drink that Rupert had poured for her, Cybil was arranging the coffee table in accordance with the evening's entertainment and the woman was giving her full attention to what was in her bag.

Gem looked around the room; the panic still within her, she tried hard to rationalise what had happened, but her mouth was dry and the palms of her hands were damp. She wiped them on her skirt and the act of doing such a normal thing helped to calm her down.

Nobody was looking at her askance, something she was extremely grateful for. Nobody had seen what had gone on between the woman and herself, but then again what had actually happened? Had she imagined it all, her senses heightened by the unusual visitor?

As her breathing finally came back to normal so did her judgement and she found she could actually put what had just happened to one side, to be examined and reviewed later.

Gem decided to join in the fun, suddenly wanting to be entertained so that she could push what had happened to the back of her mind.

She picked up her glass and wiped the moisture away that had formed on the outside; raising it to her lips, she drained it. Glad that nobody had seen her, she raised her hand to catch Rupert's attention, asked for another glass of wine and then settled back to see what else the evening had to offer.

The table before them had been cleared and the woman leant forward and addressed the friends.

"Before we start, let me introduce myself," she said softly, looking around at each of them. "My name is Remne Segs – unusual, I know.

"Now that's out of the way I can carry on," she continued, glancing round at Rupert, who was just filling his glass with a hefty slug of Jack

Daniels. She asked, "Are you joining us, Rupert, is it?" Although she smiled sweetly, her tone showed she would take no prisoners.

Somewhat embarrassed, Rupert hurried over to join the rest of them and seated himself at the foot of Cybil's chair.

They all watched in fascination as Remne produced an assortment of paraphernalia from her large leather bag. Selecting a deck of cards from amongst her items on display, she swept what was left to one side.

Raising her hand and showing the cards to the assembled friends, she continued, "Various suggestions have been made to explain the original meaning of the word 'Tarot'; they range from old Egyptian origins to a card maker from the French village of Taraux, who may or may not have produced the original Tarot cards. Whatever their origin they remain an enigma."

She laid the cards upon the table, saying, "Tarot, as we know today, is a collection of images and symbols from a wide variety of cultures, from the ancient Greeks and Romans to the prehistoric Norse peoples, from the ancient religions of India and Egypt to the medieval courts of Italy and France."

She looked around the assembled group and smiling at each in turn, she graciously tilted her head towards her hostess, offering to give her a reading first.

"Oh no, no, no, not me," Cybil almost squealed in alarm, squirming in her seat. "Well, not yet anyway, let someone else go first."

"Okay, who shall we pick?" Remne asked; her thoughtful dark gaze wandered over each of them and came to rest on Beth. She smiled warmly and Gem could see a little of the tension leaving Beth when she returned the woman's smile.

Remne placed the stack of cards in front of Beth and asked her to cut the deck three times with her left hand.

Beth leant forward and did as she was asked.

With each cut of the deck, Gem could see Remne staring intently at Beth. Her gaze passed over Beth's face and when their eyes met above the cards it looked for all the world to Gem as though she was trying to see into Beth's very soul. Beth was oblivious to what Gem had seen and seemed quite happy to go along with the act of choosing her own cards.

She picked out three cards, having chosen a simple spread after listening to what was available. The cards were laid on the table face downwards, and then Remne suddenly grew quiet, concentrating as she turned the first card over.

It was the "Hanged Man," and Beth stole a glance at Gem and gave a little grimace of distaste.

She then gave her attention back to Remne, who in her soft polished voice was explaining the meaning of the card: "This card, Beth, describes you as being in a state of limbo, a transition if you like between one stage of your life and the next."

Leaning forward to give emphasis to her words, Remne said, "This card counsels the need for patience and to focus on living in the here and now, not in the future. It also describes the ability to view life from a different perspective."

As she finished these words her hand was already turning over the next card. All four of them seemed to wait jointly with bated breath.

"This is a good card, Beth, it is 'Strength'; it is about beating the odds, or maybe performing difficult feats with ease. There are of course different types of strengths, Beth."

As Remne looked at Beth, Gem had the odd sensation she was trying to give Beth some sort of message. How could any of them have known about what had happened to Beth? Neither of them had said anything on their return to the city. They were all new friends, and even though Gem had shared a few idle childhood memories with Rupert, she had never said a word about Beth, who had felt too ashamed to say anything.

Gem could hear Remne continuing her lesson, but the doubts still troubled her. She took a sip of her wine as she listened to Remne continue.

"There is of course moral courage, strength of will, mental grit and physical stamina; all these strengths could apply to you and if you don't mind me adding, it can also indicate convalescence after an illness."

Gem's eyes flew to Beth's face and she could just register the sudden paleness of her cheeks as the words hit her. Beth's smile did not falter and Gem's heart went out to her as the meaning of the card was actually put into force.

"Shall I continue, Beth?" Remne asked solicitously, noticing her pale cheeks.

"Get on with it, woman, Beth's okay, it's probably the drink," interrupted Cybil. "We shall be here all night at this rate." She leant over the side of her chair and waved her hand in Beth's general direction. "You're okay, aren't you, Beth honey? Tell the woman to get on with it. Rupert here is dying to hear his cards, aren't you, pet?" Leaning forward she placed a loud kiss on top of his unruly mop of hair as he sat at her feet.

Rupert just laughed and took another gulp of his Jack Daniels. He adjusted his tall frame to lean more comfortably against Cybil's chair and Gem found she was disappointed to see how close the two of them seemed.

The third and last card to be turned over was the "Emperor," and even Gem was at a loss as to what that could mean.

"This card," explained Remne "means someone in authority, someone in your life who has authority over you, a parent or guardian for example. They may seem stern or dictatorial, but in reality they are reliable and trustworthy."

Remne gathered the three cards together and returned them to the pack; when she had finished she looked directly at Beth and asked, "Are there any questions you want to ask me? Do you understand what I said about the cards?"

"Not really," replied Beth softly.

"Well, it can be said we are dealing with the past, present and the future, this is what your cards represent. Their meaning is only clear to you because you hold all the answers to your own life. Do you understand a little better now? The cards are telling you what path to choose; eventually you will see their true meaning."

She abruptly turned and faced Rupert, saying in a heavier tone, "Now Rupert, would you shuffle the cards and cut them three times with your left hand and then pick three cards from the deck?"

She sat in silence while he finished the job; having decided on the three cards he wanted, he handed them to her and she placed them, like Beth's, face down upon the table.

She turned the first card over and gave it her full attention. There was a general gasp of trepidation when they all saw his first card: the "Devil."

"Contrary to popular belief," Remne said, smiling, "this card does not represent the devil incarnate, but it means enslavement or addiction, or even to be held in thrall of someone or something and being unable to break away."

Gem stared at Rupert and was fascinated by the play of emotions that crossed his face at Remne's words. As far as Gem knew, Rupert was his own man. He came and went as he pleased and was answerable to no one.

He had told her once that he did not want to settle down or be "tied down," as he said it, preferring to stay single and play the field. She felt they were kindred spirits on this occasion, as she herself did not want to be tied down either. That was probably why they got on so well together and had remained close friends instead of lovers, so to hear Remne say he was enslaved or addicted brought a frown of concern across her features, making a line appear between her eyebrows.

This is getting to us all, Gem thought and once again she was left to wonder about the true nature of the friends that surrounded her.

Her voice crystal clear, Remne continued to present all the hidden meanings of Rupert's chosen cards: "This could be a self-destructive habit or it may mean a job that makes you feel imprisoned."

The room suddenly went quiet and you could hear a pin drop; nobody made a move, so they were all a little shocked to hear Cybil's laugh ring out around the room and to cover her mirth she leant back in her chair and said, "I'm sorry, darlings, but it was just too much thinking about Rupert being all enslaved and tied up and such like." She giggled again as she took another sip of her drink.

The evening had long since lost any of the remaining sunlight and the room had started to be lost in deep shadow.

Gem reached over to the small table beside her half of the settee and turned on the lamp. A warm soft glow spread across the group, banishing the few shadows that remained in her half of the room.

Its light fell like velvet over Remne's features, softening the angles of her face and smoothing out the lines of concentration on her brow.

Remne waited until Cybil had finished laughing before she continued; turning over the next card, the frown on her face deepened as she said, "The 'Tower'; well, it seems, Rupert, that there are some sudden and dramatic changes on the way and they appear to arrive out of the blue."

Remne suddenly stopped talking and looked straight at Rupert, who Gem noticed was taking all this in intently.

"But it seems that intuitively you have sensed them coming for a long time," continued Remne, still staring at Rupert.

Rupert bravely met her gaze, full on, but even he dropped his eyes eventually, unable to win their battle of wills.

With more bravado than courage, he covered his embarrassment by downing the last of his drink and saying rather too loudly, "Come on then, I'm such a hopeless case, let's see what the last card brings. Let's hope for my sake it's a bit more cheerful."

"Here, here," replied Cybil. "We don't want any party poopers."

They all waited for the turn of the card, all leaning forward slightly to see what Rupert had in store for him. Remne cut through their suspense, revealing the last card: the "Moon."

"Goodness me, Rupert, don't tell me you are a lun … a … tic," said Cybil, spacing her words and laughing at her own joke.

Beth, who had remained quiet since her reading, looked at Gem, this all seemed to be getting a bit overwhelming her look seemed to say, but Gem just raised an eyebrow in mock amusement and carried on listening to what the strange woman had to say.

Remne's voice seemed to calm even Cybil, who was getting a little raucous with all the drink she had consumed.

"The Moon indicates deception and the ability to see a situation in its true light. As often happens at night, landscapes look different in the moonlight and this may mean your viewpoint may not be accurate."

She stopped to take a sip of water before continuing, her eyes not on Rupert's face but on Gem's. When she had finished the water, her gaze returned back to Rupert and she said, "You may be choosing to ignore the facts, or for some reason they have not been revealed to you. Whatever the reason, someone is tricking or deceiving you. Do you wish to ask me any questions?"

Remne lowered her eyes and crossed her hands in her lap, waiting for a response from Rupert.

Rupert merely shrugged his shoulders and said, "Not really, I only said I would make up the numbers of the party I'm not really a believer. All a lot of bull really; I think I will just get myself another drink instead."

With that he gracefully got to his feet and strode off in the direction of the kitchen and the bottle of Jack Daniels.

Cybil straightened her legs to ease them after having had his large frame leaning up against them.

As Cybil lounged in her chair, her gaze wandered over to Remne and Gem was surprised to see, if only for a second, something cloud her features. Was it because Rupert had been made to look a bit of a fool, or what? Gem couldn't quite make it out. As she was watching Cybil, she suddenly turned towards her and Gem could see the ghost of an emotion left behind on her pretty face. It wasn't anger and it wasn't jealousy; it was something she couldn't put her finger on, but it left her with a feeling of uncertainty.

Cybil smiled and once again she was the playful, attentive hostess.

"Now it's your turn, Gem. We've all been waiting to hear what the future has in store for you."

By this time, having her fortune told was the last thing Gem wanted.

She had seen the others go through myriad emotions and to be quite honest with herself, she felt she was better off not knowing what the future held for her.

She was just coming to terms with the past!

Gem felt their eyes on her and felt obliged to say something; as she went to open her mouth to turn the offer down, Remne forestalled her by saying, "I'm very sorry, but that will have to be all tonight. I am very tired, it is getting rather late and I have a long way to go."

As Remne gathered all the cards, two fell on the floor; Gem did not know whether this was done on purpose or not, but they landed near the settee, where she was sitting. She unwound her long legs from under her and slid to the floor to help pick them up.

As Gem handed her the cards, Remne slipped a small piece of paper into her hand. Obviously Remne had not wanted the others to see and Gem obliged by slipping the note into the pocket of her skirt. Not a word or gesture was acknowledged and Remne did not make eye contact, remaining as cool and aloof as before.

Gem managed to keep the look of curiosity from her face as she studied Remne's features up close. Gem acknowledged to herself that Remne was very beautiful; her skin glowed and her hair was thick and lustrous, which was not unlike her own had it been down. She also realised they were about the same age.

Suddenly Cybil's voice shattered the silence and the mood, saying, "What are you two doing down there? Remne darling, Rupert wants to know if you can read the bumps on his head instead. Didn't you, darling?" Flinging out her hand, she grabbed hold of Rupert's jacket and tried to pull him down to sit beside her again.

"Give it a rest now, Cyb, we've all had enough for one night," Rupert replied tersely, walking round to stand behind her chair.

Remne and Gem exchanged glances and the look that passed between them was one of mutual respect. Gem liked this woman. There was something very honest about her.

Rising to her feet after gathering all her belongings together, Remne turned to Cybil and said, "Thank you for tonight, I hope everything was to your liking; perhaps we shall meet again. I'm sorry I have to dash off but it is rather late. I would very much like to do your reading; you have a very interesting face."

Cybil by this time had risen to her feet and was swaying slightly in front of Remne. When Remne had finished speaking, she held out her hand for Cybil to shake and Gem was taken by surprise as she watched the two women.

Remne grasped Cybil's hand and leant down towards her. The height difference was more pronounced now that they stood side by side and Gem saw the mask slip away from Cybil's face, if only for a second.

Once again she saw strange emotions flit across Cybil's face and then they were gone. Clasping her hand to her mouth, Cybil let out a little yelp; plunging her hand into her pocket, she brought out an envelope and said, "Silly me, I nearly forgot to pay you; here you are, your wages for services rendered. Thank you so much for coming; I hope to see you again soon."

Remne smiled as if heedless of the look, her tall elegance towering over Cybil.

Straightening her bag that had slipped from her shoulder, Remne turned and said her good-byes to the rest of the company, her eyes staying a fraction longer on Gem's in silent agreement and with a slight nod of her head, she turned and left the room.

Rupert followed Remne to the door and they could hear his low murmurings as he said his final good-byes.

On seeing Cybil flake back down in her chair, her eyes closing in apparent intoxication, Gem took the opportunity to leave. She slipped on her shoes and nodded to Beth to do the same; after pulling Beth from the settee, she pushed her towards the front door and Rupert.

"Sorry Rup," Gem said, "I think we are all a bit tired and, well, you know." Gem's head nodded towards the lounge. "I think madam has had a bit too much to drink. Thank her for a lovely evening and tell her I will be in touch soon."

Gem leant over to Rupert and planted a kiss on his cheek; Beth, who was much shorter, had to contend with tugging playfully on his lapel jacket.

Rupert laughed and the evening's tension seemed to slip from him like rain off a new Berber Mac. He hesitated for a moment and then seeming to make up his mind, he grabbed hold of Beth, leant down and planted a kiss full on her lips. Beth was taken completely by surprise and flushed a resounding pink.

Gem was just as surprised and not wanting to stand and watch like a gooseberry, she hurriedly turned away and opened the door, waiting in the hall until Beth emerged.

As Rupert leant up against the doorframe, his body filling the gap, Gem could see he had a rather dopey look on his face, so she just raised her hand and smiled and Beth did the same, as it seemed his kiss had rendered her temporarily speechless.

Stifling her laughter, she ushered Beth back along the corridor to the lift.

"What an evening that turned out to be, not at all what I expected," Gem said as she pushed the button for the lift.

Beth's fingers absentmindedly traced an arc round her lips in memory of Rupert's kiss and Gem smiled as she watched her.

Something nagged at Gem was it the relationship between Rupert and Cybil? Was Rupert having a relationship with her or was she mistaken by it all? Not if the kiss he gave Beth was anything to go by.

Still she was sure Beth would make the right decision, she had to stand on her own two feet sometime and little steps like this one were just what Beth needed.

The lift shuddered to a stop and they clambered in, both eager to be away from the place, both wanting to be alone with their thoughts, both with entirely different reasons.

Chapter 6

The note she had received the night before was now just a rolled up piece of paper thrust in the bottom of Gem's coat pocket. Every five minutes, she got it out and reread it, trying to read some sense into what the message conveyed:

> "Meet me at Ripon Racecourse Marina.
> Come alone. We need to talk. Ask for
> a boat called the Guiding Light."

What worried Gem more was the fact that the letter was obviously prewritten before she had even gotten to Cybil's house, so how did Remne know she was going to be there? More to the point, how did Remne know anything about her?

What exactly was going on?

She had hardly slept a wink all night and had come down in the early hours to pace around the sitting room. She had even sat for a while with the headphones on, listening to some music, but it was no good; there were too many things tripping around her brain, and she could not concentrate on what was playing.

As she wandered out into the kitchen she decided to make a cup of coffee and when this was done she opened the back door, sat on the stoop and sipped its warming brew. She got out the note from her dressing gown pocket and reread it, but it was no use; even if she read it a thousand times, it would not tell her any more than she knew already.

When they had gotten in last night, Beth had gone straight up to bed, feeling a little worse for wear from the wine, or rather that is what she had told Gem, who was of the opinion that she wished to be alone with her thoughts of Rupert, so she had not detained her.

She had thoughts of her own and they were still bothering her now. The early morning mist still lingered about the garden and the blackbirds were singing to the newly rising sun.

It's going to be another fine day, thought Gem as she thrust the note back into her pocket. Shall I go or not? That was the question bothering her. What if she turns out to be a nutter or it's some sort of scam and as Gem sat there she thought of every possible scenario, but it was no good, her curiosity had been piqued and she just had to go. Not only that, there was the question of that birthmark or whatever it was; now what was all that about?

It was no use sitting there, so she got up, threw the remainder of her coffee over the grass and went back into the kitchen, locking the door as she went.

Gem had peeked into Beth's bedroom earlier, saying she had to go out on a few errands and she would be back later.

She had to smile at Beth's sleepy reply, her face glued to her pillow. The slow wave of Beth's hand was all the answer Gem received, so she closed the door silently to let her finish her sleep.

Happy now that she had finally made a decision, Gem hurried down the stairs, retrieved her keys from the hall table and then went out into the early morning sunshine. Mrs Thomas, her neighbour, was just returning after being out for her early morning stroll with her faithful Jack Russell glued to her side and stopped to pass the time of day.

"You're out early, Gemini; don't usually see you at this time of day. Not like Badger and me; we love it, don't we, boy?"

As Gem looked over the wall she could see the ancient dog half sitting to one side and wheezing like a bronchial falsetto.

"Just been for our paper, haven't we, boy?" said Mrs Thomas, tapping the rolled up newspaper against her twill trousers and looking down at her beloved dog. Gem could see that the dog was less than interested and felt sorry for the small canine.

"You off out, then; anywhere nice?" asked Mrs Thomas; Gem had learnt from long experience that she did not really want an answer and did not even care to know, it was just her way of neighbourly conversation.

"No not far, I have got to pop into work and pick up a few things," she lied, but she needn't have bothered because Mrs Thomas was turning away as she spoke. Gem had to smile as she saw the woman chivvying her dog inside the house and with a wave from the elderly woman's hand, Mrs Thomas was gone.

Gem stood there for a while, wondering if Mrs Thomas had all her marbles and deciding she had wasted enough time already, so she hurried down the steps of the house to her car before she could be stopped again by another elderly resident. There were a few along the stretch of road where she lived, all around the age of her parents, which was not surprising considering the price of the houses. There were not many youngsters that could afford them now. They had been lived in by the same families for donkey's years, like her own parents, but it was always sad to see one of them come on the market and get turned into flats instead of staying a family house.

It was just fortunate for her that her parents had given the house to her and that she had not had to buy it herself, it would have cost her a fortune.

As Gem walked along the pavement she looked up at the sky; the promise of a storm had not materialised. The wind had gusted a bit during the night so that all the clouds were dispersed across the moors, leaving the day bright and fresh and as the sunlight filtered through the trees it made dancing leaf patterns on the bonnet of her car.

The Stag sparkled and gleamed, and Gem could not help but run her hand along the paintwork, pleased with herself that she had paid extra for the new respray. The leather seat creaked as she settled herself into the driving position and with the key in the ignition and the handbrake off, Gem gently eased the powerful car away from the kerb and headed towards Ripon.

The traffic was easy at the moment, but she knew from long experience that it would be hectic later on in the day as shoppers made their way towards the City of York. It was nice to be heading out into the country; she just wished the errand was of a happier nature. Doubts still beset her and as she drove along she went over the conversations of the night before.

The whole evening had seemed a bit strange, but she couldn't for the life of her put her finger on anything specific.

The honking of a horn told her she had been daydreaming at the lights and so she slammed the gear stick into first and hurriedly pulled away from the annoyed four by four that was inching closer to her back bumper in an attempt to hurry her along.

The villages around the city sped past and Gem found herself through York and onto the motorway in next to no time. The trees were taking on the colour of old gold as the summer neared its end, but there was not the parched look about the countryside as could be found in the south of the country where the hosepipe ban had been in force most of the year.

The corn stood tall and ripe, and the combines were in the fields now, harvesting a bumper crop; she surmised they had been there since the start of the day, using every bit of daylight they could to bring in the harvest.

She loved this time of year, when the summer was coming to its end and she suddenly remembered all the happy harvest festivals she had attended at school, bringing in the large box her mother had made up for the occasion, the contents of tins of fruit and jars of homemade jam and vegetable produce all brimming over the sides and destined for the less privileged in the community.

Her thoughts were brought back to the present when the signpost indicating her exit flashed past on the left. It hadn't taken her long to reach Ripon from York, it was only a jog down the motorway and the happy thoughts from her childhood had taken her mind off the purpose of her visit.

Now that she had nearly reached her destination, she started to feel anxious and the fluttering in her stomach did not help. In her haste to get out of the house, she had forgotten to eat breakfast, and the cup of coffee she had earlier only succeeded in giving her a bit of a caffeine rush, fuelling her anxiety; as it grew so did the feeling of nausea.

Cruising along the B6265 towards Ripon, the road meandered downwards to the town like a drunken English sailor (her father used to say this about the twists and turns of the old roads).

The signpost said it was only four miles to the town, so she reined in the speed of the car, fearful now that she would miss her turning, which was just as well because she very quickly came upon a small bridge across the River Ure and had to slam on her brakes to give way to a very large lorry that had no intention of stopping.

As the road continued to slope down towards the valley, Gem suddenly saw the large imposing building of Ripon Racecourse and knew that she was nearing her destination.

The large building on her right, with the legend "Travis Perkins Timber and Building Supplies," caught her eye and she had to brake suddenly as she realised she had missed the small road on the left that said "Ripon Racecourse Marina and Private Moorings."

She had arrived so suddenly and very stupidly had nearly missed the turning altogether. She slammed her brakes on hard and skidded to a halt; after glancing in her rear view mirror, she was relieved there was nothing following her. She reversed the few feet she had overshot and with the Stag down to a crawl she negotiated the turning and made her way across a cattle grid that was flanked by two wrought iron gates. She had to smile when she saw a sign pinned to the gates that read, "Please drive carefully, frogs crossing."

Gem carried on along the tarmac road that was lined with trees, making it seem quite a rural setting even though they were so near the town and the racecourse. She was actually quite amazed at how close the racecourse actually was; personally she wasn't into horse racing, but this was such a pretty spot that she was sure her parents would like it.

Dad liked a flutter.

She once again went through her head what she was going to say, but it never seemed quite right and she didn't want to give too much away.

Especially about Beth!

In her frustration, Gem slapped the steering wheel and pulling herself to order, she decided to play the game and see what Remne wanted with her.

Her anger had helped to quell her nausea and now that she had arrived and had something positive to do, the fluttering in her stomach had ceased also.

The tarmac road suddenly gave way to gravel, so she slowed the car even more, fearful that she might flick the stones up if she went at any speed.

She decided to carry on up to the end of the road and parked the car near a small brick building which bore the sign, "Smeaton Information Centre." Gem turned the engine off and got out of the car; leaning her arms on the roof she gazed around but nobody seemed to be about. So shutting the car door and locking it, she made her way up the bank to the river and the lock to see if she could find someone; as luck would have it she spied two young lads fishing.

Gem imagined they were mini versions of their dads, if their dads fished, even down to the beanie hats plonked rakishly on their heads.

She half expected to see a six-pack amongst their bait. It was hard to believe that fishing was the biggest participating sport in the UK. It was obviously a man thing, as Gem as had never taken to the sport herself but had spent many an hour with her father when he fished. Being together in comfortable silence was one thing, but she could think of nothing worse than sitting around for hours waiting for a bite if you were on your own.

The silence was quite profound, broken only by the occasional song of a thrush and the heat was beginning to rise; she could feel it starting to beat down on her head. She resented having to break the mood of the place by asking the boys directions.

"Sorry to disturb you lads," she began, "but do you think you can help me?"

Two pairs of eyes swung round to face her and as she stood there, both boys jumped to their feet and came over to where she was standing.

"There's nothing biting at the moment," one of the lads said, "and we're only too glad of the distraction; was only saying to my friend here, it's a bit quiet round here today. There are normally more of us than this; still, what is it you want, like?"

Gem had to a smile as she listened to his Geordie accent; it was always nice to hear a regional one instead of the plumy ones she had to listen to in court.

"I'm looking for a boat called the *Guiding Light*; do you by any chance know where I can find it?" asked Gem, dazzling the boys with a perfect smile.

"Certainly can, it's back down the road a bit," said the other boy, jostling his friend out of the way as he spoke.

They both walked back down the road with her, swigging from their water bottles as they went.

"Would you like some?" the first boy asked. "It's right cold and I'll even wipe the top."

"No, thank you all the same; just point to the jetty I have to take and I will be on my way; thank you for your help."

So they pointed to the third jetty, back down the road she had driven up.

Gem waved a fond farewell to the two lads and set off down the road, but not before thanking them for the time they had saved her.

She made her way down the road until she came to the gate they had pointed out and as she pushed it open it gave a unrelenting creak as if it hurt to open.

A wooden slope led down to the jetty; there were only two long boats tied up and as she walked along, her shoes were silent on the wooden slats. Gem hoped as she peered along the side of one of the boats, looking for the name, that she wouldn't be mistaken for a thief or a trespasser.

It wasn't the one she was looking for, it was called *Blue Belles,* so carrying on she assumed that it must be the other one on the end and there it was, the narrow boat called the *Guiding Light.*

Two swans glided pass the boat, their wake sending little ripples out across the water. Their heads bobbed up and down in the murky liquid, searching for food and they were totally unperturbed by her presence.

Gem watched in fascination as the large white birds floated effortlessly past and smiled sadly at the pair, as she always did, because it always made her sad for some reason, knowing that they mated for life. She didn't want to think of such a beautiful bird being heartbroken if it happened to lose its partner.

Gem gave a small sigh and carried on her way down the jetty until she reached Remne's boat; having never been on a narrow boat before, she was at a loss as to what to do.

There was hardly a bell to ring, or a door to knock, not that she could reach from the pier, anyway. Remne must have been expecting her, because from out of the bowels of the boat she could hear her name being called.

After the rattle of a chain being removed and a bolt being thrown, the back door opened and out popped Remne's smiling face.

"I knew you would come; step aboard," Remne told her. "Did you find me okay? I bet Josh and Dean told you where to come."

"Is there anything you don't know?" replied Gem, somewhat put out that her visit was not more of a surprise.

Remne looked up at Gem from the bottom of the cabin steps, shading her eyes as she did so in the strong morning sunlight.

Twisting her eyes in the sun's glare, Remne answered gently, realising that talking to Gem was not going to be plain sailing.

"It's not hard to guess; you are naturally curious and so I knew you would turn up in the immediate future, it being Saturday and you're not working. As for the lads, they are always there fishing and seeing as how there was nobody else about, as I looked earlier, it was safe to assume you would ask them the way."

As Remne talked she had turned into the cabin and Gem had to descend the few steps to catch what she was saying.

Feeling somewhat foolish now, Gem was about to open her mouth to apologise when Remne said, her back still towards her, "Don't bother to apologise," and as Remne turned to face Gem and the surprised look on her face, she added, "Because there are times when I *do* know everything."

Remne ushered Gem further into the cabin and pointed her to a seat surrounded by cushions. As Gem looked around she was surprised at how much could be put into such a small space to make it look homey and comfortable. There were beads and crystals hanging from the windows – or were they called portholes? Gem wondered; anyway, whatever they were called, light flooded through, making the place look golden and surreal.

The fractured light from the crystals gently spun round the room as the soft breeze from the open back door wafted down. Gem had a feeling of peace sitting there, peace she hadn't felt since Beth's assault and since the feeling of impotent rage had started to bubble up inside her.

The tinkering of tea cups from the galley brought back memories of the teas she shared with her mother in her childhood. She often sat on the lawn with her favourite toys, waiting excitedly for her mother to bring out the tray.

Listening now to the cups and saucers being put together, it was a happy sound, one Gem had almost forgotten about and the memories it evoked.

"Do you take Sugar?" Remne asked, breaking into her thoughts.

"No, thank you," replied Gem, regretfully returning to the present.

She accepted the tea Remne offered and settled down in the chair's fluffy abundance and waited. Gem studied Remne over the rim of her cup and while the other woman was preoccupied with pouring her own tea, Gem noticed that Remne had divested herself of all her jewellery and ribbons, even the ruby nose stud. The flowing clothes of the night before had been changed for a pair of jeans and a simple crossover top, which left her arms bare.

Instantly Gem's thoughts went back to the night before, when she had first seen Remne and the vision of the birthmark that had initiated her feeling of vertigo. As if Gem's mind were indeed an open book, Remne leant forward and showed Gem the mark that was nestled on the inner part of her right arm.

Her curiosity now piqued, Gem leant forward to get a better look and what she saw made her take a sharp intake of breath.

There before Gem's eyes was her own name, written not by a tattoo artist but in the natural phenomenon of pigmentation.

The cup Gem was holding started to rattle in the saucer, as her nerves finally got the better of her. Remne studied Gem's features all the while, her eyes never leaving her face. Eventually she lowered her arm, and as if gathering her nerve to speak, Remne leant back in her chair.

What she said was not what Gem was expecting.

"I could tell you a long confuted story, one I am sure you would not understand."

"What has that got to do with you having my name on your arm?" retorted Gem, angry now at being patronised.

Remne stopped and looked down at her hands before she continued, ignoring Gem's last remark. "Terrible things have happened, now and in the past."

Before she uttered her next words, she looked up and tried to convey to Gem her sympathy for what she was about to say.

"Your grandfather knew exactly the terrible price one had to pay in keeping the evil ones at bay."

Noticing Gem blanch at the mention of her grandfather, Remne struggled to explain.

"Since the dawn of time, since humans first walked upon the earth, there have been forces at work trying to persuade them from living, as you solicitors would say, ethical, moral and virtuous ways and I would call righteous ways. It is a battle, and one we are constantly waging."

Here Remne stopped and gently smiled at Gem; she continued in the same tone, watching all the while the emotions playing on Gem's face.

"It might come as some surprise to you that there are angels and demons mentioned in all the religions of the world; why is that, do you wonder?"

Gem looked at Remne and shrugged her shoulders, not trusting her voice to remain neutral. She didn't come here for this; she wanted answers to the questions that had been bothering her for so long, not this load of twaddle, but she remained silent, letting Remne carry on talking, in the hope of hearing something of interest.

"It's because for every demon there is an angel to counteract it, to even the balance, so to speak. But now it seems in this modern age, where the stakes are so high, things are starting to come to a head. The evil ones are starting to take control; you yourself are in a profession where you come across evil all the time. Am I not right?" Remne waited for Gem to nod her head, which she did reluctantly before she continued, "But I am talking about wars, plagues, and religious hatred. I am talking about the four horsemen of the apocalypse being unleashed on an unsuspecting world, not about some juvenile mugger or opportunistic rapist."

As Gem listened to Remne speak, her brow was furrowed in concentration. Now she leant forward and placing her cup and saucer on the table before her, she asked Remne, in a tone akin to annoyance, "What exactly has this got to do with me? I'm just an ordinary girl, living admittedly through some extraordinary circumstances. What on earth can I do? Save the world? Create peace and harmony? I don't think so! Or maybe I should start a petition; that's it, I shall go out now and round up hoards of people and ask them if they wouldn't mind recanting evil and going out and performing good deeds because a woman I met at a party asked me to."

"No, it's far more difficult than that," replied Remne, still staring at Gem but trying to stifle a laugh.

"That's it, I've had enough of this crap," Gem answered back.

She had both hands on the edge of her chair, ready to push herself upwards in preparation of getting to her feet, but Remne's next words made her collapse back in her seat: "You knew when Beth was injured, you felt her pain, you also had an experience in the car park that night; an experience that made you feel fear like you have never known before. Am I right?"

Gem nodded weakly as she glanced over at Remne, who continued, "It is my duty to put you on the right path; you have been chosen to fight against someone who can only be described as pure evil. There is also a very good reason as to why we brought you back up north; I can't tell you at the moment, the time is not right. I …"

"Hang on a minute," interrupted Gem, her face drained of all colour. "Are you saying I haven't even got free will? I thought I made the decision to come back to York from London. I thought free will was what you lot were all about."

"You will never attain free will, not even from the outcome of this battle; your destiny was made long before you were born. Your grandfather knew that, and he died to keep your presence a secret."

Gem tried very hard but the tears spilled over her lashes and onto her cheeks; in a small choked voice, she asked the inevitable question: "Was … my … was my grandfather murdered by this … this thing that attacked Beth?"

Remne reached out a hand to comfort Gem, but she pulled her hand away, not wanting the contact with her.

"Your grandfather found a Book, along with three others. But the Book spoke only to him, so he kept it hidden. He and one other person worked on deciphering its message in secret. I went to see him on the night he died; he knew that his end was near and that by his death he could finally bring to fruition your destiny. I let him think the Book was destroyed, burnt in the fire at his house, but I brought back a different Book from the person whose turn it was to help decipher it … a copy. He had to think it was the real one because your destiny had to be fulfilled."

"Destiny, destiny, what are you talking about, what destiny? Who am I if not my father's daughter?" Gem replied, with as much venom as she could muster, her chin thrust out in defiance. Her long blonde tresses had escaped the confines of the large tortoiseshell clip and were tumbling down over her shoulder to the small of her back.

"Firstly let me explain something to you," Remne said, trying to sound calm, in a room where the tension hung in the air like an early morning mist. "This thing that we are hunting has crossed the realms between their world and here. It has become flesh. Not content with trying to tempt mankind with all the false promises they offer, he wants to dominate, subjugate and prevail over all things good and when he has finally done this, that will open the gates to all the others like him and then the time of man will be at an end."

Remne stopped talking to take a sip of her tea, acting, Gem thought, as though this was just a normal woman-to-woman chat.

This was far from normal!

Remne continued, "For now he is learning to walk amongst men, learning their ways so that he can defeat them. He is not as powerful as he would like to be, that is why we must act now, before he gets too strong. You are nearly ready, although you do not realise it. You feel things and your powers are getting stronger; you know from the little displays you give yourself. Your demonstration in the restaurant with the waiter did not go unnoticed."

Remne stopped talking to take another sip of tea, trying in vain to hide the sudden twitch of her lips where a smile was lurking.

Gem was suddenly mortified that even her slightest actions were being monitored. Racked with embarrassment, Gem steered the topic of conversation round to what she wanted to know.

"You were going to tell me something when I mentioned being my father's daughter. If there is anything more to hear, you might as well tell all. Is my father involved in this somehow?" asked Gem, trying to sound brave and feeling far from it.

"No, your father is not involved, not directly," Remne replied, hedging her answer.

"What do you mean ... not directly?" Gem wanted to know one way or the other, and the look she gave Remne brooked no more hedging.

"You are not your father's daughter; you were given to the people who brought you up, because they could not have children of their own. It was safer for you. The evil ones did not know where to look, and they thought the Book was entombed in the Minster at York. When they eventually found out it had survived, your grandfather's death was sealed and they just hoped that they could kill him in time, before he could do too much damage. So you see, you have to fulfil your destiny, because, Gemini darling, you are in fact one of us."

"And who is that?" replied Gem, still battling to come to terms with all the things Remne was saying.

"You will see soon, very soon. Be patient and all will be revealed."

That was the only reply that Gem received and by the look on Remne's face, that was the end to the morning's extraordinary conversation.

Chapter 7

Gem slowly walked up the steps to her house, unresponsive to what was going on around her. The drive back from Ripon seemed to take no time at all, so engrossed was she in going over their conversation.

Her mind was in utter turmoil about all the things Remne had told her. Not least of all being that her parents were not really that.

Now that was quite unbelievable!

Earlier on the boat, she had wanted to scream with rage, call Remne a charlatan and all the names she could think of for turning her life upside down.

Now she was home, all she could do was lean her head against the door jamb and close her eyes. Her head throbbed in such an uncontrollable fashion that she thought she must be getting a migraine. Her thoughts turned from her pain to the end of their conversation as they stood at the back end of the boat.

Gem was about to step onto the wooden jetty, her long legs easily spanning the gap, but before she did so Remne caught her arm and delayed her.

Gem had turned to find out what Remne wanted and was surprised to find her lost for words. Their heated discussion showed Gem that Remne was at least a worthy opponent when it came to winning an argument.

At last Remne spoke, saying, "I know you are full of doubts at the moment, but believe me: I do speak the truth. If you want confirmation about what I have said … then go … to Henry Ernest Peterson."

"Beth's uncle?" Gem had said. "What on earth for? He's some crusty old don living in the middle of nowhere. He hasn't seen the light of day for years, even Beth rarely sees him, what makes you think he can help me now?"

Gem almost laughed at the scene her popping up out of the blue would make.

Remne looked at her shoes and as her foot traced a pattern on the decking she replied, "He was a lifelong friend of your grandfather; he was there when they found the Book! It was he who helped him hide it! It was he who helped him to decipher it! Why do you think they took Beth and did the things they did to her?" As she spoke, Remne looked up from the floor, her eyes shining like hard brittle emeralds, her lips parted in what was almost a snarl and she could see instantly the effect her words were having on Gem.

The colour drained from Gem's face and she had to cling to the large tiller to stop her legs from giving way and falling into a heap at Remne's feet.

"What are you telling me? This was not an accident? This was premeditated by … someone … or something?"

Gem's hand flew to her mouth as she felt the bile rise, her eyes glistening with unshed tears. Remne reached out her arms and gently gathered the young girl to her and this time Gem did not object to the comfort.

After a few moments, Gem felt able to carry on, so leaning away to break the contact between them, she asked Remne, "If what you are saying is true and I am the one, why did they take Beth? Why?"

Gem felt her words lodge in her throat; unable to carry on she dropped her head forward onto her chest and cried.

The tears she had been holding back spilled through her tightly closed eyes, down onto her cheeks and dripped onto the deck below. Gem was devastated that somehow she was to blame for what happened to Beth, no matter how small a part she played.

"They were searching for you," Remne said. "They knew it had to be you or Beth; it was just trial and elimination. But they did not count on you coming to your friend's rescue so soon. They got worried when you showed up. They are not sure of your power yet, that is why they disappeared quickly."

"Are there … are there more than one of … these demons then?" Gem stuttered her question, fear raking her insides at the memory of her encounter in the car park.

"We do not know; they may just have a single overlord, but I know for a fact they gather people to do their evil works. That is why you must be careful," warned Remne.

Gem caught the edge in Remne's voice and could see she was agitated.

She had not seen the cat when she had arrived, it must have been stretched out amongst the buckets of flowers, but now it was sitting upright and staring at the far bank. Gem saw its hackles start to rise and from deep within its throat, it issued a low rumbling growl.

Remne's eyes raked the bank of the canal where the cat was looking, as if she was searching for something ... or someone.

"What's the matter, Remne? What are you looking for?" said Gem, picking up on Remne's nervousness as she fearfully looked around the empty causeway.

"They can be anyone. They are so tricky. My insides feel uneasy, which a sure sign something is wrong."

Her voice softer now, she hurried Gem from the boat, saying, "Go now, go home, but take great care, trust no one. It is not safe here. I fear we are being watched."

Remne's eyes darted backwards and forwards along the bank, but Gem could see no one; even the swans were still floating around the boats. All seemed peaceful and quiet, much the same as it did when she first arrived, but things were not the same; her life had been altered to such a degree that she did not know who she was any more, but still there were questions that needed answering.

Feeling suddenly apprehensive about leaving Remne all alone, she took hold of the girl's arm as she made ready to untie the boat from its moorings.

"Will you be all right? Will you be safe?" replied Gem, anxiety sounding in her voice.

Remne looked down at the restraining hand and smiled softly to herself and then turning her attention back to Gem, she said, "Yes, I will be safe; they don't like water, so I shall moor away from the bank tonight in a safe haven I know. It is you I worry about; take care, Gemini. Trust only in yourself."

Gem let her hand fall away, but she could not help saying, "Will I see you again?"

"Don't worry, I shall be in touch," replied Remne, smiling warmly at Gem.

As Remne made ready to sail away, rushing from one end of the boat to the other, Gem jumped onto the wooden jetty and waved a fond but sad farewell.

When she got back home, Gem thought all this was going far too quickly. She rubbed the side of her head, trying to ease the pressure and with her right hand she fumbled for her door key on her key ring, trying haphazardly to put it in the door. There was no need, as the door slowly glided open at her hand's pressure; cold chills of alarm raced up and down her spine.

Checking her watch to see how long she had been away from the house, Gem noticed she had been gone a little over five hours.

It had only just gone half twelve now. By rights Beth should still be in bed. Someone had been or still was in the house, someone tainted with evil. Gem's senses were on full alert as she stepped into the hallway. She turned and silently closed the door and locked it.

If someone was still in the house, then the deadlock on the door would hinder their escape. Sliding her bag to the floor, her body took up the natural pose of someone preparing to fight. It all came so naturally to her now that she didn't even bother to analyse it. She accepted it all with gratitude, and if it meant helping to get them both out of tricky situations, then all the better for it.

She felt her muscles tighten as the adrenalin started flowing through her and she curled her long slender fingers into fists.

She smelt the air like a dog on a scent as she cautiously peeked into all the downstairs rooms.

Nothing!

Returning to the foot of the stairs, the hairs on her arms rose as she felt the closeness of the intruder. Waves of hatred permeated the area where she was standing, waves spilling down from the level above.

This was nothing like she had ever felt before … no, this was different. No coldness evaded the house; this was something else and this was something more tangible.

Gem felt in her inner core that this was something she could see and fight.

Silently and slowly Gem climbed the stairs, automatically avoiding the step that creaked. When she finally reached the top, the landing was as it should be. Gem could see into her bedroom from her vantage point on the stairs and the mirror in her room reflected emptiness, a room devoid of anything, human or otherwise.

As her eyes raked along from one door to another she noticed that Beth's door was slightly ajar.

That was not how she left it, but perhaps Beth had left it open. Gem knew from long experience that Beth liked her weekend lie-ins; nothing short of a bomb explosion would get her out of her bed on a Saturday.

Steeling herself for this final assault, Gem inched her way along the corridor to Beth's room, her back flat against the wall, trying to melt into the surroundings, fear knotting her stomach at what she might encounter.

Whatever it was was here!

She could almost taste its vileness.

Gem pushed open the door gently and through the crack of the door she could see part of the inside of Beth's room. She could just make out Beth sprawled on the bed, her arm dangling over the side. Gem could see Beth's eyes were tightly shut but not in natural sleep.

Please God, Gem silently prayed. *Not again.*

A movement caught her eye and it was then that she noticed the figure in black bending over Beth, ready to scoop her up. Gem did not give herself time to think; her body reacted with the speed and clarity which she suddenly felt at home with. Here was something she could fight and those months of frustrated anger welled up inside of her.

Gem swung the door on its full arc and then she saw the intruder. He wore a black mask that covered the whole of his face. Then she saw him look her way as he leant over Beth's inert body. She could feel his rage at being interrupted, but Gem was not concerned. She rushed forward, her impetus rapidly closing the gap between them and she felt her fist contact the intruder's stomach and was exhilarated by it.

She felt the rush of air explode from her adversary's lungs and the way his body doubled on impact, she knew she had inflicted an injury. She was not worried about being outclassed, even though he was much taller, Gem rained blow after blow upon her quarry. She saw him raise his arm across his eyes as if warding off more than her blows but she carried on regardless because she knew after delivering the first punch that this was just a man in a black mask. So the fear of the unknown that she had felt earlier disappeared and in its place was an overpowering urge to vanquish her opponent, to beat him to a pulp, to stomp on his miserable body.

Finding he was unable to fight back against this blonde avenger because the blows were coming too thick and fast, Beth's attacker managed to give one almighty push that made Gem lose her footing; she stumbled backwards and would have fallen if she hadn't clutched at Beth's iron bedstead.

He made for the door before she could recover and quickly prised it open; running swiftly down the landing, he made his escape two at a time down the stairs. Gem instantly gave chase, secure in the knowledge that the front door was bolted and she would finally have a solution as to who was behind Beth's attack. As Gem swung round the newel post at the top of the stairs, she could see the figure in black trying to force the front door open. When this proved impossible, she was surprised to see him run through the house to the kitchen.

Gem allowed herself a small smile of triumph when she saw this, knowing that the back door was locked as well. So racing down the stairs two at a time, she finally reached the kitchen, hard on the heels of the figure in black.

What she hadn't banked on, though, was seeing the figure launch straight through the glass of the locked back door. As the glass shards flew everywhere Gem was forced to fling herself behind one of the kitchen units and by the time she re-emerged all she could see was him disappearing over the wall at the bottom of the garden. Swearing softly to herself as he made his escape, she slowly made her way over to the shattered door to view the extent of the damage.

Her feet scrunched amongst the glass and debris and she kicked at it in her frustration.

Her attention was drawn to a piece of glass jutting out from the door jamb as she momentarily leant against it. Her sides heaved from the exertion of the fight and she felt small rivulets of sweat running down between her shoulder blades; she absentmindedly rubbed her knuckles as she leant forward to inspect the small shard of glass.

Blood dripped from the jagged piece. So he did not escape uninjured after all.

Good, I hope it hurts, you bastard, thought Gem, finally getting her breath under control. Giving the door one last inspection for any more clues and not finding any, Gem turned on her heels and retraced her steps back up the stairs to Beth's room.

He stopped running only when he was sure he was not being followed. The pain in his side was nothing to the cut he had sustained jumping through that glass door. There had been nothing else for it; he had felt cornered and panic had set in, forcing him to make the decision on the spur of the moment.

Something he didn't like to do.

He liked to plan things, make sure everything went his way without a hitch.

He was not expecting that long-haired harpie to come charging into the room, much less be outpunched by a mere girl. He ground his teeth in hatred at the thought of her. Who would have thought she could deliver such blows? As for that light, he rubbed his eyes in remembrance, feeling the sting even now. He would have to inform the Master about this new turn of events. His body slid down the wall he was resting against and he momentarily dropped his head on his arm, thinking of the wrath to come from the Master when he found out he had failed in his mission.

He felt himself start to tremble, knowing it was not the adrenalin still coursing through his body but rather fear of what was to come. He would have to think of something else and quickly, something that would not arouse the suspicion of that blonde bitch. If he could go back with even half a plan, then perhaps his life would be spared. He tried to think what his Master would do and a smile spread across his face at the deviousness of his plan. The Master had told him that killing the little one was not an option; he wanted her alive and that was good enough. It was not for him to reason why. The pain in his arm throbbed, making him forget about what was to come and concentrate on trying to stem the flow of blood.

He searched in his pocket for something to tie round it, but there was nothing there. He painstakingly removed his jumper and shirt and, with his teeth, tore off a long piece of material from his shirt and wrapped it around the wound, tying it hard into a knot. *That will do for the time being,* he thought and quickly pulled the jumper back over his head, tidying himself as best he could.

He then pulled off his mask, as it would not do to frighten the good people of York. Carefully wrapping the mask inside the torn shirt, he folded them both in a neat bundle and tucked them under his arm, content to carry it until he could find a convenient wastepaper bin.

Rising to his feet, the throbbing in his arm returned and he felt weak with the loss of blood. Steeling his thoughts for what he had to do, he pulled himself up to his full height and stepped out onto the street, retracing his journey back to the Master and the punishment he knew was awaiting him for his failure.

Her heart thudding painfully in her chest, Gem entered the bedroom and leaning over, she gathered her friend to her chest. Beth's eyes were still shut and fearing the worst, Gem could feel the hot tears forming in her eyes. She brushed away the hair that had fallen over Beth's face and gently rocked her in her arms.

"Has he gone?" Beth's voice sounded faint and unsteady from within her arms.

Overjoyed that she was alive, Gem gave Beth a hard, unrepentant squeeze.

"Yes, yes, yes, the bastard has gone," she said, laughing through her tears. "He jumped out through the kitchen door."

"You can let me go now, Gem, before you do more damage than he tried to do," replied Beth, struggling to escape her friend's firm embrace.

"I thought you were dead," said Gem, releasing her and settling herself the edge of the bed.

"So did I," replied Beth, her voice now stronger. "I thought it was you returning, so I rolled over to shout hello to you and that thing burst through the door."

Beth sat up on the bed.

As she straightened her nightgown she gave Gem a sly smile. "I thought my best form of defence was pretending to faint, because I thought he would have difficulty carrying a dead weight. It would have been so easy for him to walk me to the door, no matter how unwilling I was to go." Leaning over to her bedside table, she grabbed a hair bobble that was sitting there and gathered her unruly hair together and tied the bobble into it, so revealing her animated face.

Gem was surprised at this turn of events; she half expected to find Beth in some cataleptic stupor or at least rendered speechless with shock. This new Beth was something else and it would take a little time to get used to it.

"You, by the way, were absolutely wonderful, brilliant even." Beth's eyes shone with pride as she looked at Gem; she carried on talking, her excited energised face showing no signs of stress. "And that light, wow, where did that come from? It sort of radiated from you. I kept my eyes shut for most of the time, but trust me I'm sure that was what frightened him off." Beth almost bounced on the bed with glee.

"Slow down a minute here, Beth," Gem said, confused. "What are you talking about? Admittedly I found I could fight within an inch of my life, but light radiating from me? Come on Beth," said Gem doubtfully, "It must have been a trick of the sunlight."

"No, it was you," said Beth. As she replied, she leant over and squeezed Gem's arm. "Don't let's worry about this now, shall we call the police or what?" said Beth, her concern now for her friend as she saw Gem's brow furrow as she listened to her babbling on.

"No … I think we shall keep it to ourselves," replied Gem, taking charge again. "And while we are on the subject, how come you were so brave?" Gem leant in towards Beth, covering the hand that still lay on her wrist with her own. "Actually, it was mostly down to Remne; in the cards she told me to only live in the present and to be really brave when I needed to be, and hey presto, the rest as they say is history."

The smile swept from Beth's face and for a moment Gem was transported back in time to that night eight months ago. She wanted to comfort Beth, but this time she knew she was stronger, more capable of looking out for herself; she had proved that a few moments ago.

"Also," continued Beth, "I was not prepared to be a victim anymore; once was enough, but tell me, Gem, that was not the same person, was it? I felt he was different, not so evil. I remember so little of that night, but I do remember nearly suffocating with the vileness of whoever it was."

"No, Beth, it wasn't the same person and I think the time is right for me to tell you a few things that have been happening and about my visit to Remne."

"When did you go to see her? It must have been when you left early this morning. That reminds me, I have something to tell you about our friend Remne."

Before Beth could carry on, Gem interrupted her, saying, "Let's jump to it, because we have an awful lot to get through today, not least of all having someone come out to change the locks and replace that glass in the kitchen."

Gem walked over towards the door, intent on ringing for a locksmith.

Beth's voice stopped Gem in her tracks. "Please let me tell you, Gem, it's about Remne, it was bothering me all last night. It's her name, don't you see it?" Gem's stomach started to knot as she listened to Beth speak.

Gem slowly turned and faced Beth, who was almost triumphant in her discovery. "See what?" replied Gem, fearing that all she had listened to that morning was going to be found inexplicably true and there would now be no room for doubt.

"It's her name ... her name, don't you get it?" Beth paused for dramatic effect before continuing, "Remne Segs ... it's an anagram ... it spells out 'Messenger.'"

With that Gem turned on her heels and ran to the bathroom, spewing forth the contents of her stomach.

Chapter 8

From his place of concealment he could see most of the opposite river bank and the jetty where the long boat was moored. He had been following the girl for a while now, and much to his annoyance she had managed to give him the slip more than once, sneaky bitch that she was, but he would deal with her when the time came.

For the present he would remain where he was, see what she was up to and then report back and if all went well, he would remain in the Master's favour. To protect himself he had not mentioned she had been out of his sight on a couple of occasions and for quite a long period of time as well. It would not do to fall from grace too many times and he rubbed his wrists, still feeling the pain of the last time he had not done what the Master asked of him.

The ground where he was sitting was dry and full of dandelions, their fluffy heads full of seeds which blew away gently when the soft morning breeze tickled them. It was getting very warm as the late summer sun rose higher in the sky and he was starting to feel very uncomfortable in the dark suit he so loved to wear.

It had been so long since he had roamed the earth and he revelled in his newfound freedom. Adam had chosen his body, he had explained, not for its looks but because a man could move around more freely; women, it seemed, still had a lot of restrictions on them. What use had he for good looks? Adam had given him what he so desperately desired and he could take what else he wanted, when he wanted.

He had wandered at will around the different towns he had been sent to and nobody had given him a second glance. He had gone into the drinking houses, although Adam had expressly forbidden him to drink and sat there for hours just watching, absorbing everything around him, memorising and listening so that he would learn to fit in.

Now all these months later here he was, ready to do whatever Adam asked of him. As he squatted down amongst the foliage of the bank, his legs began to ache but he was loath to sit upon the ground and get his clothes dirty.

So carefully rising, he kept himself down in a crouched posture and ran, his short legs pumping like piston rods, back to the car that he had hidden in some trees over near the racecourse.

When he had unlocked it, he reached inside and took out an old blanket; he relocked the car and made his way back to the bank, still in a crouched position, to continue his surveillance. Happy now that he had got what he wanted, he laid the blanket out over the crumpled vegetation and threw himself down on it. Lying on his stomach, he bent his arms and cupped his hands so that they formed a cover over his eyes, shielding him from the brightness that was reflecting off the water.

He hated this job, hated the fact that he was so near the water. Trust that witch to live on a boat. As he lay there he saw the woman come out on deck and stand quietly, looking up and down the road as if she was expecting someone. He saw her raise a hand and wave to two small boys with fishing rods over their shoulders as they made their way up the road.

"That's it, little boys and stay on that side of the bank if you know what's good for you," he whispered softly, but he couldn't help licking his lips at the thought of the fun he could have with the two of them.

A bee hovered near his hand but he was too lost in his own thoughts until it landed on his fingers. Suddenly aware of the insect's fat little body, he gently lowered his hand until it was level with his mouth, and before the bee could raise itself into the air, his tongue had shot out, wrapped itself around the bug, and pulled it, wriggling, into his mouth.

Laughing silently to himself, he placed his hand back over the top of his eyes and resumed his watch.

The woman was nowhere in sight; he cursed himself for losing sight of her, but just as he went to raise himself from the ground he saw her straighten up on the far side of the boat.

She must have adjusted the ropes, he thought to himself; anyway, she had not gone, that was the main thing. He watched her water the geraniums that were in buckets along the roof of the boat and scratch behind the ears of the cat that was stretched out in the sunshine, and when this was all done to her satisfaction, she went back inside.

Boring!

Why do I get these jobs? He mused, but Adam had been most specific that he did not lose sight of this harpy and to make matters worse, Adam always lectured him on what he could or could not do.

"Doesn't he trust me?" he brooded as he idly scratched around in the dirt with one of his fingers. He lowered his head onto his folded arms and his thoughts drifted back to the time he had arrived.

He owed everything to Adam; he knew that; if it wasn't for him he wouldn't be here. Adam had called him to his side when he had killed the old man, holding the still beating heart over the pentagon that he had drawn on the library floor.

Adam had given him life just as surely as he had snuffed out the life of the old man that had crossed him about the book.It had to be done quickly; he had been writhing in agony, feeling the heat of his incarceration searing his body in never ending torture.

Then there was nothing, the pain had left him and his twisted little heart had rejoiced not to be in agony anymore. He gave no thought to why it had stopped, only was pleased that it had, but his joy was short lived because he then felt a different sort of pain as his body was stretched and pulled, as it travelled through time and space to land, small and naked, on the floor of the library.

Spirals of smoke were still rising from his body and as he looked up he saw a Fallen One lean down towards him; he covered his head with his small scaly hands, oblivious to his own talons digging into the side of his bald head.

He felt weak and defenceless like a newly born being and his body still felt the heat from his incarceration, but suddenly he began to feel renewed as the Fallen One blew breath from his own body over him. The breath replaced the heat with an icy coldness. It permeated his old and tired soul with a renewed hatred and as his new life was given to him, so was his loyalty totally given over to the Fallen One. He asked no question about why he was there; he just did whatever Adam asked of him.

He was a lesser entity; he had always known this, for it was only the Fallen Ones like Adam who had the full power. Even so he had his own capacities for evil, and with his new body that had been given him, who knew what the future held?

He knew that someone had arrived when he heard the creak of the old gate through which anyone could then walk down to the jetty. He wondered if this was the visitor the woman had been waiting for.

Alert now to what was going on he raised himself back up onto his elbows and covered his eyes once more so that his view was unhindered by the sunlight.

He watched this new woman walk down the jetty and peer at one of the boats; obviously this was not what she sought because she moved on and then suddenly stopped when a couple of swans floated past.

What was she up to, just standing there? He could just see from his hideout that she was not unlike the woman she had come to visit. Yes, they were both tall with blonde hair, but it was too far away for him to distinguish any facial features.

Maybe it was just from a distance they were the same and up close they didn't look anything alike. Anyway it was not up to him to make judgements; he would tell Adam about this visitor when he saw him later and leave it to him to decide what to do. For now, though, he must lie in the undergrowth and keep watch and that was what he intended to do, even though the nearness of the water made his flesh creep.

Suddenly there was movement on board the boat and the woman came out, but he could not hear what she was saying, more's the pity. Anyway, whatever it was had the desired effect because the new arrival swung one of her long legs over the side of the boat, clambered aboard, and followed the woman down into the bowels of the boat.

Well, that's it then for a while, he thought. *When two women get together, who knows how long they will be? There is no way I can find out what they are talking about without being seen, especially with that darned cat aboard.*

That was one of the things Adam had warned him about: cats, they just hated his sort and would go out of their way to expose them. How they did this, Adam had not elucidated, but suffice to say the warning was enough to keep him lying where he was.

As the sun rose higher he felt himself dropping off to sleep, so he flipped over onto his back, and as the heat warmed his body his thoughts turned to what would be his when finally the day came when his Masters ruled the world.

He had been promised whatever his heart desired and he desired young, fresh flesh, just like the two boys he had seen earlier and as the desire rose in him he slipped his hand down the inside of his trousers to relieve himself.

"What on earth do you think you are doing, you filthy little pervert?"

The words came thundering down to him as he lay and writhed on the blanket that he had thrown across the hard packed earth. His eyes flew open and his hand slid from within his trousers, but he was not quick enough to move out of the way and he felt the man's boot kick him viciously in the side.

It was not the pain that shot through him that made him wince, it was being found by someone and the consequences it would entail.

The sun shone down on him, blinding him for a moment as he looked skywards and then as he leant over him, the man's shadow fell across his own face and he could see the twisted features of the person who had kicked him.

He could hear the man swear and cuss at him and once again he raised his boot to strike him; as it swung towards his prone body, he flipped to one side and caught the foot with both hands as it neared his face.

The man was big and burly and he hit the ground with a thud, but that didn't matter to him. He had twisted the man's leg round until he heard it snap at the knee joint and the instant the man was on his back, he threw himself on top of him to stifle the scream that he knew would be coming.

He watched as the man's eyes filled with tears and was fascinated as he watched them pour down the sides of his face to his ears, but he was even more careful not to let the liquid touch him.

He knew from bitter experience how much water burned his skin.

The man's face had turned from pink to purple in a matter of seconds and as he lay there, covering his face with his hand and the man's body with his own, he stealthily raised his head to look around, concerned that someone had noticed the commotion, but all was quiet.

Damn!

The women had come back out and were standing at the end of the boat, still talking. He could not finish the man off until the visitor had gone, because he could not take the risk of removing his hand in case the bastard started yelling; voices seemed to carry farther across water for some reason. Mind you no matter how much he strained his ears, he still couldn't hear what the two women were saying.

As he lay there he felt the wind shift direction slightly and suddenly the cat sat upright and looked directly over to where he was; even though it couldn't see him, he knew the bloody thing smelt him. He tightened his grip on the man's mouth as he watched the woman looking around, tipped off by the cat's behaviour. He watched as the visitor took hold of the woman's arm and more words were exchanged, but that was it; the visitor then stepped from the boat. He had taken his eyes momentarily off the woman and so he was annoyed to see she had already cast off the restraining lines and was backing the boat out of its mooring. That was what she was probably doing when he had lost sight of her before.

Damn her and her cat he was sure now that was what tipped her off. He could see the mangy thing stalking up and down the boat as if looking for him.

Now he would have to wait until she went past him before he could dispose of the man held in his deadly grip. He did not worry about whether he had the strength to do it; even though he was short, he had the strength of five humans. It was the fact that he would have to dispose of the body and that took time.

Time he did not have if he wanted to keep tabs on the bitch and she knew this; she had timed it well, making her escape when he was incapacitated with this fat lump and he punched him in the side, adding to the man's distress and pain.

He watched as the boat slipped past him and he could hear the cat yowling as it walked along the decking, looking up at where he was hiding. So ducking down even more he was unable to see the expression on the woman's face as she left, but he was sure she must be gloating.

He waited for about fifteen minutes before he thought it was safe to move and in all that time his anger towards the woman reverberated through his body; he needed an outlet. Looking down at the man in his grasp, he smiled and thought, *what better way of venting my anger?* The man saw the smile and knew his time was up; closing his eyes he mentally kissed his wife and children good-bye and laid there, waiting.

He did not have to wait long; he felt his assailant's cold breath on his neck and for an instant he was intrigued by it, so he opened his eyes and saw to his horror that the face that loomed above him was not that of a man.

The man's mind fought to take in what was happening; that hideous face … where had he seen the likeness before? His body tried to shrink away but there was nowhere to go all he could do was wait for the inevitable outcome.

As the creature opened his mouth sunlight glinted off his sharp pointed teeth and as he drew nearer to the man's neck, he felt him struggle to escape and a tingle of ecstasy passed through him knowing that he couldn't.

He closed his eyes, savouring the moment as his teeth sunk into his victim's neck. He knew the man wanted to scream, because he could feel his lips moving under his hand, but his grip was too tight for any cry to come out.

He ripped and pulled at the flesh on the man's neck and then he threw back his head in silent triumph as the blood started to pump from the wound. As he lowered his head to look at the man, blood and flesh dripped off his lips and his darting tongue slavered in and out of his mouth gathering up the fleshy gore.

Then as the coldness began to creep over his body, the man knew he was dying and the realisation of where he had seen the thing before came to him … the church that was it. He must have looked at it every week of his life and as he slowly died, he knew he was looking at the face … of a gargoyle.

It did not take him long to die, only a couple of minutes, but to add to his dread he had to listen to the Thing lapping and licking as it drank his blood that was slowly being pumped from the hole in his neck.

When it was all over, he prodded the dead man with one of his long bony fingers and was satisfied that he was indeed dead. So releasing his deadly grip, he then pushed the body away from him and stealthily got to his feet.

He peered over the top of the vegetation, looking round in a full 360 degrees. All was as it should be; the sun still shone and the bees still buzzed, but he dreaded having to tell Adam about this little indiscretion.

So he carefully wrapped the body in the blanket and slinging it across his shoulder, he carried it back to his car. Flicking the automatic button on his key ring for the boot lid, he waited for it to rise and then threw the body inside. Getting rid of it would be no problem; he could dump the body anywhere. It was the rest of the stuff that was so annoying. So he hurried back to the place where he had been and gathered together the dead man's fishing rod and bag and slung them across his shoulder. Giving the area one last look-over, he kicked the ground where the man's blood had soaked down into it and scattered the earth so that none of it was visible. After straightening the area as best he could, he made his way back to his car.

He then looked around, straining upwards to his full height to determine if the man had brought a car with him. There were one or two parked in the back road that led to the racecourse, which meant he would have to go and check the body again to see if the man had any keys on him.

He raised the boot lid again and flung the fishing gear inside, glad to be rid of the smelly bag; as luck would have it, he could find no keys in the dead man's trouser pockets or in his waistcoat.

So closing the lid he heaved a big sigh of relief and as he leant up against the car he looked down at himself and swore.

What a state he was in; his nice suit was ruined, so taking off his jacket he wiped it round his face, which helped remove what was left of the blood from his face. He then opened the rear door and pulled out a plastic bag, which he carried around with him for small emergencies like this.

He rummaged through the bag and selected a nice white shirt, all freshly cleaned and ironed and as he pulled the rest of the blood soaked clothes from his body, he folded them and placed them meticulously in another bag and placed them back into the car. Then pulling out the white shirt and smoothing it down over his body, he made up his mind that Adam need not know what had transpired here today. He would just tell him about the other girl that had arrived and explain that he had not been in a position to move when the woman had slipped away in her boat, as there had been too many fishermen about to risk his surveillance being discovered.

Giving the place one last look, he then walked round to the driver's door and got inside, but before he started the engine, he put on his dark glasses and baseball cap and then drove at a slow pace out of the area. It would not do to aid anyone if they had to give a description; they would not have much to go on now, as the glasses and hat covered most of his face.

Also he did not want to arouse anyone's suspicion by driving recklessly, so he wound down the window and rested his elbow nonchalantly on the sill. He slowly made his way out onto the main road and headed off to a landfill site that was not in use anymore. He would also switch cars just in case someone had taken note of the plate number.

Chapter 9

"You're not coming with me," Gem said for the umpteenth time as she packed a small case for the journey. Beth had refused to listen a long time back and she dogged Gem's footsteps round her bedroom, making her point as she went.

"He's my uncle," Beth said, "so that gives me the right and I think from now on we should stick together; if what Remne or whatever her name is says is true, then we are both in danger."

They had sat up half the night discussing what they had learnt. Both tried to reach some sort of logical conclusion about all that had happened. In exasperation Gem had decided to go alone to visit Henry Peterson and since learning of Gem's decision, Beth had been adamant about going with her.

Gem finally stayed in the middle of the room and stared down at her, but Beth bravely stood there, even though Gem towered over her.

She stood with both hands on her hips, looking for like a prize fighter eyeing up an opponent, a female David to Gem's Goliath.

Gem hadn't seen her so animated since, well, she couldn't think when.

"I'm going with you and that is the end to it," added Beth. The annoyed look on her face faded when she saw Gem dissolve into laughter.

"You brute, here I am fighting my corner and you're laughing at me. You know full well that you haven't got a chance in hell of seeing Uncle without me." With this Beth swung a punch at Gem's arm.

"Okay, okay, you win," giggled Gem, rubbing her arm. "You throw a mighty punch for a little person."

"So it's all right then, I'm coming with you?" responded Beth, practically hopping from one foot to the next with excitement.

"Doesn't it put you off, what Remne said about my parents, the Book, and well ... everything and your near abduction yesterday?" replied Gem, suddenly more subdued.

"No, it means there is a reason for all this, don't you see? It was the not knowing ... the randomness of it all that was so frightening. Now we have a purpose, we shall go and see my uncle and get him to talk to us."

With the words hardly out of her mouth, Beth suddenly turned on her heels and hurried out of Gem's bedroom.

"Where are you going now?" Gem shouted after her.

Beth's head popped back round the edge of the door and she replied with a big grin, "Just to my room to pick up my bag, because I have already packed."

"You cunning little imp, you knew all along I would say yes," replied Gem, realising that she had been conned.

The laugh echoing down the corridor was all the confirmation she needed.

Gem had let the Stag have its head as the car flew up the A1, and then along the A591 towards Cumbria, their overnight bags stashed comfortably in the boot. Dusk was falling as they reached the Lake District and Gem hoped there would be enough light left to find their destination.

Their conversation in the car had been light as neither wanted to break the mood of happy camaraderie, each fooling the other if only for a while, that this was a happy outing.

The weather, typical for August, had turned from blazing hot on Saturday, the day before, to the fine drizzle that was now falling as they drove around Lake Windermere. The car's headlights picked out the signposts they needed and Beth, who was looking around with amazement at the countryside, said, "I can't believe how much has changed; there are so many buildings since the last time I came."

"That's progress for you," replied Gem as she carefully steered the car round a large puddle. She gave Beth a gentle prod to get her attention back and added, "Come on, you can sightsee another time, where is the house? I don't want to be driving all night and seeing as how you couldn't get through to any of the neighbours to tell your uncle we are coming, we had better get on with it."

No sooner had she spoken that Beth shouted out triumphantly and pointed to the small lane leading off to the left.

"There! It's there! That was lucky; we nearly missed it."

Beth turned and grimaced at Gem, adding, "It's a bit overgrown; obviously my uncle doesn't use a car or anything; sorry, Gem." Letting her voice slide away, Beth braved a sideways glimpse at Gem's face and didn't much like what she saw. Beth knew the lengths Gem went to protect her car and the thought of the new paint job she had done just before they came up north had her biting her lip with unease.

Beth started to utter a few words of consolation but Gem cut her short, saying, "I'm warning everyone," and her eyes turned heavenwards, "nothing had better happen to my car, nothing! Do you hear me?" Turning to Beth she hissed, "And God help your uncle if he is not in or won't see us!"

With that she dropped the two front wheels down onto the overgrown lane and proceeded with caution. Finger long branches, wet with rain, protruded outwards and with only her main beam to see where she was going, Gem navigated as best she could.

She cautiously edged the car farther through undergrowth that had not seen pruning shears in years; Beth heard Gem tut-tutting as the car skidded on the wet leaves blown down by the rainy breeze.

"How long is this damn lane?" Beth heard Gem mutter.

Beth, through her long experience of knowing Gem in all her moods, thought it prudent not to say anything that would further annoy her.

She just sat there and prayed Gem was a good enough driver to miss all the obstacles that she saw advancing towards them in the car's beam. They both heaved a large combined sigh of relief when they arrived unscathed at the front door.

Gem turned to face Beth, her features returning to normal, the scowl disappearing and Beth could only shrug and offer a weak smile in return.

Laughing at Beth's gesture, Gem gave her a gentle shove, adding, "Come on then, let's see if your uncle is up, or slipped off to bed like most old people his age."

Beth emerged from the car with agile ease and ran over to the door. As Gem got out of the car she could see Beth pulling on the old doorbell and she could even hear it resonating throughout the house. As she leant up against the car, absentmindedly patting its roof with affection and listening to it cool down, she noticed the downstairs curtains twitch and for a brief second a face appeared.

Beth turned to face Gem, her shoulders shrugging and her hands rolling over to show her palms in a gesture of "I don't know where he is."

Before Gem had time to tell Beth about the face at the window, they both heard bolts and chains being released, and before Beth had gone two paces she swung back towards the house and came face to face with the recluse of Windermere ... her uncle.

"You had better come in, I've been expecting you," he said to their amazement.

Gem retrieved their cases from the car, locked it and turning to follow Beth and the old man, mumbled, "Is there anything we do that is not expected?"

On hearing her words, the old man turned to face her and replied, "Yes, well, there is, actually; I didn't expect you would make it down the lane with that car," and turning, he retraced his steps back into the house.

Her face glowing with embarrassment, Gem, now chastened, quietly followed.

They followed the old man down the dimly lit hallway; passing doors that looked as if they hadn't been opened for years, so great were the cobwebs round each one. The hall carpet had seen better days as well, with quite a few places threadbare. Gem was amazed at how frugal Beth's uncle lived, considering the amount of wealth the old man had, but then she smiled, he was so like her own grandfather. He never wasted money on incidentals either and only spent his money on what was necessary; Gem supposed a hall carpet was not really on the top of Uncle Henry's list of priorities.

Finally they turned a corner and dropped down a couple of steps and as they negotiated the wide corridor in the semi dark Gem saw Beth straightening a few of the paintings on the wall as she walked along.

Gem saw Henry disappear through a door and when she finally arrived, she found herself in the library. The warm glow that emanated from inside suggested that it was the only room in use throughout the old rambling house. Both the girls welcomed the open fire after the cold drizzling rain outside and seating themselves either side of it, they held out their hands to its warm embrace.

Henry stood between the chairs of the two girls; with his hands behind his back, he looked every inch the Oxford don. His clothes, although not new, were clean and tidy, so it was obvious that someone was looking after him. As he stood there in silence, looking from one to the other, Gem and Beth exchanged glances, not quite knowing how to broach the subject they had come to find out about.

The crackling of the fire and the ticking of the mantel clock were the only things they could hear, giving the room a centuries-old feel. The leather bound books rose above them to the ceiling and by the quick glance she gave them when she entered the room, Gem could see that this was where Henry spent his money. Now from the comfort of her seat by the fire, she noticed one of those moveable step things resting in the corner which allowed him to reach the books on the higher shelves.

At the end of the room heavy drapes were pulled shut on whatever view lay in wait beyond them. The light from the table lamp on the desk cast a warm yellow glow over their half of the room and Gem felt herself succumbing to the comfortable chair and warm surroundings.

Her eyelids started to flicker after the long drive and as she nestled back in the chair, she was brought instantly back to the present because suddenly Henry spoke.

His voice was warm and vibrant, not the voice of an old man at all. "I have made you some sandwiches," he said, pointing to the small table situated next to Beth, "and there is a pot of coffee on the hearth. When you have finished we will talk. I will leave you for a minute, because I have to go and fetch something."

With his message complete, he turned round and left them, pulling the heavy door shut behind him as he left the room.

"How do you think he knew we were coming" Gem mused as she looked at the door Henry had just departed through.

Beth just shrugged her shoulders but she was forced to laugh when Gem's stomach started to growl. So settling more comfortably in her chair she turned to Beth and said,

"Do the honours, Beth and pass me a sarnie, I'm famished," she said as she leant over and pointed to the full plate.

"Only if you be mother and pour the coffee," Beth replied with a smile like sugar.

The embers crackled and spat as Gem leant forward and placed another log on the fire. The flames licked the wood with hungry tongues of blue and red as Beth handed her the sandwiches; Gem was surprised to find the coffee was rather good also.

Henry had been back in the room sometime, waiting for the girls to finish.

The package he had brought back with him sat like an unwelcome guest in the corner of the room. He sat down in the big chair at his desk, his fingers interlocked across the stomach of his thin frame. His long legs were crossed at the ankle and were stretched out in front of him in a relaxed fashion.

Gem studied him while she sipped her hot coffee.

He was as old as her grandfather and his head was now bald on the top, but Gem could see it must have been quite a mane considering the amount that grew at the sides. He obviously had not been to the barber's for a long time.

His horn rimmed glasses kept sliding down his nose and she suspected it was more from habit that he kept adjusting them. Gem was surprised to see that Henry was inspecting her in much the same way and where she thought he was dozing, he was actually, like her, analysing and evaluating.

"Let us get down to the business in hand," Henry eventually said as he saw that they had finished their meal.

He rose from his chair and came to stand in front of Beth, reaching down for her hand as he spoke.

"It grieved me beyond measure to hear about the assault on you all those months ago, but I was not in a position to offer any help." He smiled fondly at Gem as he added, "Also I knew you were in very good hands. It would have been dangerous if you knew too early what you are up against. You acted just as you should have done ... with innocence. They were put off guard and that gave us enough time to put our plans into action."

As he spoke Henry let go of Beth's hand and retreated back behind his desk, but not before Gem noticed his eyes behind his glasses were glistening with unshed tears. As he walked around the desk Gem noticed his hands were shaking as he steadied himself before he sat down.

"Now then," he said matter-of-factly, "what exactly has Remne told you?"

Gem, now all attention, leant forward in her chair towards him, adding excitedly, "So you know Remne? Who is she?"

Henry held up his hand to stop the flood of questions about Remne; he saw that even Beth was getting quite animated.

"Remne is not the question here. She is part of the solution; that is all I am saying about her. First let me tell you about your grandfather," he said, looking at Gem. "He was my best friend, my colleague and my fellow researcher into all the wonders the Book held."

Henry ran his fingers across his bald pate and smiled gently at the two girls.

"We were so excited when we found it, never dreaming it would affect so many lives. Jonathan knew straight away that it should be kept hidden, away from the other two. He never did trust one of our group, a man calling himself Adam!"

Henry stopped talking and motioned to Gem to pour him a cup of coffee; after doing so, she leant over and placed the cup and saucer on his desk.

After taking a small sip, he continued, "Have you ever wondered why our early ancestors and medieval man built such large churches and monuments to their faiths? Why not be content to build modest, small, inexpensive places of worship?"

Henry leant further forward, his palms flat against the desk before he replied, his eyes darting from one to the other, "I shall tell you what we learnt, Jonathan and I. We learnt that these places of worship were built on an older religion than any of ours. A pagan religion ... devil worship."

He stopped to let his words sink in.

"Men built their places of worship to cover up these pagan sites. The bigger the monument, the more evil the thing that had inhabited the place and when they had built these masterly buildings, they set their saints and their faith all around them, to guard and protect themselves against this evil ever coming to the surface again."

Gem and Beth remained quiet, listening in awe to what Henry was saying. Gem started to say something, but Henry held up his hand to silence her.

"You can save your questions for later, Gemini; for now you must listen."

He rose from his chair, walked round the front of his desk and leant his thin frame against it before continuing, "Everyone thought that with the coming of the New Millennium, it was the perfect time for those evil ones to strike out, rise up from their underworld and reclaim what had once been theirs thousands of years ago. The world was waiting, watching to see what would happen; it held its breath and with the century passing and nothing happened, everybody felt relieved.

"What could possibly happen, they said.

"We were fools to think such stupid thoughts; perhaps there is nothing there after all! That is what is so clever about these evil ones, why do something when the world is watching? Surely it is better to catch everyone off guard.

"They were forced to wait and nobody knew it but Jonathan and me. They are still trapped in their earthy pits under our wonderful beautiful churches, because while the Book exists and our faith is strong, so does their banishment from our earthly realms. What we hadn't banked on was the waning of people's beliefs; do you know how many churches have come up for sale in the last year alone?"

As Henry stopped talking he noticed the girls' heads shaking in unison to his question. He reached over for his coffee and took a large mouthful, grimacing at its coldness. When he had drained the cup he continued, "Fortunately the church here in England has banned the destruction of the churches, making them listed buildings, but even so it is just a matter of time before there is a force unleashed upon the world that will be its own destruction."

Henry folded his arms and directed his words straight at Gem, who was sitting back in her chair, listening with every fibre of her body.

"Apathy is something that is very hard to fight against," Henry continued. "It is the new modern idiom. Faith is a thing of the past. Falling congregations show this. But tell me, who do people pray to in times of need?

"Who do they blame even when things go wrong? Someone once told me that there are no atheists on a sinking boat; we are up against something more terrible than the selling off of a few churches. We are talking about the total destruction of all our churches and unleashing the devil within.

"It is written in the Book that they will begin their mission with the destruction of York Minster; that much we do know.

"They tried once before when the fire raged through it. Today the authorities are selling off stone artefacts from the very walls of the church. Bit by bit it is being eroded and what lies in wait underneath, one does not want to contemplate."

As Henry stopped speaking he shook his head at the enormity of the problem.

Gem took advantage of his silence to ask a question: "Is that why you brought me back up here, to the place of my ..." Gem hesitated before continuing, suddenly confused about who she was. At last she found the courage to continue, "I was going to say birth, but now I am not so sure ..." Her words seemed to die on her lips and she looked to Henry for help.

"No, you were not born here," replied Henry. "It is of no consequence where you came from at the moment." He looked very tired, but he continued, "You are the North's last hope; Jonathan gave his life to protect your identity; only you can fight this thing. Your family's roots are here, generation after generation and you are part of that family; the northern churches are in your hands. You must protect them."

"Who are 'they'?" replied Gem, suddenly eager for an answer.

"He is a servant of his Master. His identity is unknown to us, but He can walk through the days of man as one of them. He has managed to cross over. He has learnt our ways, but He retains all of His powers. He gathers others to Him, by fair means or foul and they work for Him totally under His control. He is waiting until the day comes and He can release his Master and that is soon, Gemini, soon. Trust no one!"

Gem looked down at her hands and gave a small laugh; Beth and Henry looked at her, unable to hide their astonishment.

Looking up at both of them, they saw her smile did not reach her eyes; it was as if she was holding something in that was too great for her.

"That is exactly what Remne said," Gem replied, still with her forced smile. "So Dr Henry Peterson, retired don of Oxford, tell me how I go about finding this thing. You hold all the answers between you, both you and Remne; what do I have to do? Tell me, please, because everyone keeps saying I am the one, but nobody gives me any clue as to what I am supposed to do and how I go about eliminating this thing!"

Suddenly feeling hemmed in, Gem rose to her feet and started to pace the room, annoyance showing in every step. Beth was disturbed watching her and looked to her uncle for guidance.

"In the corner over there, you will find an old parcel; bring it to me," said Henry, pointing to the package he had brought in with him.

Gem strode over to the parcel and when she picked it up she took on a radiance that was almost blinding.

Beth squealed in alarm and hid her face in the cushion behind her; Henry placed his head in his hands so as to block out the blinding rays.

Gem was stunned by what had happened to her and although the parcel weighed a great deal, she placed it gently on Henry's desk.

Gem knew instantly that it was the Book her grandfather had died to protect. She took a step back away from it, instantly feeling bereft at losing contact with it. The light evaporated, leaving the room the way it was, in the warm soft glow of the table lamp.

Beth finally raised her head that she had buried in the pillow and Henry's face emerged from behind his hands, his eyes blinking rapidly behind his glasses.

Beth jumped from her seat and ran towards Gem.

Upon reaching her, Beth flung her arms around her and squeezed her hard, saying as she did so, "See, I told you about the light and you didn't believe me."

Gem wriggled out of her embrace and faced Henry across the table. Their eyes met, but Gem was the first to speak.

"But that's not all, is it, Henry? There's more, isn't there?" Her stare never wavered from Henry's face.

He was the first to drop his gaze and slumping tiredly back in his chair, he answered, in a frail voice, "Yes, there is. A lot more. The light that emanates from you is only the beginning; it will not last, it is just your body preparing itself because the prophecy will not be complete until a week from now. All I can tell you is very soon you will have your very own epiphany, the last piece of the puzzle will be complete and you will see the whole picture and witness for yourself what you will become."

Gem leant nearer to him, forcing him with her will to answer all her questions.

Henry shielded his eyes with his hands, but Gem was too powerful; her words, spoken through gritted teeth, finally got through to him.

"Tell me what I have to look out for, what sort of epiphany?"

Henry shrugged but knew he had to answer; he said, "I don't know, but it is the hardest test that you are given, that much we were able to decipher from the Book."

Gem reached over the desk, grabbed Henry by the lapels of his jacket and pulled him out of his seat and towards her. The muscles in her arm knotted with the tension and Henry could see that to struggle was useless.

Beth now beside herself with worry grabbed hold of Gem's hands and tried in vain to prise them away.

"Stop it! Gem, stop it! You don't know what you are doing!"

Beth's words acted like a splash of cold water and Gem's eyes, shining like brilliant diamonds from her anger, suddenly returned to their normal colour.

She released Henry, who staggered backwards into his chair and looked gravely at Gem before he said, "I'm glad I don't have to face you as an adversary; that was very frightening. All I can say now is trust in the Lord and in your own judgement; these things will happen at the given time."

He held up his hand to forestall the questions he saw springing to Gem's lips and in a low voice he repeated what he had first read long ago: "'who are we? He has favoured our undertakings, 'A New Order of the Ages.' These lines were found in the beginning of the Book and Davy, our friend who found the book, did not look further. That was just the opening; those few lines were written by someone sent by God."

Gem, all anger receded, staggered back to her seat; even Beth, who looked at her uncle with amazement, felt round behind her for her chair, not wanting to take her eyes from his face.

Henry seemed to sag; his head rested in his hands, he seemed suddenly very old; even the life seemed to have left his voice.

"I am so very tired," he admitted to them both. "I have done this work for an exceedingly long time and want to rest now; I think I deserve it. It was a serious blow to me when your grandfather, my dearest friend, died and it has been hard carrying on without him. We worked night and day to try to bring some sort of order to the writings in the Book, but I lack the courage and the excitement that I once had."

But Gem was not prepared to let him rest; she wanted to know more. She had to know more.

Realising the limits of Henry's physical strength and not wishing to be the cause of any more stress, Gem leant forward in her chair instead of jumping up and raving. She moderated her voice so that Henry would not feel intimidated.

"Who exactly wrote the Book?" Gem asked. "What is it?"

Looking across the desk to where she was sitting, Henry nodded his head and said, "Yes, I suppose you ought to know, although I am surprised you haven't guessed. Firstly, it was written, if not in the hand of God, then by his disciples."

"Do you mean his angels?" interrupted Beth, somewhat taken aback.

"Yes I do and like the tablets of Moses, this was written with the express reason of protecting mankind. That is why they want to destroy it so much and that is why, Gemini, you have to protect it."

Gem dropped her head in her hands, feeling the weight of commitment on her shoulders already. Henry felt sorry for her, knowing the things he did and prayed with all his strength that she had the courage and fortitude to see it to its bitter conclusion.

Suddenly standing up from his chair, he gestured Beth over to him; placing an arm around her shoulders, he said, "Stay here for the night and in the morning I advise you to go home and be prepared for anything. I also advise you to stay together; for some unexplained reason I suddenly fear for you, Beth, but stay close to Gemini, she needs you."

Beth raised herself on tiptoe to give her uncle a kiss on the cheek; looking over at Gem, she said, "See? I told you. You need me and from now on we shall be joined at the hip."

"We shall see," was all Gem managed to mumble, shaken to the core by Henry's revelations.

Chapter 10

"Who are you calling?" Beth enquired as she came up behind Gem. They were standing on the rooftop balcony, overlooking Lake Windermere, the following morning.

"Only work, to tell them that I won't be in for a while and to pass my work over to Oliver; he's been dying to get his hands on that hit and run case of mine."

Before she continued Gem looked at her phone, lying small and silent in her hand, her mood heavy as she added, "I suppose this is the end of the line as far as work is concerned. Who knows if I will even live to see the outcome of all what Henry was banging on about?" She gave a small tut before she continued, half talking to herself, "Who would have thought it, eh? I've worked so hard as well; now it's all gone, as if it had never existed."

Beth wandered over to the railings surrounding the large patio and stood next to Gem; as her gaze followed the contours of the lake, it seemed she was lost in thought, but Gem was taken aback by the passion in Beth's voice as she said, "Is that all you can think about, your bloody job and your bloody car? Hello! Has what we were talking about last night sunk in yet? I was nearly killed twice." Noticing Gem's raised eyebrow, Beth continued even angrier, "Well, you know what I mean, on different occasions."

Like a deflated balloon, Beth sank into the nearest seat, a rickety old cane chair still damp from the previous night, before she continued, "I always took my religion for granted, and it was there when I needed it like some old jumper that had suddenly come back into fashion."

Beth leant back in the chair so that she could see Gem properly, adding, "All this has made me question everything I thought was wrong about religion, because I now find it is all very right indeed. It is so easy to blame something or someone else for when it all goes wrong in your life. So why not blame God? After all he can't answer back, he's just there taking it on the chin. Perhaps we all need to feel we belong to come together in harmony to praise an entity greater than ourselves."

Beth started to warm to her subject and as she spoke she leant forward in the old chair and expressed her feelings for the first time in a very long time, saying, "Take Glastonbury for example."

Gem was intrigued and was also curious as to what Beth was going to say; she asked, "What do you mean the place, or the concert?"

"The concert, silly; why do you think so many people troupe there year after year, putting up with all the mud and disgusting toilets?"

"Err! The bands!" replied Gem, humouring her.

"Well, I don't think so. I think it is more the coming together, a joining of all those like-minded people. A sort of spiritual meeting of minds and bodies; is that not what the church tries to do? Except in this day and age it is not cool or hip to be religious or go to church, so people have to find their own religious path in the things they do and call it something different, something more acceptable. Those people come away from the concert feeling different; they had bonded with all the other people that went there, a joined experience. Whether you are rich or poor, whether you like all the bands or not, it is a very levelling experience and take a moment to think …" Beth paused before she continued, "Why do you think it all happens at Glastonbury?"

"Because a farmer thought of a very good way of getting rich quick!" teased Gem.

"But there are hundreds and hundreds of farmers all over the country in the same predicament who needed to diversify; how come they did not think of it or even copy the idea? And even if they did, they are not half as successful as Glastonbury. People talk and we know from experience, Gem, after we went, that you're not really 'in' until you have been to Glastonbury." Beth eased herself back in the chair as she waited for Gem to speak.

"I don't know, you've lost me now. Is it because he was the only farmer with the contacts? I don't know much about how it all began," replied Gem, raking her brains for an answer.

"My theory is religion was brought to England with the legend of Joseph of Arimathaea and the staff that he planted in Glastonbury. Not all things are shown to us at the beginning, as you so well know yourself; you have to wait and see the outcome. I think our generation is not as godless as some people think. I think we are very religious; we are more spiritual than the old time religious folk. So now I don't feel lost or anything; quite the contrary, I feel marvellous, because I can suddenly see a plan to all this. I feel as though I have cast off some grubby old coat of doubt and have put on this bright shiny raiment like Joseph's coat of many colours."

Beth's face had a radiance that Gem had never seen before and she was envious of her.

Beth turned and saw Gem looking at her.

She looks so sad, thought Beth and she called Gem to her side and said, "It's you I'm worried about; you are the one who seems lost."

Gem walked over and knelt at Beth's knees; her long blonde hair loose for once and flowing like a live entity down her back. Beth loved to see Gem like this, all young and natural instead of pulling her beautiful hair back from her face in the style Gem liked to wear for work. Beth was sure she could have won more than one courtroom battle if her hair had been flowing freely; then again they might have just thought her another blonde bimbo with only enough intelligence to go shopping rather than a top class barrister who held an Oxford first.

Gem always knew what was right and she would know what to do now, Beth had no doubt. She believed in Gem and it was now up to Gem to believe in herself.

Gem's furrowed brow deepened, but her voice was gentle as she said, "I am lost at the moment. It's not my faith that is in question; it is my ability to perform the things I have to do. It seems that a lot is riding on my shoulders, and the thought of failure frightens me to my very core. What if I haven't got what it takes? I'm only in my twenties; what do I know about fighting demons?" Gem smiled in spite of her fears, adding, "But don't worry about me; after all, I have my very own epiphany to look forward to."

Gem lowered her head onto Beth's knee and felt Beth's hand gently stroking her head.

It seemed quite impossible to believe, as they rested there listening to the early morning birdsong, that anything evil could be manifesting itself. Gem stood up and dragged a similar old wicker chair over to Beth's and the two of them sat in quiet contemplation, watching the lake turn from monochrome to green and blue and then golden as the sun crested the hills.

Not wanting to break the mood with her sombre thoughts, Gem

decided to turn the conversation round onto more mundane things and said, "What about that room we slept in last night? I thought we had been transported back to the 1930s. It would make a glorious film set."

Beth turned from looking at the view and laughingly replied, "I don't know about your grandfather but my uncle has never thrown anything away in his life. If it wasn't for the woman who comes in occasionally and cleans round, it would look like Miss Haversham's house in *Great Expectations*."

"Well, it's not far off it now, did you see the cobwebs in the hallway when we came in last night?"

They both laughed in easy companionship, glad that the moment of doubt had passed. Beth eased herself out of the low chair and walked over to the edge of the patio that overlooked the front of the house; as she glanced down, Gem turned in her chair and saw her raise her hand and wave to someone out of her view.

Then turning suddenly, Beth said to Gem, "That was Uncle but he didn't see me; he was heading off into the shrubbery, carrying something. Still it can't be anything very important or heavy, otherwise he would have called us down to help him."

Gem raised herself from the chair and walked over to stand next to Beth; when she got to her side she rested an arm around Beth's shoulders and said, "Did you mean all what you said about Glastonbury and the people who go there?"

Beth turned her face to look up into Gem's worried expression; she smiled sweetly before she replied, "Yes, I did. Glastonbury was chosen for a reason and I have no doubts about you or about the fate of the rest of mankind. Their time will come and they will not be found wanting, trust me, I work in advertising."

Gem could not help but laugh and after dropping her arm from around Beth's shoulders, she gently gave her a punch on the arm for her humour and now laughing together, the pair turned away from the edge of the parapet and made their way downstairs to breakfast.

Henry watched them leave the edge of the rooftop patio from his place of concealment in the overgrown shrubbery. He knew Beth had seen him enter because he had seen her wave, but he was so annoyed with having been caught out that he pretended not to see her and pushed his way into the undergrowth with his bundle.

After he reached the inside of the large rhododendron, he discarded what he was carrying by throwing it off to one side. Nobody would find it unless they were actually hunting for it. It was a good place to conceal something; the rhododendrons had not been pruned for more than fifteen years and had taken over much of the area around the house.

Although it was cool in amongst the greenery, small beads of sweat still managed to drip off his forehead with the exertion of carrying the large unwieldy object. The overhanging branches formed a sort of dome above his head and he found it easy to walk underneath. The peat deadened the sound of his footsteps, making it impossible for them to be heard.

He pulled out a large white handkerchief to mop his brow and standing there in the semi darkness, he was grateful for the respite. As he looked up through the branches and leaves, he watched Gem and Beth in close discussion as they leant against the parapet above him.

The early morning sun radiated behind them and he was forced to smile at the sheer beauty of both of them. They were young and eager and he had no doubt they would work things out and carry on the work of Jonathan and himself.

Their voices drifted down to him; he could not hear them very clearly but he automatically stopped mopping his brow, forcing his hand to stop in mid wipe and when he heard Beth mention the name of Glastonbury, it sent a small smile creeping across his face.

Beth had a lot of intuition; even now she was starting to work things out; she felt things and this would stand her in good stead in the days and weeks to come.

He used the handkerchief now to wipe away the tears that had sprung to his eyes and his shoulders hunched in sudden despair. He had given the pair of them a lot of information last night about Gemini and what awaited her, but he did not have the heart to warn Beth.

She was the apple of his eye and he had doted on her from the moment he had first seen her as a baby, but Jonathan had warned him to take care and not show too much interest in her, for her own safety.

When his brother and his wife had died in a car accident, it was Jonathan who had cautioned him to be careful and let the girl go to distant relatives, but he could not bring himself to do that.

He had wanted her near and if Mrs Dunn had not been around, then he might have thought twice, but she knew the situation about his work and between the two of them they managed to raise the little dark haired beauty.

He had forced himself to back away, immersing himself in his work when she had gone away to university, but he would rush to collect the post and read the letters that Beth sent. This she did faithfully every week and his dear friend and confidant, the redoubtable Mrs Vera Dunn, whose death he still mourned and himself would read and reread every word over a cup of coffee in the kitchen.

They basked in her achievements and laughed with her about her fellow students' antics; she told them all about Gemini and he and Mrs Dunn worried anew, but they both knew that nothing could change the outcome.

Fate had brought Beth and Gemini together and fate would lead them hand in hand to whatever awaited both of them. He thought he would die the last time Beth had been attacked and he thanked the almighty that Vera had not been around when the news had reached them. He had been physically sick with worry and all he wanted to do was rush to her side; he had wanted to go to her in London and bring her home and keep her safe with him, but he knew he had to keep a low profile.

That was the question, though; was it safe with him? He had been warned that they were closing in and the death of his best friend Jonathan had proved that.

It was all a question of time and he prayed they would have enough. He had done his bit to further the cause and it had left him weak and defenceless.

He reminded himself that what was coming was Beth's destiny as surely as it was Gemini's.

As he stumbled blindly out of the shrubbery and headed to the back door, away from their prying eyes, he silently prayed that Beth had the strength to endure what awaited her, but did he himself have the strength to see it all through to the bitter end? He thought not; he felt so weak, as if all his energy was leaving him with the tears he was shedding, but he must stay strong for a little longer, just until they leave anyway.

They parted from Henry with hugs late in the afternoon and Gem even managed a kiss on his old wrinkled face, now wet with tears at their departure.

"Forgive me, Gem," he whispered in her ear at their final embrace.

"Forgive you for what?" she asked. "For telling me No, I realise you had to do it. It is me that should ask forgiveness for frightening you last night and my bullyboy tactics. I'm so sorry; Grandfather would never have forgiven me if he had heard me." Gem gave him a little squeeze, fearing that she would hurt him if she applied too much pressure.

She was surprised to hear him add, as they released each other, "No, not for that. Oh, it doesn't matter now; have a safe journey home and Beth darling," he said, calling his niece over to him for a final word, "you know you have always been in my thoughts. I love you as if you were my own daughter."

Beth's eyes welled with tears and she flung her arms around him, hugging him to her with love and affection.

Overcome with so much visible signs of affection, all Henry could say was, "Look after her, Beth, she is going to need you … now go … the pair of you … and Gemini," he called as Gem was about to enter her car, "mind the lane, it can be a bit tricky after a storm."

They smiled at each other and with a last wave they climbed into the Stag and were gone.

Henry stood there long after they had left; going over in his mind the things they had talked about. He knew what he had done was wrong, but he was getting too old to continue with it all. It was time for someone else to take up the baton.

Sadly shaking his head, he muttered, "Go with God, Beth and Gemini and go with God."

"Well, well, well, look who that is leaning up against our door," said Gem as she swerved into the kerb to park the car. Beth had her head down and was checking the contents of her bag, hoping she had remembered to bring everything back from her uncle's. On hearing Gem's words she lifted her head and Gem could see a faint flush creeping over her cheeks.

"It's Rupert," she whispered.

"What are you whispering for? He can't hear you," added Gem with a laugh.

"I know, but all the same, do you think he has come to see me?" asked Beth.

"Well, I can assure you he hasn't come to see me," replied Gem, adding,

"Not after that kiss he gave you a couple of nights ago." Gem turned to Beth and said seriously, "Look Beth, I know this is all a bit sudden and if you feel uncomfortable then don't do anything you don't want to."

Beth turned and smiled at her friend, patting Gem's hand as she said, "Thanks Gem, I appreciate that, perhaps we can just go in the lounge for a while. I'm not up to going out on a date with anyone just yet."

"Suits me, honey, I shall make myself scarce and go upstairs and soak in a nice hot bath, then I shall start the dinner. You can invite him to stay if you want," said Gem as she switched off the engine and prepared to step out of the car.

Beth was about to add something further but the gentle tapping on her passenger window stopped her. She opened the car door and Rupert offered his hand to help her onto the pavement.

"I did ring a couple of times yesterday, but there was no answer, so I thought I would just pop round tonight to catch you after work. I hope that's okay. Have you been away?" Rupert said, noticing the bags Gem was lifting out of the boot.

"These? No," lied Gem, feeling she was getting quite expert in it, adding, "We have just been pampered for the day. We decided to take a day off and make it a long weekend; you know how we women like to look good." She held up one of the bags, smiling warmly as she said, "Just our towels and swim things, but this one contains quite a few bottles of lotion that Beth found she needed for those early signs of aging."

Gem walked up the steps, swinging the bags as she went; she could feel Beth's eyes boring holes in her back.

They waited around while Gem opened the front door and as they entered the hall Gem shouted a quick farewell and headed for the stairs, taking them two at a time. She finally reached the top before dissolving into hoots of laughter.

She left them to make their own arrangements for tea or coffee, knowing that Beth would not want her getting in the way, not now anyway.

Gem soaked in the bath until she was practically a prune and after washing her long hair that always seemed to take ages nowadays, she stepped from the bath and briskly dried herself. She rubbed the moisture off the mirror and gazed at herself, amazed that her eyes were clearer and bluer than ever before; for some reason she didn't need her glasses.

I wonder why, she thought to herself. She could feel the hard muscles on her arms and stomach as she dried herself. She had always kept fit but this was something else; she could actually feel herself morphing.

Into what that was the question? What?

When she was dried and dressed, Gem bounded down the stairs, happy now to be home, clean and relaxed.

She entered the kitchen and started to rummage around in the fridge. Laying the ingredients out on the central worktop for a Caesar salad, Gem set about chopping everything up. She was so engrossed in what she was doing that she did not hear Rupert come into the kitchen behind her until he said, "Hi, I just thought I would pop in to say hello. Beth has just run upstairs to the bathroom, so I thought I would take this opportunity to have a quiet word."

He leant his tall frame up against the side of the units and started to pick at her chopped salad.

"If you value your fingers, Rupert, I suggest you stop doing that," said Gem teasingly, holding a very sharp knife up in front of her.

"Sorry," he said, holding his hands up in mock surrender; Rupert smiled his lopsided grin.

"What did you want to have a talk about anyway?" said Gem, turning back and starting to cut up some chicken.

"I thought you could have a word with Beth and convince her it's okay to come out on a date with me. You know she will be safe with me."

Rupert leant towards Gem and smiled again.

Rupert's smile had always been disarming; those two cheeky dimples were like twin sensors, testing people's ability to see if they could see the boy within. Gem knew Beth would have fun with Rupert, but it was up to Beth to call the shots; obviously her friend had said no and she would not go against her.

"I'm sorry, Rupert, honestly I am, but Beth has obviously said no and it is down to her, is it not?" Gem smiled over her shoulder at Rupert and she was surprised to see a fleeting look of annoyance cross his face.

Realising that Gem was looking at him, he replied quickly, "I'm sorry Gem; it's just that I have two tickets for a show in Newcastle and I thought Beth would love to see it. It doesn't matter ..." He leant across where she was standing and quickly stole some more peppers. He said, "If she doesn't want to go, I won't force her; I shall just wear her down with my ardent attention."

Blowing her a kiss and giving a small wave, Rupert left the kitchen to join Beth once again in the lounge, eating his stolen prize as he went.

She shook her head, laughing at his outlandish behaviour. You couldn't stay angry with Rupert for long and she wondered how long Beth could keep him at arm's length. She was surprised to hear the door slam ten minutes later and Beth herself entered the kitchen and stood leaning up against the unit that Rupert had not long vacated.

Gem stole a quick glance and noticed she was deep in thought. As she took the pan down from the overhead hook in preparation for frying the chicken fillets, she ventured a few words, breaking into Beth's meditation, "I take it he is not staying for dinner then?"

"What?" Beth replied.

"Rupert, he's not staying for dinner?"

"No, he's not. He's very nice and all that, but …"

Her voice just seemed to trail off and Gem was starting to get a bit concerned, considering Beth's previously buoyant mood. She went over to stand next to her and handed her a cold glass of Pinot Grigio that she had poured.

She waited until Beth had taken a few sips before she said, "You okay? Did Rupert say anything to upset you?"

"No, it's not that, it's … well, I might as well tell you. We had a bit of a kiss and a cuddle, nothing serious," said Beth, noticing the twitch to Gem's lips. "And I … well; I was running my hand up and down his back and …"

"This is not going to be too much information for me, is it Beth? Because I think I would rather not hear," said Gem in mock horror.

"No, you daft nut, it was just he flinched when I touched him; he said it was because he had been pot-holing yesterday and caught himself on a rock."

Gem immediately turned to face Beth, all humour leaving her face at the news that Beth had just imparted.

She placed her glass of wine on the side unit and began to pace the room.

"Well, what do you think? Can we trust him?" said Beth, her voice full of concern.

Gem stood in front of her, her own face mirroring the concern she saw on Beth's face. "We shall have to wait and see it's true he does go pot-holing; I should know, I have been with him, but I suggest we carry on the same, you seeing him here only while I am around. As for now, let's eat," said Gem as she started to gather the dishes together, although her mind was far from food.

Chapter 11

He stood behind her, his breath cold and heavy on her neck; for some reason she was not afraid. On the contrary, she welcomed his attention. His hands caressed her shoulders and ran down her arms to her elbow, where he cupped them both and gently raised her arms above her head. Like a lover, she leant her head back and rested it against his, feeling his soft kisses on her cheek.

She had longed for this moment, longed for the time when she would eventually be his. They had never met, but she knew him, she had been waiting for him. Deep within her soul she knew they would eventually unite.

His hands started to explore her body, sending shivers up and down her spine with the sheer pleasure of it.

She turned in his arms and his lips came down and covered hers and like someone discovering an oasis in the middle of a desert, she kissed him.

His mouth was hard and urgent against hers and like a flower craving the sun, she opened up to him and her heart sang with the joy of it.

She opened her eyes for just a second and the tall handsome stranger was all she expected him to be, but then she was lost again in his kiss, closed her eyes and gave in to the bliss.

She felt his hands run up and down her naked body and she was overcome with a burning desire for him. She was surrounded by soft grey mist and as she stood there in her nakedness, she wondered why she did not feel the cold. His kiss ended and he turned her once more in his arms so that she had her back to him and still wanting the nearness of him, she leant her body against him.

But as she leant against him her thoughts began to clear and suddenly the feeling of him being her one and only started to leave her. One thought kept entering her head: *Trust no one!*

But he was her soul mate; she could feel it!

Or was he feeding off her?

Was he Feeding off her thoughts and desires like some obnoxious creature that was unable to feel for itself?

She wanted to be wrong; she wanted her soul mate, not this parasite, a feeder on human emotions. She was the opposite of him; she suddenly felt this in her soul.

Where he was ice she was fire.

Where he was cold hearted she was passionate.

Where he was evil she was pure.

Words sang in her head like a trapped animal.

Trust no one, remain pure!

It was as if the scales had dropped from her eyes and as she looked down at the hands that were caressing her breasts, they were not the hands of her lover but the claws of a beast.

She tried to break away from him, but he held her to him, eager to satisfy his own lust.

She opened her mouth to scream, but nothing came out.

Fear welled up inside her like water from a broken dam; it rushed over her body in a thousand ways; along with her fear came her strength.

The strength to do what was right.

Her fingers encased his and her horror helped her to break his grip on her naked body. She slipped from his grasp and turned to face her adversary, but like before in the car park, there was no one there ... he had vanished.

Feeling the tears slide down her face, she was not sure if it was because she had escaped from him once again ... or because he had gone and with his going he took with him the fleeting presence of someone she could love.

It was like reaching for a shadow, a will o' the wisp, a fleeting spectre of something wonderful and good and for that one second his kiss was all she ever wanted, but who was he?

It was not the beast that fed off her emotions, it was someone she knew deep within her that she was destined to meet and love with every fibre of her soul.

She turned and turned, trying to find him in the mist, but it was too thick. She couldn't find her way through it and now she was frightened she would lose her way altogether.

She fell to the ground and rested her head on her knees.

Her long blonde hair covered her nakedness and her shame. She would rest for a while before she began her search again. Yes, she would rest and as her tears fell, her long lashes descended and she slept.

"Come on sleepy, you going to stay there all day?"

Beth bounced on the bed, seemingly ready to take on another new day. Gem lay there, stretching and yawning, trying to come to terms with the dream she had just had. She still felt the horror of those hands upon her; it was so real.

Sensing her mood Beth asked, "What's wrong with you? You look as though you've been up all night; didn't you sleep well?"

"No I didn't, actually; I had the most awful dream."

As Gem threw back the sheet to get out of bed, she heard Beth say in a shocked voice, "What's that!" as she pointed to Gem's side.

Gem swung her long legs out of bed; because she had been so warm of late she had taken to sleeping in the nude. She hurried over to her long mirror on the door of her wardrobe and looked at her reflection.

Brushing her hair over her shoulders, she turned first sideways and then full on, all the while staring in fascination at the long scratches running along each side of her breasts.

They were not particularly deep, more like slight scratches and as she raised her arms above her head, she was again reminded of the hands that had caressed her.

"It's nothing," she said, turning to Beth. "I must have done it myself while I was asleep."

Beth look suspiciously at Gem as she slid across the bed and came to stand next to her, saying as she did so, "What aren't you telling me? You look very guilty about something."

"Nothing," she said; looking at Beth's face, Gem had to laugh. "Honestly, it's nothing. Now do me a favour and go and put the kettle on for a nice cup of tea; I'm gasping. My mouth is as dry as a bone."

Beth stared at Gem's reflection in the mirror for a while, perplexed at her friend's attitude and then she turned on her heel and left the room, muttering to herself. As Gem put on her robe, uncertainty gripped her; had the Thing invaded her dreams?

Those weals seem to suggest it had, but she could have done them herself?

Beth's voice calling up that the tea was ready broke into her reverie and tying the belt of her robe firmly around her waist, she hurried down the stairs. During breakfast they both decided to have a bit of a lazy day, after the running around of the last few days. Gem changed into a pair of shorts and a t-shirt and Beth donned a pair of leggings and a large baggy shirt. They were both sprawled out in the lounge on identical settees.

Lying on her back, Beth was propped up by some cushions; she had her knees pulled up, and one leg was crossed over the other, her foot swinging as she talked. She wanted to know what Gem was keeping from her and Gem was too relaxed to complain. Also the events of last night seemed a long time ago now and Gem wondered to herself why she had gotten as upset as she tried to convince herself it was just her imagination.

Beth wanted to go over it again, saying, "Do you think it's a hidden message, or was the Thing trying to tell you something?"

"No I don't and It wasn't trying to tell me something, no ok" replied Gem, getting bored with the whole subject. "I wish I hadn't told you now."

Beth raised herself up on her elbow and looked across at Gem with a worried look in her eyes.

"Gem, you must tell me everything; two minds are better than one in solving all this and we might miss something if we don't compare notes and such like."

"Yes I guess you're right." Gem raised her right hand and added, "I do solemnly promise that I hereby ..."

The cushion that came flying across put paid to anything else she was about to say.

"Say it properly," said Beth, getting ready to aim another pillow at Gem.

"Okay, okay, joking aside, I promise you, Beth: I shall share everything with you ... except ..."

"Except what?" Beth was bemused at what she could mean.

"Except my car," Gem said hurriedly as she raised her arms to fend off another pillow that was heading her way.

Their laughter was cut short by the ringing of the front doorbell. They both looked at each other, and Gem was the first to say, "You get it."

"Oh no," replied Beth, "I made the tea."

"I cooked breakfast," countered Gem, sticking out her tongue.

Beth knew she had lost, so she scrambled to her feet, tut-tutting as the bell rang again. Gem could hear muffled voices through the partly open lounge door and was surprised to see Beth come back in the room, all traces of hilarity wiped from her face.

Gem struggled to sit up properly and as she was floundering about, she saw who was behind Beth and exclaimed, "DI Grantly! What a pleasant surprise."

"It's a pleasure to see you again too, Miss Hawker. May I call you Gemini?" said the policeman, extending his hand to Gem in greeting.

"No please, call me Gem, everybody else does," said Gem, giving Beth a quick glance.

Beth hovered near the door, suddenly not wanting to venture back to her seat. She nervously ran her fingers along the edge of the door and when Gem and the officer stopped talking, she ventured to ask him if he wanted anything to drink.

"Tea would be lovely," he replied warmly. "I can always drink a cup of tea."

Beth, glad to escape, disappeared back round the door and they heard the distant clink of china as she prepared the tea in the kitchen.

"Well, what brings you to our neck of the woods, DI Grantly?" said Gem, studying the policeman.

"Please, call me Nathan," he replied, trying not to look too much at Gem's long legs stretched out in front of her and the mass of hair lying around her shoulders and tumbling down her back.

"I'm sorry, where are my manners? Please, do sit down," said Gem, pointing to the seat Beth had vacated.

As he sat down Gem wondered what had brought him here. She seemed to remember telling him all she knew about Beth at the time of the attack. Unless something new had come up and she knew now that would be impossible, then what exactly did he want?

Gem was saved from asking further questions by Beth returning with the tray of tea cups. After having served everyone, Beth chose to sit next to Gem, suddenly needing the security that she offered.

Gem turned and said to Beth, "I was just asking DI Grantly," and seeing him about to rectify her, Gem corrected herself saying, "sorry,

Nathan, what he was doing in our neck of the woods." Turning back to Nathan, she added, "You're a long way from home, or are you on holiday?"

"This may come as a bit of a shock to you both, but actually the powers that be in London have set up a bit of a task force," replied Nathan, looking rather nervous.

Instantly Gem was alert, her inner radar going at full pelt, feeling nervous now that he might have found out something.

"What do you mean, a bit of a task force? Aren't you sure?" answered Beth, suddenly joining in the conversation.

"It's not that, of course I am very sure; it's got more to do with your attack," he said, nodding to Beth and looking at Gem, he continued, "and your grandfather's death. We think there may be a connection."

Beth's hand crept along the settee and linked with Gem's; Gem squeezed it softly in moral support. Nathan continued talking, telling them about the things the police had found at both scenes of crime.

"It wasn't much in both cases," he explained, "except for the fact it linked in with another death a few years back."

"Is that connected to our case? I don't recall anyone in Beth's family dying under suspicious circumstances," said Gem, trying to sound matter-of-fact.

"No, the connection we have found out is with both of them, your grandfather and, I believe," said Nathan, turning his attention to Beth, "with your uncle, who is still alive and, if I am not mistaken, you visited him yesterday?"

Gem could see the colour slowly draining from Beth's face; to cover her friend's waning demeanour; she suddenly stood up and walked over to the fireplace so that Nathan had to look away from Beth to her.

"So are you telling us that all three things are connected?" said Gem, turning to face Nathan, her hands on her hips in her usual no-nonsense pose.

"We believe so, yes. I had an officer watching your uncle's house, to see who came and went." Noticing their faces, he continued quickly, "Purely as a precautionary measure, I can assure you. We are there for his protection."

"Protection what do you mean?" said Beth, sounding agitated.

Nathan started to feel slightly uncomfortable; he did not anticipate being questioned so intensely. Gem could see a slight sheen across his face, as he sat there in his suit and tie, most inappropriate for this time of year.

She felt sorry for him, suddenly realising that she liked this tall policeman very much.

"What we have ascertained is that your grandfather and your uncle," and here Nathan nodded to each girl in turn at the mention of the names, "were friends at university along with Horatio Penn-Wright and another gentleman called Adam Cunningham, who we know very little about. Penn-Wright was found dead in his car five years ago, or I should say that what remained of his body was found.

"Unfortunately we couldn't do any DNA tests on him at the time, but things have progressed immensely over the last few years; had we been allowed to keep the body ..." He shook his head at their failure in procuring any decent leads.

"Lord Horatio Penn-Wright did not have a family of his own, so the title went to a distant cousin and they insisted what was left of him should be cremated and the ashes interred at the ancestral home. There was little we could do about it and so we lost any vital clues his body might have given up, but we are pretty certain now he was murdered."

He leant forward on the settee, his face solemn as he spoke his next words: "Did you know or have you met this Adam Cunningham, who was friends with all three?" Seeing them shake their head, he continued, "It seems that this Mr Cunningham is an enigma, because as far as we can make out he died in 1944, somewhere in the middle of France.

"His body was located after the war and his relatives had him buried in a churchyard in Suffolk. But we have physical evidence linking him with your grandfather's death and that of Penn-Wright." Noticing their bemused faces, he continued, "That would make him about thirty-four when he attended Oxford University with the others, if he had lived, I might add and we know from the college records that the second Mr Cunningham was only twenty-two. So who is this mysterious Mr Adam Cunningham who has the same set of fingerprints as the first Mr Cunningham? And where did he go after he graduated? It seemed the ground just opened up and swallowed him."

Nathan looked from one woman to the other, but the blank look on their faces informed him better than anything that they knew absolutely nothing about the mysterious man.

He continued speaking, glad that for once he had their attention, saying, "What we do know is that the four of them were quite an item; they went everywhere together. If your grandfather organised a dig or a fact finding mission like the last one they went on, then it was pretty certain the other three would go with him. We have records stating that they spent a good part of the summer here in York, but that is where it all ends. For some reason the group split and they all went their separate ways. We know what happened to three of them; their work history was easy to follow, but as for Cunningham, he just dropped off the radar."

Gem walked back to her seat and flopped down next to Beth; trying not to sound too eager about the information he was imparting, she said, "Is that so unusual, Nathan? It was the end of their time at college; I would have thought they would naturally have drifted away from each other."

"Does that happen? You amaze me. I did not have the privilege of going to university; I made it through the ranks on merit but it seems to me that if you were with someone for that number of years, including all the holidays, then I would have thought that they would have at least kept in touch. I personally still keep in touch with a few of the lads I went to school with and if I am not mistaken, you yourself are here with your old roommate from university."

"How do you know that?" replied Gem, somewhat embarrassed at trying to knock him off the scent regarding her grandfather.

"I made it my business to know; after all, what happened to Beth here was unusual to say the least."

Gem had edged closer to Beth as Nathan was talking, needing her presence for comfort, as Beth had wanted hers previously. Gem was about to say something when a catchy little tune rang from Nathan's mobile.

Both Gem and Beth found this distraction amusing and momentarily felt it lighten the tension in the room. They both decided to study their feet, while he hunted for the phone in his jacket pocket. Mumbling an apology, he looked at Gem and then at his phone; Gem said, "Yes, of course, go in the hall, it is more private."

He leapt to his feet and quickly left the room, saying as he went, "Hello, yes Collins, what have you got for me?"

As soon as he left, Beth turned to Gem and whispered, "What do we do? Shall we tell him what we know? He seems to know an awful lot already." She ran her hand through her hair, in a worried gesture of anxiety and added, "And who is this Cunningham fellow?"

Gem patted Beth's knee; keeping her voice low as well, she replied, "What does he know, when you think about it? Not a lot really, just a load of stuff anyone could have got from college records. They know a little about this Cunningham chap but that's all. He's on a fishing expedition, hoping we might know something, so we have to be careful. Anyway it would be too dangerous to involve anyone else. Let's face it, he wouldn't believe us anyway, he would think we were mad!"

Still whispering, Beth replied, "Yes, I suppose you are right." Glancing over at the door to make sure he hadn't returned, Beth said, "Hunky though, isn't he?" Looking back at Gem, she said, "Go on, admit it, you fancy him!"

"Whether I fancy him or not, I have not got time for anything." She gave a significant sigh before continuing, "I never had time for anything, what with my studies and everything, and you should know that. My mind was caught up with a lot of other things in London and now all this; it looks like I shall die the oldest virgin in England."

Beth gave her a smile of encouragement and added, "Still he is hunky, though; perhaps when all this is over."

"We shall have to see, but let's look at what is happening now. We must keep positive; we —" Gem's words were cut off as Nathan re-entered the room. He had taken off his jacket and as he took his seat his face was very grave.

"I have some news although we are not sure of the outcome yet; it may be nothing …" "What is it?" said Gem, suddenly feeling agitated.

"It's Beth's uncle, Mr Henry Peterson. He's missing. We don't know whether he has taken himself off somewhere, or if something has happened to him."

Beth's small cry of alarm cut off what Nathan was going to say next. Gem placed her arm around her shoulder and in a quiet voice, trying to ease Beth's panic, she said, "Now, don't start to worry too soon, let the police check it out first. There are all sorts of avenues we can explore."

Nathan interrupted her platitudes by changing the subject, inquiring, "Your parents, Gem, have you heard from them recently?"

"My parents well no, not recently, they have gone to the country to live since I moved in here, to give us a bit of space. I know Daddy was feeling a bit poorly so they took themselves off to the seaside for a few days. I think Mummy thought the sea air would do him good. They usually contact me when they get back; they don't have mobile phones, you see and I haven't heard from them yet. Why do you want to know?"

"If you don't mind, we would like to check on them as well, just to be on the safe side," said Nathan.

"Well, if you think it's advisable," said Gem, letting go of Beth.

Gem stood up and went to the table near the window and wrote down the country home address for Nathan; as she turned to give it to him, she noticed something through his shirt on his upper arm.

His back was to her as he sat on the edge of the seat and Gem couldn't quite make out from where she was standing, but it looked like a dressing of some kind.

Please God, no, she thought, *don't let it be him.* Turning back to the table, she slipped the address back underneath a pile of papers.

Nathan showed no sign of unease as he quietly sat there talking to Beth, giving her gentle words of encouragement regarding tracking down her uncle.

Gem walked back to her seat and as she sat down she composed herself enough to say, "I know it's silly of me, but I left my address book at work. They have only just bought the place and for the life of me I can't remember off hand what the address is or the telephone number. I can give it to you later when I've popped into work; I have to go there soon anyway."

Beth glanced sideways at Gem and saw by the look on her face that now was not the time to question her about this lie. Beth was fully aware that Gem knew it by heart; they'd had the place for years. Something was going on and it had to do with the handsome policeman. She just had to wait until he left.

Gem knew that Nathan suspected something was wrong but was either too polite or too shrewd to say anything; she wondered which one it was.

She hoped it was the former.

Nathan searched Gem's face, trying to read from it what she was thinking but to no avail; eventually he gave up and with a small shrug of his shoulders he stood up.

"I'll leave now then; perhaps you would like to see me to the door, Gem." Leaning over to pat Beth's hand, he said, "Don't worry, your uncle will turn up; we have our best people on it."

Beth thanked him but continued to look concerned.

Gem walked him to the front door and when they reached it, Nathan turned and said, "I've thought about you a lot since London and I jumped at the chance to head this investigation. Seeing you again has confirmed what I feel about you. I was wondering if perhaps you felt the same." He smiled down at her and was disappointed to see she wasn't smiling back.

He went to put his hand on her arm, but she pulled back away from him; it was a small gesture, but one that did not go unnoticed; his face showed his dismay in witnessing it. He was further disconcerted when she abruptly changed the subject and it took a couple of seconds for him to get his head round what she was saying: "Why do you want to see my parents?" she asked. "I thought this was all to do with my grandfather."

"It's only to see if they could shed some light on the situation, they might know something about Beth's uncle. It is more to do with a fact finding exercise than anything else. Are you going to answer me about us?"

Gem refused to answer his question and once again changed the subject to what she wanted to hear. "How did you hurt your arm?" she asked tentatively, raising her hand to touch the spot where she assumed the dressing to be.

It was his turn to pull away this time and as she looked in his eyes she could not make out if he was lying or not; this bothered her more.

"My arm?" said Nathan, confused.

"Yes, your arm," replied Gem, lowering her hand to her side and waiting patiently for his answer.

"It's nearly healed now," he said. "I did it tackling someone who had a knife and did not want to come quietly. I had to convince him otherwise. Unfortunately I didn't come out of it without injury, but at least the chap is going to get life for what he did to a young girl."

He sounded convincing, but that was the problem; she had been told often enough: trust no one and that is what she was going to do, no matter how attracted she felt to this man. Gem raised her hand and placed it in the middle of his chest; she wanted desperately to believe him, wanted him like she had wanted no other, but the time was not right. Even so she felt herself drawn to him and sensing her indecision he pulled her gently to him.

Standing there in the hallway, she lifted her face so that Nathan could kiss her and it was everything she hoped it would be. It was a kiss that was full of promise, his tongue explored the inside of her mouth and she felt herself moan with pleasure.

He gently ran his hands down her bare arms and it was as if someone had thrown a bucket of water over her; her dream came back to her with such force, she was astounded by its impact.

What am I doing? Her mind screamed and she clamped a hand over her mouth, frightened the words had come out. Gem leant back against the wall, fearing that he would think she was a complete lunatic. She closed her eyes for a second, praying that he would not see the effect his kiss had on her.

Finally with her breathing under control, she opened her eyes and looked at him. Nathan too was leaning up against the door, looking to the entire world like someone who had won the lottery.

Taking her hand anyway from her mouth, she said, "I'm sorry, I didn't really mean that to happen, it's just …"

"There's no need to explain, that kiss meant a lot to me and if not for you now, I'm sure it will in the future when you get to know me better," he said, interrupting her, smiling all the while and finally adding, "I shall go now, but promise me you will give me that address, we don't want to leave things too long." Reaching over, he ran a finger down the curve of her face; cupping her chin, he said, "You are an amazing woman, Gemini Hawker and I am definitely going to get to know you better."

With that he opened the door and was gone, leaving Gem in fear of him and wanting him all at the same time, just like her dream. She heard Beth calling her from the lounge; standing back from her position against the wall, she leant over and ran her hand down the place on the door where he had been standing.

She lowered her head, her emotions in turmoil.

The answer came back plain and simple … No!

She questioned the reason for Nathan wanting her parents' address and although it sounded feasible, it was also suspicious this late in the investigation. Gem walked back into the lounge, her mind set on the thing she had to do. Beth looked at her from the settee and seeing the set look on Gem's face, she instantly jumped to her feet, clasping her hands in agitation in front of her.

"Is it more news? Have they found my uncle?" said Beth, on the point of tears.

"No. We were just talking," replied Gem, standing by the window, her mind not on the view in front of her but rather on what she had made her mind up to do. As Gem turned towards Beth, she smiled to ease what she had to say, hoping that Beth would not put up too much of an argument.

"Well, you've decided on something, I can see by the set of your face; am I going to like what you are going to say?" said Beth, almost reading her mind.

"Not really," replied Gem; walking over to where Beth was, she pulled her down to sit beside her on the settee. Before she continued she took hold of Beth's hand. "I have decided to go to my parents' place; I lied when I said they were going away, I was just buying myself a bit of time, so you see I just have to check for myself to see if they are okay."

"What is it, Gem? Is that why you didn't give Nathan their address? Is there something wrong about him?"

"I can't tell I'm just concerned." Replied Gem feeling suddenly agitated.

Before she continued Gem squeezed Beth's hand, trying to put her feelings into words. Beth sensed something was wrong and as she pulled her hand out of Gem's grip, her mood changed to anger as she said, "You're planning on going there alone, aren't you? By the look on your face you have no intention of taking me!"

Gem looked pleadingly at Beth, her eyes welling up with tears as she said, "It's for your own good; if something is wrong, I might be forced to fight my way out of the situation and I would never forgive myself if anything happened to you. You know that, don't you?"

As she was speaking Gem leant across and took Beth's hand again and held it tight. Beth's anger evaporated as if it had never been, because she knew Gem was only looking out for her. She bent over and gently kissed Gem's cheek, saying, "I'm sorry, it's just … well … I thought we were in this together. I know you are looking out for me, so I shall do as you say, just this once and just stay here. I'll not answer the phone or even open the door till you return."

Gem's relief was evident; jumping to her feet, she hastily crossed the room and headed for her bedroom to get ready. As she reached the door she suddenly turned back to face Beth and softly said, "Thank you."

The promise she had made Beth to tell her everything was already forgotten.

Chapter 12

The drive to her parents' house was one Gem had done numerous times before, but now the anxiety of getting there as quickly as possible was eating at her. Beth had stood in the window waving good-bye and as Gem pulled away from the kerb she had her doubts about whether leaving her behind was the right thing. However, that was too late now; the need to get away overtook her concern for Beth and nudging the gear into second, she sped off down the road.

She took the familiar route to Ripon and then took the A6108 north to Leyburn, turning onto the B6270 and heading as fast as the road allowed to the village of Reeth in Swaledale. Her parents had purchased Dale House at an auction just before she was born. They had lived there until she started school, but because it was so remote, they had decided to purchase a house in York.

It was more convenient for both her father's work and her school; her father had once told her. It was used as a bolt hole when the pressure of her father's work got too much for him. Neither of her parents liked holidaying abroad and the quietness and remoteness the house offered was just what they wanted. Her father had told her often enough that they planned to retire there, but now she had returned to the north he was more than pleased to give her the York house and retire permanently to Dale House.

Passing through Reeth, the Arkengarthdale Road rose sharply into the old lead mining country, an industry that had thrived there until the last century. As the Stag headed to the northernmost part of the dale in the valley of Arkengarthdale, Gem wondered again why her parents had chosen one of the most sparsely populated of all the dales.

The house, Gem knew from experience, was surrounded by a bleak but dramatic landscape, its hillside dotted with the hardy native sheep.

Many a time during a hard winter, her parents' home had proved invaluable as a refuge for the local farmer; who had managed to bring his sheep down to their lower pastures. She knew her parents loved the place because of its remoteness, but in times like this, its isolation was a worry and a hindrance.

Gem felt her stomach churning at the thought of anything happening to her parents and her hands tightened on the steering wheel, turning her knuckles white.

It did not matter to her what Remne had said, they were her family and she felt the car leap forward as her anxiety returned; her foot pushed the accelerator pedal to the floor in answer.

As she drove round the edge of the valley, she could see down below the house, lying silent and peaceful on the valley floor. The old Yorkshire stone was turning golden as the sun was setting and a lump came to Gem's throat as she looked at its beauty. Beside the house stood a small copse of trees, where many a time as a child she had run wild, much to her mother's annoyance, who chided her for running around unchaperoned. Anything could happen, she would say. Nothing ever had; she always felt safe and secure up here. Along with the house came a large section of land that encompassed not only the small copse but a section of the lake that bordered their land.

Gem could still remember the pleasure she felt when she ran through the little wood to find the lake beyond. It seemed quite magical to her as a child. Her father was a keen fisherman and many a time she sat with him while he fished, the silence between them one of love. They talked nonstop at the house, but here it was different.

There was no need for words here. They felt the lake had a calming effect on them and both felt relaxed and happy after being together there most of the day.

As the car sped along the road she could see up ahead the turning she needed and the small oak board bearing the name of the house still sitting on the fence where she and her father had nailed it. She had it specially made in York as a little present for the both of them at Christmas and she had the name, "DALE HOUSE," picked out in gold letters.

She remembered the day as if it was yesterday.

It was Boxing Day and her father had called her out of the warm kitchen where she had been chatting to her mother. He had stood patiently in the hall with his big coat on and his hat with the ear flaps and with the board under one arm and hammer and nails in the other hand.

"No time like the present," he had said and Gem had laughed as she scrambled to get into her coat to follow him. He had opened the large front door and strode off down the drive even as she was tying up her boot laces. The wind had blown down from the hills, freezing their hands as they worked and she had laughed when her father's nose had turned red with the cold. It did not take them long, but they felt the cold starting to penetrate their warm clothes, so when their job was done her father had flung his arm about her shoulder in an effort to keep her warm. As they had walked back to the house, their feet crunching on the snow and their breath hanging in the air, she had seen her mother standing on the door step with big steaming mugs of coffee in both hands for them. As Gem's thoughts tumbled backwards she found she could still smell the dash of whiskey her mother had put in the mugs to "help warm them up," she had said.

The Stag skidded slightly on the loose stones of the lane as she made the turn without braking from the road; paying no heed to caution, she picked up speed for the long drive to the house.

Everything looked all right, nothing untoward. The rambling roses climbing up the front of the house were blown, their petals ready to drop and as they intertwined with the Virginia creeper it gave the house a feeling of permanence and beauty she never got tired of looking at, because as one colour faded the other took its place.

How silly she was going to look when she went flying into the house. Her mother would tell her off for not wiping her feet, but she would not be able to keep the smile from her face and her father would shout from the lounge, happiness in his voice, that she had dropped in to see them. Gem pulled up in front of the house, calmer now that she was here. She parked the Stag so that it was facing back down the lane, a habit she had gotten into since it had refused to start one day.

As she locked the car she was smiling at what excuse she could give and decided that she missed them and wanted to see how Daddy was. The last time she had spoken to her mother on the phone, she had said that her father was indeed feeling a bit poorly but they had no intention of going away, as she had told Nathan.

Gem sniffed the air, her nostrils flaring at the smell.

125

The light breeze that wafted through the open door and set the tubular bell chimes dancing and their pretty tinkling sound was at odds to what Gem was experiencing. Her body reacted instantly to the threat and she could feel her muscles bunch and tighten; her breath was coming in small shallow draught as her heart started racing.

She gently pushed the door open to its full width and tried to see inside the dim interior. She stood to one side of the door as it opened, trying to shield her body as best she could, but her view was limited. There was nothing else for it: she had to enter the house. She thought about going round the back, but that would be just wasting time. Cautiously entering the large hall, she glanced at the parquet flooring; it was polished and gleaming, giving testimony to her mother's cleaning prowess, but more importantly there were no footprints heading towards the lounge or the kitchen. That did not mean anything, though; someone could have got into the house from any of the doors or windows. She eased her car keys into the dish on the oak hall table, trying not to let them jangle against each other. She did this more from habit than anything else and when she had done it, Gem stood silently for a minute, listening to the sounds of the big house, listening for any giveaway noise, trying to ascertain who was in there.

The smell of Him was everywhere; there was no way she could turn without the stink of Him pervading her senses.

She knew He had been here as certainly as she knew He had gone!

Why had He gone?

Why wasn't He waiting for her?

The answer she knew awaited her in this house!

The fear for her parents rose within her and taking a small step forward she decided to try the kitchen first, knowing that was where her mother would be at this time of the evening. Her pace increased as she walked down the corridor, looking for any tell-tale signs of disturbance along the way, but the small framed photographs of happier times were still in their places; no shoulder or arm had moved them, so reaching the end and faced with the closed kitchen door, she forced herself to enter the room without hesitation.

For a moment Gem thought it had all been a mistake.

Her mother had her back to her, sitting at the table where she always prepared dinner. The Le Creuset set of saucepans she always used were laid out ready for the vegetables she was preparing.

Gem softly called her name as she walked towards her, saying, "Mummy, it's me, I've come to see you, to see if you and ..."

As Gem walked round her mother's chair to stand in front of her, she saw now why her mother did not answer her. The flesh from her face had been torn off and hung in long slippery shreds past her chin. She had no mouth to utter words of comfort to her daughter, her eyes, those beautiful, soft brown eyes, were missing.

Gem placed her two hands on the table for support, unable to tear her gaze away from the abomination that was once her mother. Her eyes roamed across her body, seeing other horrendous wounds. The front of her mother's neat blouse was torn and bloody and as Gem cautiously pulled the front of it aside, she could see that her mother's heart had been ripped from her body.

The blood lying on the floor had already started to congeal and she could hear the lazy buzzing of the flies as they moved from wound to wound. As she backed away from the table Gem looked down at her hands that had been resting in her mother's blood, the redness in stark contrast to her fair skin.

She looked at both her hands, unable still to take in the horror. As she gazed around the kitchen, it all seemed so quiet and peaceful, even the vegetables lay at one end of the table ready to be put into the saucepan. Ready for a meal that nobody would eat.

Soft rays from the setting sun streamed through the window, giving a lie to the horror sitting at the table. Her mother's body was now in the shadows and when she stepped back from the table Gem could almost imagine that everything was normal.

Rage poured through her, blind, stifling, unadulterated rage; her hands balled into fists wet with her mother's blood and she wanted to scream her anger and her fear, but her legs buckled underneath her and she went sliding to the floor, her back resting up against the large Welsh dresser. She felt herself in the grip of something monumental and suddenly feared that the shock was taking away her sanity as she stared continuously at her blood-soaked hands.

The scream that she felt building up inside needed an outlet and was almost primeval in its outpouring, but only one word escaped her lips: "M ... O ... T ... H ... E ... R!"

She only stopped when her throat felt so raw that she feared she would never speak again, but strangely the tears did not fall and slowly getting to her feet, she made her way over to the range, picked up a tea towel, and tried – with little success – to wipe her hands clean of her mother's blood.

She dropped the stained and bloodied towel where she stood and then retraced her steps back to what was left of her mother sitting at the kitchen table. When she was next to her mother's body she leant down, kissed the top of her head and gently stroked the fine white hair.

She turned suddenly from her ghastly findings in the kitchen and swiftly went in search of her father. A new energy had entered her, a new purpose. She felt her heart harden as she left the kitchen; she had been dealt the blow she had been dreading and knew deep down the same fate awaited her father.

There was no need to search the rest of the house, because she knew he liked to sit in the conservatory and watch the sun go down. It was his favourite spot and whenever Gem had stayed over, the two of them would sit there together.

Her father would have his usual, Glenmorangie with two chunks of ice and she would have a chilled glass of white wine. Mother would join them and her father would hand her a glass of sherry and the three of them would watch the last rays of the sun disappear behind the distant hills, spreading its dying beauty across the lake.

Memories invaded her thoughts, a thousand different ways, as she hurried through the house each one happy and loving.

Gem headed back along the corridor, her trainers silent on the parquet floor and bravely entered the lounge, no longer in fear for herself. The room was in shadow as the setting sun left the sky, but Gem could see instantly that the room was empty. The large ornate mirror hanging over the fireplace reflected the peace and quiet of the room. Large logs burned and sizzled in the grate during the winter, but her mother had put generous bunches of roses, both wild and cultivated, in a vase inside the empty fireplace and their perfume valiantly tried to mask the odious aroma of Its progress.

She made her way across the Persian carpet, her shoes sinking into its fullness and as she passed through she saw long trails of scuff marks on the chairs and settee, where nails had raked along it and here and there on the whiteness of the plump pillows she saw spots of blood; her anger knew no bounds.

As she pushed the French doors open, there in the gloom by the side of the chair, where he liked to sit lay her father. Gem couldn't see from where she was standing if he was alive or dead. Moving quickly across the room, she reached his broken body and sitting on the floor beside him she slipped an arm under his head and raised him to her chest, rocking him back and forth as though he was the child and she the parent. She did not want to see the extent of his injuries just yet; she was content to have found him and to hold him. When he gave a little murmur, she was overcome with joy, but her happiness was short lived when she looked down into his face.

The blood tasted good on his tongue, and he licked his bloody fingers with relish. It seemed he would never tire of the things he had to do. He had given himself up to the pleasure of killing a long time ago.

The place was not too hard to find and it had taken him no time at all to get there. He knew the blonde one would be hard on his heels when she had worked things out. He knew when she had left her sanctuary, knew that she had left the little one all alone.

What he didn't know was how much time he had to complete things.

His blonde nemesis was unpredictable and that was dangerous. He had to be careful, check and double check, leave nothing to chance. Killing the woman had been too easy; she gave her life up with little or no resistance, believing she was saving her daughter.

Her daughter! What did she know?

Now the father, he was a different matter, he lasted longer than he thought he would and he would have finished the job if she had not interrupted him.

He had stubbornly refused to tell him what he wanted to know.

The Book must be around somewhere. He had searched the house for it.

Someone must have it!

He had paid Henry a little visit in Windermere. Fully expecting to retrieve the book, he had even laughed when he saw the policemen standing at the top of the lane.

For Henry's protection, no doubt!

His humour did not last long when he found Henry had gone and the book was nowhere to be found in his rambling old house. In fact, he was incandescent with rage. That was why it was such a pleasure coming up here to this lovely old house and being made welcome as a friend of their daughter's. Her mother had made him more than welcome when he had

lied, saying he was an old friend from university and she had no inkling
of the things to come when he had offered to help prepare the dinner with
her.

Now he was going back, away from her and her rage. Because he knew
it would be the same as his when he was thwarted. He was still not sure of
her powers, so it was safer to get away as far as possible before she found
what he had done to those two snivelling, rotting bodies. But he had
enjoyed himself, going through her belongings in her bedroom. Running
his hands through her silky underwear, feeling the essence of her in the
things she had worn.

He had found himself bent double with hatred at the thought of the
people closest to her.

It should be him.

That was why it was such a pleasure killing them off one by one. They
were not a match for him; they had died easily.

Unlike her!

She was his match and he relished their next encounter.

Gem could see by the angle of her father's body that serious damage had
been done. His legs protruded out at a funny angle and it was not until she
tried to drag his body further onto her lap that she realised that both his
legs were broken. Her mind questioned why he was not writhing in pain
until she heard him speak, the blood frothing at his mouth, forming small
bubbles as he said, "Gemini, you came; don't worry about me … I'm …
I'm … not in pain. In fact I can't feel anything …"

It was then Gem realised his back was broken, snapped like a dry
stick.

"Don't say any more, Daddy, let me phone for an ambulance."

His voice grew a little stronger in his anxiety saying, "No, it's too late
for me, but you must find your mother, protect her … she will be lost
without me."

Gem comforted her father, saying, "Shh now, lay still, Mother is fine.
I told her to lie down while I went to find you."

She could see the relief flooding through him and felt his body relaxing
in her arms. Fearing he had died, Gem softly called his name, "Daddy …
please don't leave me."

He responded by opening his eyes slightly, as if this simple gesture was too much for him. He opened his lips to say something, but Gem had to lean forward to catch what he was saying: "I didn't … tell him what he … wanted to know," he stuttered. "I don't know … where the Book is."

Again Gem tried to comfort him, stroking his grey hair as his head lay in her lap.

"Shh now, don't worry, the book is safe. Henry Peterson has it. Beth and I went to see him and he explained a lot of things. So please darling, don't worry any more about the Book."

"It is not the Book … that I was in … safe keeping of … it was … you."

A small spasm of coughing racked his body and Gem could see dark red blood trickling from his mouth.

"Please Daddy … please don't talk; wait till you are stronger."

Gem felt his body give a little shake and she was stunned to see that he was actually laughing.

"Stronger? No, Gemini … I am dying." He felt her arms tighten round him as if to keep the inevitable away; he smiled gently as he said, "Go to the lake … Gemini … trust in yourself … and you will find what is yours."

Gem could see his eyes trying to take a last look at her, but the life in him was fading away until finally nothing remained but the empty shell she was left holding.

How long she sat there rocking his body like a grieving mother, she had no idea. But the moon was high in the night sky when she suddenly looked around her. The numbness that had hit her when her father died in her arms was now replaced by the chilling, all-consuming rage she had felt when she had found her mother, but now it was back a thousand fold.

Gem laid her father's broken body gently on the floor. After straightening his legs as best she could, she folded his arms over his body, clasping his hands together as if in silent prayer. She leant forward, brushed a few strands of hair from his forehead and softly kissed his brow.

Her good-byes done, she got to her feet and headed out of the conservatory to the lake.

Chapter 13

The grass was damp as she made her way through the garden and from the moonlight it looked as though she had left silvery footprints in the turf. She pushed her way past the large hydrangea, her mother's favourite, with its large mop heads of lilac-blue. Stopping for a moment, she held in her palm the delicate lilac-pink bloom of the buddleia tree. How often had she lain in the garden, watching the butterflies collect around this particular plant, but now in the dead of night it looked how she felt: devoid of all colour and emotion just like a shadow passing through.

Gem's thoughts shied away from remembering happier times; her father had sent her to the lake and so she hurried on, not knowing why but feeling urgency inside of herself, nonetheless. Moving quickly now, she straddled the old stile that separated the garden from the fields beyond; she could see the sheep huddled together in the far corner, frightened now that the storm was so close, their white woolly coats standing out in contrast against the surrounding darkness.

Her feet made their own way instinctively across the field. When she was a small child she had skipped her way and later as an adult she could have walked it blindfolded. In her troubled state of mind she covered the rough ground between the garden and the wood without even thinking, but she stopped suddenly upon reaching the outer edges, reluctant for some reason to enter.

She turned and looked back the way she had come; the house seemed a long way away, but its appalling contents seemed closer to her now and the further away she got from the house, the nearer they seemed to her.

Gem felt herself doubling over and she put her arms around her middle to assuage some of the hurt building up inside. Taking a deep breath, she straightened up and placed her foot on the path that would lead her through the wood.

The moon cast an eerie glow, coldly lighting her way; branches picked at her clothes and small furry things scurried out of her way. One part of her mind wanted to blot out all she had seen and another part wanted to hold it close, seeking vengeance. She shook her head to try and clear the terrible things she had seen, but the faces of her parents still swam before her eyes. How could somebody do the things she had witnessed? A chill ran deeply though her as if his presence was suddenly close to her.

Bile rose in her throat but she forced it down, swallowing hard on the burning liquid. She compelled her mind to think of other things to stop herself from throwing up and as she stumbled on she could hear the storm brewing in the distance, creeping closer, breaking the warm air with its thunder. Dark clouds rolled in over the bleak landscape and the wind suddenly whipped up, making the trees bend and shake, forcing them to shed their leaves long before they were due. She could see long flashes of blue and white lightning as she entered the wood and now as she went deeper the lightning flashes made the trees seem like long ghostly fingers reaching upwards to a bruised sky.

The path she travelled along was overgrown and the brambles of autumn were already claiming the ground back for its own. She was uncaring of the scratches and burrs that clung to her, her mind trying to accept the horrors she had witnessed. How could her mother be dead, butchered in such a way and her beloved father, snapped and broken like a rag doll?

She stumbled over a tree root and would have fallen had not the moon suddenly shone its light through the trees, leading her to where her father urged her to go. Instinctively her feet guided her through the wood on old familiar paths, now so overgrown from lack of use. She tried to think back to the last time she had visited the lake with her father; it had been a long time ago. He had been unwell for a while now and had found the trek down too strenuous for his thin frame, even with Gem's arm to lean on.

She had sadly watched as he had packed all his fishing gear away, stowing all his hooks and reels in the handy little box she had bought him for one of his birthdays. His fishing gear had remained in the cellar, neatly put away until the time came, he had said, when he would be fit enough to carry it all, but that time never came and he became more and more frail as the months went on.

Now though, instead of the peace and contentment of earlier visits she'd had with her father, there was only pain and her heart felt like a lead weight in her chest.

Each stumbling step brought her nearer to the lake, but it seemed as though the very woods were trying to hinder her journey. She forced herself through the dense undergrowth, momentarily losing her way as she stumbled off the path. It all seemed so different at night; the landscape had altered, or was she just remembering wrongly?

She stopped for a moment to get her bearings, but it was so dark in the woods that she began to worry if she might be going round in a circle. Gem looked up through the branches and through a small gap in the overhanging trees she could see the dense black clouds scurrying across the sky; then suddenly the moon came out and for a moment it illuminated the area around her. What was she doing here? This was useless; she might as well turn round and go home, then her thoughts went crashing back to the night of the party and she placed her hands on either side of her head as she remembered the words that Remne had spoken: "All things look different in the moonlight; you get a different perspective."

Had she been saying that to Rupert or her? She tried to think why it was so important. *She had been looking at me when she said it*, she thought; *it was a message to me not to give up.* Suddenly she felt renewed.

She was on the right path … and she would continue to the lake, where her father had urged her to go. Something important awaited her there and it was the duty to obey her father's last words that forced her through whatever obstacles remained. As she broke through the restraining brambles, Gem could see she was now out in the open and bending down she felt the courser grass that surrounded the lake.

She had arrived! … And she lifted her face to the dark forbidding sky and cried out in her anger. As if in reply, the thunder answered back; standing there, her arms outstretched to the shattered sky, she vowed her revenge.

Wave after wave of intense anger swept over her, consuming her with its passion. So great was the need to fight the thing that had done this to her parents that she was forced to her knees by the strength of that emotion; she felt defenceless and tears of rage did nothing to lessen the feeling of impotency.

Oh, she knew she could land a few blows and at times she felt the blood racing through her, making her strong, but what she needed now was something different and it was that something that she didn't have. She was heedless of the tiny drops of rain that had started to fall and kneeling there beside the lake, she could feel a change starting within her. Her heart pounded with panic as she fell onto her side and as she opened her mouth to scream, the pain became so intense that all she could do was lay next to the water, panting for breath, praying it would pass.

A small current of wind played around her body, momentarily cooling her burning skin and on that draught she thought she heard her father's voice.

Forgetting the pain, she raised her head, desperate to hear him once again.

Sand and grit were embedded in her hair and long strands fell in disarray around her shoulders as her plait came loose. The night closed in around her. The moon had retreated behind the clouds again and as the storm gathered pace, the darkness was almost complete, shutting her off from all that was familiar. She felt frightened and alone, lying there in the darkness with only pain for company.

As she mumbled her father's name, her eyes brilliant with unshed tears, she prayed for comfort, knowing in her heart it would not be forthcoming. But then she heard again his voice, as soft as a summer breeze and they helped to give her the strength she needed to raise herself upright:

"Go in the lake, Gemini! Enter its waters before it is too late! Go quickly!"

Pain tore through her, as she ripped the clothes from her body. She pulled her jumper over her head and scrabbled around her back to undo her bra, which she discarded to one side and then she sat again on the cold shoreline and pulled off her trainers. As she stood the pain once again swept through her with such intensity that she thought she would succumb to it.

Fearing she would not be in time, the urgency returned; she ripped the jeans from her legs along with her panties and kicked them both off; they landed at the water's edge with a plop. Then naked and shivering, she entered the water.

The thunder and lightning were getting closer, their duet almost simultaneous, as Gemini headed towards the shelf that lay just several feet from the edge of the shoreline. The freezing water lapped around her thighs and she involuntarily sucked in her stomach as it crept higher and as her feet felt the edge of the ledge; she knew from experience that it dipped steeply to twenty feet or more.

Her father had taught her to swim in this lake and she knew every inch of it.

Without hesitating, she filled her lungs with air and dived beneath the surface of the water; her strong strokes took her down into the murky depths of the lake. The coldness of the water eased the pain in her body at first, instantly cooling her skin, but as she swam deeper, the pain suddenly increased.

Deeper and deeper she went each stroke a torture to her. Holding her breath and fighting the pain together was taking its toll on her and she finally felt herself succumbing to the agony.

Why was she here?

Was this part of what she was supposed to endure?

Or was she down here to look for something?

As she neared the point of giving up, her eyes caught a glimpse of something metallic hidden amongst the weeds. Her hair that had streamed behind her like a long golden banner swirled and drifted around her, obscuring her vision as she floated above the glint of metal. Her lungs were starting to object and she felt herself wanting to open her mouth and take in a lungful of air, but her senses were deceiving her: all that awaited her was a cold and watery death.

Gem shook her head from side to side, trying in her last efforts to get some oxygen to her brain; turning in the water she headed downwards, kicking her feet in an effort to gain more momentum. She pulled herself through the water arm over arm; her muscles ached with the strain, each one burning with the effort she put into diving deeper. She swam until her hand clasped the metal object and pulling with all her might, she felt it come loose, along with a large clump of weed which floated ethereally about her. Her vision at this depth was next to nothing, so not bothering to inspect it; Gem held it with her left hand and swam to the surface, dragging it behind her.

Swimming was difficult with only one hand and the weight of the metal object hindered her, the clouds must have parted because she could see the ghostly shape of the moon shining on the surface of the water above her. All she could think of was getting free of the water and taking in mouthfuls of air as her lungs burned for release.

As her head broke the surface of the water, she was greeted by a loud clap of thunder; she tossed her bedraggled hair behind her, raised her right hand and wiped the water from her face and eyes, gratefully filling her lungs with the precious air.

Exhausted by her swim, she turned on her back and gently kicked her feet until she drifted towards the shore and shallower waters. Turning over, she felt the ground under her knees and, with a great deal of effort, slowly raised herself out of the water.

Gem stumbled naked from the lake, dragging the metal object behind her. The water ran in rivulets down her body and her hair was plastered to her head and body. She did not feel the cold, for once again the pain took her in its grip and she felt on fire.

Wave after wave of pure agony, joined in conjunction with the pain of losing her parents, drove her to her knees and as she reached the edge of the water she was forced to stop moving.

Her body was changing; she could feel her skin stretching and tearing.

Fearing that this was the end, she closed her eyes and lifted her face to the heavens and the cry that came out was torn from her very soul. Rain beat against her as she knelt, washing the sand and mud from her. The blood from her mother's body that had stained her hands was washed away; her whole body felt clean … and pure.

She felt her fingers curl around the handle of the object she had dragged from the water, and she raised her arm and lifted it to the sky. She opened her eyes, in the glare of the lightning and saw she was holding a flaming sword.

Its glow transcended anything she had seen before.

It was beautiful and its earlier heaviness was gone. It was lightness itself and as she felt its litheness and balance, she knew she had held it before.

It shone with a brilliance that was not of this world.

Rising to her feet, she could feel the pain receding and her body becoming revitalised. She lifted the sword in front of her and transferred it to her right hand and as her feet and her body found their own balance on the sandy shoreline, she raised the sword again and slashed it first one side of her, then the other.

This was hers; it had always been hers.

Her father had just kept it safe until the time was right, hiding it away until she could claim it for her own.

And this was it, this was her time.

The lightness crept up her body and she closed her eyes once again as she felt herself grow faint; then turning back to face the waters, she threw back her head and gave herself to the night. As the storm crashed and thundered around her she felt herself rising on the storm's downdraft.

She felt herself rising above the shore and the earth below.

Rising!

Gem threw her arms wide, the sword still in her hand and as she opened her eyes all fear had left her.

Her heart sang in tune to a thousand angels.

The song was learnt from time immemorial and her heart was bursting with the love of it. As she floated down to earth the rain ceased its incessant beating and turned once again to a light summer rain.

When her feet touched the dank ground she walked to the lake's edge and looking down at her reflection in the choppy waters, she saw what she hoped to see.

There behind her was the symbol of all she was. Wings that were so white, pure and strong pulsated gently behind her.

The blinkers to her memory had been lifted and all was made clear to her.

She had been born again.

Although she was part human, she now knew her ethereal inner being had been lying dormant until this time.

Her time!

And now it spread through her, filling her with its energy. The white wings spread out behind her, beating and trembling to their own rhythm. The raindrops looked like jewels as they beaded down their feathery lengths.

Gem ran her hand down their outer edges, glorifying in their beauty. Then rising with the flaming sword in her right hand, she once again lifted her head to the skies and the cry she sent forth was of defiance and challenge.

"Behold the Angel of Retribution!

"Fall to your knees all those who seek forgiveness, for the Lord thy God is merciful, but make ready all those that fight against me ... For I shall avenge all those that have suffered and my justice will be swift."

As the storm passed the skies began to clear and in the moon's glow Gemini dropped to one knee; laying the sword reverently on the ground, she clasped her hands together and prayed to her God for the safe delivery of her parents' souls and for the fight to come.

Her body shook with the wondrous knowledge that she was now in a position to undertake that fight. Her eyes glowed like brilliant diamonds and as her hand reached across the sand she clasped the hilt of the sword with a grip like iron.

She smiled because now she knew she could right the wrong that the day had brought her and no matter where he went or where he tried to hide, she would hunt him down and destroy him.

This much she promised herself.

Chapter 14

Beth stood at the window, far from happy as she waved good-bye to Gem. She knew from long experience that Gem was hiding something from her, because as she had started to make her way down the steps, Beth saw her hesitate as if she was going to come back in, but then she gave a little shrug of her shoulders and raced on. Beth turned from the empty window and leant against the desk, her thoughts still buzzing.

She ran her hand through her dark locks and closed her eyes to try and concentrate. Why didn't Gem give her parents' address to Nathan? What was she afraid of?

Beth could see by Gem's face when he walked into the room that his presence was welcome; what had happened in the space of a few seconds to change all that? She racked her brains, trying to figure out the sequence of events that led up to Gem's strange behaviour.

No! It was no good; a piece of the puzzle was missing.

She would just have to give it time; it would come to her eventually. Heaving a large sigh, Beth straightened up and walked over to the settee she had been sitting on earlier. So much was going through her mind. Gem taking off as though her life depended on it, her uncle going missing; it was all getting too much.

As she walked round to the front of the settee she realised there was nobody she could turn to for help; she couldn't even ring Nathan if Gem didn't trust him. Planting herself comfortably down on the cushions, she had a sudden thought about the Book.

If her uncle had gone missing, had he taken it with him? Was that why he could not be found? It seemed strange that the day after they had visited him, after he had produced the Book to prove a point to Gem, he should then up and vanish. Had he known about the police watching his house and thought it safer to disappear, knowing they had little chance of protecting him?

Over and over the questions tumbled in her mind. Her head ached with trying to sort them all out. Each one vied with another for priority. Beth glanced down at her watch and tried to estimate what time Gem would arrive at her destination. She tried to work out the miles per hour Gem would be travelling, making allowances for traffic, but her mind couldn't concentrate on it, and she punched the nearest cushion in her frustration. The house seemed too large when Gem was not with her; even when they were together they both seemed to rattle around like a couple of peas. They rarely used the dining room, as they either ate in the kitchen or had something on their laps. They didn't own a television, which everyone thought was so unusual, but they just didn't have time to sit down and watch it.

Gem often came home late from work and all she wanted to do was listen to a little classical music, or else she was sitting at her desk, studying for her next case.

As for her it was much the same; she had taken over one of the spare bedrooms and turned it into a design room, where she could work at what she loved best: interior design. It was funny how you could end up in a job where you were not happy and that is precisely what she was doing now in advertising. She was very good at her job, but she didn't enjoy it the way she enjoyed matching fabrics, choosing colours and accessorising a room.

No, "enjoy" was too tame a word, she loved it, revelled in it when a room came together. For the present she was just getting together her portfolio. She had taken pictures of the room downstairs, getting things ready for when she had enough courage to leave her job and start up on her own. There were other things, too, that grated on her at her work, making her long to leave, especially when Simon from paste-up always managed to brush his arm up against her breast when he leant across her board. She hadn't dared tell Gem, she had visions of her storming into the office and tearing him off a strip; what if it was just her imagination?

No, it was best to say nothing.

It wouldn't be long now and she would be her own boss and not have to put up with the sleazy office Romeos. They had been in the house for a while now and they still hadn't gotten round to decorating it how they wanted it. Gem's parents had very good taste, but it was not really to Beth's liking. She had managed to change a few of the paintings, replacing wild highland watercolours with modern, more up-to-date pictures.

When they had first moved in, she had talked into letting her have free reign in redecorating the lounge, considering it was going to be their main room. She had asked Gem to stay in one of the hotels in York for the night and worked feverishly for two days with a small decorating firm to get the room how she wanted it.

She had used soft greys and cream on the settees, with cream and light pink cushions. She had painted the walls a very pale pink and had a rich ruby red pure wool carpet put down. Beth had left the coving in place and had painted it magnolia but had picked out the pattern with gold leaf, the same with the large central rose and she had painted the ceiling white to add contrast.

She was loathe touching the grand Victorian fireplace, so all she did was paint the surrounding woodwork white and gave the original tiles a polish. She had added a shelf in the alcove next to the fireplace and put the Denon stereo on it; underneath she had alphabetised Gem's vinyl records and her CD collection.

The only old thing in the room was Gem's desk and this was totally sacrosanct, as it had belonged to her grandfather; she knew Gem would go mad if she moved it. So to soften the area around the desk she changed the curtains to heavy, dark grey silk with soft pink tie backs and changed the desk lamp to a softer bulb.

Beth had flopped into one of the settees and heaved a great big sigh when they had finally finished. She had only just paid off the decorators when Gem's car had pulled up outside and she had rushed to open the front door.

She watched Gem struggle up the front steps with a large package under her arm. Gem kissed her on the cheek as she entered the front door and Beth asked her what she was carrying.

"No, let me see your room first," was all she had said, so Beth had led her into the lounge and waited with her hands clasped together for Gem's verdict on the redecoration. Gem didn't answer and Beth started to feel very uneasy; she could feel the apologies spring to her lips, but Gem had held up her hand and handed her the large unwieldy package.

"What is it?" she had asked and Gem had replied, "Open it and see."

As she had ripped open the package, there before her was the most wonderful modern oil painting in all the colours she had furnished the room in.

"It's to go over the fireplace," was all Gem said.

"How did you know? Have you been spying?" Beth had asked.

Gem had shrugged her shoulders and said by way of an answer, "Don't ask me, I just knew; I love it, by the way, it is so much softer than those National Trust colours my mother favoured." The matter was never spoken of again; Beth had just put it down to another one of those spooky things that Gem did every so often.

Now that she was on her own with nothing to do, Beth decided to go round and check that all the windows and doors were all properly latched, a job that Gem always did before retiring to bed. Rising from her seat Beth walked back over to the window and ran her fingers along the centre cross of the sash window to check that the latch was secure; for some reason she gave a little shudder as she looked out of the window at the darkening sky. One down, countless more to check, *this should take me some time,* she thought sadly but at least it would waste a few more hours until she heard from Gem.

As she wandered through the house, thinking about nothing in particular, the thought came to her of Nathan coming back in the room after making his phone call.

Strange that she should think of that.

She had checked all the downstairs windows and doors and then made her way slowly up the stairs, her fingers running absentmindedly along the hand rail until she reached the top; grabbing hold of the newel post, she swung herself around it so that she was now facing her bedroom, which was at the end of the corridor. She strolled into her bedroom, feeling lazy and bored and lay on the bed, letting her mind roam aimlessly. She knew it was useless to force these things; it would come soon enough.

She must have dozed off because the room was in deep shadow when she awoke and as she lay there between waking and sleeping, it suddenly came to her. Gem had seen something when she went to write her parents' address down. She had gone to the table and as she turned ... yes, that was it!

Beth sat upright on the bed, pleased with herself to have worked it out. She had seen it too but had paid it no mind, because she was so wrapped up in the news of her uncle's disappearance. She had thought he was wearing a t-shirt under his top shirt, but she had been wrong. Gem had guessed straight away and had seen the dressing on Nathan's upper arm.

The ringing of the phone interrupted her train of thought and thinking it might be Gem, she raced from her bedroom and down the stairs to the hallway, her dark locks bouncing around her shoulders.

She snatched up the phone and shouted, "Hello!" into the receiver.

"Whoa there, steady on, tiger, you almost blew my ear off," said a familiar voice.

"Oh hello, Rupert; sorry, I thought it might be Gem. What can I do for you?" Beth replied, embarrassed.

"I thought you might like to go out somewhere tonight, to a pub or a restaurant for dinner; what do you say? I know a few places where just the mention of my name would get you the best table in the place. You can't keep turning me down; a person could get a complex," he said, laughing.

"I really … really am sorry, Rupert, but I have to stay in; I'm expecting an important call," said Beth, trying to put as much sincerity in her voice as she could.

"Did you say Gem was out? Are you waiting for her call? Is something wrong? Do you need help? Shall I come round?" enquired Rupert concern evident in his voice.

"No, that's all right, Rupert, there nothing wrong," Beth lied. "Gem just had to go and see a friend who is in a spot of trouble; she'll be back soon I expect and we have plans this evening." Looking down at her watch, she added, "What's left of it."

Beth closed her eyes to give credence to her lies.

Lies always sounded better when you shut your eyes, she thought; they did on the phone anyway. Rupert seemed to believe her, that much was certain and she gave a small sigh of relief when he said he would call back tomorrow.

She promised to make it up to him when all this was over.

He deserved that at least.

Beth placed the phone back in its cradle and stood there, staring at her own hand as it lingered on the phone's back, one finger tapping the ivory plastic casing, as she thought what to do next.

Should she call him back, say yes to his offer? She was sorely tempted!

No! She had promised Gem she would stay in; what if there was news of her uncle, bad news, while she was out gallivanting? She would never forgive herself. Well, that's that then; happier now she had made her mind up and giving the phone a last look, she turned and made her way down the dark hallway to the kitchen to prepare herself a snack.

Beth was halfway through cutting some bread when the phone rang again, its insistent ringing shattering the silence. As she retraced her steps back to the phone, she flicked the light switch on and the shadows retreated, banished to the upper landing, as light flooded the hallway.

She snatched the phone from its cradle on the fourth ring and decided to moderate her voice in case it wasn't Gem again. "Hello, Beth speaking," she said, gripping the phone.

"Hello, Beth; do you remember me? It's Remne," said the soft voice at the other end of the line.

"Remne! Oh my God," said Beth, relief flooding her voice. "Thank goodness you rang; have you any news for me? Gem has told me everything so you can speak freely."

"I phoned to check up on Gem to see if she was all right, but I do have some other news, yes!" Remne replied.

There was a small pause as if she was talking to someone else in the room, whispering, but Beth could not quite catch what she was saying.

"Sorry, Beth, I was just checking to see if it was safe; you see I have your uncle here with me." Beth gave a squeal of delight, greatly relieved that her Uncle was not in fact missing but safely in Remne's care. She clutched the phone tightly in her hand with pleasure and said, "Oh I am so glad he isn't really missing, may I speak to him?"

"No, not over the phone, it is not safe," Remne said. "I am taking a chance as it is. Will Gem be there if we were to come round?"

"No, I am afraid not, something came up and she had to go and visit her parents' house in the country," answered Beth.

"What do you mean, something came up? Has someone been there? Why did you think that your uncle was missing anyway?"

Beth could hear the anxiety in Remne's voice, so she decided to hold nothing back, saying, "A policeman called round today, a DI Grantly. He was the policeman that dealt with my attack in London and he told us, he is now heading a task force looking into the death of Gem's grandfather and another chap who died, I can't remember his name off hand," said Beth in a flood of information.

The phone remained silent at the other end and Beth started to worry if she had been disconnected, then Remne's voice came down the line once more. "Is there anything else I need to know?" she asked Beth.

"Well yes … Gem was a bit suspicious … and to be fair, so am I."

Beth closed her eyes, not wanting to tell Remne what she had to say.

Her fingers curled the phone cord round and round, trying to delay the inevitable.

"Beth, I don't have time to play games. What is it you have to tell me?" replied Remne, annoyance sounding in her voice.

"For one, it's Rupert. I was attacked here in the house, when Gem came back from seeing you and she fought the attacker off, hurting him in the scuffle and ..."

"And?" Remne's short sharp reply came down the phone.

"And we thought it might be him, as he had a sore side." She realised she sounded foolish and added, "but then DI Grantly came round and he had a dressing on his upper arm and well ... we don't know who to trust now. You did tell Gem to trust no one ... and ..." Her voice trailed away as she stood there holding the phone, feeling slightly foolish.

Remne's voice came back down the line, strong and passionate, as she said,

"Now listen, Beth, we have suspected DI Grantly for some time, we often wondered how he managed to turn up so quickly when you were attacked and it may not be a coincidence that he is heading this task force. You did right not to trust him; if Gem is away all night and I suspect she will be, then we are coming round to collect you. You will be safer with us."

Her happiness in knowing that Rupert was not her attacker was short lived, when she realised that the man Gem had fallen for ... was!

Beth's eyes gleamed with unshed tears and she mumbled into the phone, her lips shaking as she tried to get the words out: "How long are you ... going to be?"

Beth gave a little cough to clear her throat and to make the words come out stronger. She pushed the mound of hair back from her hot face and blew air from her mouth, curling her lip so that it was directed to her forehead.

"Not long," replied Remne, adding, "Don't worry anymore, Beth, you will be safe with us."

Then the line went dead and Beth was left alone again, but this time she knew help was coming. She would leave a note for Gem just in case she returned early; replacing the phone once again in its cradle, she turned and entered the lounge. She walked over to the desk by the window, leant across and pulled the curtains shut, closing out the night. The room was plunged into darkness and she thought she heard the distant rumble of thunder as she switched on the table lamp.

The soft glow spread across the paperwork and Beth pulled out the chair to write the note in some semblance of comfort. She folded the paper in half and left it lying at the front of the desk, where Gem would instantly see it, now all she had to do was wait. She went and sat back down on the settee, all thought of food banished from her head by the excitement of the phone call. She tapped her feet impatiently, but the seconds slipped slowly by.

At least her uncle was safe, that was something to be thankful for and Rupert, dear sweet Rupert; perhaps after all she could allow herself the luxury of a relationship.

Beth tucked her feet up under herself and curled up on the settee, letting her head fall back on the cushions behind her. She still had on her baggy shirt and leggings and the thought crossed her mind to throw a few things into an overnight bag, just in case. After all, she did not know how long she was going to be away.

Annoyed that she had spent too much time sitting around, she jumped up from the settee and ran to the stairs. Her legs would not allow her to take them two at a time like Gem, so she ran up as fast as she could. She did not bother with the light until she got to her bedroom; pulling open drawers, she proceeded to pack a few essentials into a large soft leather bag.

The doorbell rang, stopping her in her tracks; smiling broadly, she left what she was doing and ran back down the landing to the stairs. She quickly retraced her steps down the stairs, careful not to fall and as she reached the bottom step, the bell rang for the second time.

This time, though, the person kept their finger on the bell and its insistent ringing started to grate on her long before she reached the door. Beth swung the door wide, expecting to see her uncle and Remne standing there.

The smile slowly evaporated from her face and she was at a loss at what to say when she saw who was standing in front of her.

"Well, are you going to ask me in?" said Cybil, her foot tapping an annoyed tattoo.

Taken completely by surprise, Beth stood to one side and let her pass. After Cybil had entered the house, Beth stepped out onto the doorstep and swept her gaze up and down the road.

Nothing! There was nobody there.

At least she'd have time to get rid of Cybil. Beth was wondering what she was doing there anyway. It was not as if she had an invite! Had she come to see her because of Rupert? As Beth closed the front door, she quickly thought best how to tackle this new problem. She did not want Cybil there, but on the other hand she did not want to upset her.

Beth's eyes had to readjust from the bright light of the hallway to the soft glow of the desk lamp as she entered the lounge. She could see Cybil moving to the other end of the room in the semi darkness, so to give herself more time to think; she switched on the main ceiling light and then strolled over to turn off the table lamp.

Cybil was standing near the cold fireplace, its grate filled with fresh flowers instead of coal this time of the year. She looked immaculate as usual, her outfit co-ordinating exactly. Her red hair was swept up in a slide; she looked both elegant and sophisticated. Beth felt completely self-conscious as she joined Cybil, smoothing down her baggy shirt in an effort to look at least a bit presentable. Noticing the look of Cybil's face, she gave up and listening to the approaching storm, Beth said, "So much for summer, eh?" as she nodded towards the window and continuing, "It wouldn't seem out of place to light the fire, there is a bit of a chill in the air already, don't you think?" She felt herself give a small shudder as if suddenly feeling cold. She knew she sounded stupid, making idle talk, but she continued bravely, "I'm sorry to have to cut this visit short, but I am expecting someone and well … I shall be leaving soon."

As she finished talking Beth stole a quick glance at her watch and as she raised her head she smiled sweetly.

The blow, when it came, sent her reeling backwards and she was only saved from smashing her head on the floor by the soft cushions of the settee.

Dazed and disorientated, Beth raised a hand to her face and when she bought it away she could see bright red blood lacing its way through her fingers.

Too stunned to cry, Beth raised herself on her elbow and looked up at Cybil, who somehow still appeared elegant. She still stood there in silence, not a hair out of place. As Beth got to her knees with the help of the furniture, she could taste her own blood as it trickled into her mouth. She wanted to spit and looked around for a convenient place.

Yes, Beth thought, looking over at Cybil's feet, the very place.

The round lump of bloody spittle landed squarely on the front of Cybil's expensive shoes. *I may not be able to whistle,* she thought, *but I can certainly spit when it comes to it.*

Gem would be proud!

Her victory was short lived. Cybil bent down and grabbing Beth by the hair, she delivered her another stunning blow. She would have suffered a severe whiplash if Cybil had not been holding her hair so tightly; even so Beth felt the muscles in her neck straining at the onslaught.

Surely this was not over some man?

Cybil raised Beth's face with her free hand, holding her chin and forcing her to look eye to eye. The blood in Beth's veins turned to ice and the fear she was feeling was replaced by something a million times more dreadful.

Beth opened her mouth to speak, but the words caught in her throat. Suddenly Cybil started talking; gone was the self-taught elocution voice and in its place were the soft cultured tones of Remne: "Hello Beth, do you remember me? It's Remne."

Beth's eyes widened in horror, as she listened to Cybil recount her phone conversation of a couple of hours ago: "I just phoned to check on Gem," she heard her say.

"No! Pleeeease ... who are you? What do you ... want?" sobbed Beth, her tears mixing with the blood and fleshy tissue of her broken face.

"I, my dear ... I am your worst nightmare. My little ruse fooled you into thinking I was that whore," Cybil gloated.

Beth tried to raise her hands to gouge away the grip, her nails ready to rake through Cybil's flesh, but Cybil twisted her hair savagely and Beth felt her back arching with the agony of it.

"Oh, it's true, little one, I've got a knack for imitating voices; do you want me to do Gem's, to make you feel safe?" said Cybil, a smile fleetingly brushing her lips.

"No, you bitch ... I want you to curl up ... and die," replied Beth with every ounce of hatred she could muster.

Beth's eyes blazed with hatred and frustration at being subjected to such a beating, but this intensified when Cybil casually tut-tutted, "Now, now little one, being nasty doesn't suit you." With her free hand Cybil wiped the damp strands of hair from Beth's face before she continued, "I only had to check to see whether Gemini was with you or not and if she was likely to return at some inopportune moment." Cybil stopped talking and looked around, her eyes searching the room, before she turned back to Beth and said, "Like now ... and hey presto, she's not and she's not going to be either, from what you say. So she's not going to come galloping to the rescue this time."

Cybil's face broke into a wide grin, her pleasure almost palpable. She pushed her face closer to Beth's and Beth tried to turn away from her, but she was still held in Cybil's vicious grip. As Cybil's face inched closer, Beth felt her cold breath on her exposed neck and when finally Cybil had her lips up to Beth's ear, she said, "We are going on a little trip; I need to set a trap and you, my dear," Cybil paused and her tongue slowly and sensually licked the pink tenderness inside Beth's ear before she continued, "and you, my dear ... are the bait!"

Chapter 15

How long she knelt there in silent vigil Gem could not say, but when she raised her head she felt the first flush of a new day. Weak golden beams of light that came from behind her drifted across the water, sparkling and dancing across the gentle swell.

She glanced around, taking in her surroundings; everything looked fresh and green after the storm. The lake was gentle once again, its waters like glass in complete contrast from the night before when hell seemed to scorch across its surface, the wind whipping the white horses, turning the once calm surface into a boiling cauldron.

Now, though, small sand pipers dipped and nodded about, searching in the sand and mud for their breakfast. They seemed oblivious to her presence and carried on about their business with total unconcern. She watched them for a while, letting her mind drift off with the peace of it all, but now she knew what she had to do.

She knew what paths lay before her. The only thing she didn't know was who her adversary was. But that time was coming, it would not be long now.

She'd had her epiphany! She had become the stronger for it. She had not weakened; she had embraced the horror and the pain.

Now as she stood looking across the lake with the early morning sun caressing the back of her naked body, she felt whole and complete. She knew to what lengths her parents had gone to keep her identity a secret and the price they had paid for their silence was something she could never repay.

All she could do was what was right and so she spread her beautiful white wings and basked in the glory of a new day and new beginnings.

There was just one more thing she had to do, though, and the thought of it brought her brows knitting together; she refolded her wings close to her body and they disappeared, leaving her as she once was.

She leant down and picked up her abandoned clothes and the long silver sword, thinking hard about how she was going to tackle this next problem.

She had not noticed before but the sword was really quite beautiful, with a design all along the shaft and the hilt had a highly ornate, half crescent piece of metal as a guard that protected the back of the hand. The design was four interlocking angels, their wings touching and their arms entwined and as she ran her fingers over it, their faces seemed familiar to her, but she put this down to just speculation on her part.

Gone were the long streams of luminescent flames that had glowed along the length of the sword when she had held it the night before; now its phosphorescent radiance had dimmed, leaving the sword dull and undistinguished but still beautiful in her eyes.

Smiling now as she gathered up her belongings, she turned round into the sun's warm rays and raised her face, letting the sun warm it. Then she headed towards the woods and back to the house.

As Gem moved through the wood, small showers of raindrops, left over from the storm, fell from the branches onto her naked body, soaking her anew. Her long hair lay in sandy, tangled strands down her back, while small leaves and grass stuck to her legs and feet, but she was unconcerned, her mind elsewhere and the nearer she got to the house, the more the smile slipped from her face.

As she neared the conservatory she could see that the door was still open and that a small puddle of water had collected inside, where the rain had come in.

Gem stood there for a moment, forcing her body to enter and as she stepped over the puddle she found herself staring down at the body of her father.

Father, he was never her father, but what did that matter, she had loved him all her life. She had never wanted for a better one; he had lavished all his love and attention on her and she had never suspected she was not his own.

The room was still in shadow, because the sun's rays would not reach this part of the house until late in the afternoon. Standing there looking at her father's still face, Gem felt the hot scalding tears flowing down her cheeks.

Her shoulders shook with her muted crying, but this eventually gave way to great gasping sobs as she forced the air into her lungs.

Gem threw her clothes to one side, laid her sword gently on the floor and knelt down beside him. Her eyes were blinded by her tears and in her sorrow she was forced to cling to his inert body, feeling with her fingertips the contours of his beloved face. She tasted the salt from her own tears and cried till she could cry no more.

Gently she slipped one arm underneath his head and the other beneath his legs and slowly she raised herself upright with his body held close to her. She did not feel the weight in her arms, all she could think about was this was the man who had thrown her up in the air as a child when they played together. Who had taught her how to swim and ride and had sat in quiet contemplation when they fished. He had always been there for her and had never failed her, so how could she fail him now?

Her muscles did not even flinch as she carried him tenderly out into the garden, so powerful had she become. She made her way out to the place where the wild roses grew and lovingly laid his body on the ground. A soft breeze from the moors caressed her body and she could smell a hint of heather in its essence.

Not waiting any longer, Gem swiftly turned on her heels and made her way quickly back to the house and the kitchen. It lay to one side of the house, a small extension incorporating a small breakfast room her mother loved.

She could hear the half-hearted argument her mother and father had over the position of the room. Her mother wanted to have it facing the direction of the early morning sun and her father, who would have given her anything anyway, made a token gesture of refusal, saying it would be too warm.

"Nonsense," she had replied, until she saw the gleam in his eyes and knew that he was having fun with her. Gem had watched them sink into each other's arms, their love for each other very much alive.

Now looking at her mother, sitting stiff and erect in her chair, she pushed all happy thoughts of them together from her mind until she had done what she had to do. The lazy buzz of one or two flies that she had seen earlier had been replaced by dozens, as the warmth of the kitchen grew with the rays of the early morning sun.

Little fat black flies crept in and out of her empty eye sockets and landed on and took off from the exposed pieces of flesh. They were oblivious in their need to decimate the dead body and Gem was filled with loathing as she watched them crawling all over her mother. She pushed the table away, exposing the full length of her mother's body and the black cloud of flies rose as one to hover in the air, waiting for a chance to return to the corpse.

Scooping up the stiff body from the chair, Gem made her way back through the lounge and before she went out through the conservatory, she knelt down on one knee; she held her mother to her chest while she picked up her sword with her other hand. Tucking it under her arm, she continued on her way out into the garden.

Upon reaching the spot where she had left her father, she knelt down on one knee and laid the body of her mother next to him.

"In life so shall you be in death. I will let nobody separate you!" said Gem as she kissed each face in turn.

Raising her sword high above her head, she brought it crashing down against the earth and it cut through the soil like a hot knife through butter. She knelt on both her knees and as the sword sliced through the grass and the soil, she watched as a large opening appeared in the ground.

Small flames of gold licked around her hand as she held the sword, but they did not burn her; she could hear its keening as she made the hole the right size for her parents' bodies. She laid her sword to one side, and the sword's mournful song ceased. As she lifted each body in turn, she kissed them one last time and laid them tenderly in their grave.

When she had finished, she pushed the earth over their bodies and felt the stones cutting the flesh of her palms as she scraped and patted down the cold earth. She almost welcomed the pain, rather that than the ache in her heart that she was feeling now. Stretching out full length on top of the grave, she flung her arms across the dirt mound, her wings extended to their full width and she gently held her parents in one last loving embrace.

The sun was high in the sky by the time Gem finally walked back into the house. She did not want to enter by the kitchen, so she chose to go by the conservatory once again. She dragged her heavy sword behind her, making little trail marks in the carpet as she silently walked across in her bare feet.

She automatically averted her eyes from the spot where her father had died, intent now on doing only what she had to do. Quickly now she walked through the house, into the hall, and up the stairs.

She propped the sword in the corner of the bathroom while she turned on the shower.

With her wings once again folded away from view, she stepped into the steam and let the hot water cascade over her. She carefully washed her long hair and inspected her body for any cuts or abrasions. There were none; even the bramble scratches from when she buried her parents had now all gone.

She turned off the water and stepped out of the shower; grabbing a large white fluffy towel, she proceeded to pat herself dry. When she had finished, she discarded the towel on the floor and, reaching up into the medicine cupboard, found what she was looking for.

The locks of hair floated to the floor and lay silently in a heap where they fell. Each snip of the large scissors sent more of her beautiful golden hair to join the other strands. Looking at her reflection, she did not see herself, so intent was she on completing the job. Her hair, the pride of her mother, was gone.

She was not Gem, the little girl or the loving daughter, any more.

This was her way of saying she was ready for the task ahead; live or die, whatever the outcome, she would be ready.

When she had finished she finally looked at herself through the steamy reflection of the mirror, seeing a woman whose close cropped hair showed the fine beauty of her features. The dark circles of sorrow under her blue eyes were the only hint that all was not right.

She heaved a small sigh and, turning from the mirror, automatically picked up her sword; leaving the bathroom, she made her way to the bedroom that her mother always had ready for her. She had always kept a small wardrobe of clothes here when she came to stay with her parents; it was easier that way than lugging a large suitcase up with her every time she came to visit. Now as she ran her fingers through the fine expensive material of her clothes, she realised that she would no longer be dressing up to dine with her parents.

It was the one thing they had insisted on whenever she came to visit – that they should all dress up formally for the evening meal. She had thought it was rather last century like a scene from an Agatha Christie novel, but she went along with it, humouring them in their eccentricities.

What had it mattered anyway if they enjoyed dressing up in clothes from the early part of the twentieth century? What did it matter that they wanted to recapture their youth, if only for a moment? She had always enjoyed herself and Beth was over the moon to be involved when she had stayed here during her convalescing and after a few weeks of rest she had totally immersed herself into the part. She had even ordered special material from her laptop so that she could make some dresses based on an original 1920s pattern she had found.

Gem slammed the door shut, turned round and leant against the wardrobe; everywhere she looked there were warm and loving memories of her parents and her friends. Her parents had welcomed everyone wholeheartedly when she had someone stay over during the school breaks.

As for Beth, her parents had not uttered one word about her being there; they had just welcomed the broken girl into their home and gave her a reason to carry on one day at a time. Her mother had taught her how to bake scones and her father, even though he was frail, had taken her round the garden and pointed out all the wild flowers to her. Or he had sat in the conservatory with her and just held her hand when she had felt the tears coming.

Finally Gem could stand it no longer.

Dragging open the chest of drawers, she searched through their contents until she found her underwear. Another drawer she was rewarded with jumpers and track suit bottoms and choosing one of each, she quickly pulled them on.

After raking through the bottom of the wardrobe, Gem came across an old pair of trainers which she had discarded some time ago. Now fully clothed, she grabbed her sword and charged from the bedroom, along the landing and down the stairs to the hall.

Her car keys were where she had left them and scooping them up, Gem raced out to her car. The Stag was still facing down the drive; it was hard to believe so much had happened in such a short time. She unlocked the car door, placed her precious sword on the back seat and covered it with a blanket she had kept there since Beth's attack. With the task completed to her satisfaction, she closed the car door and leaving the keys in the ignition, she once more headed back into the house.

The door she was looking for was under the stairs and upon reaching it she yanked it open so hard that it crashed against the wall. A flight of steps appeared; before she went hurtling down them she flicked the switch at the top of the stairs. The stairwell flooded with light and even so she descended cautiously, as many a time in her youth she had tripped down them, much to her mother's consternation and her father's anger. That was the only time she had seen him lose his temper, when she disregarded the dangers and made light of putting her life in danger.

"You should be more careful, Gemini, look before you leap," he would say to her. "It's the little things that lead us into danger."

Now she knew why he had always tried to keep her safe and the memory of his wise words comforted her. As she entered the cellar Gem looked around her; this was where her father kept all his weed killers and fuel for the occasional bar-b-cues they had. He had not liked them much, preferring her mother to cook the evening meal, but occasionally he made the effort and they ate outside during the hot summer months round the long wooden table under the large umbrella. Everything was neat and tidy and meticulous, just like everything he did through life. All the bottles were labelled in his spidery solicitor's handwriting, erasing any doubts of misuse. She found a half empty box of matches and slipped them into her pocket.

She eventually found what she was looking for; shaking the bottle to see if it contained enough liquid and finding it had, she then turned and raced back up the stairs to the hall. She unscrewed the top as she entered the kitchen and walking round the table, she poured the liquid as she went, careful not to slip on her mother's blood. Walking backwards towards the hall, she turned and entered the lounge, pouring the liquid as she went. Not wanting to tread in any of the flammable liquid, Gem raced round the side of the house and entered once again through the front door. She only had a quarter of the liquid left, so she flung the contents far and wide, splashing the stairs, banister and hall floor until nothing remained.

She hoped the flames would spread quickly into the other downstairs room, as she didn't have enough liquid to pour into all of them. The fumes were becoming extremely powerful and with one last look around she pulled the half empty box of matches from her jogging bottoms. Scene after scene of happy childhood memories came crashing down upon her and as her fingers struck the match, all she could see was her parents' loving, caring faces smiling back at her.

The flaming match descended as if in slow motion as the memories washed over her and when it finally hit the ground, sending forth blue and purple sheets of flame, Gem was already walking out of the door.

It was late evening when Gem finally got to where she was going. The traffic had been horrendous and with each passing mile her sadness had increased.

She had gotten into the Stag as if in a dream, already feeling the heat from the flames on her back as she had left the house. It was like a tinder box; the red angry flames that had so matched her mood had streaked across the hall floor and into the lounge and had risen up the curtains and devoured them. She had only stayed to watch it start to creep up the stairs; she knew that nothing now would stop its complete destruction.

There was not a fire engine in the land that could put out the fire, so she had turned and walked out through the front door, never wanting to enter its portals again. She drove down the long driveway that stretched from the house to the main road; carefully pulling out onto the road so that she was not seen by anyone, she headed in the opposite direction from the one she had arrived and drove until she came to a lay-by, with a board that boasted of wonderful scenic views.

All she could see was the fire, snaking out through the roof like some giant red devil consuming its prey.

She knew she had done the right thing, as she did not want the police to come poking round the place too soon. No long poles, sniffer dogs, or infrared soil testing would ever find her parents' bodies. She had now made sure of that.

Their grave was hallowed ground and it would remain so, their bodies joined together and left undisturbed for all time. It was her gift to them for the long and loving care they had taken over her and it was the least she could do.

She had sat and watched for longer than was safe. Someone must have phoned about the fire because she heard the first scream of the fire engines heading up the hill from the town, sighing gentle with sadness she started the Stag and headed north.

She had timed her arrival just right and it seemed even the tides were in her favour. She pulled up outside the large unimposing house; a small light in the downstairs window shone its beam bravely out into the darkness, beckoning her forward. She did not know why she had come here, only that the force urging her to do so was too powerful to ignore. A great weariness overcame her and she found herself too tired to care, this was the last phase of her journey and then she could rest. As she got out of the car Gem leant back inside and over the back seat retrieved her sword, wrapping it cautiously in the blanket.

As she straightened she held the sword in the blanket so that it pointed downwards and close to her side. After locking the car, she made her way up the path to the front door.

Her light tap was answered almost immediately and as the door swung open, Remne gathered her into her arms, saying, "Welcome to Lindisfarne, Gemini; welcome to Holy Island."

Chapter 16

Gem could hear voices whispering. They penetrated her subconscious like determined little burrowing animals, tunnelling through her mind. She had to wake up! She had to face this new day! Finally she forced open her eyes. Daylight spilled through the window and a gentle breeze lifted the curtains, making them float backwards and forwards and on that breeze, she could smell the sea. She recalled the rough salty tang of seaweed and beaches with little children making sandcastles, all the things that a pleasant summer's day could conjure up.

She smiled, remembering holidays spent in Scarborough and as she lay there she became fascinated by the way the sunlight made patterns on the old-fashioned wallpaper and raised her hand for a moment to trace their golden lines. She adjusted her head on the pillow and her eyes roamed around the room, taking in the dark oak furniture, their starkness softened by the lacy doilies and runners on their tops. *Some hand had sat and made those,* thought Gem. *They had sat in peace and quiet harmony and made doilies.*

"I'll never make doilies," she said out loud.

She was suddenly brought back to reality by Remne's soft voice: "You'll never make what? Gem, look at me; it's time to get up. The afternoon is nearly gone and you have company downstairs. I've sent Margaret down to tell them you'll be down soon."

Gem twisted her head to gaze at Remne, startled that she was there in the room with her. Her memory of the previous night was a little hazy; all she could remember was falling through the door into Remne's arms and being half carried up the stairs. She had been exhausted with all the emotional turmoil and changes that had occurred in her, but now she was refreshed and ready.

"Where's my sword?" she asked.

"Safely wrapped in the blanket under your bed; I thought perhaps you would not want to be too far from it," replied Remne.

She moved to the end of the bed as Gem threw back the covers. She watched as Gem was moved to laughter by the sight of the top-to-toe nightgown she was wearing.

"Yes, well, sorry about that, it was all they had to offer at such short notice," remarked Remne, joining in the laughter.

"Never mind," said Gem, pulling it off over her head. "Where's the bathroom? I'm in need of a shower."

"I don't advise going around in the buff; this is a religious house, after all," said Remne, throwing her a large towel. "And what have you done to your hair? You look ... well, you look ..."

Remne's voice trailed away and Gem moved closer to her before she spoke.

"I have made myself ready for battle. I do not want anything to hinder me and those flowing locks were getting in my way."

Gem ran a hand over her shorn head, suddenly remembering her mother singing as she brushed her hair as a child. Unwanted tears sprang to her eyes and turning quickly she angrily dashed them away; this was not the time to show any weakness, especially not in front of Remne.

"It's okay, Gem, please don't feel you can't show hurt, particularly in front of me," said Remne as she placed a hand on Gem's shoulder.

Gem turned back and looked Remne full in the face before she suddenly moved away, making Remne's hand fall to her side.

It was a look that Remne had never seen before.

Gem's happy blue eyes of a couple of weeks ago were gone and in their place were eyes that held a look of pure steel. Remne dropped her head for a moment, sad at the loss of such a beautiful, natural girl, but Gem was right: that girl was gone, never to return and in her place stood this tall, valiant soldier of the Lord. When Remne raised her head, Gem had left the room and she could hear the soft hiss of the water as Gem started her shower.

Remne wandered round the room, straightening the bed and laying Gem's clothes out for her. She had sat and prayed all the previous night, knowing what Gem was going through. The premonitions had come to her all through that night. She had prayed that Gem had the courage to get through what she found at the house, as the premonitions came more and more frequently.

Remne had not doubted that Gem would get through her own transition.

She knew she would accept the changes to her own body, knowing, as she herself did, that the road was now open before her. Gem had chosen that road, chosen the path of knowledge.

She had grasped her sword with both hands and had stood tall and ready for the fight. She now hoped the rest of them were as equal. Was it only two nights ago they had all sat together, praying for Gem? She was grateful now for the respite and as she sat on Gem's bed, her mind drifted back over the last two days.

Remne sat in silent vigil with Margaret and Lloyd, the owners of the house, each of them silently praying for Gem's safe deliverance. She had sat and called Gem to her, over and over she had called Gem's name, calling her to a place of safety after her personal storm. As dawn was breaking the previous day, Remne knew Gem's ordeal was over and all that remained was for Gem to come to her.

Margaret had lit a small candle and placed it in the front room window, allowing its small lonely beam to shine out and draw Gem towards their place of safety. Lloyd had cooked the three of them a fish supper, its light fragrance of dill and tarragon doing little to tempt Remne's appetite. She poked and prodded her food round the plate until she finally gave up and pushed it away from her with a small apologetic smile. Margaret and Lloyd stoically carried on eating, but even they had to admit defeat and they all sat and watched the hands of the clock tick slowly by.

Remne was the first to jump to her feet, pushing her chair back with such force it nearly fell over when a small knock sounded on the front door.

"Oh praise the Lord, she is here," said Margaret, wiping a tear from her eye.

"Now, now, Margie," said Lloyd, the emotion in his voice evident as he said, "Let Remne see to her and you be away and turn down that bed. I'll clear these things away; later she might need a cup of something warm. Yes, that's what I'll do, I'll make cocoa for everyone."

Lloyd set about clearing the table, scraping the uneaten food onto one plate and carrying everything out into the kitchen, glad of something to do at last.

Usually there would be several people staying at the retreat at this time of the year, people with all sorts of emotional problems. This year was different; he had to turn people away for the first time, to cater to their unusual guest.

It was their policy not to interfere or inquire as to why anyone visited; the "guests," as he called them, just paid a nominal fee for their bed. If they wanted to, they could cook their own meals or join Margaret and him.

They could also pray alone in their room or join in a small communal prayer group in an informal family gathering. Spiritual healing was their forte, but he had noticed over the years the numbers of people coming to the island had increased. Something was going wrong with the world if people felt the need to come and pray in private away from all the trappings of society, but who was he to judge? There were people like him and Margaret all over the country, opening their doors and giving succour to all those in need, no matter what religion or creed they followed.

Unlike the others, he and Margaret belonged to a special alliance that was almost an underground movement. They watched and prayed and when the time was right, like now, they closed their doors to the public and offered help and sanctuary to the Chosen Ones.

Margaret's voice calling from the landing above sent Lloyd scurrying from the kitchen down the hall to the foot of the stairs. His breathing came in long laboured breaths as he realised that he was not as young as he used to be.

"Yes dear, you called?" he answered, his voice not quite as loud as he would want it. His hand rested on the large carved acorn that formed the top of the newel post. He cleared his throat with a small cough as Margaret's head and shoulders showed over the top of the dark oak banisters that ran along the landing, its panelling cutting off from view her lower half and as she smiled down at his upturned face, she said, "Lloyd, do be careful, you're all out of breath. I just wanted to say that Remne has put Gemini to bed, as she is exhausted, so she won't need that hot drink. Thank you all the same."

"I'll just clear up here and then I'll join you upstairs," he said. "We could all do with an early night."

Remne stood in the dark, looking down at Gemini and knew exactly what trials she had undergone. Gem's beautiful face showed no sign of the anguish she must have been through, but as Remne had helped her up the stairs, she had felt the changes to her body. *Perhaps she might open up and tell me one day so that she can start to heal*, she thought. As she turned away from the bed and the sleeping girl she looked out of the window and a single tear slipped unnoticed down her face as she herself relived all that Gem had been through.

Remne was sitting on the bed when Gem re-entered the room, water dripping down her bare shoulders. The towel was tied neatly around Gem's torso and another smaller one was tied round her wet head. Sunlight danced through the open window and shafts of red from the coloured glass at the top played on Gem's nakedness as she removed the towel from her body to dry herself.

Small dust mites floated and danced in the streams of light and everything seemed quiet and peaceful. There was no noise from traffic and the only thing to break the silence was the occasional singing of a blackbird, outside the window on the branch of a tree. The soft carpet dampened the sound of Gem's footsteps pacing round the room. She had retied the towel around her body and Remne silently watched until Gem finally made up her mind what she wanted to say.

No smile or emotion crossed Gem's face.

As she stood before Remne she said, "Not everything is known to me yet except my heavenly name, but I shall continue to use the name of Gemini; do you wish me to do the same with you? I know you are my messenger by your very name, but do you have a proper earthly name?"

Remne could hear the coldness in Gem's voice and as she smiled up at Gem she answered, "I like my new name; it is unusual, like me. Our heavenly names are not to be spoken, as they give away too much of our power," said Remne said in a voice grown suddenly stern.

Gem backed away from her.

Feeling she had used too much force in her answer, Remne quickly apologised, "I'm sorry, Gem, I did not mean to sound terse, but as you went through your ordeal, so did I."

"I thought you had all your powers," replied Gem.

As she stood at the end of her bed Gem traced the lines of the iron bedstead she was standing against with her finger. She looked as if she was bored, but Remne knew different.

Trust!

That was what Gem found hard: trusting people. She herself had told her not to trust anyone, but now was the time for Gem to trust those who loved her.

"Gem, look at me," said Remne, her voice suddenly gentle. "Without you I cannot function. It is only now that you are with me as your true self that I can see into the hearts of those who stand before me."

Remne rose to her feet and walked to where Gem was standing and as they came face to face Remne took Gem's hand and said, "You have not questioned how you got here; that is good and it means that we can now communicate with each other by telepathy. We have forged an unbreakable bond. We are now as one."

Remne let go of Gem's hand and gathered her into her arms. They were both the same height and the similarity between them was most striking. Both had blonde hair, except now it was only Remne whose hair flowed down her back. She had taken out the long ribbons and its natural beauty was not unlike the mane that Gem once had. Gem could feel its silky softness against her hand and for a second she almost regretted cutting her own.

Remne pulled away but still held onto Gem's upper arms and as she looked into her eyes she said, "Let us get down to business."

Dropping her hands from Gem's arms, Remne proceeded to pace about the room while Gem dressed.

"Your mobile phone rang while you were asleep and I took the liberty of answering it. It was a policeman named …"

"DI Nathan Grantly?" answered Gem before she could finish.

"My, you're getting good," replied Remne, somewhat impressed.

Gem was forced to smile in spite of the seriousness of the situation and added as she pulled a soft top on over her shoulders, "It's not telepathy and the only policeman I know is a Nathan Grantly. He came to see me the other day and told us that Beth's uncle was missing. Why was he ringing? Has he any more news?"

"Yes, it was about your parents, so I told him you were here and he came straight over; he's downstairs now waiting for you. Another thing I have to tell you: Beth's uncle is not missing. I put him in one of our safe houses; he is being very well looked after."

"Why didn't you let us know? Beth was going out of her mind with worry; admittedly I had other things on my mind, regarding my parents …"

Gem stopped talking and stole a quick look at Remne, who was studying her hands and was not looking at her. As Gem rubbed the towel across her hair she continued talking, "Was that why you didn't tell us, because of me?"

Gem's voice was slightly muffled and Remne was hard pressed to hear what she was saying. Remne knew it was hard for Gem to carry the burden of guilt she felt regarding her friend and the assault, and she did not wish to add to it.

"My first priority is your welfare," Remne said. "Without you we are lost; I had to do what I thought was best at the time. You left Beth at home and that made good sense, but I feel something is wrong. I have felt bad since I woke up this morning; all is not well. They are gathering against us and we must prepare ourselves. In the meantime let us go down and meet this Nathan Grantly and hear what he has to say."

Gem had finished dressing in jeans and a t-shirt and was just adjusting the laces on her trainers as Remne, similarly dressed, headed out of the door.

DI Grantly had his back to the door and was resting his arm on the high ledge above the fireplace when Remne and Gem came through the door.

To say he was speechless was an understatement; he just looked from one girl to the other in total disbelief as they settled themselves on the sofa.

Eventually he found his voice and clearing his throat with a light cough, he said, "Gem, what on earth have you done to your hair?"

The look on his face brought a reluctant smile to Remne's face and she leant nearer to Gem on the sofa and whispered, "Not quite the formal relationship you were implying, Gemini, hmmm?"

Gem raised her hand and ran her fingers through the tight little curls, already embarrassed that Nathan had drawn attention to it.

"I fancied a change," Gem replied somewhat abruptly, still wary of him.

She felt Remne's hand on her arm and turned her face towards her. The words when they came were as if they had been spoken out loud, so clear were they in her head.

"Do not fear this man, Gemini," she heard Remne's voice say. *"He is a good man, an honest man. He told you the truth about his arm; he bears the scars of a knife wound fighting against a man who had done harm to young girls. All these things are known to me now that he stands before me, because I can see all things that are hidden. Do not be afraid, Gemini, trust him."*

"If you know all, then you know how I feel about him," Gem replied through her own thoughts.

"Trust him with the things you want him to know; it is up to you to trust him with your heart, but bear in mind the task you have to complete. Is it fair to him to make him suffer? Knowing what he would do when you have to meet this unholy adversary?"

"Yes, you are right," said Gem. *"I will tell him only what he needs to know; thank you, Remne."*

They both turned as one to face Nathan and he looked a little uneasy in their presence. The afternoon sun spilled into the room, making it hot and uncomfortable and as if she could read his mind, Gemini's friend got up from the sofa and opened all the windows in the room. Letting in the cool gentle breezes from the sea beyond caused the curtains to swing and sway. He could see the cloudless sky through the window and suddenly realised he shouldn't be here, giving out this information. Not on a day like this. Everything in the room seemed safe and a million miles away from the nightmare scenes he had just witnessed.

When Gem spoke again, her voice held a hint of softness: "Remne, my friend," said Gem, pointing to the girl sitting next to her, "has just told me that she has taken Mr Henry Peterson, Beth's uncle, to a place where he is being looked after due to his advanced years."

"Well, I'm very glad to hear that; it's a load off my mind. We were a bit stretched regarding manpower trying to track Beth's elusive uncle, but we have more unsettling news for you, I am afraid, Gem."

Gem steeled herself for the news that she knew was coming, but even so hearing it put into words was still something of a shock. The colour drained from her face, but she remained perfectly still on the sofa as she listened to Nathan speak.

"We found the address of your parents, it wasn't very hard and fearing that they might be in danger, I decided to go with a team of men up to the dales to check it out for myself." Nathan lowered his head, unable to meet Gem's penetrating gaze, but he carried on regardless, saying, "We were nearly there when we heard that the fire brigade had been called out to their address. It was blazing when we got there. There was nothing that could be done and I am afraid your parents were in the house at the time. We could not recover their bodies."

Gem watched as he raised his head and she could see him waiting to see what effect this news would have on her. The look on his face was one of surprise when she showed no emotion at all.

"He is wondering what is wrong with you," said Remne's voice in her head. *"He's wondering if you are in shock."*

When Gem spoke it was not what Nathan was expecting: "Do you believe in right and wrong, Nathan?" Gem coolly asked.

"Yes of course I do; that's a strange question. I am a policeman, after all."

Gem held up her hand to stop any further conversation between them and asked, "Do you believe in good and evil?"

"I believe that people have the ability to choose between good and evil. I have never found anyone who was too good, mind you, but I have found plenty that were downright evil."

Gem could see Nathan wondering where this conversation was taking them.

"What if that choice was taken away … what then?" Gem asked him.

"Well, in that case it would be up to me to find out who was corrupting who," replied Nathan, frowning.

"He thinks you are beautiful," said Remne.

Gem glanced sideways at Remne, who was now sitting on her hands and was rocking backwards and forwards next to her on the sofa; by the look on her face she was enjoying herself.

"And he wants to go to bed with you, but doesn't know how to ask you," said Remne, returning Gem's look.

"This is bad enough without you butting in," said Gem.

Gem noticed the look of surprise on Remne's face and realised she had spoken out loud. She did not want to turn her head back to face Nathan as she was sure his features would be set in total confusion.

"That's it, out you go, Remne. I will try to handle this on my own," said Gem, pushing Remne off the sofa.

Remne reluctantly got to her feet and, smiling sweetly at Nathan, made her way to the door. As her hand reached for the handle, her soft voice in Gem's head said, *"Go gently with him, he thinks he loves you,"* and before Gem could answer she was gone.

Nathan was staring at the closed door, a look of total bewilderment etched across his face.

"What was that all about …? I could have sworn that you and she were …"

His words were forgotten as Gem moved off the sofa in one long sinuous movement. His eyes feasted on her and he could not believe that it was only a couple of days ago that he had last seen her. As Gem came to him, his arms swept around her and gathered her to his chest. He ran his right hand across her head and ruffled her short curls.

"I like it, it suits you," he murmured into her ear.

Gem raised her face and his lips descended on her lips with a hungry and desperate need that almost overwhelmed her. She answered him with the same fiery passion and as their bodies locked together she could feel his swollen member pressing against her. Nathan raised both hands and cupped her upturned face. "God, you are so beautiful," he whispered. "You know how much I want you right now?"

"Yes, some things do give it away," said Gem and she was forced to smile at his embarrassment. She patted him gently on his suit lapels, her face serious again as she said, "Nathan, sit down please; there is a lot I have to tell you."

He turned away from her worried now that he had overstepped the mark and taken advantage of her, she was obviously in a state of shock regarding her parents and he foolishly had pressed his attentions on her. He went and sat in the place that Remne had vacated, but Gem stood where he had been, near the fireplace.

"This is very hard for me and it is going to be very hard for you," said Gem, her hands on her hips in her usual no-nonsense way.

Nathan looked down at his hands embarrassed now he had kissed her and tried to regain his composure before finally saying,

"Fire away then and let's get everything out in the open," replied Nathan, little expecting what he was going to hear.

Chapter 17

Gem paced backwards and forwards in front of the unlit fireplace as she explained to Nathan about the four young men who had met at university and, through their research, had uncovered a rare and valuable book. She could feel her heart pumping the blood vigorously through her veins and she felt perspiration breaking out all over her body as she tried to justify why her grandfather and Henry Peterson had hidden the book from the other two, fearing that they meant to have it for themselves. As Gem talked she started to wander round the room, worried that if she stayed in one place too long she might forget about discretion and start to tell him all the things she didn't want him to hear, but she could see by the look on Nathan's face that he was itching to say something.

Turning to face him, she eventually said, "Well, I knew there would be questions, but this is a bit quick off the mark; I haven't even got into the story yet."

She tried to sound unconcerned but wanted to tell him quickly before her nerve gave out and before she regretted having told him anything in the first place.

"Sorry, Gem, but that is what this sounds like: a story," Nathan replied, fidgeting in his seat.

He leant forward and a stray lock of his dark hair fell across his brow. She watched as he brought his lean tanned hand up to brush it away. Totally captivated by his movements, Gem stood and gazed at Nathan and was unaware he was speaking until he called her name.

"Gem answer me! I know all about the fab four's relationship, but are we only talking here about two young men pinching a valuable book from the archives of York Minster? I think it has gone further than that. What about the identity of this Adam Cunningham, for instance? That man is dead and buried in a graveyard in Suffolk, so how did his fingerprints turn up in your grandfather's study and at the murder scene of Lord Penn-Wright? If you know something you must tell me. I want to help."

"Yes, yes of course," Gem quickly replied. "Just give me a minute and I will try to explain, but it's difficult."

Gem drew a deep breath and hurried on with her account of what was happening. She decided it would be better to sit on the sofa next to him, so she manoeuvred round the furniture and positioned herself next to him.

Taking his hand in hers, she continued, "Please keep an open mind to all that I am about to tell you. There are more things between heaven and earth," Gem stopped and gave a small laugh before she continued, "or so they say."

She found her courage ebbing away as she looked into his soft green eyes; the fear of doubting him was replaced by the heavy burden of protecting him.

He sat there, so strong and vibrant and she suddenly realised that she could not draw him into this terrible situation; it was bad enough that Beth was involved. So she decided to skirt round the main issues and concentrated on the things she thought he could cope with.

"I know nothing about my grandfather's death, but I do know that the person who killed him is the same person who is searching for something and I think it's the Book and I think that he is linked to the assault on Beth and my parents."

She wanted to add, "And is searching for me, trying to draw me out into the open," but she could not bear to see the look that she knew would creep into his eyes. He thought she was an innocent, someone caught up in all this murder and mayhem. He had assured himself that she had nothing to do with anything; how she could tell him now and destroy that belief?

So they talked about the assault on Beth in more detail and he told her that the official verdict he had given about the mobile phone was that the assailant had stolen it before he made his escape.

"You know I doubted you when you came to my house," she said. "I did not trust you well enough to give you my parents' address." Gem saw his eyes harden and the small lines around them crease with emotion at her confession; as she laid her hand on his arm she said, "I'm sorry but there is more I have to tell you. As soon as you left I went to my parents' house and when I arrived I found …" She could not help but falter in her account of what she had found. It was all still too new and raw and she couldn't help her eyes filling up with tears.

Nathan leant forward and gently brushed the falling tears from her cheeks, concern written all over his face; so as not to frighten her he said, "You don't have to carry on if it is too much, you can always tell me later. We did get the gist of what happened there and I am only sorry you had to witness it."

Gem shook her head and said, "No, you don't understand; they were already butchered when I got there. Whoever did it had left some time before. They had gone to my parents' house and ripped the life out of the pair of them and left them there to rot. I could not see them desecrated any further, so I buried them in the garden."

"My men went all over that place and didn't find anything amiss in the garden. There were no fresh diggings that we could find so, if you don't mind me asking, where exactly are they?"

"They are not far; you just have to look. It is in a special place," replied Gem, masking her lies with a trembling little smile.

Nathan patted her hand in an effort to comfort her and said, half to himself, "I suppose it was over near that great big hydrangea. My men had to be called back from there as there was a danger of the house collapsing."

Seizing the opportunity that had presented itself to her, Gem gave a sad little nod. Half of her was glad that he seemed to believe her and the other half did not have to act in mourning for the death of her parents. Gem sat there in silence and watched the play of emotions on his handsome face. She had feared that he might suspect her of being involved in the murder of her parents and it was something she did not want to contemplate.

Her eyes raked over his face, looking for clues as to whether he believed her or not and it was not until he pulled her into his arms that she gave a big sigh of relief.

Gem could feel the steady beating of his heart as her head lay against his body and she wanted to lie there forever, but she heard the words rumbling in his chest as he said, "Gem, there are still a few unanswered questions. Who is it you think that wanted your parents and grandfather dead? Also who killed Lord Penn-Wright, the first of the four to die? Just one more question, this book you keep going on about; it seems to me that it holds the key to what is happening to everyone."

Gem pushed herself away from his chest, using both hands to do so and looked him in the face, hesitating before she said, "I do not know where the book is; the last time I saw it, Henry Peterson had it. I shall have to ask Remne."

"How much is Remne involved in all this?" Nathan asked. "Can she be trusted?"

Was now the time to tell him everything? No! She would wait a little longer and take the advice Remne had given her; she would not tell him about their part in all of this, "Remne? She is the least of our worries. No, don't worry about Remne; she is totally on our side. She's been a good friend to me."

At last Gem could speak the truth about something. She hated the way she had been lying to him and feeling guilty, she lowered her eyes so that he could not read the deception in them. She need not have bothered, because his mind was obviously racing ahead as she heard him say, "Don't worry about your parents, it is a small matter. I will deal with it." Noticing the expression of genuine hurt crossing Gem's face, he grabbed her hand and brought it to his lips and before he kissed it he hastily added, "Not their murder, my silly girl, I'm talking about your part in it all. I shall say the balance of your mind was disturbed by what you had discovered at the house. Your parents perished in the blaze, their bodies totally destroyed by the searing heat and you were to save them, this will stop any questions about an autopsy."

Gem sat there ramrod straight as she listened to Nathan concoct an alibi for her. She wondered if he really believed her deep down in his policeman's soul, because even she had doubts believing herself sometimes, but he seemed to have accepted what she had told him.

He continued, "And while you were still in shock you came here to your friend's house for comfort, knowing she was here. You were out of your mind with grief and were not thinking straight, but you later phoned me instead of the local Bobbies because I am in charge of the task force dealing with your family's affairs. So I rushed over here to take your statement and to make sure nothing had happened to you, as someone seems hell bent on wiping your family and friends out."

Realising he might have sounded a tad harsh, he pulled Gem into the circle of his arms again and kissed the top of her head.

"Do you think they will believe that?" she asked. "After all, I do seem to turn up when the people I love are getting hurt."

Nathan smiled down at her and cupping her face with his free hand, he pulled her forward towards his waiting lips. It was not a kiss of deep passion, it was a kiss that carried his very heart to her, a kiss that conveyed his love and devotion and his need to protect her. He was not kissing her for his bodily needs; he was kissing her because he loved her and something in her heart did a little flip of joy. Like a phoenix out of the ashes of her parents' death, her heart had found a healing balm in his love, but as their lips parted she heard his voice change and once again he was the policeman taking charge.

As he spoke, he emphasised each word, trying to convey his authority. He took his arm from around her shoulder and said, as if she was a little girl, "I want you and your friend Remne to go back to York and along with Beth, I want you all to stay put until I have worked something out. This is all getting very complicated; do you promise?"

Gem could see the concern for her written all over his face so she bit down on a retort that had risen unbidden to her lips and wondered what he would say if he knew the full story and not just the bare bones. What would he say if he knew that hidden under her bed was a sword that spat fire? What would he say if he knew that she had an itinerary that did not include him?

He thought she was a weak and vulnerable female and his male ego would not let him see past it. It was wise that she did not let him know the truth about everything, because that could work in her favour. Let him continue to see her as a helpless woman in need of his strong arms. Gem felt she should distance herself from his embrace and kisses and getting to her feet, she wandered over to the window. The sun was slowly moving round the house to the west and the atmosphere of peace and harmony was totally at odds with how she was feeling. She allowed herself a small smile, thinking about how Nathan believed her to be fragile and defenceless.

It was just as well she had her back to him because her features hardened and the look of steel crept back into her eyes when she thought of the battle to come. She must not let her fondness for Nathan interfere with what she had to do; it would weaken her.

What if It found out?

The thought left her momentarily stunned; she had not thought of that. Feeling momentarily nauseous, she rested her hands on the old oak sideboard situated in the bay window and lowering her head, she gave herself time to think and reassess the situation. Gem knew she could not take the chance; Nathan would have to go back to London but how could she manage it?

She did not want to stay in the house anymore; she wanted to go back to York. Time now seemed of the essence. For one thing she had to check on Beth; she had not heard from her for a few days and Remne had not been able to contact her this morning. Gem swung away from the window back to Nathan, masking her feelings with a smile. Nathan was now standing by the old tall fireplace and was running his finger along the eye level edge, waiting patiently for her to respond to what he had practically demanded, so without hesitation she went up to him and said, "Yes, you are right, I shall leave straight away. Remne and I will be in York later tonight. I will feel safer there; please don't worry about me. We shall all be able to look after each other in the house. Trust me." She raised her face and kissed his cheek.

The relief was evident in his face and she saw him heave a large sigh at her acquiescence. "The last thing I want is to lose you before we can properly get to know one another," Nathan said, pulling her into his arms once again.

"Hey you," said Gem, "don't be so morbid."

But he could see her face change and suspected she was thinking about her parents. Gem's thoughts ran along a totally different line and she reached out to Remne, whom she knew would not be too far away,

"Help me, Remne; help me to send him away!" her mind screamed.

Gem felt powerless; she wanted to keep him with her, but her common sense told her to send him away. In answer to her plea, Remne walked into the room. "Sorry to disturb you, Nathan, I can call you Nathan, can't I? I feel I know so much about you even though we have just met."

Gem stood silently and watched as Remne approached Nathan. A sudden feeling of jealousy coursed through her at the sight of Remne smiling at him. Gem found she was annoyed with Remne's assertive and forceful nature, annoyed that it was Remne who had the ability to save Nathan and not her.

Gem felt the anger bubbling within her and dropped her gaze to study the floor, but her eyes were swiftly back on Nathan's face when she heard Remne say, "We have just received a call on the house phone and it was from your boss, Hugh Smith; such an ordinary name, don't you think, for such a high flier?" said Remne in a voice that was almost purring.

Gem felt Nathan's arm leave her shoulder at the mention of his boss's name and watched as he turned his back on her so that he could face Remne.

Gem stood in silence, her back to the fireplace, as she heard him ask what the call was about, but she was forced to turn away from the pair and walk over to the bay window again when she heard Remne say, "Something about collating new evidence; anyway it sounded very important and I told him I would give you the message straight away."

Gem could hear Remne's soft footsteps as she left the room, her job done.

Instantly forgetting her anger, Gem forced herself to face Nathan and she saw the same expression mirrored on his face.

"It won't be for too long," he said softly. "Apparently they want to gather all the evidence from this episode and put it with all the other information; well, you know what's happening. I have to attend but I will be back up before you know it."

Nathan smiled bravely, but she could see his heart was not in it. Gem did not question the whys or wherefores of their relationship; they had found each other in a world that was preparing to be torn apart. Found and torn apart on the same day; that was some going, she thought, but she was glad he was leaving. He would be safe in London and she would not have to worry about him getting hurt or killed; the very thought brought a choking lump to her throat.

Misinterpreting the emotions on Gem's face, Nathan rushed to her side and gathered her once again in his arms. "Nothing is going to happen to you, I won't allow it," he said gently. "I have to go now; my driver's waiting, but just remember one thing."

"What's that?" said Gem, her eyes desperately trying to take their fill of him as she gazed into his startling green eyes.

"That I love you very much," he said as his lips descended onto hers.

After he left, Gem slumped down on the sofa and ran her hands through her soft curls. She did not hear Remne come into the room until she said, "It was for the best, Gem. You know that, don't you? It's better to have him far away and safe than near and unprotected."

"I know, I know," answered Gem, "but it's so hard. I thought it was bad enough finding my parents but this … this …"

Gem's voice faltered and Remne could see her eyes fill with unshed tears. Remne knew that she was near to breaking. Gem had undergone a lot in the last couple of days, more than any normal person could stand, a roller coaster of emotions, but she was forced to put a stop this self-pity. Grabbing hold of Gem's arms, she forced her to her feet and gave her several good shakes, making Gem's head roll backwards and forwards.

Stunned by Remne's behaviour, Gem reaction was immediate; the blow she gave Remne sent her reeling away to land heavily on the sofa. Gem's eyes blazed with anger at Remne's treatment, but she was shocked to hear Remne's sudden burst of laughter.

As Remne lay sprawled out Gem could see her rubbing the side of her face. "That's better; I was getting rather sick of your wallowing. You have a job to do, Gemini and if you are successful then your friend Nathan will be your just reward," said Remne, all humour gone from her voice.

Gem's eyes still blazed fire as she bent down toward Remne, but her words dripped ice as she said, "Never for one minute think I have forgotten my destiny and don't ever touch me like that again or I might forget why I am here." Gem raked her gaze over Remne's face; she paused in what she was saying, her anger still volatile and then added a warning: "Don't ever try to make me jealous because I have no humour regarding that situation. Do you understand me, Remne?"

"If you don't give me cause then I won't interfere with you, but you do not frighten me, Gemini, with your posturing; my powers are as great as yours, although somewhat different, I must admit," said Remne angrily, rising to her feet from where Gem had knocked her down. "I am your conscience, if you like; I am here to see that you do indeed fulfil your destiny and whether you like it or not you are stuck with me and as for Nathan I couldn't care less about him. I was just doing what you asked me to do."

Gem could see the furious expression on Remne's face and immediately regretted her outburst.

It was too late, with her piece said Remne walked away, but before she went through the door she turned and said, "I'm going to pack our bags. I've already put your sword in the car. We can leave when you are ready. I fear we are needed in York; we cannot sit around here anymore and it is time, Gemini."

Chapter 18

Gem said good-bye to Margaret and Lloyd and thanked them for their hospitality. Margaret had looked sad and lonely as she stood on the doorstep, her hand tightly clasped in Lloyd's. The emotion of the moment all seemed too much for her and Gem could hear Lloyd making soothing noises and gentle murmurings to bolster her courage. The light had already started to fade as Gem made her way to her Stag, eager to be away and as she turned for one last look at the old house, she could see Remne in a tight embrace with both Margaret and her husband. She watched as Remne touchingly wiped the tears from Margaret's faded cheeks and after one last hug with Lloyd, Remne turned and made her way to the waiting car.

The clouds in the sky had turned red and heavy, looking as if their weight would pull them suddenly earthwards. As the sun dropped away the air became still and quiet. With the expectation of rain the occasional bat was swooping around, catching the myriad small insects that the promise of damp weather was starting to generate. The heat of August was finally over and now that September was upon them the early evening mist, or "fret," as the locals called it, came up from the sea and was starting to rise, obscuring the road down through the town.

Gem climbed into the car and started the engine, forcing Remne to hurry; she was surprised to see her wiping tears from her cheeks as she entered the car.

The wheels of the Stag grated over the shingle drive as Gem slowly reversed and as she applied pressure to the accelerator small stones flicked up, hitting the car's underside, making Gem frown with annoyance.

It was all going wrong! Everything she did went wrong! Gem felt she couldn't even open her mouth without it sounding spurious and insincere.

She desperately wanted to say something to Remne, to clear the air, but just looking at the bruise that was beginning to show on her cheek forced her into silence.

As she backed the car out of the drive Gem could hear Remne whispering good-bye to the old couple and she watched, crestfallen, as more tears ran down Remne's face as she waved through the windscreen. Once across the causeway and on the open road, Gem hesitantly questioned Remne about why she was so upset, using this neutral ground to open up the conversation. Gem knew all the things she wanted to say, but her tongue seemed to have a will of its own and she found herself hesitating before she said, "Do you know Margaret and Lloyd well ... er ... you seemed ... well, you seemed very upset when you left them." She tried to concentrate on her driving at the same time as talking.

"Oh, I know them very well," Remne snapped a cold edge to her voice.

Gem tried not to be put off by her tone, knowing full well she deserved it, so persevering, she added, "They are a nice couple; they seem to like you very much."

"Why shouldn't they?" Remne replied sharply.

"Oh no reason, it's just, I wasn't expecting it that was all."

"What were you expecting, Gem? Tell me, I'm interested; oh, but I forget, your powers don't extend to looking into people's hearts, do they?" said Remne, adjusting her seatbelt to a more comfortable position, her voice still frosty.

"Look okay, I was wrong, I admit it, I jumped to all the wrong conclusions and I am very, very sorry," said Gem as she swerved the car over to the side of the road and switched the engine off. The driver that had been following blasted his horn at Gem's sudden manoeuvre and as the vehicle went past Gem could see the look of indignation on the driver's face; she was slightly shocked at the words he mouthed at her. She waved her hand to acknowledge her error and then turned in her seat to face Remne and said as humbly as she could, "You have been at this a lot longer than me, it is all so new. Admittedly I have gone through some incredible changes, but sometimes I still feel like the old me, with all the old inhibitions. To make things worse I have never been in love before and I admit I panicked a bit when I saw you talking to Nathan."

"A bit... Try a bloody lot!" replied Remne, refusing to look at Gem, her gaze riveted on some point beyond the windscreen. The heat from their bodies had started to steam up the window, which was at variance with the atmosphere between them and as Gem turned slightly away from Remne she rested her hands on the steering wheel and idly doodled on the glass in front of her.

Remne sneaked a quick look in Gem's direction and watched the play of emotions on her face but decided not to say anything. Gem sat there racking her brains for something appropriate to say as the fingers of her right hand traced a long meandering curve in the mist.

Come on; come on, Gem thought, *this was never going to be easy.*

Swallowing her pride, she turned back to Remne and said in a rush, "I promise I will never strike you again, if it makes you feel any better I feel mortified about it." Gem reached her hand over and gently touched the mark on Remne's face and when she didn't flinch she said, "Does it still hurt?"

Remne turned in her seat and finally looked at Gem, but it was some time before she answered, "No, it doesn't hurt at all, it shall be gone in a minute. Like you, I can repair any minor injuries. I just left it there for you to see. You hurt me in more ways than one, though, Gem. People are putting their lives in jeopardy for you, so you must remain focused."

She slowly shook her head as she looked at Gem, who was worried she had overstepped the mark. Remne released a small sigh as she continued, "We were chosen from so many for this work. We were not chosen to do good deeds and we are not the manifestation of your typical holy entity.

"We were chosen because we were found to have the attributes needed to walk in the world of mankind. We have been endowed with human qualities so that we would not throw suspicion on ourselves and draw the attention of those that wish to kill us."

Remne stopped talking for a second, reached over and took Gem's hand; holding it tightly, she said, "We have to be brave and not let our nerve fail us." She smiled sadly at Gem before she continued, "We have to work together because there are worse things to come, Gemini and my fear is growing the nearer we reach York; we must be serious now and put this petty squabble behind us." Seeing her words were having the desired effect as Gem's face started to show the anxiety she herself was feeling, Remne let go of her hand and said more kindly, "We have both been going through changes and I must take part of the blame for aggravating you." Remne's face suddenly broke into a large smile as she continued, "It's just that I was having such a good time out in the hall listening to both of you refusing to put into words your feelings. I admit I homed in on what you were both thinking; pretty steamy stuff, I can tell you."

Noticing the look on Gem's face, Remne held up both hands in an attitude of surrender before she hurried on, "Well, if we are confessing to each other, then I thought it was only fair to tell you. It's new to me as well, this power ... I thought I might ... have a little ... fun."

Remne bowed her head in mock submission and Gem could not find it in her heart to be annoyed.

"That's it now! No more reading my mind when I am not aware. Like you said, we have more serious things on our plate. You must focus as well as me, so let's make up and be friends."

"Oh, we were always friends, Gem, you just didn't know it," laughed Remne, but she continued in a more serious way, saying, "and as for those people back there, that was my mother and father, the people who raised me and the people that put their lives on the line so that you would have a safe haven to come to."

All Gem could do was nod her head in acknowledgement at their continual sacrifice and as Remne spoke; she looked over at Gem and saw her dash the tears away with the back of her left hand. As Gem turned the key in the ignition, the powerful engine roared into life. A light drizzle started to fall so Gem turned on the wipers and their intermittent swish was all that could be heard as Gem nosed the Stag out into the stream of traffic for the final leg of their journey back to York.

The darkness was forced back by the street lights, their amber luminescent glow shining intermittently on the wet pavements. The streets were empty of pedestrians, the rain keeping them indoors and only the parked cars along the street gave any indication that her neighbours were at home.

As Gem slowly edged the car into her normal parking space outside her house she was filled with trepidation and glancing over, she could see the tension building up in Remne also; every line of her body was taut as she sat in the passenger seat, gazing up at the large building. Gem leant across Remne and peered up at the dark, empty windows. Not a glimmer of light could be seen; Gem knew that Beth hated being in the dark, so if the lights were not on ... then ...

No, I refuse to admit it, Gem thought to herself. *Beth might have gone out. There could be any number of reasons and sitting here won't answer them.* Panic gripped her insides and turned them to water. Gem's fingers shook as she turned the car's engine off, glancing quickly at Remne for assurance; getting none, she opened the car door and hurriedly stepped out onto the road. She waited impatiently as Remne did the same and after she locked the car, they both made their way cautiously up the steps to the front door. Gem expected to find the door off its hinges, or worse, anything but this large wooden obstruction, barring her way with not a mark on it.

In the soft glow of the street lights Gem ran her hand over the door, looking for any clues, but she found none and there in the semi darkness she turned to Remne and said, "Let me enter on my own to check the place out; you go back to the car and get my sword."

Giving Remne a half smile, Gem removed the door key and handed her the car keys, saying, "Just in case; who knows what we might find inside?"

Remne hesitated for only a second before she ran back down the steps on her errand, her hair streaming out behind her and Gem watched her get to the safety of the car before turning back to the heavy wooden door.

The key lay in her hand and Gem forced herself to place it in the lock, suddenly fearful of what she might find on the other side.

The smell that Gem was now so familiar with was inside her house. It was the same smell that had been in her parents' house. But now the smell had faded slightly, its pungent odour that so antagonised her was weaker.

It was long gone!

Gem's nose tested the air like a hound on a scent and knew that it had been at least two days ago when It had come for Beth.

Two days!

That must have been straight after the death of her parents. Beth might have been in the clutches of evil while she had been kissing Nathan.

"No, no, noooo!" she screamed as she headed for the stairs and took them two at a time in her usual fashion.

She headed straight for Beth's bedroom and saw the clothes scattered across the bed as if she had suddenly been interrupted in her packing; the leather holdall she always used lay discarded on the floor. Gem picked up one of Beth's scarves and ran it through her fingers, trying to ascertain what had happened, but it was no use so she made her way to the spare room Beth used as her workroom.

Nothing! It was empty like the rest of the upstairs.

Gem flung the scarf down on Beth's drawing board with a curse and hurriedly made her way downstairs. She quickly scoured the remainder of the house, praying that she would not find Beth's body, but knowing that if she didn't, the alternative was too ghastly to contemplate. The kitchen was the only place where Beth's movements were visible in the two slices of bread cut from the small loaf they always used, but they lay discarded on the central unit as if she had cut them and decided not to eat. Their edges had started to curl, and when Gem placed her fingers on one of the slices, it was hard and stale, a testament to how long it had been lying there. Gem's brow knitted with worry and turning away, she made her way back to the hall to check on the dining room and the lounge. When she had decided it was all clear, she walked through the darkness to the front door and called Remne inside. It had entered her sanctuary and now Gem knew for sure that something terrible had happened to Beth.

Remne stood in the hallway, clutching the covered sword to her chest, as Gem bolted the door; her face was white with anxiety but her voice was strong when she said, "Don't enter into recrimination, it won't do any good. I called you to me because you had to rest after your ordeal. You were in a fragile state between this world and the other. I could not take the chance of anything happening to you." She followed Gem into the lounge.

Not wanting to flood the room with illumination, Gem decided to turn on the small table lamp on the desk, preferring its softer beam. Remne walked over to the settee, shivering as if from the cold; she leant forward and placed the heavy sword down onto its softness. As she was leaning forward, something caught her eye and she dropped to one knee to investigate.

Gem's voice broke through her reverie, sounding excited, excited enough to stop Remne from what she was doing and looking up over the rim of the settee she saw Gem standing by the desk, flapping a piece of paper at her. "Look at this," Gem said in a rush. "It's a note from Beth saying she was going to meet you and her uncle and if I came back I was not to worry,"

"But she didn't meet me, though, did she?" replied Remne, dashing Gem's hopes.

"No, but she could have met her uncle; you don't know she didn't meet him. You only said you had put him somewhere safe, perhaps she has joined him," replied Gem, knowing she was clutching at straws.

"I do know she is not with him, because he suffered a stroke just after your visit; the whole situation was just too much for him at his age. He is now in a private nursing home being cared for by a Carmelite Order as per his wishes. He also has neither the power of speech nor the use of any of his limbs," Remne said gently, noticing the droop of Gem's head.

"There is more," said Remne, glancing at the floor where she stood, before she continued, "I found blood on the carpet. It can only be Beth's; it looks as though she put up quite a struggle and didn't go quietly. I know it's no consolation to know she is injured, but at least it gives us an insight to her state of mind."

"How can that help me, knowing my friend is injured?" said Gem angrily.

"It is not the injury I am talking about, it is her state of mind," replied Remne, copying Gem's challenging attitude by standing up straight with her hands on her hips. "Listen to me," said Remne, trying to soothe the situation; she walked back round the settee and came to stand next to Gem at the desk.

Remne raised her hand and settled it on Gem's shoulder and applied pressure until Gem was forced to face her. Remne looked Gem straight in the eyes and said, "I know it's hard but this means that Beth was willing to fight for her life; she had not given in to what has happened to her so neither must we."

"Yes, of course you are right," said Gem sadly. "It's just that I promised nothing would ever happen to her again. I couldn't even keep that promise; I should have taken her with me."

"No, you shouldn't have," replied Remne with feeling. "Your transition was not for human eyes, Beth would have been damaged or gone mad or something."

Gem looked at Remne, cocking her head to one side, saying as she did so, "You're making that up, I can tell."

"Well maybe," said Remne, "but you know what I mean; it's unfortunate, but it has happened and now we must find her."

Gem patted Remne on the arm and was forced to acknowledge that she was trying to help; turning away, Gem made her way over to inspect the blood stains. It was when she was on her knees with her fingers running across the hardened fibres that it suddenly came to her; jumping to her feet, she shouted across to Remne, who was studying Beth's note.

"It's the note, don't you see?" said Gem excitedly.

"See what?" said Remne, turning the paper over to study the back.

"No you fool; Beth left us a great big clue even though she didn't know it at the time. It's the note; she would only have written a note if she was going off with someone she knew, so when she opened the door … Bingo! She thought she knew who it was," said Gem, please with her deduction.

"So where does that get us?" replied Remne, still at a loss.

"It could have only been one or maybe two people she opened the door to and my guess is it was Rupert. I expressly forbade her to open the door to anyone, but after Nathan's visit I think Beth half guessed I was a bit wary of him," said Gem, dropping herself down onto the settee as she remembered the scene of their good-bye.

"And …" said Remne, joining her.

"Well, don't you see, if I mistrusted Nathan that meant Rupert was okay and vice versa," said Gem, leaning forward and running her hands through her curls.

"Well, that's okay then," said Remne. "We shall just have to pay Rupert a little visit."

"There is something else I just thought of as well," said Gem, the strain finally showing in her voice.

"What's that?" said Remne, grimacing as she moved the large sword from where she was sitting.

"The Book where is it? If, like you said, Henry had a stroke after you picked him up, then he would have had it with him. He would not have left it in the house for anyone to find," said Gem, turning round to face Remne and seeing her hands scrabbling around on the seat behind her. She said, "What are you doing? Leave my sword alone." Gem tapped Remne's hand.

"What! Oh sorry, yes, well, it was getting in my way. I really don't know how you manage to lift that thing, it weighs a ton," said Remne, rubbing her hand; seeing that Gem expected an answer to her question, she hastily said, "Oh, the Book; well, he didn't have it with him when I picked him up, what do you suppose he did with it?"

"That's what I'm asking you," said Gem, feeling herself wanting to tut but adding instead, "I think the best thing to do is for you to go and visit Henry and use your telepathy powers on him; I shall go and visit our friend Rupert, both I think have a lot of explaining to do."

"But don't you want me to come with you to Rupert's? I could tell at an instant if he was lying or not," said Remne, grabbing Gem's arm and stopping her from rising to her feet.

Gem shrugged off Remne's restraining hand with little effort. If she was honest with herself, she did not want Remne with her; for some reason

Remne annoyed her and Gem couldn't understand why; not only that, she preferred to tackle Rupert alone. Gem left Remne sitting on the settee but her curiosity was piqued as she looked down at her. *Is she reading my mind?* Thought Gem, because she could have sworn she saw something in her eyes just now as they were talking.

No, she promised, thought Gem, and turning her attention back to the immediate problem she said, "No, it is important that you track down the Book; we cannot let it fall into the wrong hands or all of this would have been for nothing. They would have won without us raising a finger. Where is this nursing home?"

"Just outside Thirsk, it's a partly closed order, but they take one or two terminal cases. Henry has been a devout Catholic all his life and his wishes were that he saw out the remainder of his days in their care," explained Remne as she leant back into the comfort of the cushions.

Gem could not see Remne's face from where she was standing, so she could not tell if she was annoyed or not; the tone of her voice gave nothing away.

As Remne hadn't moved Gem walked over and leant across the top of the settee, saying, "Well, are you going to move? We can grab a change of clothes and a quick bite to eat and then we can both be on our way."

"There's only one problem with all this planning," said Remne as she craned her neck to gaze up at Gem.

"And what's that?" Gem replied, forcing a smile while her hands gripped the back edge of the settee, feeling suddenly unsure of Remne's behaviour.

"How do I get there? You are going off on a nocturnal visit to Rupert, so how am I supposed to get to Thirsk? I don't do that flying thing, I prefer water and boats as a means of travel," replied Remne, smiling sweetly before turning her face away and looking at the fireplace.

Gem could feel the annoyance rising within her body. Why did she feel that Remne was always irritating her?

Gem was now forced to make a decision that stuck in her throat no matter what the reason. Painfully she said, "You will have to take my car." Remne could hear by the tone of Gem's voice that the words were practically wrung from her; she smiled to herself as she sat alone on the settee, listening as Gem carried on behind her, "I can go by the aerial route to Rupert's, it's only on the outskirts of town and you can drive my car ..."

Then Remne felt Gem's breath on her neck as Gem leant forward and accentuated what she had to say into her ear: "*very carefully*, and find out what we need to know from Henry. Is that okay with you now, everything to your liking?"

Remne sat there with her eyes closed, biting her bottom lip and trying not to show any inappropriate humour considering their situation, but really this infatuation with the car was going a bit too far. Swallowing hard, Remne composed herself as best she could and turned in her seat to face Gem, who was standing behind the settee with her arms folded.

"Of course I will take care of it silly and I shall meet you back here in the morning," said Remne.

As Remne sat there on the settee silently for a moment, Gem could see the humour draining from her green eyes to be replaced with worry and anxiety at their separation.

Gem's annoyance at Remne's baiting was forgotten and as she unfolded her arms into a more relaxed stance she heard Remne's voice come out in a whisper, as if the words were just too painful to express: "Please take care, I shall worry about you all the time we are apart; please be on your guard." Her eyes welled with tears.

"Don't worry about me, just take good care of my car," said Gem, but this time the smile that she returned was genuine.

Chapter 19

Slowly Beth opened her eyes and panic gripped her. She was blind!

Everything was in total darkness; she could not see a thing. She raised her hand and waved it in front of her face, but she could see nothing, so slowly and gradually she felt with her finger to see if her eyes were actually open.

Her eyelashes fluttered as she felt the wetness of her eye and as her hand travelled down her face she inadvertently winced as she encountered her bloody and badly bruised cheekbone. Fortunately it was not broken like she had thought although the pain was just as bad.

Laying there in the darkness, Beth tried to get her breathing under control, but the sobs that racked her body did not bring the relief she was hoping for.

Had she gone blind?

It was possible; that second blow that Cybil delivered had sent her spinning into unconsciousness. Had it also damaged her eyes?

How long had she been here?

It was impossible to tell and gradually as her tears subsided Beth fought to get control of her mind and the situation she was in. As she cautiously raised herself into a sitting position Beth flayed her arms about in a moment of panic, fearing that she might be entombed. There was nothing around her, so Beth guessed she was in a room somewhere, but how big was hard to tell.

Her hands ran along the edge of cold metal and realising she must be sitting on a low bed, she swung her legs over the side and sat in a more upright position and immediately felt sick.

Even with no eyesight she felt disoriented and swayed backwards and forwards as she sat there. Her fingers clutched at the rough blanket until she felt herself returning to normal and the feeling of vertigo receded.

"Breathe, girl, breathe!" she told herself. "The only thing to fear is fear itself."

Beth wanted to chant this like a mantra, but the sound of her own voice in the room echoed strangely and the fear of sounding manic even to herself was too much to bear, so she closed her mouth and thought about what to do next. As the cold crept up her legs Beth realised she was barefoot, but fortunately she was still dressed in the clothes she had on when Cybil came to call. Her body was warm enough because it was not particularly cold, but then she had no idea how long she was going to be here.

There was nothing else for it; she had to find a way out of this room, so she eased herself off the bed until her bottom hit the floor. Beth ran her hands around the area she was sitting.

"It's dirt," she said as she rubbed both hand together, feeling the grittiness. *That must mean it's a basement or an outbuilding,* she thought excitedly and she inched her way sidewards until she hit the cold hardness of a stone wall. Then slowly and steadily, by sliding on her bottom, Beth managed to circle the room. As she dragged her bare feet over the dirt floor she felt her heels tear and feeling with her fingers she touched the wetness of what could only be blood.

Wiping her fingers down her trousers, she carried on regardless and gradually wound her way backwards round the room. Halfway through her endeavours her back bumped into something metallic and the noise resounded in the closed room with a loud clang; as she felt with her hand behind her she was surprised to find a large metal bucket. Beth dragged the heavy object in front of her and after feeling all round its perimeter; she dropped her hand in over the side and felt the cold dampness of what seemed to be sand.

Sitting there and letting the coarse mixture run through her fingers, she was at a loss for a moment as to why it should be there. It would hardly be for a fire and then it dawned on her, and she was forced to laugh out loud at her foolishness and ignorance.

"It's a toilet!" she said into the darkness and realising she was playing with the contents, she immediately took out her hand and wiped it once again down her leggings as her face contorted in disgust. Replacing the bucket in the corner, Beth continued moving and her spirits soared when she finally came across a wooden door that barred her exit.

As she rested for a moment Beth raised her feet one at a time and gently rubbed the torn and broken skin on her heels. With her fingers she flicked away any of the bigger pieces of dirt that she found sticking to the cuts.

With this completed and feeling more comfortable, Beth turned towards the door and, resting her hands against its frame, slowly raised herself onto her knees and ran her hands as far as she could reach, until she came across the spot where the door handle should have been.

There was nothing; the door handle had been removed and all that remained was a small raised square area.

What had she expected?

That it would be open?

Sinking slowly back down, Beth felt the tears welling up once again and actually that was exactly what she was hoping.

Foolish, stupid person, she thought and no matter how much she wanted to be brave she felt her chin starting to wobble uncontrollably; as the hot scalding tears started to fall her head sank down onto her knees. It was in this position that she saw the faint glimmer of light shining underneath the locked door. Hardly believing her eyes, Beth rubbed her knuckles into their sockets to clear the tears away and then she ran her hand over her face to clear the dirt and snot which had stuck to her.

She flattened herself fully on the cold floor and pushed her face up against the bottom of the door, praying she was not mistaken. It was not clear enough; she had to enlarge the gap. Beth dug her fingernails into the dirt to clear away as much as possible, heedless of the pain; lowering her head once more to the sliver under the door, there it was!

There, shining out along the passageway was the smallest of beams, but to Beth it was as big as a lighthouse and just as welcome. This time it was tears of gratitude that streamed down her face. She was not blind after all!

"I'm not blind, I'm not blind," she mumbled over and over again.

Beth wanted to stay in that position forever. She did not want to have to return to the awful darkness of her incarceration. That one little light shining there gave her hope and faith that all might be well after all. How brave it looked, flickering there; she wanted to hold it. She wanted it to banish the darkness of the room and above all she wanted it to banish the terror that was waiting in the darker recesses of her mind.

Finding it now too cold lying on the floor, Beth slid across the room to where she remembered the bed was and at least a suggestion of warmth and grasping the rough blanket, she pulled it round herself as she sat back on the bed. It did not offer much in the way of comfort, but at least it was something.

"I wonder how you are getting on, Gem, have you got a little light to help you?" Beth said to herself.

Then suddenly the light was gone, extinguished in a moment, as if it had never been there.

"Bye bye, little light," said Beth sadly and as she lay there in the darkness, suddenly feeling the temperature dropping, trying to keep warm, she pulled the blanket tighter. The light was gone and once more she was plunged in impenetrable darkness but now she knew she was not blind. At least she had seen the light and proved beyond doubt that she could see; that was something, wasn't it?

She knew that she would be kept alive because Cybil had said she was going to be the bait for Gem.

Bait for what?

Her mind wandered over what part Cybil was playing in all this, but for some reason, sitting there on the edge of the bed, she felt her heart begin to quicken.

She felt the pulse in her throat throbbing and the adrenalin coursing through her body; it flooded her with the energy for flight, but where to? She felt trapped and helpless; where was there to go?

Someone was in the room with her!

How did they get in there without her knowing? She could not see who was with her, but she could feel them, feel the temperature plummet. Her flesh started to crawl and her eyes darted all ways as she inched herself farther onto the bed, tucking her feet underneath her and squirming into the corner, her back pressed firmly against the cold stone. Beth felt the hairs on her neck starting to prickle and her mouth suddenly became extremely dry.

She wanted to scream and scream and as she opened her mouth, suddenly someone spoke to her.

"Are you warm enough?"

The words slowly filtered through her numb brain; she was equally shocked to hear words of comfort, as she would have expected to hear hateful words.

"Can I get you anything?" the Voice continued to say.

"Why would you care?" replied Beth, the words coming out in a whisper.

"Now now, what a thing to say; your comfort is all I care about," answered the Voice. "Have I not prepared everything for your arrival?"

"You can get me another blanket," replied Beth and as an afterthought she bravely said, "and something to eat, I'm starving."

"Isn't that better? See, we can communicate nicely if you allow yourself."

"Can I ask you something?" enquired Beth.

"Yes of course, by all means."

"Why are you keeping me in total darkness? Who are you?" said Beth, trembling even though the voice sounded so pleasant.

It seemed as though he was mulling over the question, as if he did not want to answer immediately. Eventually Beth heard him speak again and her body shuddered as he said, "Who am I? Well, that is the question, isn't it?" The Voice continued in the same casual manner, "I am all things to all people and I like the dark because it is less confusing for you. If you take one of the senses away, the others become more stimulated. Perhaps I shall do a little experiment and take all your senses away one after the other, perhaps permanently. How would you like that?"

Beth knew now that she was in the presence of evil and that he was toying with her. There would be no blanket and no food, this was his game and it was going to be played to its fullest outcome. Suddenly Beth felt strange and it came to her from the weirdest thought. Ever since the assault she had dreaded anyone coming near her, dreaded the thought of being taken captive again and like someone coming to terms with a terminal illness, Beth faced the fact that she was indeed captured again.

She had finally come full circle.

It was as if time and space stood still and she was back to where her horror first began; everything had gone in a loop back to the beginning. With the horror came a sort of acceptance to her fate and Beth bowed her head and let the tears fall onto her folded arms.

"I feel a change within you," said the Voice. "Perhaps this is going to be more interesting than I thought. You are an intelligent woman, Beth."

"Answer me this one thing," Beth said through her tears, ignoring his remark. "Was it you that attacked me?" She had uncurled her feet from under her and now as she dragged herself across the bed she felt the coldness of the floor permeate up through the ground, into her bare feet.

Beth let the blanket slip slowly back onto the bed as she stood in the dark room. She closed her eyes, as they were useless to her and clasping her hands together, she prayed as she had never prayed before as she waited for his answer.

"Yes, it was me who attacked you," said the Voice calmly.

"Why did you have to cut me?" replied Beth in a small choked voice.

"I cut you to see if you were hiding anything under your skin; it was the only way to see who you were, or in your case, who you weren't. I had to cut you to see what sort you were; there are several, you know and you could have been any one of them. Except you were not, you are human and of no consequence to me at all. I would have killed you there and then, but I was interrupted by the blonde one. She saved you even though she was unaware of her powers and she will try to save you again." Beth could hear his tone changing as he spoke of Gem.

Beth's head reeled with all this new information; why was it saying that Gem was not like her? She knew Gem was different; she had since they had first met, but was this dissimilarity something that could defeat this monster?

"I feel you assessing my words; you are good, perhaps the taking away of your sight has aided you more than I thought it would," said the Voice with genuine amusement.

As Beth stood there in the darkness she clasped her hands in supplication; touching her mouth with her fingertip, she instinctively screwed her eyes tighter as she felt his evil presence walking round her and her body reacted to his presence by involuntarily shivering.

"There isn't much longer to wait, things are moving ahead nicely and soon I will get what I desire the most," said the Voice somewhere behind her.

Beth could feel the coldness blowing on her neck as he spoke.

"Are you not going to ask me what that is?" said the Voice.

Beth could feel her neck starting to freeze as he got closer and she willed herself to stand perfectly still.

"I'm sure you will tell me if you want me to know," said Beth with as much bravado as she could muster.

"Ah, that is very true; well, I shall tell you anyway, seeing as how I am enjoying myself so much. The ultimate goal is to release my Master and then all the rest that are buried deep within their tombs, but my reward is the beautiful blonde one. She will be my equal and I will make her mine."

Beth could hear the emotion in his voice and was stunned to hear what he was saying.

"Are you saying that you would unleash such a force onto an unsuspecting world because you believe it, or are these just the ravings of a madman?"

"Think what you like, it is of no consequence to me. It will not alter the outcome. I do not have to convince you; that is not the reason why you are here. Let us say, for now, that in this modern day and age, people like you are naturally sceptical and I find that only works in my favour."

Beth lowered her head, but it was hard to think clearly with him standing so close. "Are you talking about Gem? Is that the blonde you are obsessed with? And are you saying that you are in love with her? You said she would be your reward; is that when you complete your little job here?" said Beth, amazed at all of what she had heard; she inadvertently gave a little laugh.

"I hear you laugh; you think it is funny that I could want a woman like her, yet you do not question the fact that I will fulfil the reason I am here." He said this casually, but Beth knew she had overstepped the mark and grimaced at her own stupidity.

"No, no of course not, I just find it so unusual that you even know about her let alone love her," replied Beth, trying to fix the mess she had inadvertently gotten herself in with her thoughtless words.

"Love?" he said questioningly, but then the tone of his voice changed dramatically, "I do not know what love is. No, I will dominate her; she will be mine to do with as I want," he replied angrily into her ear as he stood close behind her.

"Then I truly feel sorry for you," said Beth, once again speaking without thinking.

"Sorry for me?" replied the Voice quietly; she felt him move round her to stand once again in front of her.

"Yes, sorry for you, for not knowing the glory of love," said Beth sadly.

The blow when it came sent her staggering back onto the bed and the taste of copper flooding her mouth told her that her lip had split. A hand gripped her face, digging the nails into her soft flesh and Beth instinctively raised her hands to break the grip, but when her hands touched the skin of her attacker, they felt hard and scaly like those of a reptile. She was not brave enough to touch them again.

So she lay there in submission; all she wanted to do was scream, but the pain was too much for her and as It lowered itself nearer to her face It said, "Do not ever preach to me again, bitch, or speak of love, because I know nothing of it." With venom dripping from Its every word, It continued, "I have watched and waited for what is coming. I knew she was out there; it was just a matter of finding her. We are destined to be together, she cannot hide forever and the people protecting her are getting fewer as we speak."

Beth carefully drew in a small breath between her pinched lips as It continued to crush her face in its steely grip. Her inner self wanted to writhe and scream and shout abuse, but that would be useless, so all she did was gently nod her head.

She wanted to know more, and there were more ways to skin a cat, as Mrs Dunn was wont to say when she couldn't get her uncle to do what she wanted; Beth now took this advice to heart. She had overstepped the mark a couple of times, and each time she had paid the price for it.

Now she would analyse and assess each word It spoke and only give an answer when she had thought it through. After all, her life depended on its good will; It could easily finish her off if It wanted to. If she was to survive then she had to use the talents that God had given her and she prayed that they would be enough to play the mind games It had in store for her.

Beth felt the cold scaly hand relax its grip and then release her and though dazed from the blow, Beth knew that it had left her alone in her prison. The darkness did not contain its evil presence; she could feel it in every inch of her body and in every nerve ending and she sagged inwardly with relief upon the bed.

One touch of that scaly hand told her that the thing was not human and she would never think of him in that way ever again. His voice had fooled her but now she was aware of what he was but this did little to lessen her horror. Her hand searched around in the dark and found what she was looking for. Dragging the rough blanket up around her, Beth curled her body into a foetal position and tucked her bare feet under it. She was now completely covered, so she pulled the remainder of what was left over her head, burying herself in a cocoon of hurt and fear. All bravado had left her, all the feelings of standing up to whatever It was had left with that one punch and that feel of its disgusting hand.

She did not feel brave anymore, she felt sore and tired and very, very scared.

She did not doubt its intentions anymore, one feel of its scaly hand and the coldness of its breath was enough to confirm all it had said.

She trembled under the blanket as she thought about Gem; she was all she had left in the world. She had no parents, her uncle was missing and to all intents and purposes Gem and Remne were in hiding, otherwise it would have known where to find them. So there was no one to help her. What if It was right and It got Gem as its reward? Who was there to stop it from doing so?

It was too powerful, there was nobody ... nobody.

If there was nobody to stop it, then there would be no reason to keep her alive for longer than was necessary. Beth realised in that moment that her survival depended solely on Gem's ability to defeat this creature and as the cold hard facts started to hit her, Beth felt herself rocking to and fro in a vain attempt to stop herself dropping completely into insanity.

"Gem, where are you? I need you so much," said Beth as she sobbed into the bedding and as she closed her eyes, her mind whirled around in an effort to find some comfort and eventually the words came to her and she softly whispered the 23rd Psalm to herself:

"The Lord is my Shepherd, I shall not want ..."

Chapter 20

Gem left by the rear of the house after deciding it was too dangerous to leave by the front; the last thing she wanted was to be seen by anyone walking late at night like Mrs Thomas next door, who insisted that her little dog's bladder was all for the better for its midnight strolls.

Earlier Gem had doused the street lights and plunged everything into darkness so that Remne could leave unobserved. She had watched from the front step in the shadows as Remne accelerated away from the kerb, gunning the car down to the end of the road, only to be lost from view as the road curved to the left. Gem felt herself tut-tutting as she listened to the car's engine fade into the distance. With a small shake of her head, she turned and re-entered the house, but she was still worried that Remne was not as good a driver as she said she was. There was nothing she could do about it now so she closed and locked the front door and then walked into the lounge.

Gem's face was set and determined as she walked over to the settee and retrieved her sword. She fastened the strap she had found earlier, over her shoulder and round her waist like a bandolier.

It was a long leather strap she had used when she had taken up archery. The strap had lasted a lot longer than her enthusiasm for the sport, as she had become easily bored when she had mastered the long bow in record time.

There was no challenge in the sport for her; now she knew why.

When Gem had found the strap tucked away in a drawer, her strong fingers had caressed the dark leather. When she saw the slot in the middle of the strap she knew straight away that it would be ideal for carrying her sword and now with it in position round her body, Gem found that it did not impinge on the opening of her wings. Like a metal cross strapped to her back, the sword hung down between her shoulder blades but was ready when she needed it. Now as Gem stood in the darkness of the garden she scanned the closed curtains of the houses around her for any signs of movement; finding none, she decided it was time to move.

The light drizzle that had been falling all evening had changed to a heavier downpour and as Gem flung her head back the rain washed over her face, plastering her curls to her head. She was unaware of anything except the energy flooding through her and she opened her arms wide in total acceptance of her new being. She felt her muscles bunching together and as she bent her knees slightly, she expanded her glorious white wings to their full width; with one bound she was airborne.

Flying swiftly to her destination, Gem was focused and ready; nothing would stand in her way to retrieve the information she needed. It was only a matter of minutes before she arrived at her destination. Gem hovered in the air high above Rupert's home and erring on the side of caution, she extinguished all the lights in the surrounding neighbourhood.

Can't be too careful, Gem thought as she made her descent. She watched as the streetlights fizzled and died, plunging all around into total darkness; there was not even the moon to worry about. Everything looked locked and barred, no glimmer of a light anywhere, but she was not surprised; it was late and Gem assumed that Rupert had gone to bed hours ago if he was there at all.

Rupert had bought the house from his parents, who he said had now moved abroad. Gem was at first surprised that he had bought it and then she was glad. She had visited the house on several occasions when his parents lived there and it always had a nice homey feel about it. Its honey coloured stone walls were typical for the area and the more Gem saw the place, the more she liked it. She had always thought though that Rupert would have preferred a modern apartment somewhere in the middle of town, which made this pleasant old house a bit of a surprise, as it did not quite gel with his personality.

Gem landed in the large garden at the rear of the property and as she stood there refolding her wings in the shelter of the trees she gazed up at the dark, soulless windows. Not a glimmer of light could be seen, but she was not surprised because of the lateness of the hour.

Gem made her way over to the French windows; rubbing the pane with her fingers, she peered into the lounge.

It was empty!

There was nothing in the room except an old chair and newspapers strewn about. Gem decided there was no point in waiting any longer, so she placed her shoulder against the middle of the door and steadily pushed. She leant against the door until she heard the wood splintering and it gave way before her.

She sprang forward and clasped the doors before they had a chance to bang against the inside walls; as she released them she stood for a while and tried to guess what room Rupert would be in.

All was silent so she stealthily walked across the dirty parquet flooring, remembering the Persian carpet and valuable antiques that had once graced the room.

The rain had soaked Gem through and little pools of water formed on the floor as she made her way over to the door leading to the centre of the house.

Her shoes squished repeatedly and it sounded too loud to her ears in the dark empty house, so bending down, Gem removed each shoe in turn and then her socks, leaving herself barefoot, but at least she was quiet. She decided to take a look about the place; it surprised her that Rupert had let the house get into such a state. He was usually so meticulous in his cleaning, being a doctor and into cleanliness and his mother had always been so house proud; she assumed it had naturally just rubbed off onto Rupert but this … this was awful!

She pushed open the door on the right that led into the kitchen and although she could not see much it was the same in the kitchen as the rest of the house, except the smell that came from the overflowing waste bin made her pinch her nose in disgust. She pulled open the drawer nearest to her and pulled out a small torch that she knew Rupert always kept there. Shining the small beam around the wall units, she went over and opened a few; there was nothing inside and the more she opened the more the truth dawned on her. There was not a tin or box of breakfast cereal in sight; they were all empty. Gem imagined that Rupert had not used a kitchen appliance to cook himself anything for some time and by the scurrying of the furry rodents she could see she was right.

The overflowing bin was full of take-away cartons. The smell increased the deeper she went into the kitchen, and Gem felt herself gagging and decided it was better to take small shallow breaths. She looked around herself, perplexed and placing her hands on her hips, she shook her head from side to side and was not convinced that the one bin could have caused so much stink.

Something was not quite right the smell had a sweet smell to it and as walked towards the large walk-in larder even more rodents scampered out of her way. They did not seem frightened of her and carried on about their business once she had passed. The darkness was almost impenetrable and the small beam of the torch did nothing much to keep the nagging doubts at bay. She reached forward and slowly opened the cupboard door and she stood in silent horror as the brave little beam swept over what was left of Rupert's parents!

They were slumped in the corner as if dragged there haphazardly and then unceremoniously dumped. She quietly closed the door on the atrocity and made her way back out into the hallway, placing the small torch on the worktop as she left. The door gently bumped against her legs as she dragged in a lungful of cleaner air, but nothing could take the smell of the rotting bodies from her nostrils.

The hallway was darker than she remembered, so Gem had to run her hand along the panelling until she encountered the newel post at the foot of the stairs; glancing up at the front door, she could see that the light was blocked out by sheets of newspapers that had been taped over the windows.

Gem poked her head into the dining room and it was the same in there as well: empty of all furniture and the windows were taped the same as the front door.

Wasting no more time, Gem returned to the hallway and bounded up the stairs, two at a time in her usual fashion, until she reached the top. She stood there for a few seconds, listening, with her back pressed up against the wall and as she gained control over her thumping heart, she heard a noise in the far bedroom. As quietly as she could Gem inched her way along the landing until she was standing outside the room. Cautiously Gem pushed the door open, but she was unprepared for the screaming figure that hurtled towards her and it was only thanks to her heightened senses and quick reflexes that she was saved from being mown down.

She quickly sidestepped out of the way and the figure went flying past her, smashing into the opposite wall on the landing. Realising that it would be difficult to fight in such a confined space, Gem backed into the bedroom and stood there watching as the figure shook its head to clear it. Leaping to his feet again he came charging into the dark bedroom.

Gem could feel its taut, hard muscles and smell his maleness as he tried to overpower her.

He tried to fling his arms around her to try and hinder her movements, but she was too quick. Her energy had increased to such an extent that she found the dark figure was no match for her and not wishing to prolong the bout she swiftly brought her fist up and landed a powerful blow onto her opponent's jaw, sending him sprawling across the bed.

Now she would see who she was dealing with; Gem strode across the room and flicked on the light switch. As the room flooded with light, she found herself looking down the barrel of a gun.

"For what do I owe the pleasure of this little nocturnal visit?" said Rupert as he eased himself off the bed onto the floor, waving the gun as he spoke.

"Aren't you pleased to see me?" said Gem.

"Not really," replied Rupert, rubbing his chin. He waved the gun over in the direction of a stool and indicated that she should sit there, saying, "You will have to let a chap get dressed, so sit down there like a good girl."

Gem did as she was told and kept her back as straight as possible as she sat on the stool, hoping that the end of her blade would not scrape on the floor.

Gem wanted to keep the sword out of Rupert's view, so to draw his attention away from herself she asked, "It was you, wasn't it, that I had a fight with in my house? Why did you try to kidnap Beth?"

"Do you know you caused me endless complications?" he replied. "I had to put six stitches in my side and it was not easy, I can tell you; I had to do them myself and when I failed to get her like I was ordered to … well …"

Rupert's voice trailed off and Gem could see a light sheen of sweat break out on his forehead at the memory she had just evoked.

"He wanted her," Rupert said, "that is all I can tell you and he must have what he wants, otherwise he can get very nasty, I can tell you." He nodded his head sagely.

"You even came to my house and tried to seduce Beth, you low life bastard!" replied Gem, her temper for a minute getting the better of her.

"Yes and I would have succeeded if the little bitch had not wanted to talk everything over with you first; see what I mean? You get in the way all the time," said Rupert, waving the gun about as he spoke.

He had succeeded in getting his trousers on with one hand and was just pulling on a t-shirt when Gem said, "I know what you have to do, Rupert; it's not rocket science, but do you think you could answer a couple of questions before you finish me off?"

He would not meet her gaze for long and continued to straighten his appearance, adding as he did so, "That is what I like about you, Gem: you are straight to the point, no messing around; well, what is it you want to know?"

Rupert had moved while he was talking and had positioned himself at the foot of the bed, directly in front of Gem. He seemed almost jovial and looked as if he was enjoying the encounter; as Gem spoke he settled himself more comfortably on the end of the bed.

"I do like your hair, Gem, it suits you, shame you won't have it for long," he said, smiling fondly at Gem as if it was the nicest compliment in the world.

Was he losing it? Gem thought suddenly; if so she wanted to steer him back to what she wanted to know and so trying not to alarm him, she quietly said, "Who am I dealing with, Rupert and how did you get involved in all this?"

Rupert became even more agitated when he heard her questions and he could not help glancing over towards the bedroom door, as if he expected someone uninvited to walk through. It was as Rupert was glancing away that Gem noticed for the first time his dishevelled appearance. It looked as if he had not shaved for three or four days and by the smell of him he had not washed for a lot longer.

"All I can tell you is his name …" he began. And again Rupert glanced at the door; finally making his mind up, he turned to Gem and said, "His name is Adam, but he is known by different names and different faces; he is very clever, brilliant even; he said you would know the rest and that you are a clever woman and not to be trusted; he said you will know the meeting place."

Rupert gave a small nervous laugh and Gem was suddenly worried for his sanity. "What about you, Rupert?" said Gem softly.

"Me, oh, that's easy: plain and simple greed. He promised me lots and lots of money and drugs and all my heart desires."

Rupert laughed again but this time his eyes had taken on a manic gleam.

"Have you got all those things, Rupert?" asked Gem, sitting straight and tall on the stool.

"No! And I even thought you had guessed the truth when we all had our cards read; that witch Remne, if that was her name, she knew!"

"She knew what, Rupert?" Gem asked trying to keep him focused.

"She knew about the drugs and that I was being sucked in, but Cybil was there and she blocked a lot of things so that witch could not read everything. Cybil is clever and helps me when my need gets too much for me."

It was as if Rupert was repeating well-rehearsed lines; his eyes started to take on a glazed appearance and the gun in his hand wobbled slightly. Gem prayed it would not go off before she was ready.

"What has Cybil got to do with Adam, Rupert?" said Gem, leaning slightly forward on the stool, eager to hear his answer.

Rupert's eyes swung round onto Gem's face and he sat there for a few seconds, watching her, before he answered, "You don't know, do you? You don't know the connection."

Rupert broke into a high pitched laugh as he watched Gem trying to work out what he was talking about. Gem sat there, knowing she was missing something; it was one of the missing pieces.

Think girl; think, she told herself as she looked at the faded piece of carpet under her bare feet. What would get Rupert so excited and animated? Then slowly the truth came to her, it was what Rupert had said earlier about Adam, about him having different names and faces.

That was it!

Adam and Cybil were one and the same!

Rupert could see the truth slowly dawning on Gem's face and as she raised her head to look at him, he nodded to indicate she was right.

"Yes, you are right, I am afraid, so you see now how this changes everything."

Rupert looked down at her beautiful face and said sadly, "He has taken everything away from me as a punishment, but now with you here I can get back to where I was, as his favourite. He will thank me for killing you, to get you out of the way."

Gem could see the tears threatening in his eyes, but before he could continue Gem quickly replied, "I've seen what's left of your parents, Rupert. Why did you do it? They were good people."

If Rupert was shocked at her discovery he did not show it; he merely shrugged his shoulders.

"I had to prove to him that I was prepared to do anything for him and when he asked, I agreed. They are better off not knowing what I had become. My life is in ruins and things will never be the same, ever again. So I have to do this, don't you see?"

Gem heard the depth of sadness in his voice and compassion washed over her. So speaking softly, she tried to reach him with her words; perhaps it was possible to save him after all … she had to try.

"Would you like it all to be over?" she asked softly. "Would you like to find redemption and forgiveness?"

"Yes, yes of course I would." Rupert lowered the gun, his eyes glistening with tears that eventually spilled down his cheeks.

"Then pray with me, Rupert," pleaded Gem. "Pray and God will forgive you; come, I will help you."

Gem leant forward, extending her open hand as a sign of peace between them. It was at that moment, when Rupert lifted his eyes to her and she looked into them, she saw to what depths of depravity and wickedness his soul had descended to. There was no going back, there would be no forgiveness sought or given. That tiny spark of humanity that had burned so bright for a few seconds had been extinguished and in its place was someone she did not want to contemplate. Gem sadly lowered her head, mortified that the moment of forgiveness had passed and listened with a heavy heart as Rupert said, "He warned me that you were clever, that you would have a silver tongue; well, it won't work with me, you are going to die right here and now and he will thank me for it and I will be his favourite again."

Rupert waved the gun and his eyes gleamed with the vileness that had rotted his soul and as he stood and pointed the gun at Gem's head he laughed when she said, "I will give you one last chance to redeem yourself; please, Rupert, ask forgiveness and it will be given you."

"Shut up! Still you spout your stupid words; my Master and his Master the Supreme One will be the lord of all men, not yours, so you say your own prayers and prepare to meet your maker." Spit dribbled from his lips as he shouted his words at Gem's bowed head.

It was as Gem raised her head and looked back at Rupert's demented face that he realised that she was armed; she had bowed her head too far and Rupert had been given a clear view of the hilt of her sword.

It was a simple, stupid mistake and one that she could see had tipped him over the edge. There was no going back now; she could see it in his face, as it twisted with rage, that he had to kill her, he had to get back all that he had lost and her death he thought would procure this.

Gem saw as if in slow motion his hand rising to take aim and the finger of that hand squeezing the trigger.

Sadly, she had no choice.

As Gem stood up from the stool, she raised her arms and took the sword from between her shoulder blades and in one fluid motion she sliced Rupert in two even before he could level the gun at her head.

The flaming sword cut through bone and gristle like a hot knife through butter and Gem watched as it entered at the base of Rupert's neck and travelled down until it reappeared on the opposite side of his waist.

She saw the surprised look on Rupert's face as the two halves of his body crumpled and slipped wetly to the floor.

As Gem knelt over the body she gently closed his eyes and whispered, "Rest in peace, Rupert, your trials are over. Mine are just beginning."

She leant her hands on the sword handle while the point lay embedded in the floor and using the sword as a cross she said a prayer to his departing soul. When she had finished she cleaned her sword on the bed and returned it to the leather strap.

Her work here was done but she was no nearer to finding Beth; with a heavy heart she quickly departed from the bedroom and its grisly occupant, making her way once more down the stairs to the lounge. As she passed through the hallway, she pulled on her socks and shoes and went out of the open French windows to the garden.

Turning for one last look at the house, Gem hoped that Remne was having better luck than she was; with her thoughts turning to Beth and where she might be, she unfolded her wings and headed back to her house while it was still dark.

The large black car had been parked farther up the lane for some time and its occupant remained sitting in the back seat. His legs were stretched out in a modicum of comfort as he read the evening paper.

He remained where he was in the lane until sunrise, but now feeling the effect of sitting too long in one place, he decided it was time to get out and see what had happened inside the house.

He had heard a bit of a commotion when he had got out of the car to take a leak, but that was many hours ago. He had his orders, he was not to interfere and why would he he'd like to know. There was no love lost between that smelly unkempt doctor and himself. He would be glad to see the back of him, it was just all this sitting about and waiting; surely Adam knew by now he could be trusted. He had managed to get away with what had happened at the river bank, but Adam had shown his anger in quite a subtle way when he had told him the woman had escaped. He now knew the reason why they had to keep clear of cats after Adam had placed him in a room with one. He walked down the lane in the half light, his small frame unable to see over the hedgerows growing on either side; he had to give an occasional jump in the air to get his bearings.

The house appeared before him and he made his way through the gate and, like Gem before him, walked round the back and entered through the broken doors of the French window. He touched the broken and shattered frame with his childlike hands and then, shrugging carelessly, made his way through the house. Small shards of light filtered through the torn newspapers that had been taped to all the windows and by this weak light he made his way upstairs to where the freshly spilled blood beckoned him.

He didn't have to search the upstairs; he knew immediately what room to go to: the smell called to him. He gave no gasp of surprise on seeing Rupert's dead sanguinary body, even though one half lay separated from the other by several inches.

Things like this were his joy, but for now he would not to touch the body, even though the flesh cried out to him to be tasted and sampled. The fear of the cat kept him from bending down and running his fingers through the blood and licking them.

He ran his tongue over his lips at the thought but then slowly backed out of the room and made his way carefully downstairs. He had to get back and report all he had seen; he hurried down the stairs conscious of the passing time and it was then that the smell came wafting out to him as he passed a door on the left of the hallway. He had not noticed it earlier because the smell of the fresh blood had overpowered it, but there it was, beckoning him. He carefully pushed opened the door and found himself in the kitchen and as if he was tracking, he made his way purposefully across the kitchen to the larder door.

The smell was so ripe he drooled and as he opened the door his pleasure was heightened at seeing the two decomposing bodies.

He made allowances in his head for what he was about to do; after all, Adam had only said not to touch Rupert's body if he was to find him dead. He could always say it had taken him longer than expected; after all, who would know? Adam had said nothing about these two stuffed in the larder and what an appropriate place to keep them, he thought with an evil grin. As he entered the larder, he silently closed the door behind himself.

Chapter 21

Beth knew the exact dimension of her prison cell. She knew that it only took five normal paces from the top end of her bed to reach the bucket to relieve herself and exactly two paces from the end of the bed to the door. As to what time it was or whether it was day or night, she had no way of knowing; the darkness was still all pervasive. She had instigated a soft regimen of exercise whilst lying on her back on the small bed. Her muscles had started to feel weak and as she didn't have the strength to do very much, she thought this was better than doing nothing at all. She had always thought that being in solitary confinement would be a doddle and had always laughed when she had seen someone in a film being dragged off for that particular form of punishment.

"I'd love it," she used to say to Gem, who always looked at her over the top of her glasses, shook her head and tutted.

"Well, I would," she had replied indignantly. "What's not to like? You're not bothered by anyone; the place is your own."

But Gem had always refused to be drawn into an argument, no matter how much Beth baited her. *I wonder how much she was aware, even subconsciously*, thought Beth, *and that was why she never talked about it.*

She turned the thought of her incarceration over in her head and put it down to her own juvenile stupidity; who was she kidding now? Nobody!

It was awful, the most diabolical thing that could happen to a person, to be shut off from all human contact. Beth had not realised until that moment how much she missed even the smallest form of contact: the kiss on the cheek when Gem hurried out the door, the smile she received from the newsman when she went to get her paper, even Mrs Thomas going on about her dog and Mr Bentley on the other side, endlessly explaining how to prune roses.

She missed it all and wanted it back!

She wanted to be back at her drawing board, planning and designing new rooms. She wanted to go through swatches of fabric and books of wallpaper designs. She wanted to match and co-ordinate … She wanted to be free!

She was just getting her life back on track … and now this!

To make matters worse, she had become obsessed with looking for the light again and had regularly gotten down in the dirt to look under the door, but she didn't see it again. That one little beam had come to her in her hour of need and she had gotten down on her knees and thanked God at the time for looking out for her. Now time seemed to stand still; she knew that it had been a while since the evil thing had visited her.

It had come to her at the start of her incarceration, but that seemed ages ago now; she could hear her stomach growling with hunger. Beth rolled on to her side and squeezed her arms around her middle in a vain attempt to ease the pain of its emptiness, but it was the lack of water she was finding hardest to bear. Her tongue stuck to the roof of her mouth, and she had tried all sorts of things to try and lubricate it. She had even thought of biting into pickled onions and it had worked for a while but now she could feel the moisture draining away from her. She had searched in the dirt for a suitable sized pebble to suck, but the ground was too fine and she gave up and slumped back on the bed. Beth pulled the blanket around her for comfort and wondered how long she could go before she was either driven mad or died.

Could she drink her own urine?

The thought disgusted her, but she had heard of other people doing it. No, she was not that desperate, not yet anyway, but who knows?

She shivered at the prospect and it was not until she heard its voice that she realised it was in the room with her again. Beth had thought it was because her body had weakened that she felt the cold, but she should have known it was because of its presence.

Her body tensed as it spoke and she wondered how it was going to toy with her this time.

"How are you keeping?" the Voice said as if her welfare was its top priority.

When she did not answer she could hear the slight change in the tone of its voice as it said, almost laughingly, "Are you not going to answer me? Do I have to punish you?"

As Beth concentrated she realised she could pick up each little inflection and nuance in its speech. She knew that this humour was at odds to what it was truly feeling and she suddenly realised that she had an ace up her sleeve, even if it was a very small one. She waited until she knew it was going to speak again. Beth now found that her hearing was greatly improved, mainly, she suspected, because it compensated for her lack of sight. She heard a small intake of breath heralding the fact that it was going to speak.

She waited a fraction longer and then she spoke, breaking off its words before it had a chance to finish.

"I'm sorry … but it is … the lack of water … I cannot get my … words out … properly."

"Well, that is a problem, isn't it? Here, take this, I cannot have you dying on me, not yet anyway," the Voice replied almost jovially.

Beth sat up on the bed and swung her feet over the side; as she leant forward she held out her hands and her fingers curled round a large cylindrical object. She felt her arms tense as they took the weight and her shoulders strained as she bent to put the heavy object on the floor. As she leant over the jug she had placed on the floor, her hands crept up either side and finding there was no top, she slid her fingers in over the side and felt the cold liquid.

Water!

She squeezed her eyes tight and forced herself not to make a sound, as she knew he would be listening.

"Thank you," said Beth, grateful beyond measure for the water.

She never before realised that water had a smell; she knew you could smell the rain coming and you could smell the wetness afterwards, but now she felt she could actually smell the beautiful, life giving water she was holding in her hands. She wanted to sink her head into its depths and drink till she was fully sated, but something stopped her from doing this. Something stopped her from being too eager and so carefully she curled her bare feet around the base of the container like an extra pair of hands and held it securely and then she straightened her back and sat upright.

There it was!

She could feel the tension building within the room again, something else was coming and she had the feeling she was not going to like it.

"I have news of your friend," the Voice said and Beth could hear the tone changing again like thunder rolling in from a far off distant storm.

Beth braced herself, but still she waited until she could feel him ready to speak again and forestalling him, she said, "What friend is that?"

"Your blonde friend, the one you call Gemini," and this time It smiled as he heard Beth's small but sharp intake of breath; continuing, the Voice said, "Yes, she paid a little visit to someone we both know and unfortunately one of them came off the worse."

Beth could feel the smile in its words and promised herself not to let a slip like that happen again; replying as calmly as possible, she said, "It would seem to me that if you're bringing me water and I am still alive, then it was not Gem who came off the worse."

"Oh well done, well done, you are a sharp little button, aren't you? Yes, you are right, it was not Gem, as you call her, but someone who had outgrown their usefulness."

Beth held her breath while he had been speaking, and very gently she let the air flow silently out from between her lips, immensely relieved that she had been right.

"This person who came off the worse, did they ... die?" asked Beth, suddenly nervous.

"Oh yes, he is very much dead, as dead as anyone can get and it's all thanks to your tall blonde friend," the Voice replied, but Beth could still feel the undercurrent of emotion in the room.

"I suppose you are angry because you have lost someone," said Beth, testing the waters and trying to make It give more away.

"Angry? No, I am seething!" the Voice shouted down at her and as Beth sat there she regretted her baiting; her whole being shook as she felt the venom in the words that now poured out at her.

She forced herself to sit there as it came within inches of her face, but she could not help herself from closing her eyes and turning her head to one side as its cold fetid breath washed over her.

Then she felt It turning away to pace about the small room as the Voice said, "The stupid arrogant fool could have ruined all that I had set up. No, I am glad that he is dead. Glad that he got what he stupidly deserved because he could have taken my prize away from me. If she had not killed him then I would have done so."

Beth leant forward and placed both her hands round the jug, protecting it in case in its anger the precious water was knocked over.

It was in the quiet after its tirade that Beth had a chance to speak and summoning up her courage, she said, "You said you had news of a friend but you also said that we both knew them, who is the other person?"

Like the changing of the wind its voice went from anger to pleasantries in an instant and Beth heard the tone change straight away. She heard the pleasure it took in its words; she could tell it was enjoying itself knowing the words were hurting her, but she had braced herself for what it was going to say.

She sat there immobile while it said, "That is very remiss of me; did I not say who the other person was? Well, I won't keep you guessing, it was Rupert, stupid, dull, arrogant Rupert. Rupert is no more, cut in two by your friend and now he lies rotting on his bedroom floor. So don't expect him to come calling on you anymore because he won't, or can't ... I should add. Don't waste your tears on him; after all, he was the one I sent to get you and he was foiled by your friend; mind you, he paid a price for that little lapse."

Beth concentrated on holding the water, she channelled all her thoughts to the time when it left and she could drink her fill, but she knew the thing was waiting for an answer, so she straightened up, forced her fingers to let go of the jug. When she starting speaking, she could tell it was not expecting to hear what she said; once more the ball was in her court.

"What is your name?" she asked. "What do I call you? I cannot call you Thing or It, so tell me your name." Beth put as much inflection and curiosity into her voice as she could.

"My name? And here I was expecting you to grieve for your boyfriend; my, you are a dark horse. I could even get to like you. My name, since you asked so nicely, is Adam. I am of course known by a lot of other names but I like this earthly name, so please call me Adam."

Beth could hear an equal amount of curiosity in his voice also.

"Adam that is a nice name. Thank you for the water, Adam; it was good of you to think of me," said Beth, leaning down once again and holding the jug, fearful it would be snatched away from her at the last minute.

"I shall leave you now to drink your fill; I have the distinct impression that I have been slightly outmanoeuvred, but what does that matter? I have enjoyed our little chat, until the next time, Beth." Then he was gone.

Beth felt her body shaking uncontrollably with the sudden release of tension and fear. She had not even been aware that every muscle in her body had been tensed and ready for action.

Beth almost laughed aloud. "What action?" she said into the darkness.

Her hands brought the precious liquid up from the floor that she had so long desired; raising the jug to her parched lips, she carefully sipped the water.

Beth had feared that it might be something other than water, that Adam was playing some horrendous game with her, but the liquid tasted sweet and welcoming. Never in her life had she tasted anything so wonderful. She could have filled her life with all sorts of objects and needless accessories and it all came down to faith and a drop of water. Perhaps life was just like that: you go along gathering useless junk, telling yourself that is what you need, and when it all comes down to it, you find it is not important after all.

Poor, poor Rupert found that out and her heart grieved for his death. Tears squeezed out from her closed eyes and she prayed for the Rupert she once knew. He had been Gem's friend, one of her oldest but to her he had been just happy, fun loving Rupert; to what depths had he sunk to make Gem kill him? She knew it would have had to be vile and loathsome to make Gem take his life. At least she knew one thing and that was that Gem was alive and on her trail; she was amazed with herself for getting Adam to share this information. Perhaps that was the way to go, a token acceptance of the "Stockholm syndrome."

Admittedly, the calmer she was when she spoke to Adam, the better he was to her and also with her heightened ability to analyse his speech, she suddenly found herself not quite as paralysed with fear at the thought of his next visit.

Feeling calmer, Beth took another long swig of the water; she could feel herself becoming more hydrated as the water flowed into her empty stomach.

Not wanting to make herself ill, Beth forced herself to place the jug back on the floor by the edge of the bed, near the wall. She could not help herself from dropping her fingers into the water from time to time as she lay on her bed, just to confirm it was still there; after all she had no reason to trust Adam, just because he had told her his name. Finally sleep overcame her and pulling the blanket up and over her head, Beth drifted off and dreamt about the days when she used to walk in the sun …

Chapter 22

As Remne pulled away from the kerb she valiantly tried to keep control of the powerful car. It would do no good if she crashed it just as she was getting started; what Gem would do, she did not want to contemplate. She could just see Gem in her rear view mirror standing on the top step inside the shadows of the porch. Luckily for Remne the road curved and she was soon lost from view, but she did not ease up on the accelerator, finding a childish delight in aggravating Gem, as she knew she would be listening as the noise of the car disappeared into the distance.

Laughing to herself at the way she had convinced Gem she was an excellent driver, Remne slowed the car down to a more sedate pace. Her hands shook with tension as she released the grip she had on the steering wheel. She longed for the gentle cruising of her boat, where the riverbank drifted past at a leisurely four miles an hour. She had never been so long away from the river she'd loved so much and the bittersweet pang she felt spurred her on.

The journey to Thirsk would not take too long, just over half an hour, but she did not want to encounter any speed cops, as she had neglected to tell Gem that she did not actually hold a driving licence. The less Gem knew about her driving the better.

Remne rubbed her eyes, feeling the effect of too little sleep and the hypnotic flow of the white lines disappearing under the car as she sped through the rain and up the old A19 to Thirsk. Large lorries intent on making their delivery deadlines thundered past the car and Remne's grip intensified each time it happened. She switched the wipers on so that they were going at a demon pace, their swishing adding to the hypnotic effect, but at least they were doing their job and clearing the spray from the windscreen.

I don't like this at all, thought Remne as she manoeuvred the car round the larger puddles that had started to block the road. She turned off the A19 onto the A128 and followed the signposts to the centre of Thirsk; all was quiet and still as she entered the large market town; casting a quick look around the square, she noted that it was devoid of all but a few cars. There was nobody about to hear her crunch the gears down into third and then second and she felt herself wincing as the car gave a little kangaroo hop as she let her foot off the clutch too soon. She quickly applied the pressure to the correct pedals, but evenly this time and made her way across town; turning right at the roundabout, she carried on for another couple of miles until she reached her destination. It was still raining when she got to the outer gates of the large imposing house and at the front of the drive, by the gates, there was a small oak board that read:

Woodhay Priory
Respite Care and Nursing Home
Run by the Carmelite Order of St John

Remne turned the car into the drive and headed up to the house, the tyres crunching on the gravel as she went. Then parking the car as near as possible, she readied herself for the dash in the rain to the front door.

Not bothering to lock it, knowing it would be safe, especially here, Remne slammed the car door and ran up the steps to the large imposing front door. Even so she was wet through; shaking the offending drops from her coat, Remne reached up and grasped the solid brass knocker and tapped as quietly as she could, considering the hour.

The door was immediately opened by an elderly man in a long grey flowing robe and Remne nodded to him in recognition but neither spoke. As he walked ahead of her, she noticed his sandals did not make the slightest noise on the marble tiles. As they crossed the foyer they turned down a carpeted hallway; as Remne looked into the rooms that she passed, she could see several members of the order, their heads bent piously as they chanted their devotions.

They carried on to the end of the hallway; reaching the room where Henry lay; the elderly monk held the door open for her and smiled, saying in a soft Austrian lilt as he laid his hand on her arm, "Velcome back,

Remne, it is good to see you. Nothing much has changed; he is still as veak as he vas. I fear he vill not be vith us much longer."

"I am sorry to hear that, Johan, but I must visit with him; alone, if you please," said Remne, looking over towards the figure on the bed.

"That's okay, just tell me vhen you are finished, but there is little you can get from him, poor man."

As Johan spoke he retrieved his rosary from his pocket and started to say the Paternoster. The room was dimly lit; the light that was there came from a small florescent tube on the wall just above the head of the bed. The shadows in the room were just held at bay by the dim little light, but it was enough for Remne to see the still, inert body lying on the bed.

She could see a tube in Henry's mouth for oxygen and it looked like he had been pegged as a tube ran straight into his stomach, for liquid sustenance, she assumed. There were wires and machines all surrounding the head of the bed and she could tell by their monotonous beeping that they were monitoring Henry's status. The room smelled slightly of lavender; Remne assumed it was what they washed the lino tiled floor with, as she could see no flowers in the room.

As Johan was leaving he turned back towards Remne, who was still standing in the doorway, looking at Henry; cocking his head to one side like a curious sparrow, he looked at her thoughtful expression and placed a hand on Remne's arm again saying, "Vhere are my manners? I am so sorry, Remne, please help yourself to a towel on the stand over there, you are soaking vet." Smiling gently at her, he finally turned and walked out of the room, leaving her with what was left of Henry.

Remne walked over to the bed; not bothering with the towel the little monk had offered, she leant over Henry and peered down at his immobile face. Tiny drops of water fell from her long hair onto his forehead and she softly brushed them away with her fingertips. Remne's hand reached around behind her and finally located the chair that had been placed there for visitors. She pulled it closer to her and sat down, but her eyes never left Henry's face. She leant forward across the bed, feeling the crisp sheets beneath her hands as she steadied herself.

Her lips were nearly touching Henry's cheek as she spoke through her mind, saying, *"Hello Henry, how are you? It's Remne."* Her lips did not move but her mind probed deep within Henry's; finally she got an answer.

"Ah Remne, how nice of you to come you are just in time; I fear I am not long for this world, but still this old body keeps me earthbound," replied Henry's mind to Remne's.

"Nonsense, you will outlive us all," she thought, *"but there are more important things to talk about. Listen to me, Henry: what happened to the Book that I entrusted to you? We cannot find it and you know it cannot fall into the wrong hands."* Remne had to draw him back to this earthly realm, but his mind was focused on heavenly glory and he did not want to come back.

"The Book is safe; let me go, Remne," replied Henry.

"No! I will keep you earthbound forever, I will have you lying in this bed for all eternity unless you tell me what has become of the Book," said Remne angrily.

"Don't be angry, Remne, I told you the Book is safe. Gem has it," replied Henry.

"No she doesn't, Henry, she doesn't! That is why I am here," said Remne, probing deeper into his mind as she felt him slipping away.

"Yes she does, Remne, but I admit she does not know she has it. I put it in the boot of her car under where the spare tyre goes. I removed the tyre and placed the book in its place. So you see, it was always safe; you know how much she loves that car."

Remne could see how much effort this was taking out of Henry; the machines on the wall started to give off more than one alarm.

"Henry, Henry, you can't go yet; I have to tell you that Beth is missing; they have taken her and we don't know where she is."

"This is the final chapter, Remne; it will not be long now before It makes its move; you must be ready for Gem's sake," said Henry, his voice coming to Remne as if from a long way away.

As he continued Remne lowered her head onto the bed, her hot forehead finding relief from the cold stiff sheets.

"Beth is playing her part," he said. *"There is nothing you can do for her, except pray for her. This is just the beginning; have faith, Remne. Now you must let me go; my work here is done and I wish to join my friends; they are waiting for me."* Henry's thoughts grew weaker and Remne had to concentrate hard to hear his voice.

She raised her head once again and studied Henry's face; not a flicker of life could be seen; he had done his best and now he was leaving her. She would not make him stay any longer; he had earned his rest and as she gently smoothed the sheet in front of his face, she said, *"Thank You, Henry, go with God and be at rest; your work here is indeed over."* As she spoke the monitors in the room gave off a high pitched whine and Remne knew that Henry had drawn his last breath.

"Come, come to me, Angel of Death and show yourself. I can feel your presence. Henry is ready for his journey home," Remne said to the figure that was just beginning to appear from out of the shadows.

"Thank you, Remne," said Death. "His friends are waiting for him; it will not take long. We are but a blink of an eye away from this realm and the next."

Remne looked down at the old man's body and smiled. There was nothing to fear; Death would see Henry safely to his final destination.

"I hear you have quite a battle on, it will be interesting to see the outcome," said Death as she walked over to where Remne was sitting, her robe giving off little beams of light as she walked.

"Do not fear for me, my old friend, your services will not be needed for myself, but be prepared to escort the others to their fiery realm." She patted the elegant hand that had come to rest on her shoulder.

Gazing up at the beautiful angel, Remne wondered why mankind had always depicted her as not only male but as a skeleton in a black robe, when in reality her beauty was beyond compare. Perhaps, if they knew what she really looked like, they would go with her too readily and not cling to life as they were meant to do.

"Take care, Remne, you know I cannot help you, but when your time comes to shake off that mortal shell, at least you know there will be a friendly face waiting for you."

The Angel of Death gently squeezed Remne's shoulder as she spoke.

"Thank you," replied Remne, "but go now before anyone arrives and starts to wonder why I am talking to myself."

As Death started to walk away Remne swung round in her chair to steal a look at the door in case anyone should come in, then she quickly turned back to face the beautiful angel. Death stood there with her arm round Henry's shoulder and Remne smiled warmly at the pair. Henry and Death smiled warmly back, then as suddenly as she arrived, Death and her charge were gone.

Remne straightened up in the chair; she did not feel sad anymore because she knew Henry was going where he longed to go and the beautiful Angel of Death was with him, he was not alone. What she was disturbed about, though, was not having any information about Beth to give Gem.

What were they to do now?

As Remne sat there the door sprang open and she was suddenly surrounded by figures dressed in soft grey as they came hurrying into the room, alerted by the monitor's long final beep; Remne, her good-byes already said, stood up from the chair and made her way out through the open door.

Turning for one last look at Henry's body, she thought about the long sessions they had had, poring over the contents of the Book. She would miss him and his intellectual mind, but as the order's efficient staff started the process of undoing all the equipment and laying out his body, she turned and made her way back to the foyer.

She had to smile though at the thought of Henry hiding the book in Gem's car. All this trouble and it was right under their noses; she found it funny that everyone who knew Gem knew how much she thought of her car.

Well, I suppose it is up to me to make sure I get back safely, she thought because the last thing she wanted was to run into any trouble.

Remne felt a slight tug on her sleeve and turning she found Johan, the senior monk who had shown her in earlier, standing there, shuffling his feet. As she looked down at him he said, "He's gone then." Johan sadly nodded his head as he spoke.

"Yes I am afraid so, but it was what he wanted. Pray for him please, Johan," said Remne, reaching over and patting the old monk on the arm.

"Oh, dat goes vithout saying, Remne," said Johan, his head bobbing away, "you are all in our prayers. Ve know that your vork is perilous unt ve try not to think about zee outcome if you should fail. Let me add dis."

Before he continued he grabbed Remne by the arm and pulled her into the chapel.

It was unused at this time of night and the quietness and solitude was ideal for the mood Remne was in. Small candles burned and Remne could smell the beeswax as the scent drifted round the semi dark chapel. The flickering light brought in and out of focus the beautiful stained glass window and Remne saw the depiction of Jesus carrying a lamb upon his shoulders, surrounded by saints and angels.

Johan saw Remne staring at the window and said, "It is beautiful, ya, I prefer dis God, a God of Peace."

Remne gave her shoulders a little shrug; how could she tell him that now was not the time for a God of Peace? She let Johan escort her to one of the chairs at the back of the chapel and kept her counsel to herself.

Johan waited patiently as she got comfortable on the hard seat, he scooted his bottom along the seat to be closer to her before he continued, "I have been in dis vorld an awful long time unt I have found human nature, being vhat it is, a very complicated affair. Tell a man he can do something and he vill pass it by, tell him he can't then he vill fight tooth and nail until he can. It is the same vith religion, when zee churches ruled zee day, man was told vhat to do and vhen to do it, because he had no choice. It was a violent time. But vhen he had a choice of going to church or not, he did not want to, saying that God can be found anyvhere. This may be so but, *mein Gott*, so can zee Devil, except for one place." As Johan spoke Remne became even more aware of his bobbing head as he emphasised each point with a nod.

"One place and one place only and dat is in zee holy shrines man has built, to keep zee Devil and his minions contained." As Johan stopped speaking, he leant over and took Remne's hand in his, continuing, "Do not think you are fighting diz battle alone, ve are vith you every step of zee vay unt dat goes for all zee brotherhoods. Ve are many houses but ve speak vith one voice unt dat voice is raised in prayer for vhat you unt Gemini are doing. Ve know dat dis is a time of var unt my God of Peace has no place amongst whom you seek. Take care, Remne, I fear for you."

Remne felt the emotion overwhelm her and she leant forward and placed her forehead on Johan's hand. While she was in that position Johan raised his free hand and placed it on top of Remne's head and in Latin he blessed her and all her endeavours. They sat there together, talking quietly about Henry and his life for a while, content in each other's company and then Remne stood up and Johan followed her.

She clasped the small monk to her in a final embrace; bending down, as he was quite a bit smaller, she said, "I must leave now; Gem will be waiting for me. I shall leave Henry's funeral arrangements to you, as you have his final written instructions. Thank you, Johan, for all you have said and done."

Johan released her slowly and as he raised his head to look at Remne, she could see his lined face creased with worry. As she made her way out of the door of the chapel she noticed Johan trailing along after her as if his age had finally caught up with him; his shoulders were slumped and Remne was suddenly upset to be leaving him in this frame of mind.

As Remne walked along the passage back the way she had come she could hear a murmur of voices up ahead and when she entered the foyer there before her stood what looked like all the monks from the order. Remne was amazed that so many were up at this hour and as she walked towards them they turned from their individual groups and massed together as a whole.

They stood silently before her; a sea of faces seemed to watch her every move, some faces were full of hope and faith but others, she noticed, were filled with fear and uncertainty. As she approached they all turned towards her and knelt on the cold hard floor; as one, they lowered their heads in deference to her.

She could hear the gentle clicking of rosary beads and the soft murmuring of prayers as they knelt before her. Remne looked over her shoulder at Johan; drawing him close to her, she bent down and whispered in his ear, "What are they doing, Johan? Why are they here?"

"I'm sorry, Remne, but dis is a small order unt vord gets out; they know you are someone special unt dat you belong to a higher power," said Johan, his brow creasing in concern as he looked at his fellow monks.

"I hope that is all they know," replied Remne.

"Oh trust me ont dat, your secret is known only to a very select few." Johan moved in front of her and was about to clap his hands to disperse the kneeling monks, but Remne stopped him with a small tug on his robe.

Turning to see what she wanted, Johan was surprised by what Remne said, his expression changing to pleasure at her words. "Let me have a moment with them, Johan," said Remne and he politely stepped to one side, his small head nodding continuously. "Thank you all for the honour that you have bestowed upon me," she began, "but I cannot go on my journey without telling you that if it was not for your faith and love, we would feel very alone in this task. I have faith. Faith that mankind will prevail and that as long as there is one spark of human decency left in this beautiful world that God has created, then all is not lost. You do not know me but I know you. I can look into your hearts, each and every one of you."

This caused a stir amongst them and she could see some of them looking at one another; she could hear the shuffling of their feet, but all went quiet when Remne held up her hand and continued, "Yes, I can look into your hearts. Blessed are you for you have not been found wanting, your faith will sustain you and me through all the difficult times to come. Now go and pray for me, brothers and pray for my companions, for their tasks are more difficult than mine. Thank you, one and all."

Johan's head was nodding away as he walked up to Remne; raising his eyes to her face, he said, "Sometimes, Remne, it comes down to the little things; it is not alvays enough to think you are holy, you have to live it, breathe it unt let it fill your life till all those dark corners of doubt are vanquished. Zat is vhat you have done tonight; zee brothers will have taken on a new lease of life, for it is not enough to just pray for someone, it is to be shown you are needed as well, unt diz is vhat you have done, my lamb. They now feel they are part of de fight; trust me they vill go out into the community unt zay vill spread the word."

"Good," said Remne. "I thought they needed a bit of a pep talk."

As she was about to leave, she staggered and leant against the doorframe; she would have fallen if Johan had not caught her and steadied her. "Vat is the matter, my little one, are you not vell?" Three of the younger monks, their eyes radiant with their zeal, came running to assist Remne, but Johan stood like a sentinel in front of her and before they could touch her, he said kindly, "Go; shoo … go about your duties; I vill see to our guest." And stepping away from the pair, the three young men obeyed his orders and left in silence.

"I'm okay, it's just that I came over a bit peculiar and I fear it has something to do with Gem. She is in grave danger at the moment," said Remne, clasping her hands to her head.

Johan stood helplessly and watched as Remne ground the balls of her hands into the sockets of her eyes. His fingers moved swiftly over his rosary; his lips moved but no words came out as he silently prayed for Gem's safe delivery.

"Gem, Gem, what is happening to you?" whispered Remne as she leant against the door.

She could hear the soft click of Johan's rosary beads and as she took her hands away from her face to glance about the empty foyer, the feeling of death washed over her, and she sank to the ground, her legs giving way from under her. Johan was beside himself with worry and his head nodded uncontrollably as he tried to raise her to her feet. Remne sank her head to the floor and lay there, bent over double, for a few minutes.

"Tell me, Remne, vhat has happened? Vhat can I do? *Mein Gott, mein Gott*, I feel so helpless. Answer me, Remne!" said Johan, tugging at her sleeve, his Austrian accent becoming more pronounced as he became more agitated.

Slowly Remne raised her head and Johan could see her expression had changed from one of horror to one of joy; the tears that ran down her face were tears of happiness.

"I'm sorry, Johan, but I thought for one awful minute it was Gem's death I felt, but I was wrong." As she clambered to her feet she continued, "Gem is alive and well, but the death I felt was by her hand; it has started.

Gem has come into her own and may God help those who get in her way."

When she finally looked at Johan, the blood had drained completely from his face and as his little head nodded away his shaking right hand crossed himself while his trembling left hand clicked through his rosary. Remne, seeing the state of the little man, took both of his hands in hers and said, "Do not fall at the first hurdle, Johan. Death is the only certainty in this fight and let it be theirs and not ours. I will not waste my tears or my prayers on those who die; they choose the path they lead. There are things you do not know and it is better for you not to know, except this one thing I will show you."

Remne pushed the monk away from her and walked around the foyer, checking to see if they were indeed alone and as she walked back to where Johan was standing she extended her wings to their fullest extent. Johan fell to his knees and covered his head with his hands; as Remne walked up to him, her wings beating with a steady rhythm, she heard him say, "No, no, I am not vorthy to look upon you. I am a mere mortal and full of sin. No, I am not vorthy."

"For goodness sake, Johan, you are the holiest person I know and I know a few. Look at me and never doubt what we are fighting for again. I do not like to show or use my wings; it is not the reason why I am here. My gifts, as you know, lie in reading men's hearts. I can read yours, Johan and it tells me that you are going to get to your feet and be the inspiration that your order expects. They look to you for guidance; you have seen that God loves you and is fighting for you, so rise, Johan, before I lose patience with you," said Remne with humour in her words.

Johan slowly got back on his feet but kept his head bowed; Remne was forced to lean towards him and tilt his head so that their eyes met. Johan's eyes widened as they took in the sight before him; he could not help but put out his hand and run it down the soft feathery edge of Remne's wings.

As soon as his hand dropped to his side Remne closed her wings; like a penitent Johan stood before her, his hands clasped together, his little head nodding as he said, "I am sorry, Remne, you did right to chastise me. I know now vhat is expected of me; go now unt join Gemini, unt I and my brother's vill continue to pray for you. Forgive me for my lapse in faith, it vill never happen again, but I must pray for those poor departed souls, may they rest in peace." Johan took Remne's hand and kissed it.

"Amen and thank you, Johan; now let me go, I have to get back to Gem," said Remne, making for the door. Remne pulled it open and stepped out onto the wide veranda; as she readied herself for the dash out into the rain back to Gem's car, Johan called out her name.

As she turned to face him he thrust something into her hand, saying as he did, "This vas meant for you; I vas told to give it to you vhen the time was right and I think now is that time." With a final nod of his head he raised his hand and gave her a final blessing and then turning swiftly, he closed the door.

It was almost dawn and Remne could see the first rays of sunlight appearing on the horizon as she dashed through the rain back to the car. As she sat in the driver's seat, she opened her wet hand to see what Johan had given her. There, lying dry and sparkling was the jet rosary that she had seen Johan using earlier. She knew it was his only possession; he had owned it since he had first entered the order as a young man. Remne was very touched by the gift, but her concerns lay with what Gem had found out and what to do about Beth. So slipping the rosary safely into her pocket, Remne started the V8 engine and carefully headed the Stag back to York.

Chapter 23

Gem stood at the window and watched as Remne backed the Stag slowly into the parking spot outside the house. She could hear, even through the double glazing, the sound of the car's powerful engine as Remne applied too much pressure to the accelerator as she reversed. She watched as Remne clambered out of the car and ran round to open the boot. Her head disappeared for some minutes and Gem was at a loss as to what she could be up to.

As if on cue Remne reappeared, holding a large package in her arms and proceeded to stagger up the steps to the front door. Gem did not move as she heard Remne enter the house; it felt as if she was rooted to the spot.

Gem had left the door on the latch in readiness for Remne's return. A casual passer-by who might happen to glance in at the window would have seen a young woman standing in a relaxed pose, gazing back out at the world.

The reality of the situation was much different.

Gem's mind was in a whirl and all the muscles in her body felt stretched and taut. Seeing Remne return, she realised that she had been in the same position since arriving back at the house two hours earlier. Remne hurried into the lounge as best she could, considering the weight of the parcel she was carrying and seeing Gem standing there with her back to her, she cried out excitedly, "I've got it, Gem! I've got it!" When Remne received no reply from her, she dumped the parcel on the settee and walked over to where Gem was standing.

Gem gazed vacantly out through the window down onto the street, but it was as if her eyes were seeing a different view altogether.

Remne leant her bottom against the desk just to one side of where Gem was standing; folding her arms, she waited until Gem spoke.

"I failed," Gem finally said.

"What do you mean, you failed! What happened? And who died?" replied Remne, trying to get a grip on what Gem was talking about.

Gem turned her head slightly and looked at Remne out of the corner of her eye.

It is as if she does not want to have full eye contact with me, thought Remne, and suddenly smiling, she said, "Oh, do behave, Gem, I know what I shall see if I looked into your heart. Nothing! You haven't got one!"

Gem swung round to face Remne, the anger plainly showing on her face, but before she could raise her hand to strike out, Remne quickly grabbed both of Gem's arms and shook her gently, saying as she did so, "I'm joking Gem, stop being so hard on yourself. I was terrified earlier; I thought something awful had happened to you, but I did feel someone die. Who was it?"

Remne saw the anger disappear from Gem's eyes and she could feel the tension easing away from her. Gem felt herself relaxing in Remne arms, the feeling that had sustained her since she had come home draining from her.

It was as if she had been in a trance; she could still see Rupert sliding to the floor, his arterial blood pumping from his dying body. She remembered the surprised look on his face, his eyes searching hers as if for answers, just as her sword cleaved him in half. She had seen his lips moving and Gem hoped he was finally asking for forgiveness, but it was just one more final obscenity.

Gem shook her head as if to clear it and looking at Remne, she shrugged off her restraining hands, saying as she did so, "Always the clever one, aren't you? If you must know it was Rupert who died and if you want to know any more details, he died by my hand when I sliced him in two and to make matters worse he died cursing my name."

"Please don't tell me you are wasting your time mourning him; the Rupert you knew died a long time ago. That was but a shell of the man he used to be. Trust me, Gem, he was not worth your sympathy," Remne replied in a matter-of-fact voice as she walked over to the settee.

"Yes, I suppose you are right, I did give him every opportunity to redeem himself and he spat it back at me … literally," said Gem, raising her eyebrow in remembrance.

"Well, there you are then. Let's forget about him; if he did not give you any information we must move on to the next problem and try to solve that," said Remne, beckoning Gem over to where she was standing. She pointed down at the parcel lying on the settee cushions.

"Ta daaa," said Remne, flourishing her arms about like a conjurer performing a trick.

"Ta daaa, what?" said Gem, looking down at the parcel with a blank look on her face.

"Oh, Gem, sometimes you amaze me," replied Remne as she started to undo the parcel, "and by the way, do you mind taking off that sword? You look as though you mean business and it is a bit unnerving."

Gem removed her sword from between her shoulder blades and placed it on the carpet to one side. Then she sat down on the settee on the other side of the parcel and helped Remne to untie the strings, suddenly realising what it contained.

Their fingers tore at the stiff paper and both women gave a happy cry of recognition when the Book was finally revealed.

Gem ran her fingers fondly over the leather bindings; looking over at Remne, she said, "I'm very sorry; what happened with Henry? Did he manage to tell you anything?"

Gem continued to run her fingers over the Book.

"Well, he did and he didn't," Remne replied and in answer to Gem's quizzical stare she continued, "He told me where he had put the Book, but he also told me there was nothing we could do to help Beth. Apparently it is her destiny, as much as all that is happening is yours and mine."

Remne reached over and placed her hand on Gem's shoulder, saying as she did so, "Perhaps that is why the Book has come back into our possession, maybe we can find some answers. Also, you will never guess where Henry hid it." Remne laughed as she removed her hand from Gem's shoulder.

"No, I can't guess," she said, "because if I could there would have been no point in you going to see Henry in the first place and what you might have done to my car, I shudder to think. I must have been mad to let you borrow it!"

Remne could not control her laughter and the tears ran down her face as she tried to get the words out, sputtering, "That's it … don't you see … Henry … hid … it … in …"

"Come on, spit it out, I haven't got all day," said Gem, still not amused.

Remne tried again, and managing badly to get some semblance of control, she spluttered, "It ... was in ... the boot of your car!" And with that she fell back on the cushions and laughed until her sides hurt, which finally forced her to stop. Taking in a large lungful of air, she managed to get control of herself, resorting to the occasion snort when she looked at Gem's face.

"I fail to see what is so funny," said Gem, rising from the settee. "So he hid it in the boot of my car, so what?"

"But that's just it," replied Remne, smiling. "Everyone knows how devoted you are to that car; it should have been the first place we looked."

"Oh, ha bloody ha. Is that all he said? How was he when you left him? Is he being looked after all right? Perhaps I should pop up and see him," said Gem, noticing that the humour had disappeared from Remne's face. She sat back down and waited for Remne to say what was in her eyes.

"He died, Gem. I just managed to get to him before he slipped away, but don't worry about him, he was collected by an old friend of mine. I'll tell you what was weird: I had an unusual experience with all the brothers. It was as if they all knew who I was and what my mission was about. Mind you, it was very comforting to know they are all there praying for us," said Remne. Remembering the conversation she had with Johan, she put her hand in her pocket and pulled out the jet rosary he had given her.

"What's that?" said Gem, leaning over and picking up the rosary from Remne's open hand.

"Brother Johan gave it to me, to keep me safe I assume; he pushed it into my hand just as I was leaving," replied Remne, suddenly serious and with a touch of sadness in her voice.

"It's very beautiful, it's jet, isn't it?" said Gem, gazing intently at the beads.

"Yes, I think it is," said Remne, leaning back on the cushions.

As she looked over at Gem, she was surprised to see that Gem was studying the beads quite intently. "Quick, get me the Bible," said Gem, flapping her hand over towards the desk.

"What have you found?" replied Remne, trying to peer across the settee at what Gem was looking at.

"Go, don't fool around, I think I am on to something here," said Gem excitedly.

227

Remne hurried over to the desk and after a few attempts of pulling the drawers open and not finding what she was looking for, she finally succeeded with the bottom drawer and brought the Bible over to where Gem was sitting.

"Right, turn to Revelation chapter 20, verses 1, 2 and 3; what does it say?" said Gem, peering at the beads in her hand.

"It says, 'And I saw an angel come down from heaven, having a key of the bottomless pit and a great chain in his hand. And he laid hold on the dragon, that old serpent, which is the Devil and Satan and bound him for two thousand years and cast him into the bottomless pit and shut him up and set a seal upon him, that he should deceive the nations no more, till the two thousand years should be fulfilled.' Are you telling me that there are numbers written on that rosary?" replied Remne, trying to get closer for a better look, but the large Book between them hampered her movement.

"Yes I am and believe it or not, there are more." As Gem looked over at Remne, her brow crinkled with concern and she added, "Do you think we might find something out about Beth?" Gem's face brightened and she became quite animated, saying a little breathlessly, "That's it, this must be a clue; come on, put the Book on the floor and let's see what else this rosary contains; it's just as well my eyesight is good; these carvings are very small."

Now that there was something to do, Gem's spirits soared; here at last was another piece of the jigsaw and it had fallen into their hands just when she was at her lowest ebb. Gem glanced over at Remne and could see a mirror image of hope and excitement portrayed on her face as well. She watched as Remne heaved the large tome onto the floor and then moved her bottom across the settee until she was close enough to Gem for her to feel the warmth from her body.

Gem felt the need to say something before they continued and as she sat there and watched Remne, she said in a soft voice, "Sorry I was a bit of a pig earlier; it was just that I was so worried about Beth. I tend to forget what everyone else is going through. I don't mean to be so rotten; am I forgiven?"

Remne was slightly taken aback by Gem's apology and she sat there briefly for a moment, trying to think of something appropriate to say, but all she could manage was, "What? Oh, don't worry about that, I'm used to your funny little ways and I'm learning how to duck when you lose your temper." Remne laughed and looking at Gem's contrite face, she added, "The past is over; let's concentrate on what we have to do now and when we've finished I shall go and make us some scrambled eggs and toast, because I am absolutely famished. So come on, get on with it." She nudged Gem playfully in the ribs.

"Right then," continued Gem, "chapter 12, verses 7, 8, and 9."

Remne's fingers flicked through the pages and when she finally found the passage, she read aloud, "'And there was war in heaven: Michael and his angels fought against the dragon; and the dragon fought and his angels and prevailed not; neither was their place found any more in heaven. And the great dragon was cast out, that old serpent, called the Devil and Satan, which deceiveth the whole world: he was cast out into the earth and his angels were cast out with him.' Well, we know that, what else have you got?" Remne caught hold of the bottom of the rosary and peered at the carvings.

"Chapter 13, verse 4," said Gem, squinting as her eyes ran over the beads.

"'And they worshipped the dragon which gave power unto the beast: and they worshipped the beast, saying, who is like unto the beast? Who is able to make war with him?' Well, we are, for a start," said Remne, glancing up from the Bible.

Gem frowned at Remne's comments and as she looked across at her, she saw Remne starting to fidget, a sure sign she was getting restless, so straightening her back and letting out a small sigh, she said to Remne, "I'll tell you what, you go and start the eggs and the coffee and I shall look at a few more of these; how does that sound?"

"Sounds good to me," replied Remne, placing the Bible on Gem's lap and getting to her feet, she made her way across the lounge and down the hall to the kitchen.

Gem could hear Remne clattering about as she searched the kitchen for the appropriate pots and pans. She concentrated on reading the remaining beads to see if more clues came to light now that Remne was occupied elsewhere. Gem studied each bead in turn; they did not all have carvings on them, but she found one and turning to the Bible on her lap, she ran her finger down until she came to the chapter she required, saying out loud so that Remne could hear her, "Chapter 19 verse 15: 'And out of his mouth goeth a sharp sword, that with it he should smite the nations: and he shall rule them with a rod of iron: and he treadeth the winepress of the fierceness and wrath of Almighty God.'

"Oh and here's another one, Chapter 21 verse 4, 5, and 6: 'And God shall wipe away all tears from their eyes and there shall be no more death, neither sorrow, nor crying, neither shall there be any more pain: for the former things are passed away. And he that sat upon the throne said, Behold, I make all things new. And he said unto me, Write: for these words are true and faithful. And he said unto me, it is done. I am Alpha and Omega, the beginning and the end. I will give unto him that is athirst of the fountain of the water of life freely.' That's all, there are no more; so what do you make of that?" said Gem, her voice loud and clear so that it carried into the kitchen.

Remne popped her head round the door of the lounge and said, "I'm not sure at the moment; we have to sit and go through them all again. In the meantime I shall bring in the sustenance; do you want sugar in your coffee?"

Gem was still concentrating on the beads, but she lifted her head at Remne's question and answered, "No and no milk either and I like my toast cold and then the butter put on."

As Gem was talking Remne straightened from her pose of peeking around the door, to standing, with her hand on one hip and the other hand supporting her weight on the door's edge. When Gem had finished speaking she could see by the look on Remne's face that she was perhaps going too far.

"I'm sorry, you did ask and I am a bit picky when it comes to toast; I don't like it all soggy."

"And there sayeth a woman who has just cleaved a man in two, a bit picky indeed," said Remne as she turned and flounced out of the room, the long twisting curls of her hair winding about her like squirming snakes.

All Gem managed was to mouth, "Well, you did ask," at Remne's retreating back. Remne returned, carrying a large tray and as Gem dragged the coffee table over, Remne placed her heavy burden down as a large sigh escaped her pouting lips. Gem had not realised how hungry she was and soon demolished the steaming plate of scrambled eggs and toast and as she was just sipping her coffee, Remne said, "Well, was it all to your liking? You didn't seem to have come up for air while you were eating it, so obviously the toast was okay."

Gem looked across at Remne and smiled before she answered, "It was perfect, but now we must get down to some work."

As Gem leant forward she placed her cup on the small table and picked up the beads again.

"I get the distinct feeling we are missing something; perhaps the Book will give us some more clues, because to be honest with you we are no nearer finding Beth than we were from the start," said Gem, running her hand through her short curls.

Remne started to randomly flick through the Book, then stopping at a page she started to read, "'He keepeth the paths of judgement and preserveth the way of his saints. Then shalt thou understand righteousness and judgement and equity: yea, every good path. Discretion shall preserve thee, understanding shall keep thee: To deliver thee from the way of the evil man, from the man that speaketh forward things. Who leave the paths of uprightness to walk in the ways of darkness; who rejoice to do evil and delight in the forwardness of the wicked. Whose ways are crooked and they forward in their paths. To deliver thee from the strange woman, even from the stranger which flattereth with her words. Which forsaketh the guide of her youth and forgetteth the covenant of her God. For her house inclineth unto death and her paths unto the dead. None that go unto her return again, neither take they hold of the paths of life. That thou mayest walk in the way of good men and keep the paths of righteous. For the unpright shall dwell in the land and the perfect shall remain in it. But the wicked shall be cut off from the earth and the transgressors shall be rooted out of it.'"

Gem sat upright, suddenly interested in what Remne was saying; leaning towards her, she could not quite keep the excitement out of her voice as she said, "What was that bit about delivering from the strange woman?"

And as Remne read the piece to her again Gem leapt to her feet, exclaiming as she did so, "Oh what a fool I am! We should go to Cybil's house; I forgot to tell you that Cybil and this mysterious Adam are one and the same."

Remne sprang to her feet and in a voice barely containing her anger she grabbed hold of Gem's arm and said, "And you just forgot to mention this small shred of information?"

Gem looked at the hand clutching her arm and realised that Remne had every reason to be mad; raising her eyes to look into Remne's scowling face, she replied, "Oops! Look, I'm sorry there was so much going on and what with not getting any more information about Beth, it just went clean out of my head."

Remne let her hand fall to her side and sat back down on the settee, her face still showing her outrage, but she said nothing in reply to Gem's words.

Gem flopped down on the settee beside her, but she could see by the set of Remne's shoulders that she was barely able to contain her anger. Remne's long hair concealed most of her face and Gem had to lean forward to catch a glimpse of Remne's angry features.

Gem tentatively raised her hand and pulled the soft curls away from Remne's face and as she did so she said softly, "I'm a complete idiot, I know, but please believe me, I genuinely forgot, what with you bringing the Book home and the rosary and … the … lovely scrambled eggs … and … toast."

As Gem's voice trailed away Remne turned to look at her and she could not help but smile at Gem's stumbling apology, but the smile did not reach her eyes; turning fully to face Gem, she said, "This is not a one man band, Gem. You do not do anything without talking things over with me. I cannot tell you the danger we are both in and you might feel invincible, but don't forget you are in a mortal body and can still die."

Gem tried to shake off Remne's hand, which had suddenly clutched hers and Remne knew this was not what Gem wanted to hear. Remne knew by the sudden set of Gem's features that she did in fact feel herself invincible and catching Gem looking down at her sword, Remne pushed her hand away.

"They do say pride comes before a fall; let's hope that the price is not too high for your foolishness." Rising to her feet, Remne gathered the plates and left Gem sitting on the settee, her face a mask against her true emotions.

Gem wanted to scream and shout and shake some spirit into Remne; she always wanted to stay on the safe side, but this was not the time. Yes she did feel invincible, but she was also aware of the dangers she had to face; otherwise, what would happen when she finally met the Demon?

"I'll tell you what," she wanted to scream, "because of your negative attitude, I will be thinking of all the things I shouldn't be thinking."

Jumping to her feet, Gem decided that's what she was going to tell Remne: get it over and done with. She would go to the kitchen and sort this nonsense out once and for all …

Gem swung the lounge door open with such force that she had to make a grab for it to prevent it from hitting the wall. As she started to pull the heavy door back into position the doorbell rang. Realising that Remne had no intention of coming out of the kitchen, Gem made her way over to the front door as it rang again.

Her anger was still bubbling as she opened the door, but she could feel it drain away as she saw who was standing on the doorstep. As she flung herself into Nathan's arms all he could manage was, "Hello you," before his face was covered in kisses. Gem wrapped her long leg around his and pulled his body closer to her; she could see his eyes widen at her strength.

Gem ushered Nathan into the house and as she closed the front door he tried unsuccessfully to pull her into his arms again.

Placing both hands on the front of his coat, Gem whispered, "Not yet. Remne is here and we have some news about Beth; come in the kitchen and we can tell you together." Taking hold of Nathan's hand, Gem guided him along the hallway to the kitchen. They found Remne sitting on a stool at the centre island, pouring herself a glass of white wine.

Surprisingly, to Nathan, she looked as if she meant to finish the bottle all by herself. "I'll get a couple more glasses, shall I?" said Gem, moving away from Nathan and going to the cupboard and bringing out two extra glasses.

"Please yourself," was the only reply Remne gave as she tipped more wine into her glass. "Not for me, thanks," Nathan said. "This is just a flying visit; I'm here to visit a murder scene that we think is linked to what is going on. Perhaps you knew him, Dr Rupert Winsmore?"

Remne and Gem traded furtive glances as Gem poured herself a glass of wine, but Nathan continued talking, oblivious to the sudden exchange between the two women. "In fact I have come straight up from a meeting in London with the commissioner of police," and he stood there, ticking off the names on his fingers, "the archbishop of Canterbury, Rowan Williams; the Most Reverend Cormac Murphy-O'Connor and if not him then his successor; Archbishop Sentamu of York; various MI5 and MI6 agents; and last but not least, the minister for home affairs, who also introduced me to someone I would like you to meet. He is in the car, but I thought it best to come in first and explain things."

Remne and Gem remained silent while Nathan explained as much as he could about the meeting.

"This problem has a lot of the church hierarchy greatly concerned, that's why they called the meeting. The chief of police was less than impressed when he was told about the number of dead bodies that have started to pop up all over the place. So MI5 and 6 have decided a complete news black-out is essential to stop people panicking."

Gem watched as Remne poured the remainder of the wine into her glass, taking little notice of what Nathan was talking about.

She wanted to discuss their argument but couldn't with Nathan in the house.

All Gem could do was lean up against the units and sip her wine and nod occasionally when Nathan said something, but her thoughts were entirely elsewhere and by the look on Remne's face so were hers.

They were both unaware that Nathan had stopped talking altogether and was glancing at each of them in turn. "What's wrong with both of you, what's happened?" he asked. "Gem said something about Beth." Concern was written all over his face. Suddenly he felt out of place and it was as plain as the nose on his face that there had been words between these two.

He could see Gem slumped against the side unit with a sulky look on her face and her hands rammed into her trouser pockets, as if afraid at what she would do with them if they were exposed; even her wine now remained untouched.

As for Remne, well, she looked no better as Nathan watched her swallowed the last of her wine. The silence between them lasted only a few seconds, but it was palpable and intense; with an embarrassed cough Nathan turned to Gem and said, "I want a favour from you, Gem. There is a guy I don't want anyone knowing about. Booking him into a hotel is out of the question. So will you put him up for one night? He's a lovely chap, a bit of an authority on church antiquity that the government has brought in to help clarify some of our problems."

Nathan bobbed his head down to catch Gem's eye and she turned to him with a smile. "Of course we will put him up, won't we, Rem?"

But Remne remained mute to Gem's question and continued to study her empty glass. Gem turned her attention away from her and moved from the unit to come and stand close to Nathan. She drank in his smell and her eyes feasted on him as if she wanted to remember every little detail.

He laughed at her intensity, pulled her to him in a quick embrace and placed a well-aimed kiss on the top of her nose. "So what's all this about Beth?" said Nathan as he tried his best to kiss Gem's full lips.

Before Gem could speak Remne broke her silence, ignoring the animosity between them, Gem, surprised at what she was hearing, turned round in Nathan's arms to face her.

She listened with amazement as Remne lied, "Oh, it's nothing really. We thought Beth was missing but it seems we were mistaken; she has just gone somewhere safe for a few days. Down the coast I believe; anyway, it's nothing to worry about."

Gem felt Nathan give her body a little squeeze before he said, "Well, that's all right then, one less to worry about. Now you girls stay safely indoors, leave all this running about to the professionals." Giving Gem another little squeeze, he continued, "Do you hear me, Gem? I know you … you hot head." He made her shiver involuntarily as he kissed the back of her neck.

Gem was staring at Remne with such intensity, but she merely smiled back, saying, "Well, you had better get your guest; otherwise he might think he is sleeping in the car for the night. Oh and by the way, it's nice to see you again, Nathan, even under these circumstances."

Happy now that their clash seemed to have resolved itself, Nathan said, "It's nice to see you as well, Remne, but I must admit you both look rather tired." Putting his head on the side, he looked into Gem's face and said, "Haven't you been sleeping well?" Catching Gem's small shake of the head, he gave her another squeeze and added, "Well, Remne's right, I shall have to go and get your guest, but try not to worry, Gem, we have everything under control."

With that he let go of Gem and turned her to face him, saying, "Seems as though I'm off again. Hopefully it will not be for too long and then we can spend more time together. I am owed plenty of leave plus doing this job 24/7."

As Nathan spoke he gently stroked her face, still amazed with himself that she could have such effect on him.

Remne's polite cough brought him back to reality and this time he planted a kiss squarely on Gem's lips and felt her responding back with equal passion. My God, how he wanted this woman, but his job was far too important, as the end result could mean a good promotion.

"Well, I shall be off then; don't worry, I will see myself out." As he departed he gave Gem a slap on the bottom. He said a quick farewell to Remne and, with a wave of his hand, left the kitchen. Gem sat down on one of the stools next to Remne and put her head in her hands, resting her elbows on the unit top.

She looked at Remne and said, "Are we talking now? I am so sorry for what I did and I didn't get the chance to tell you before Nathan arrived … you know … to apologise and all that." Gem dropped her hand from her face and reached over to take Remne's hand, adding, "You and I always seem to end up fighting; why is that, do you think?"

"Because we are so much alike in most things and because you are a stubborn obstinate mule, which is totally unlike me."

Gem snorted with laughter and the pain she was feeling at Nathan's departure was eased somewhat by their close camaraderie.

Remne patted Gem's hand and said, "I'll tell you what you can do, you go upstairs and draw yourself a nice hot bath and soak for a good hour while I see to our guest. You must be exhausted."

"No more than you, we have both been up all night, but to be honest I could do with a nice hot bath and get out of these clothes; it was a wonder Nathan didn't mention the state they were in."

"I'm sure he only had eyes for you; now go and get yourself upstairs before you frighten our guest," said Remne, gathering the empty glasses.

As Gem stood she looked down at Remne and asked, "Why did you say that about Beth?"

Remne sat still for a few seconds before she finally answered, "Now was not the time to tell him; it would only put him in danger. We have to do this on our own."

"Thank you for thinking of him," said Gem as she walked towards the kitchen door; as she put her hand on the handle, she turned and asked, "Everything is all right, isn't it, Rem? You would tell me if anything was wrong."

"Of course I would, silly, now go and have your bath, you are starting to smell," replied Remne, waving her hand in front of her face.

Laughing, Gem walked down the hallway and ran up the stairs two at a time, eager now to divest herself of her clothes and slide into the hot steamy water.

Remne listened to Gem's movements above and waited for the doorbell to ring.

Now was the time.

Now it was happening and now it was her time. She had to be brave and see it all through to its fullest conclusion. The ringing of the doorbell interrupted her reverie and getting quickly to her feet she swiftly made her way along the hallway, ran into the lounge and swiftly kicked Gem's sword under the settee, away from prying eyes. She decided to leave the Book on the floor and move it at a more convenient time.

She gave the room one last look round to make sure everything appeared normal, then quickly left the lounge and made her way to the front door.

Remne leant her head against the cool wood, summoning her courage and giving herself time to steady her heartbeat and then before she could change her mind, she quickly straightened her shoulders and opened the heavy door.

There before her stood a tall elderly man with a small goatee beard and a mop of glorious white hair. He had wire rimmed spectacles that covered his merry blue eyes. His smile was infectious and Remne had trouble acquainting the man with the vision that had come to her when Nathan had been telling them about his meeting.

She could not help but smile when he said, "Hello, thank you so much for putting me up for the night; my name is Reynard Holt and I am very pleased to meet you. You are Gemini, I presume. All Nathan told me was that you were very beautiful and he was not wrong."

Remne held out her hand and prayed her words carried conviction as she said, "Hello, how nice to meet you. Yes, I am Gemini; won't you come in? You must be exhausted after your long journey."

As her hand closed round that of Reynard's, all her fears were confirmed and she had trouble holding onto his hand.

Chapter 24

The drive up had been long and laborious, but he didn't mind. This was the last time he would be trusted and he would not fail. He had been forgiven his little lapse with the corpses, seeing as how they had been dead for so long.

The oncoming headlights dazzled him and hurt his eyes. He had been driving for a long time; raising his hand, he rubbed them, trying to ease the pressure behind them. His hand travelled down onto his face. It felt dirty and stubbly; he hadn't shaved for a long while, a fact which annoyed him. He liked to look clean and smart and out loud he said to himself, "Cleanliness is next to godliness."

He had read that on a toilet wall somewhere and the hilarity of it made him snigger every time he said it.

He suddenly became serious as he thought back over what Adam had told him to do. This was special, they had managed to track these Ones down and it was up to him to eliminate them. Now that the doctor was out of the way, he would show Adam that he was capable of following instructions. He had watched and learnt so many things and it was now his time to show what he could do, given the chance.

He slowed the car down, searching in the dark for somewhere to pull in, as he was dying to take a leak. The coffee he had drunk at that all night roadside café had finally worked its way through him and he was starting to get desperate. His headlights picked out a lay-by up ahead and he manoeuvred the big car into it and quickly pulled up the handbrake and undid his seatbelt. Not bothering to turn the car off, he opened the door and slid out, undoing his flies at he went. He was careful not to let the hot steaming liquid go onto his shoes. When he was finished, he fastened his flies once more and climbed back into the car. He took a quick look at his watch to see if he was still on time and was pleased to see that he was.

The blue and white flashing light caught him totally by surprise and he sat there like a rabbit caught in the headlights. The lights from the police car blazed into his car, illuminating the interior.

How he could have been such a fool not to see them coming, he thought. *Mind you they are sneaky buggers, they probably saw me here and slid in behind me and then turned their lights on,* he rationalised.

He took a few deep breaths to steady his himself and waited for the officer to get out. He saw him coming in the side mirror and as the policeman drew level he put his finger on the button and opened his window.

"Yes officer, can I help you?" he asked politely.

"No, it's okay sir, we just thought you might be in need of assistance," answered the officer, who was now bending down to look through his driver's window.

"Thank you for your concern, officer, but I just pulled over to answer my mobile. You know how it is nowadays, I didn't want to break the law so I pulled over and … well there you are," he replied, waggling the phone under the policeman's nose.

"Well, if you are sure you are okay, we'll see you on your way; take care. Have you got far to go?" the officer inquired, backing away from the car.

"No, not far at all but it is a matter of some urgency; thank you for your concern," he replied, smiling up at the officer.

The officer took a step backwards, tipped his hand to his hat in a salute and then returned to his car.

As he edged out into the road the police car turned its lights on again to warn any oncoming traffic to slow down, allowing him to drive onwards to his destination. He watched them every few seconds in his rear view mirror until they turned off at the next intersection and it wasn't until they had gone did he feel the tension finally easing from his body.

Just my luck, he thought, *Can't even take a piss without somebody creeping up on me* and he slammed his hand against the steering wheel in annoyance.

It took him another half an hour to get where he wanted to go and driving up the road, he kept looking at the directions on the piece of paper he held in his hand.

"Not far now, not far now," he sang softly. As he consulted the paper one more time he leant across the passenger seat and scrutinised the name plate on the wooden gates.

"Hi honey, I'm home," he sniggered.

Driving the car slowly up the drive and over the small pebbles gave him enough time to compose himself.

By the time he had parked and clambered out of the car he felt ready, so wiping his free hand down his jacket to smooth the creases, he adjusted his collar and then picked up his overnight bag and knocked on the door.

The door swung inwards and the woman standing before him greeted him with a warm smile, adding, "We are so glad you could make it, Reverend; we have been waiting for you. Your room is available, if you would like to go and freshen up." Margaret pointed to the stairs. "It's number 3," she added and was surprised to see him give a slight shiver.

Seeing that she had noticed his inadvertent shudder at the mention of that number, he smiled and said, "I'm sorry, my dear, but it has been a long drive and I would like to get to my room if you don't mind."

"Certainly not, Reverend and here I am babbling on about nothing when you must be so tired. Would you like a tray brought to your room? It wouldn't be any trouble."

"No, that will not be necessary, I ate on the way. Now if you will excuse me, I will go to my room." Waving his hand about in a rough outline of a cross, he hurried up the stairs and along the corridor in the direction that Margaret had pointed.

When he had gone Margaret lingered in the downstairs hallway for a minute, gazing up the stairs and wondering. She could not put her finger on the exact reason she felt uneasy, but there it lay like a piece of food in the pit of her stomach that she couldn't digest.

Clergy regularly visited the house as an alternative to a formal religious retreat. Some came just to recharge their batteries while others came silently in the night, like this one, as if ashamed that their faith was slipping away from them. A few days peace and quiet was all it took normally and they went back to their parishes renewed and refreshed. Everybody needed time out from the stress and strains of daily life and the clergy was no exception, but still she wondered.

She heard Lloyd calling from the back parlour and put the thought to the back of her mind and went to join him. "He's arrived then," he said as she entered the room. Lloyd busied himself laying the places for their supper, unaware that Margaret was standing there with a perplexed frown creasing her brow.

Realising at last that she had not moved since she had first entered the room, Lloyd straightened up and stared at Margaret, suddenly fearful. He had to ask, though; he had to know what was wrong, even if he didn't want to hear the answer. He walked unsteadily on legs that had suddenly turned to jelly, but he took a deep breath to fortify himself and carried on until he reached Margaret's side. "What's wrong, my dear? You look a bit shaken. Is it something to do with Grace? Have you heard some news?"

He placed an arm around Margaret's shoulders and before she could say anything, he led her farther into the room. He guided her over to her favourite chair and turned her round, saying, "Sit down and tell me what's wrong; I am starting to get a bit worried." Not wishing to convey to Margaret the extent of his anxiety, he went and sat on his chair on the opposite side of the fireplace.

"I don't know what it is. I just feel a little uneasy. Perhaps I am worrying too much over Grace or Remne as she said she wanted us to call her while she was here." She made a little disparaging noise in her throat before carrying on, "Remne, indeed, where on earth did she get that name from?" Before she continued, a relieved Lloyd leant across and patted her on the knee. "Daft, aren't I?" she said as she wiped the tears that had begun to fall onto her faded cheeks. "It's not as if we didn't know this day would come, but how do you stop yourself from worrying after nurturing a child for so long?"

Lloyd nodded his grey head in agreement as he remembered the sad farewell they had given their beloved daughter the day before. Grace had tried to console them both with words of comfort, but they could see she was eager to be off, even though it broke their hearts; they knew she was right. That other one was a force to be reckoned with, though, and he admitted as much to Margaret as they stood on the doorstep waving good-bye.

Grace had called the girl "Gemini" and she had stumbled into their lives, exhausted and weary, but when she had left she was tall and proud with a mission in her deep blue eyes and with their own beautiful daughter in tow.

There was no need to try and persuade Grace not to go; they knew their time with her was at an end, they could see it in her face. She had looked pale and drawn and the anxiety inside her kept her pacing backwards and forwards during the long wait for Gemini to appear.

Lloyd had only just managed to get her to eat something and then the girl had arrived and Grace was like a mother hen. He remembered asking Margaret the next morning what was bothering her and it was the way she had shrugged her shoulders in that old familiar way and she had laughed, saying how alike the two of them were when they were together.

Grace had kept them out of Gemini's presence for some reason and it was not until the two girls stood in the hallway readying themselves for their departure that Lloyd had seen the similarity also. Grace hurried Gemini out of the door and as she stood on the step she took both of them in a hug and whispered something in her mother's ear, then gently planted a kiss on her cheek.

When the car was out of sight they turned to go back inside, but Lloyd took hold of Margaret's arm and said, "What's going on, Margy? I saw what passed between you and Grace."

But Margaret had only smiled and shook her head and then reaching down, she took his hand and together they walked back into the house; nothing more was mentioned. Now, though, as he looked across at her, he felt she was holding something back and in all the years they had been married, it was the first time he had suspected her of not being honest with him.

"Well, no news is good news, or so they say," said Margaret, rising to her feet. "And we shan't have any supper at all if I don't go out there and dish it up." As she smiled down at Lloyd she held close to her the feeling that all was not right.

He wanted to get this over and done with. It was just a number; he could have asked for another room, but that would only have created more suspicion and the old woman had already looked at him in a funny way. No, he would stick to the agenda, but he must clean up first, these whiskers were driving him mad. He averted his eyes from the number on the door; it didn't do to tempt fate, not that he needed it with this job, it should be over and done within a minute. As he entered the room he noticed the small reading light at the side of the bed was switched on in readiness for his arrival. The bed covers had been turned down and the room smelt faintly of flowers, but what he wanted was the bathroom. He had especially asked for the room with the en suite, as he did not want to share his toilet facilities.

He laid his bag on the bed and proceeded to pull out what he needed. Everything was new. He had purchased what he required on the way up. The electric shaver was ideal and he tore open the package with the batteries and placed them inside, leaving the razor on one side of the bed. Next he got out the baby wipes that he used to clean himself and laid the container beside the razor. He proceeded until he had arranged everything he needed side by side. Next were the plastic bags, one laid on top of each of the items he had put in a row; as he finished using that item he placed it inside the plastic bag and put it back into his holdall.

Eventually there would be nothing to show that he had ever been here, not a single hair, whisker, or fingerprint. He looked at himself in the mirror and was pleased with what he saw. The hairline had receded a little too much for his liking, but the rest of his general appearance was presentable.

It wasn't a bad face, a little on the long side but hey, you couldn't have everything. He would have liked to have been taller if he could have chosen, but anyway it had never hindered him in what he had to do. So all in all he liked what he saw in the mirror. He twisted his face into a semblance of a smile; he had already been down the corridor and checked to see if there were any more residents, but the place was empty.

Just like they said, they had been closed for a few days and had just started taking bookings again, and he was their first.

Lucky me, he thought.

He turned the light off and went and stood in the moonlight that was filtering through the trees outside, making leaf patterns on the carpet as it came shining through the bay window. He did not want to sit down anywhere, as that would leave some evidence of himself, so he stood and waited patiently until the time was right to make his move.

Lloyd gathered the plates and took them out into the small kitchen while Margaret went and sat back down in her favourite chair. She could hear Lloyd humming a little tune and she smiled to herself as she waited for him to bring in the cup of tea he had promised her. She leant forward and looked at the clock on the high mantelshelf; it was ten past nine, it would soon be time for bed, but the feeling of unease had not left her.

Was it to do with Grace?

She knew she worried excessively sometimes, but what else does a mother do?

Mother … it had always sounded so right. They had practically given up ever having a child and were in their late forties when they had been

243

offered the baby girl. They had moved here when Grace had been a toddler. They knew she was different and had not questioned the fact. They had just loved her.

She closed her eyes and listened to Lloyd rattling her best china as he made the tea.

She felt a small draft circling about her ankles; *That's strange,* she thought, *that only happens when the door ...* and as her eyes flew open, the hand descended upon her mouth.

"Stay perfectly still," he whispered, "otherwise you will die right now, do you understand? Just nod if you do." His breath was cold upon her neck.

He did not have to lean down far to talk to her and he was pleased to see the fear already starting to form in her faded brown eyes.

"I'm going to take my hand away your face and when I do I want you to remain quiet. I am going to stand over there," he said, pointing to the far corner of the room that was in the shadow, "and if you cry out I shall slit your husband's throat where he stands, do you understand?"

She did not trust herself to speak so she just nodded again and watched as he secreted himself in the corner of the room, waiting for Lloyd to enter.

As if on cue Lloyd came in from the kitchen with a small tray of tea things and went and stood before her, but the cups started to rattle when he saw the look on her face. "Oh dear God, what is the matter?" he asked. "You look as though you have seen a ghost."

Turning to put the tray on the table, he saw the small man slide out of the shadows and come towards him.

Lloyd backed up until his legs hit the chair he had not long vacated and feeling the strength draining from him, he sank down into its cosy softness.

No words escaped his lips for the horror he was now feeling and as he quickly glanced over at Margaret he saw the same look mirrored on her features. The grotesque little man manoeuvred around the table to stand between them; Lloyd noticed he had a holdall in his left hand.

He no longer wore the dog collar and Margaret knew she had been right about her feelings. It was not Grace! It was this despicable little creature who was to blame for her feeling of unease. She remembered now, it was when he blessed her and made the sign of the cross, or attempted to.

It was as though he didn't know what he was doing; she had just put it down to him being so tired. How wrong she had been. They watched as he put the bag on the table and extracted from it several plastic bags and a long knife.

"We have nothing of value in the house," Lloyd said, adding bravely, "we have no savings here, but I can get you something from the cash point."

Margaret leant over, clasped his hand and softly said, "Lloyd darling, I don't think he has come for our savings or our silver." Letting go of Lloyd's hand, she turned to face the man and asked, "Isn't that right …? I'm sorry, what is your name? I'm sure it is not really Reverend Albright."

"You are right in both cases, I have not come here to steal but maybe I have …" Both Margaret and Lloyd shuddered when they heard him snigger. When he had finished laughing he carried on, "Maybe I have come to steal your life, how about that?" He sniggered again, even more pleased with himself for making a joke of the situation. "As for my name, it is not important …"

Margaret interrupted him before he could continue, saying, "Not important? Of course it is important …"

"Shut up, you stupid woman. It is not important because I do not have a name; I have no use for one."

"What a shame," said Margaret. "Everybody should have a name."

The man shook his head at the absurd conversation and decided that he had lingered long enough. He arranged the bags side by side along the table; Lloyd counted six in all.

"What do you intend to do to us?" asked Lloyd.

The man had his back to him and as Lloyd spoke his eyes slid to the clock above his head but he could not see the time. Margaret caught his look and mouthed, "Nearly half past nine," and the look that passed was a secret shared.

The man picked up the long sharp knife and as he held it in front of him he twisted it round so that the blue and silver sheen of the blade sparkled in the light. "I am going to cut your throats and when I have finished I am going to cut out your hearts and your livers and anything else that takes my fancy."

He spoke as if he was already relishing their deaths and they could see little drops of saliva dripping from his lips as he spoke.

A very frightened Margaret felt herself shrivelling into the cushions; would it be too late, had she misjudged the time? No, the clock started its long slow half hour chime and as the man bent over her, Margaret closed her eyes, hoping that it was not too late.

She felt him take hold of her thin neck, his fingers forcing it upwards in readiness for slicing the knife across her throat. Then the noise she was straining to hear echoed from the kitchen.

She felt the fingers release their grip on her throat, and as she opened her eyes she saw to her horror the face that used to be human had slipped away. In readiness for the pleasure to come he had let his human mask slip, and in its place was his true self, the grotesque features of a diabolical creature.

"What was that? I thought you did not have anyone else staying in the house," he snarled, and he backed away from Margaret's chair, ready to confront whoever it was in the kitchen.

Lloyd jumped up from his chair and pulled Margaret to him and they stood together with their arms around each other as Grace's cat entered through the door from the kitchen.

Its hackles were high on its back and the skin over its teeth was stretched, exposing its fangs. It walked stiff legged, its body already arching in preparation for leaping. The fear exploded through him as he instantly recognised the cat and he started to mumble in his terror as he backed towards the door. He reached behind him and his trembling hand felt for the door handle; turning it, he pulled it open. He wanted to slide out away from the beast but in his haste to see how far the gap had opened, he dropped his eyes momentarily from the advancing animal.

The cat was larger than average, its fur golden in the dim light and as it launched itself forward Margaret could see it unsheathing its claws. In their wildest dreams they were not expecting to see such fury as the cat landed on the man's back, embedding its back claws and raking them continuously down his back. Its front paws clawed at the man's neck, and its large head bobbed around as it tried valiantly to sink its teeth into the man's throat.

Small spirals of dark smoke emerged from the man's cuts as the cat's claws penetrated deep within his flesh. The man's screams were awful to listen to and Margaret placed her hands over her ears to block out the sound while Lloyd, also deeply affected, had the forethought to drag his wife out into the kitchen to safety.

Fighting now for his life, the man tore the cat from his back and as Lloyd pushed Margaret through the kitchen door, he saw the man throw the hissing, screaming, enraged cat to the floor. How he managed to get out through the door, leaving the cat screeching on the other side, was indeed fortunate.

He could hear it scratching deep gouges in the door panelling and not wanting to get near the thing again; he stumbled to the front door and yanked it open.

He felt the blood flowing down his back from his wounds and knew they would take a long time to heal, if at all. Those claws, he knew, held poison for his kind, therefore the best thing to do was to go back and find Adam. He would know what to do and as he staggered down towards his car he reverted back to his human face. He wanted to get away from this place as fast as he could; this was not how it was supposed to be.

"Why do things always go wrong for me?" he wanted to yell, but he heaved a sigh of relief when he put his hand in his pocket and retrieved his keys.

Lloyd ventured round the side of the house and waited until he heard the car's engine start and knew the man had finally left. He hurried back to the kitchen and told Margaret to wait where she was, outside the back door. Lloyd entered the kitchen and made his way back into their small parlour, where a scene of devastation greeted him. The tablecloth had been pulled off; along with the tray of tea things he had placed there earlier. Margaret's best china lay in a shattered heap on the carpet and he frowned as to how she would take the loss.

The man's bag and some of its contents also lay on the floor beside one of the overturned chairs and Lloyd was intrigued as to what was in the small plastic bags. He nudged one with his foot and heard a soft growl coming from over by the fireplace. Lloyd made his way tentatively over to where the large ginger cat was lying, not quite sure whether to trust him or not. The cat was lying in front of the fireplace, licking its paws as if nothing had happened, its tail making an occasional thump on the carpet as the last of its anger left. He could hear it purring as he leant over and nervously reached down to stroke it, ready to pull back if the cat turned on him as well.

He jumped and his heart started pounding again as he felt a hand on his shoulder. As he straightened up he turned and there before him stood Margaret, her face white and drawn; he pulled her towards him, hugging her with all the strength he could muster.

"That, my darling was too close for comfort," he said as she leant her head on his shoulder. "You know what this means, don't you?"

"Yes Lloyd, I do know; we shall move on tomorrow; as for tonight ..."

Leaving the comfort of her husband's arms, she knelt down and, without any hesitation, stroked the soft fur of her daughter's cat.

"This fellow here deserves a nice reward," she continued. "How about opening that tin of salmon I was saving for Sunday tea?"

Lloyd, his hammering heart now finally under control, smiled at his wife, turned, and went into the kitchen to do her bidding. Margaret looked down at the cat, and the cat looked back at her.

As she spoke the amber eyes squinted up at her as if it knew every word she was saying: "No wonder Grace was so keen to leave you with us; normally you and her can't be separated. Thank the Lord that your routine is so predictable. You always come in at half nine for your supper, don't you, my darling?" Once more, she gratefully stroked his dense fur.

Chapter 25

Remne beckoned Reynard into the hallway and was surprised to see he only carried a small attaché case. She was expecting him to be carrying at least a suitcase and seeing that her eyes were on his bag, he said by way of explanation, "I always travel light; it is necessary as I could be jetting off all over the place at a moment's notice. I find this more to my liking, as I can always buy what I need when I get to my destination."

Remne turned away from him as he was speaking and he obediently followed her into the lounge and said, in his jovial way, "It is so good of you to put me up like this; I hope it is not an inconvenience. Oh, what a lovely room and you've kept all the original features; that's so rare nowadays."

Remne left him to walk round the settee and sit near to where the Book was lying on the floor; she tried to push it out of sight with her foot. He immediately caught her subtle action and, coming round the side of the settee, became very enthusiastic when he saw the rare tome. Watching him carefully, she realised his reaction was not in the least bit forced.

"My, my, what have we here? This is very rare indeed." Looking down at Remne, she saw that he was genuinely filled with appreciation. His eyes gleamed and she could see by the way he rubbed his hands together that he was itching to get his hands on the volume. "May I?" he said, reaching down to pick up the Book, but Remne placed her hand in the way before he had a chance to pick it up.

To take the sting out of her words, Remne smiled sweetly back up at him, knowing that this was a dangerous game of cat and mouse, but who was the cat and who was the mouse remained to be seen.

"No, I would be grateful if you didn't; it is very old, as you so rightly assessed and the acid from your hands might damage the pages; I assume by your profession you have brought your own gloves."

Seeing that he had been forestalled, Remne's guest seated himself on the settee adjoining hers and made himself comfortable, leaning back against the cushions and crossing his legs at the ankles. He looked over at Remne and gave her an appraising look, all the while keeping a pleasant smile upon his features.

"Yes of course," he said after a while, "silly me. I was just overcome by the moment; it is not often one gets to see a book of such rarity. Please forgive me; it was unprofessional."

Knowing that she had won that little battle, Remne suddenly said, "That is a strange name you have, Mr Holt, I don't think I have come across many Reynards in my time." Remne leant forward and stared at him closely.

"Thank you, yes, it is unusual; goodness knows what my parents must have been thinking of when they named me that."

"It's the name of a fox, isn't it?" said Remne, laughing. "Reynard the Red Fox?"

"Goodness knows my literary bent is more towards historical than children's classics and my hair is more white than red nowadays," Reynard replied with a soft chuckle.

"Is there anything I can get you? You must be tired after your journey up from London, how about a nice cup of tea?"

Remne knew what he would do the moment her back was turned, but now was not the moment to be hesitant. Gem had been upstairs for a good twenty minutes and it would spoil everything if she were to come down now.

"Tea? Yes, that would be lovely. The brew that refreshes, isn't that what they say? I must admit it is the first thing I miss when I am away from England. So yes, thank you very much, tea would be lovely," Reynard said, uncrossing his ankles and sitting in a more upright position as he talked to Remne.

Remne left the room and made her way to the kitchen, where she placed the cups and saucers on a tray along with the sugar bowl, milk jug and teapot. When the kettle had boiled, she poured the scalding liquid into the teapot and made her way back to the lounge. When she entered the lounge, she found Reynard where she had left him, but now he had his attaché case placed unopened upon his knees.

Now it begins, thought Remne as she made her way round the settee to place the tea things upon the small table. As she did so her eyes went to the Book; to the unobservant it looked as if it had not been disturbed, but Remne could see a tiny line on the thick carpet where the Book had not been put back in the correct place. It was so small to be hardly noticeable, but Remne knew.

Once she was sitting down, she glanced over at Reynard and, with a smooth smile and her hands on the teapot, enquired, "Milk or sugar, Reynard, or would you prefer lemon?"

"Milk, please and no sugar; I'm sweet enough," he answered with a chuckle.

He watched as Remne poured the steaming liquid into his cup and on seeing the clear liquid, he suddenly glanced back at Remne, the smile gone from his face to be replaced with a dark frown.

Finally he spoke and Remne could hear a little tremor of doubt creeping into his words as he said, "It seems to me that you have forgotten the tea leaves. Is there a problem?"

"No, there is no problem, Reynard. I just thought as you were playing a little game with me, I would do the same."

Remne saw all vestige of humour wiped away in an instant and what replaced it was what she had been expecting. Gone were the twinkling eyes dancing with humour, replaced by a dark and menacing expression.

"So it seems you have seen through me. They said you were cunning, but I did not expect you to be so perceptive. Please accept my apologies for underestimating you. You do indeed have a strange ability; no wonder He is so keen to meet you properly."

"Who is the 'he' you are talking about?" replied Remne, egging him on as she leant nonchalantly back amongst the cushions, trying to remain unfazed by what Reynard was talking about.

"That is not part of the question at the moment. I am here to deliver a message. It is about your friend Beth and if you want to see her alive again. He grows impatient and wants to resolve this matter once and for all," said Reynard, tapping his attaché case with both hands, but Remne could see his eyes returning constantly to the place by her feet where the Book was laying. She could see the need in him growing and she watched as small beads of sweat started to break out on his forehead.

As if he could read her thoughts, he plunged his hand into his jacket pocket, pulled out a large white cotton handkerchief and proceeded to mop his brow and the back of his neck.

Remne decided to help the situation along and said, "Well, what is the message you have to deliver, Red Fox? Yes, from now on I shall call you Red Fox, because that is what you are."

Reynard forced his eyes back to where Remne was sitting and even managed a small grin at her nickname for him; he said, "He said you will know where to find Him and that He will be waiting there with Beth."

"Is that all? Is there no more to the message? Did he say whether Beth was dead or alive? Come, answer me, Foxy; this is no time to be shy with the details."

"No, that was all. He does not trust me enough with anything else," replied Reynard, who once again wiped his face with his handkerchief.

It was as he lowered his face to dry off the sweat that Remne saw his expression alter from humble servant to conspirator. She would have missed it altogether had she not been looking for it. Her senses had already told her that he was more than what he seemed and now that look confirmed it. Seating herself upright, she leant forward again and reached for the teapot and in a movement that was too swift for Reynard to gauge, she flipped the Book open with her foot and held the teapot, with the still hot liquid, purposefully above it.

She watched as a look of pure horror crossed his face as he realised the consequences of her threat. He stumbled with each word, trying to stop her from doing the unmentionable, "Plea … se do …n't do any …thing stu … pid."

His hands flapped about in a vain attempt to reach across the little table, but Remne kept the teapot tilted over the Book. "Tell me where Beth is, or better still take me to her, or else you know what damage this would do to the Book, don't you?"

She watched as tears formed in his eyes and all he could manage was a small nod; she guessed her actions had rendered him temporarily speechless.

"Now that we've got that sorted out, this is what I want you to do." She lowered the teapot but still held it within her grasp.

"And this is what I want you to do," said Reynard, pointing a small calibre pistol at her. "Do you think I would be so stupid as to let you get the better of me? I took the gun out when you went to make your pretend tea and it was just as well that I did."

Remne watched in fascination as Reynard kept the gun level and pointed at her head and then he mopped his face with his free hand.

She was not deceived by his show of bravado and smiled inwardly as he took several small gulps of air as if to compose himself before he spoke again. "Please put the teapot down on the table." As he motioned with the gun she complied without hesitation. "I thought I would leave a message somehow, saying perhaps that Nathan had called me while you were out of the room. I even had a quick glance through the Book but to no avail; you have to know what you are looking for. It does not give up its secrets easily."

"Have you seen this Book before?" Remne enquired as she watched a look that could only be described as desire cross Reynard's face as he talked about it.

"That is of no concern of yours. I could kill you myself for even threatening to damage it," he replied angrily.

Pushing his attaché case to one side, Reynard got to his feet and motioned Remne to do the same. Keeping the gun trained firmly on her, Reynard indicated that she should sit in the place he had just vacated; as she moved round the small table Reynard took a couple of paces backwards as if he was frightened she would lunge for the gun.

"You do not know the extent of what you are getting yourself into. We have people everywhere; some are in very high places." He paused in his speech to give a nervous little laugh before continuing, "Even the Vatican have thought up numerous, injurious plans to stop us, but to no avail." This time his laughter increased and he wiped an unsteady hand across his mouth, but it could not conceal his humour; Remne was at a loss as to what he was talking about.

"Well, are you going to share the joke or do I have to guess? This is all getting very tedious," said Remne, flopping back on the cushions and making her voice sound bored, but this was new information, and all her senses were alert to the danger.

"The joke is, the Vatican is making plans to join forces with all the other churches; they will be coming home, so to speak, to Mother Church. Even as I speak there are secret plans being drawn up to unite the Protestants, Methodists, Presbyterians and anyone else who would like to join the Catholics. They think by uniting the branches of the faiths they will stand a better chance to defeat us."

Remne drew in a small breath of relief. It was beginning; the major faiths were starting to take things seriously, but they did not know how imminent the threat was. This was only the outset, the advance guard if you like, the testing ground, but if Gem was unsuccessful, it left all the northern churches vulnerable.

They had to succeed!

Reynard continued speaking and Remne was drawn back to what he was saying: "You cannot stop the inevitable; the people do not want your sort any more, they are ready and willing to take on a new age."

Remne sat quietly as Reynard rambled on, suddenly wondering why he had her change seats. She did not have to wait long; Reynard reached down and pushed his attaché case along the cushions towards her.

"Open that!" he ordered, and Remne complied with his wishes, eager to see for herself what the case contained. Her small intake of breath did not go unnoticed and it brought another happy smile to his face as he watched her eyes roam over the contents of the case. There laying snug amongst a velvet lining was all the equipment needed to inject someone and Remne guessed that someone was her. There was a small phial of liquid and a hypodermic syringe with the needle already attached.

"Now you have two choices: one, you can fill the syringe with the liquid and inject yourself, or two ..." At this point she saw that Reynard could not keep the smile from his face and it seemed option two, when she heard it, was going to give him the greatest pleasure. "Yes ... option two. I can place this little silencer on the end of my gun and blow your brains out here and now. So what is it going to be?"

"Option one, I think."

Pleased that she had caused him even a modicum of frustration by her refusal of option two, Remne quickly and silently filled the syringe with the liquid and as she held the needle poised over her arm, she said, nodding towards the drug, "What is this anyway? You obviously don't intend to kill me, otherwise you could have shot me, so at least tell me what is going on; you owe me that much."

"Actually I owe you nothing, but I will tell you anyway. I am going to take you to Beth, but the drawback for you is that He will be waiting for you as well. I have done what is expected of me and for my reward He is going to give me the Book. As for the drug it is just a mild sedative that will allow us to walk out of here but will not allow you to do much else. In fact, when it takes effect, you will be unable to talk let alone walk, but trust me it will wear off, not that it should worry you. He will have you by then and you will wish you were dead."

"Why do you want the Book so much? It is just an old tome, nothing very special," said Remne, blatantly lying as she pushed the needle into her soft flesh.

"Oh, how you lie. You know as well as I that it can tell you things. It has magical and mystical properties and all those things are going to be mine. It can see into the future. You just have to know what to look for and I have been told on very good authority that it can heal as well, although I am a bit sceptical about that. Whatever, it is now mine."

His attention was brought back to the stillness of the tall, beautiful woman with her long golden hair sitting on the settee in front of him, but what did he care for a woman's beauty against the wonders of the Book? That was his mistress and the only love he had ever known or wanted. In all the years of searching, he had never given up hope and now it was his; his arms physically ached to hold it and caress it.

Reynard bent down and almost tenderly removed the syringe from Remne's hand; he placed it back into his attaché case as it lay on the settee next to her and gently closed the lid. What use was anger? Now that he had what he wanted he could afford to be magnanimous as he slipped his gun into his pocket. He watched silently for a moment as the drug started to work. When he was convinced he was in no danger, he moved over to the other settee and bent down, giving a slight groan as he picked up the heavy Book once more, holding it lovingly to his chest.

Carrying the heavy tome, he walked out of the lounge into the hallway and as he neared the door he spied a set of keys lying on the hall table.

Reynard set the Book down by the front door and picked up the keys; giving them a quick inspection, he noticed that the fob had a picture of a car and the word "STAG" written underneath. It did not take much to work out they were the keys to the car sitting outside by the kerb. This was indeed a fortunate piece of luck and one he had not counted on; feeling very pleased with himself, he hurried quickly back to the lounge, walked round to where Remne was sitting, and pulled her to her feet. This was going better than he had planned; just a few minor adjustments, nothing that caused any worries and he had in his possession both the Book and the girl called Gemini.

Remne's head lolled forward in her semi somnolent state and Reynard was forced to put his arm around her waist to help her along. With one arm around her, Reynard easily managed to reach the front door, opening it with his free hand; after a small stagger, he eventually got her down the steps to the car. The drug was taking effect quicker than he expected and she was leaning heavily against him. As he looked around he became anxious that they might somehow arouse suspicion; the last thing he wanted was for someone to call the police. He carefully looked up and down the street for any signs of pedestrians or inquisitive faces at neighbouring windows, but there was nobody about; taking the handkerchief from his pocket, wiped his face free from the sweat that was starting to run into his eyes. With one final heave, he leant Remne up against the side of the car. He fiddled with the small key and just before she started to sag he yanked open the door, lowered her into the passenger seat and then slammed the door shut.

Reynard hurried back along the pavement and up the steps to the house to claim his prize; staggering slightly under the Book's weight, he pulled the front door closed and, with the sweat starting to reappear on his brow, hurried along the pavement to his stolen car and waiting passenger. As Reynard placed the key in the ignition Remne's head rolled to the right near his shoulder and unbeknownst to him Remne's eyes flickered open slightly and looked at the car's clock. She estimated that it had taken Reynard nearly an hour from his arrival to finally getting her into the car; as the smile crept across her face she was glad that her long hair obscured her features from his view.

Chapter 26

"I'm out of the bath now," said Gem, calling down the stairs. The soft plumes of steam followed her out of the bathroom as she walked towards the landing rails. "You can go in now, if you want." She listened for a reply as she hung over the balustrade, but there was nothing. The house seemed empty for some reason, but she refused to panic at her slight feeling of unease.

"She's probably in the kitchen with the door closed," Gem mused as she made her way to her bedroom. She rubbed the thick white towel across her head, drying her curls as she went; entering her bedroom, she let the towel slide that she had tied around her breasts. The white folds fell about her feet and as she stepped daintily over them the feeling of unease invaded her senses again.

Something was definitely wrong and she was not going to linger naked and wait for that something to happen. Gem opened one drawer after another to pull out the clothes she thought would be appropriate. Tight black stretchy leggings along with a black stretchy sleeveless top: just the thing for a moonlight escapade. It seemed that was how she was spending all of her time lately, but still she was no nearer to rescuing Beth.

The thought of Beth in Adam's hands galled her so much that she felt wave after wave of fury engulf her body, forcing her to sit on the edge of the bed and rest her head in her hands. She made herself take deep breaths and soon she was feeling calm enough to go downstairs.

As Gem reached the bottom stair she again called out to Remne and taking a quick look inside the lounge and not finding her there, she carried on to the kitchen.

Empty!

Gem leant against the doorjamb and wondered where on earth she could be.

"Maybe she went out for something; no, she would have told me," said Gem, voicing her feelings out loud.

She turned back into the hall, leaving the kitchen behind and made her way to the lounge again. Gem sauntered up to the settee and looked in amazement at the tea cups on the small table. Their guest had arrived after all, but where were they both? This was getting too weird, but even as she was thinking this, the feeling that something bad had happened grew even stronger. Walking round the settee, her first thought was for her sword. She got down on her knees and looked under the settee and spotted it, nestling there where it looked as if it had been hurriedly pushed. She knew this would have been Remne's first reaction if someone they didn't know had entered their domain, but what of the Book that was far too heavy and big to slide under the settee at a moment's notice?

She went to stand over the spot where she had last seen it and sure enough, there in the carpet was the unmistakable imprint of where the tome had been.

Now it was gone and along with it Remne and their mysterious guest. Gem turned and sat down on the settee where Remne had been sitting last and as she put out her hands to balance herself on the cushions her right hand touched something strange. Gem was so startled that she pulled her hand back as if it had been stung and sliding round in her seat to view the object, she was surprised to see a small leather attaché case.

She pulled the case to her, resting it on her knees, flicked open the catches and raised the lid. There inside she found the empty phial and syringe nestling amongst the red velvet lining. Well, that explained what happened to Remne, but it did not explain who their mystery guest actually was. Or worse still, perhaps the guest hadn't arrived yet and Remne had opened the door to a stranger.

No, don't be silly, she thought; she would not have made tea for a stranger.

Gem placed the open case next to her and then rested her head in her hands; she had to think clearly, going from one thing to another was not doing any good.

It was now that she missed both Beth and Remne with their clear and logical thinking.

What did she know?

She tried hard to put the pieces together. Raising her head slightly, she looked through her splayed fingers; glanced over towards the tea cups and realised something was odd.

That was it: the tea cups!

Shuffling her bottom along the cushions, she reached over and picked up one of the cups and looked at the cool clear liquid inside. There was no tea in the liquid! Reaching over, she picked up the teapot and looked inside and sure enough, it was just plain water. Now why would Remne make a pot of plain water instead of tea? Gem got up from her seat and walked to where she assumed Remne had been sitting when she poured the tea and seated herself in the same spot. As she glanced down she noticed that the indentation of where the book had been was right by her left foot. So in that case, if Remne had a pot full of boiling water, the only reason she could think of was that she used it as a bargaining tool.

Suddenly she could see it all.

She could see Remne sitting there, threatening to pour the water over the Book and their guest, what was his name? Then she remembered that Nathan had not told them his name, he had only asked whether they could put him up for the night.

Something drastic must have happened to change the shift in power and as Gem glanced over towards the other settee the hypodermic syringe glinted spitefully in the dying embers of the day.

So it was safe to assume that Remne had been forced to go with their mystery guest, although somewhat unwillingly, by the looks of the empty syringe, but where had they gone? That was what was so frustrating. Deciding to get herself into a more comfortable position, Gem pushed the table out of the way and sat down on the floor, crossing her legs; she monitored her breathing until it rolled in through her nose and out, deeply and evenly, through her mouth. She then placed her hands palms outwards on top of her bent knees and gently let her mind travel. Her mind hopped like a demented frog from one topic to another, but still she sat there, calmly waiting for the answers to come to her. They said she would know when the time came; she would know where the meeting would be. She remembered again going over the carved jet rosary beads and reading aloud to Remne as she made lunch in the kitchen.

Was it only this morning? It seemed a lifetime ago. Each day dragged like an eternity, and each passing hour weighed heavily on her soul. Each hour meant one more hour that Beth was incarcerated. Gem forced herself to be still; her breathing remained deep and even, and as she sat there a small voice inside her said, *"I am the beginning and the end."*

Gem's eyes flew open; why had she not seen it when she was reading it? Of course, that was it, and shouting out loud she said, "I am the Alpha and the Omega, I am the beginning and the end!" Raising her eyes to heaven she silently mouthed, *"Thank you Lord, it took some time but I got there."*

As Gem started to get to her feet she could feel Remne close to her and suddenly Remne's mind called out to hers and the shock forced her back into her sitting position.

"Do you hear me, Gemini? Do not be angry with me; I had to do what I thought was best."

Gem focused all her energy on replying to Remne and as her thoughts tumbled through her head she heard Remne cautioning her, *"Steady, steady, Gem, your thoughts are running all over the place."*

Gem took a few more deep breaths and tried again: *"Remne, are you hurt? Why didn't you call out to me?"*

"It was a trap, Gem and I knew I would be better suited than you; forgive me but I had to do what was expected of me."

"Of course I forgive you and I have also worked out where you are; I shall be coming for you ... and Beth. Be ready for me."

"Be on your guard, Gem, nothing is as it seems," and as suddenly as they arrived, Remne's thoughts left her and Gem was alone once more.

This time Gem got to her feet in a single bound and immediately fell to her knees once again, remembering to retrieve her sword from under the settee. As her hand closed around the metal shaft, beams of light radiated from it and she could hear a strange noise, as if it was singing.

As she gently pulled the sword towards her it felt as though it was preparing for the battle to come. Gem was overcome with awe as the sword turned from dull lifeless metal to this shining, radiant sword that was singing within her grip. As she raised herself to a standing position she once more felt the pleasure of handling the sword. She felt its balance and lightness as she twirled and scythed it first one way and then the other. It felt good in her hands and as she readied herself for the fight then she decided to use a few moments to reflect quietly before she went into battle against those who wanted her dead. Such a sobering thought made her lower her sword and trailing it behind her; she went over to the window and looked out onto the street below. Night was slowly falling but she had already decided to not make a move until it was fully dark, as there was less chance of her being seen, and that was a good few hours away.

As she reached over to shut the curtains she swore softly under her breath. Nathan was running up the steps two at a time, his face alight with animation at the thought, she assumed, of seeing her once again. The doorbell rang just as she had finished pulling the curtains together and after turning on the small table lamp, she slid the sword back under the settee, rose and quickly went to open the door.

As soon as it was open, he scooped Gem into his arms, saying, "I finished earlier than I expected, so I decided to make a detour and visit you before heading back to London."

As he finished speaking he buried his face into her neck and started to kiss her around her ear.

Gem was thrown for a minute, but she managed to gather herself before she got swept away by the moment; pushing him away, she began to speak, but he interrupted her by saying, "Has Mr Reynard Holt made himself at home? I hope he hasn't bored you with all his talk of church antiquities, because he certainly bored me all the way from London, I can tell you. Is he in here?"

Before Gem could stop him, he strode into the lounge; as she followed she was angry with herself for leaving the attaché case open on the settee with all the hypodermic paraphernalia on show. It was obvious from the look on his face that he had spotted the needle and as he turned to face her he looked worried and confused.

"What is going on here, Gem? What's with the needle?"

She lowered her head for a moment as she tried to gather her thoughts; this was not how she wanted it to be. She did not want to involve him; he was too precious to her, but what other option did she have? Would he think her mad? Or would he require proof to confirm what she was saying? There was only one way to find out; raising her head she looked at him squarely in the eye and said, "I think you had better sit down; there is a lot I have to tell you."

"No, I think I shall remain standing, thank you. Now tell me what's going on," replied Nathan, his natural authority rising to the occasion.

Gem looked momentarily crestfallen at his reply, but her natural fighting spirit came rushing to her aid.

She placed her hands on her hips at Nathan's words and with her legs slightly apart for balance, her usual angry pose, she leant forward to give her words more emphasis.

"For one, you can take that tone out of your voice," she said, "and if you think for one minute that I have been taking drugs, you can leave right now. I have no intention of showing you my arms, although I am sure you can see from there that I have no track marks. So Mr Detective Inspector Nathan Grantly, can you please explain to me who this Mr Reynard Holt is exactly, because if it wasn't for him, Remne would still be here and not drugged and carted off as a hostage."

Gem could see the effect her words had on him; the blood drained from his face as he opened and shut his mouth like a goldfish, seemingly too overcome to put anything into actual words. Gem refused to help him and just stood there, waiting for an answer and the only indication she gave was to raise one eyebrow when it looked as if he was finally going to say something.

"God, I'm so sorry, Gem; this is getting so out of hand. It seems to be just one thing after another and to think I brought that man here and put you both in danger." Gem watched as his shoulders drooped and his face became troubled, but he continued, "I was told by someone quite high up in government that he was an expert on church antiquity; they asked me to bring him up to York, seeing as I was going there myself."

As she listened Gem was intrigued to hear what Nathan was telling her. She wrinkled her brow in sudden perplexity and wondered if the mention of someone high up in government had any bearing on what was happening.

Who had sent the man here? Were there more out there that she should know about? It was something to seriously consider; she knew it was spreading like a wildfire, consuming all who came into contact with it.

She suddenly realised that Nathan was still speaking, so she leant a hip against the settee while he continued, "Of course I agreed; what else could I say? But I swear to you I know nothing else about him. In fact he was so boring I thought he was the last person to do you any harm. It just goes to show how wrong you can be about someone."

On hearing this last part, Gem straightened up and took a small intake of breath, hoping he would still feel the same if he knew all her secrets. Nathan turned and sat down on the nearest settee; he lowered his head into his hands, mirroring Gem's action a few moments ago.

"To cap it all, Gem, I've just come from seeing the body of Dr Rupert Winsmore and it was not a pretty sight," said Nathan, by way of explanation for his sudden and inappropriate anger.

Gem felt herself overflow with compassion, seeing him sitting there with that lock of hair falling tenderly onto his brow; all she wanted to do was put her arms around him. Not waiting a moment longer, she immediately went and sat beside him, realising suddenly that it was through her that he was feeling so bad. As she put her arm around his shoulder she felt the anger drain from him as he softly said, "God, it was not a pretty sight at all, Gem, somebody had sliced him in two and there's more …"

"I know," said Gem, interrupting him, sympathetically nodding her head in remembrance.

Nathan shook off Gem's comforting arm and swung round in his seat to face her. His voice, although tired, was firm and strong again as he said, "And what do you mean by that? Now come on, Gem, tell me exactly what is going on. I feel as though I am fighting in the dark; there are things here that I know nothing about." He swung round on the settee to look her straight in the face, probing her blue eyes for lies as he continued, "Why is the church hierarchy on full alert and having secret talks all over the place?" He leant forward towards her to emphasise his words. "I'm not talking about one religion, I'm talking about all of them and what has got the Special Forces so spooked to cause a complete news blackout?"

"Exactly how much do you know?" Gem enquired as she rose to her feet and started pacing the room, worried now that he did indeed know too much for his own safety. After all, he was part of the inner circle and knew what was going on; that could be extremely useful to her, especially if she was having to battle against his own kind.

"Not a lot, really," he offered.

She guessed he was being either modest or diplomatic. In her opinion, he was an astute tactician who would not give too much away until he heard all the facts and for some reason that pleased her.

"I know all about the different murders and about Beth's attack and we now have two more to add to the list." Seeing her raise an eyebrow he continued, "We found Dr Winsmore's parents, or what was left of them and that was also not a pretty sight, I can tell you. It looked as if they had been half eaten …"

Seeing the look of Gem's face, he stopped talking. Had he overstepped the mark and made her feel squeamish? After all it was not the sort of subject you talk about to someone outside the force.

Gem remembered seeing the bodies, but when she left them they were decomposed, not eaten.

Had someone been there after her?

Again she was forced to draw her attention back to what Nathan was saying, adding before he continued, "No, I'm fine; it was just a bit of a shock, they were nice people. Go on with what you were saying."

She smiled over at him but he thought it best to change the subject, saying, "As long as you are okay."

Gem nodded her acquiescence but he continued, still not completely convinced, "I think I should tell you that even though I sat in on that meeting with the Government, I'm a police officer, Gem, not a theologian. I deal in facts! Black and white facts, not premonitions; all I seem to be getting now are various shades of grey."

She watched as he picked up the tea cup and saw his brow furrow when he looked at the clear water. She could see his detective mind putting together the pieces and some day he might, just might, pull it all together in the right order, but she could not wait that long; she had to trust him now.

She had to trust him because she needed a witness who was a human and mortal. She had to have a complete human, one with frailties and complexities.

She had to have Nathan to bear witness.

Chapter 27

"You will be moving soon." These words came whispering to her through her mind.

Had she dreamt them? Beth was not sure. She was not sure of anything anymore. No, that was a lie. She was thirsty. That much was true, and hungry, but her thirst far outweighed her hunger. Adam had brought her a little sustenance; that seemed like hours ago now. Funnily enough, when she found out it was porridge, she laughed. She hated porridge, but that was before she hadn't eaten for what seemed like days.

She was still wary of him and his gifts, but she had accepted the bowl thankfully and was grateful he had not stayed to watch her eat it. He had not given her a spoon, and in her eagerness to eat something, she drove her fingers into the glutinous mass. Beth screamed as the hot sticky substance clung to her fingers and burnt her. Swearing softly to herself, she quickly pulled the blanket round the bowl so that she could hold it properly and then she wiggled her burnt fingers, trying to ease the pain. Then popping them in her mouth, she sucked each one in turn, to ease the pain and remove the food sticking to them. After all, it would not do to waste any of it.

Beth blew over the bowl of food while her nostrils were tantalised by the smell; only when she thought it was safe to eat did she plunge her fingers down into the mass. Using her fingers like a spoon, she shovelled the hot porridge into her mouth, savouring each and every drop. When it was gone, she wiped her finger round the bowl and, fearing she might have missed some in the dark, raised the bowl to her lips and licked the inside until the last vestige of porridge had been consumed. Her stomach had ached with the unusual amount of food it had to digest, as it was not used to being bombarded with nourishment after such a long abstinence.

She had lain on her side facing the wall and the little bed had creaked as she curled her knees up and hugged herself, trying to ease the pain and wishing it would go away. Now that her hunger had been appeased, her thoughts automatically turned to water; she lay there licking her lips at the memory of draining the last of the jug he had brought her.

She had tried to make it last as long as possible and was proud of the fact that she had done just that. She had allowed herself only a few gulps every couple of hours. Now it was all gone; she had held the heavy pot over her head so that the last remaining drops had trickled down the sides and into her mouth. As she held it in her hands, Beth had thought fleetingly of using it as a weapon against Adam. She thought of bringing it down onto his head again and again. It was not a very charitable thought, but at that moment she did not feel very charitable. She heaved a large sigh and lowered the jug to the floor, realising it was impossible to satisfy her wishes, because she was tired out just holding it above her head for a few minutes.

How on earth could she use it as a weapon?

Tired and now very depressed, Beth did what she always did at times like these: she closed her eyes and willed herself to a better place. As she drifted off to sleep she hadn't thought it possible to dream of water in all its various forms, but she had.

There was sparkling water, when the sun shines on a still lake and the tops of the little waves flash and gleam as the sun strikes them. Or there was cascading water from a waterfall, tumbling and turning down a predestined path, coursing its way through rocks to land in tumultuous pools of icy blue and silver, their depths unfathomable. Or there were the soft waters of the Caribbean, where you could swim in the sea so aquamarine and warm that the sheer beauty of it took your breath away. She liked that one the best. She would lie for hours imagining herself in the warm waters of Antigua. It was her favourite spot for holidaying since she and an old school friend had flown there for a last minute holiday. Gem was off in the South of France with her parents and couldn't make it. It was one of those glorious times in her late teens when everything was an adventure and felt fresh and new.

"Did you hear me, Beth?" Adam said again, this time with more emphasis.

She raised herself onto her elbow and tried, as she had tried several times before, but her eyes just couldn't penetrate the blackness. It was always total darkness and she had long ago got over being frustrated, she just shrugged and lay back down. What did it matter? He had his own agenda and all she had to do was go along with it.

"Where will I be going?" replied Beth in a weary voice.

"That is no concern of yours at the moment," Adam said, "but soon you will be reunited with your friend and my Master will be free and I will get what I have always wanted as my reward. Everything is coming together and I am so happy that I will even grant you one request, just to show how much you have pleased me."

Beth could hear the gloating in Adam's voice and even in her weakened state, his news brought her fresh anxiety.

She tried to calm herself as she felt her heart pumping rapidly. This would not do; she had to think of something fast, otherwise he would take advantage of her as he had done in the past. She thought of the times Adam had come to her and questioned her about Gem. He wanted to know all about her and sometimes she was ashamed to say she had inadvertently let slip little things in the sheer pleasure of being able to talk about her. She knew he would take this knowledge and use it against Gemini, so now she was always on the lookout for his little tricks, but it was so hard.

Was this another one of those tricks? What could she possibly ask for that he would grant? Or would she ask for something and he would say no just for the pleasure of hearing her ask?

"Come, come," he said, "there must be something you would like. I could take you to the highest mountaintop or transport you to a tropical beach. Perhaps you would like some beautiful clothes or a marble bath with asses' milk to bathe in. I know, how about a banquet so that you could eat to your heart's content? Come now, Beth, say something."

She could hear the annoyance sliding in around the edge of his words. Beth lay on her little bed in the filthy clothes she had worn since being brought to her prison cell. She had gone from the hope of being rescued to the resignation of her situation. She had travelled a long and exhausting path to the place where she found herself now, but never in all that time had she lost her faith.

Her faith kept her sane and it kept her fighting for what she knew was right.

Would it protect her now? She was about to find out; uncurling herself from her foetal position, she swung her legs over the side of the bed and swayed slightly as she tried to gain her balance to stand erect in the dark room; eventually she managed it.

"There is no need for formality, Beth," Adam quipped, "you could have told me sitting down. Now what is it you need – or want, I should say? I am in a good mood today; I will grant you anything, within reason of course. So don't go asking for your freedom, as refusals only cause offence; now where did I read that?" Adam gave a small chuckle, amused at his own joke.

Beth clasped her small hands together and taking a deep lungful of air, she said, before she had a chance to change her mind, "Get thee behind me, you spawn of Satan. Your enticements are nothing to me. I will fall where I stand, you can do nothing else to me. I am as dust before the feet of the Lord but his hand is upon me in my hour of need, bringing me hope when I doubt and comfort when I fear. You, my evil friend, shall be cast into the pit with your Master. So tempt me no more because my life is done and I will not allow you to use me against Gemini."

The effort Beth had put into her words made her sink to her knees and turning her head to one side, she waited for the death blow she was certain was coming from Adam.

She had purposely antagonised him to the point of no return and hoped there was no other way for him but to lash out at her in temper and do what she had purposefully started. She had been shown her path and she accepted it readily. The way forward was now as clear as day. She did not want to be the lure for Gem, but she knew what she had to do, and nothing would persuade her otherwise.

"Very good, very … good," Adam said as he bent over her cowering form.

Beth could feel the coldness of his breath on her turned cheek and it pervaded her body and made her shiver violently. In a desperate attempt at being brave she placed her hands on the ground and pushed herself upright until she was standing before him.

She swayed slightly until the blood started to circulate in her legs and then she grabbed hold of the front of Adam's clothes and snarled, "Kill me, you bastard. Kill me and get it over with, you snivelling piece of shit."

She knew her words were getting to him, because she could feel the effort he was making to maintain his self-restraint. She knew he did not want to lose control and killing her would seriously jeopardise his plans, so she had to goad him further until she felt that steely reserve slipping.

Still clutching the front of Adam's jacket, Beth hoisted herself nearer

hapter 28

continued her pacing, finding that it relieved her stress if she kept ... ng. This was not going to be easy and casting her eyes heavenwards ... moment, she addressed herself to the ceiling and, almost shouting ... words, cried, "Nothing is ever easy with you, is it?"

"Are you talking to me?" Nathan asked. "Because if you are, I would ... to point out that ..." but Gem interrupted his flow with a gentle raise ... er elegant hand.

"No silly, not you, I was talking to a higher authority." She couldn't ... lp but smile when she saw Nathan raise his eyes heavenwards as well, as ... fully expecting to see someone floating round the ceiling.

She stopped her pacing and folded her arms, giving him a stern look ... s he dragged his eyes back to look at her; he said in reply, "Well, I just ... on't know anymore, a lot of strange things have been happening and you ... now as well as I that these are interesting times."

Gem had to smile at his reference to the old Chinese curse of hoping ... someone would live through interesting times; well, he was right there at ... least.

Gem wondered what was the best way to start and then realised there wasn't one, so she went straight in at the deep end and hoped she could swim. "You have obviously guessed," she said as she continued her pacing, "there are extraordinary things happening, now ... how can I put it ... that are not of this world." She stopped her pacing and waited for a moment for Nathan to say something, but he remained silent. "Well yes, quite," she said as she continued her pacing. "The Devil, or Satan, or whatever you

---

and spat her words at him and for one second she had the immense pleasure of knowing her words had hit their mark as Adam drew slightly away from her.

"Do you think for one minute Gem would look at you?" she sneered. "She will die fighting you, rather than subject herself to one moment with you and what you can't stand is the fact that she loves me as if we were blood. That is why you took me, isn't it? You are jealous of everything she loves, you ... you ... abomination."

This time Beth knew her words had found their mark. She had guessed why she had been taken and now she waited eagerly for the blow, yearned for it even. She felt Adam's hands cover hers and tear them away from the front of his jacket. She felt the power build up in him until it burnt her with its iciness, but still she stood there swaying in front of him and if it was not for his cruel, icy grip upon her hands, then she knew she would have fallen.

His voice, when it finally came, was as cold as an arctic blast and she knew now this was it; this was where he sealed her fate. "You have tempted my anger once too often, now suffer the consequences, you meddling bitch. Yes, it's true, I hate you. I hate everything about you," said Adam as he dragged her to the middle of the small room.

"You have more human qualities," Beth said, "than I gave you credit for: anger, lust, envy and jealousy; all you lack is love!"

"Love? What need have I for love when I have everything else?" he said. "Soon you will see why."

Beth stumbled as he dragged her by her hands; her long tangled hair fell across her face and caught in her mouth and she felt herself gagging. As she fell, she felt his hands go around her face, brushing the hair away and then he raised her head so that under normal circumstance she would have been forced to look at him, but the total blackness prevented her from seeing anything. Her world now consisted of the dirt floor beneath her knees and the rough hands forcing her face upwards. Beth fought for every breath as her head was steadily forced backwards. She felt as if her heart were going to burst. In the sudden fear of her predicament, each second felt like an eternity.

What had she done?

Was he going to force her head so far back that he snapped her spine? That was not what she was hoping for. She wanted her punishment to be quick, not slow and painful, as it was now. How foolish she was to think she could get the better of him; he knew all the ways of subtle torture

– hadn't he proved that over the last few days? She realised there was no going back now; she had stepped once more onto the path of destruction and her lips trembled with words unsaid.

She felt her nails breaking as she scrabbled vainly to pull his hands away; gone was the fear of touching him. Her small hands were not strong enough to break his hold on her, so she clung to his wrists as he continued to hold her head in a vicelike grip. As she looked up a light started to shine around him; she began to see him, the light grew brighter and there was nowhere for her to look other than at him. She was surprised to see how handsome his features were, but they started to melt and change the more she was forced to look at him. As the last semblance of normality was shed she started to see the real entity behind his human mask and it was more terrible than she could have ever imagined.

As the light grew more intense she could see that his eyes, once green, were now red with orange slits and the pupils, instead of being round, were oval like the eyes of a reptile. The inner eye flicked from side to side and she became fascinated by their glare. The skin on his head became stretched and taut like a skull or death's head mask, but still those eyes watched her. He grew taller and taller and rose so high within the room that Beth felt herself lifting off the ground as he clung to her head. She saw muscles and scales starting to appear on his torso. His clothes started to tear from his body as he got bigger, now practically filling the small room. The fingers that held her grew talons and scales covered the back of his hands. Beth assumed the same was happening to his legs and feet, because she could hear the tearing and splitting of cloth and leather.

Finally he flung his head back and Beth was forced to watch mesmerised as his thin, stiff, leathery lips slipped back over his teeth, and she could see the whiteness of his fangs gleaming in the increasing light.

Beth's neck muscles stretched in agony and she would have screamed aloud, but the horror of what she was witnessing kept her mute. Her eyes again filled with more tears as the light grew in intensity and they dripped off her lashes and ran in scalding rivulets down her cheeks. Then, to her shame and revulsion, she felt hot liquid running between her legs and realised she had finally lost control of her bladder.

She watched him throw back his head as his mouth opened and he gave a shuddering howl and suddenly, on his back, there appeared what she could only describe as … enormous bat-like wings.

His baying continued along with the intensifying light; Beth couldn't stand it anymore and felt herself slowly sinking into unconsciousness, away

from the horror and the pain. Something l
as she had seen Adam's true self, now she
unlike before when she had prayed for deat
wanted to live because she suddenly knew de
some miracle she did survive she knew then
destiny had planned for her but she prayed n
the last of the hideous, odious corruption in f

Adam released Beth when he saw that
watched as she slowly slipped through his claws
He was annoyed with himself for allowing this fr
to him, but he had to teach her a lesson and this
as he didn't want to kill her and so he had done
had said he was jealous of her relationship with Ge
He seethed with bitterness whenever Beth talked ab
it was not him that Gem smiled at, or laughed with

He had listened time and time again to her pra
kill her there and then, but his lust for Gemini kept
every word.

This stupid little nonentity was barely worth the
alive. Well, never again would she be able to look up
features or see that glorious mane of hair that he ha
through the night he had entered her dreams. He ran a
saliva round his thin, leathery lips and drooled at the thou
his power. It would not be long now. He had set the final
and soon he would have what he had always wanted. As for
down upon the small slumped figure on the ground and co
feel the pleasure her punishment had brought him. He wante
had exercised patience and unusual control, although admitt
no need to show her his physique, but then she had tweaked

No, he had seen to her!

He had taken away something precious … yes, he had
irrevocable taken away her sight … and Beth, as she lay unco
the rough floor, was unaware that all her prayers had been ansv

would like to call him, is looking for a way, or a bridge if you like, to enter this world from the pit he was cast into."

Gem didn't want to look at Nathan's face. *Please let him believe me,* she thought as she continued carefully, "If you were a theologian you would know that the first churches were built on pagan sites and that the largest of these was built in the North ... York was the cradle of Christianity at the time. It is the second most important church, holding as its bishop, the second in command, if you like, of this country's church hierarchy." She gave Nathan a quick glance, hoping she wasn't boring him, but he just sat there giving her his full attention. "Unfortunately for us, His minion has found a way of bridging that gap. That is why he has taken Beth and Remne; so that I will follow ... I know that now."

Gem stopped pacing in front of her desk and for a moment she let her thoughts wander back to those who had died.

Nathan's words broke her reverie and as she turned to face him he stood up and said, "What has all this to do with you? For Christ's sake, you are a solicitor not a bloody demon fighter."

She could tell by the tone of his voice that his concern for her overwhelmed what she had just told him about what was about to be unleashed upon an unsuspecting world. In fact she felt he was taking it all with a pinch of salt.

"I don't think you are fully grasping what I have just said," replied Gem, placing her hands back on her hips.

"Yes I do," he said, "but let us get one thing clear, you are a woman and, I might add, a very beautiful one but a woman nonetheless and I forbid you to go wandering off on your own thinking you can fight all and sundry. Please, Gem, leave it to us professionals."

Gem could not help herself; she threw back her head and laughed out loud and when she looked over at Nathan, she laughed again at the angry set of his features.

"Oh please," she said, waving a hand in front of her as she tried to contain her mirth; she was forced to take a few deep breaths before she continued, "You thought I was going to faint earlier after what you had told me. Just let me show you something."

Nathan leant forward as Gem ducked down out of view behind the settee and as she rose again to her full height he could see she had within her grasp a large, shiny sword. He was so overcome by the sight of it that he took a quick step backwards without looking and bumped into the small table, rattling all the china. Nathan flapped his hand in front of him as he pointed to the sword and once again the blood drained from his face.

"Whoa there; for God sake, Gem, am I looking at a murder weapon? Did you use it to kill the doctor? Now that I think of it, you seemed to handle that extremely well. Please tell me, Gem, did you kill the doctor?"

Gem could hear the pleading in his voice, but she was loathe to answer him. She eventually summoned up her courage and admitted, "Yes, if you must know. He had fallen into a pit of evil of his own making. It was Rupert who killed his own parents because his greed and hatred had consumed him. He held a pistol to my head and told me he had twice tried to kidnap Beth. I was inches away from his gun barrel and seconds away from death; what was I supposed to do?"

Gem held out her hand and was devastated to see Nathan turn away from her and sit heavily back down.

"I'm not a killer, Nathan, you have to believe me. I gave him every opportunity to repent but he spat in my face," said Gem, her voice choking with emotion.

"What makes you different from him? If as you say his life was consumed with greed and hatred, what is yours consumed with? Eh ... Answer me, Gem: who exactly are you?" Nathan's face contorted at this unexpected harangue.

It was like a slap in the face and Gem suddenly remembered, through all the passion and affection they had shared, the reason why she was there. It was not a situation she had asked to be in. Two weeks ago she was going about her ordinary business, doing a job she loved and now ... no, that was a lie, who was she kidding? Only herself ... it had started a long time ago.

She had known from when she was a little girl that she was different, she had felt and experienced things that she took for granted at the time.

Her parents had not made a fuss when she told them things that eventually came true; they knew that she was special and told her that was how special people behaved. They did not make her feel freakish or abnormal ... now she knew why. Now, after all that had happened and the promises she had made to herself, she had let herself be side tracked by this tall, handsome man and he was right ... she was consumed. She was consumed with hatred at the loss of her parents, hatred at the abduction of Beth and hatred at the loss of Remne.

Hatred of the thing that was too evil to contemplate.

It kept her on the path of vengeance and retribution; she could not let It enter an unsuspecting world and ruin even more lives. Gem knew now that mankind was going through a period of spiritual poverty. She knew plenty of people who tried desperately to find something outside themselves, trying to fill a need within themselves and not realising that it was taking away all that was inside, leaving them hollow and without purpose.

Gem suddenly realised the significance of the retreat at Holy Island and why her own people were trying to guide mankind back into spiritual and loving ways. They were trying to break the patterns and habits that mankind's aimless lives were creating. Margaret and Lloyd were taking people away from their natural surroundings and comfort zones and offering them an alternative to their solitary, sad and consumer-ridden lives.

Without this help, they were clear candidates for the evil and horrors to come.

Now as she looked at Nathan she realised that the love he was offering her was a hindrance; she knew she should put it behind her … but it was hard … very hard.

Nathan watched the different emotions cross Gem's face, but he was still appalled at her confession. He had been trained to see things as they were, to unify all the facts and evidence, to add motive and eliminate reasonable doubt. In the end after exhausting all the possibilities, hopefully you came to the right conclusion. These shades of grey were not what he was used to; suddenly he felt out of his depth, knowing he had only heard part of the story. He was at a loss as to how he should continue.

Should he take her into custody?

Shouldn't he arrest her? She had, after all, confessed to murder, but these were exceptional circumstances and the old rules did not seem to apply in this situation. He was suddenly frightened, not only for himself but for her also and that fear manifested itself into anger. He wanted to turn back the clock and forget what she had told him. He wanted to bump into her in a cosy wine bar, go out together, make love, but above all just be normal now, but that was impossible.

His anger rose again and he heard himself adding, "Well, have you finished or have you any more to add? Because I have suddenly realised that I don't know you at all."

Gem heard his words, and as they gradually sank in she lifted her lowered head and held it high as she said, "I have done nothing to be ashamed of. I was brought here for a reason, to force out these evil ones and I am doing just what is expected of me."

"What do you mean?" he asked. "On whose authority, did the Government bring you in? I was not aware they had brought in a special task force."

Gem could see the hope of a possible solution gleaming in his eyes. "My authority comes from a much higher source than you could ever imagine; nothing will stop me from doing what I have to do, not even you."

Her words were spoken calmly, but Nathan could hear the chill creeping into her voice and he realised, in that awful moment, he was on the point of losing her forever.

Fear gripped his insides and he pushed his hands into his jacket pockets as he felt them start to shake. She was his world, and the phrase "for better or for worse" had not seemed more appropriate. He could not give her up no matter what she had done, but how was he to protect her? She could be so bloody wilful at times – well, actually, all the time.

Nathan sat there going over everything in his mind; raising his right hand, which had been buried deep within his jacket pocket, he ran it absently through his dark hair. He felt the anger leaving him and what she had been trying to get across finally registered.

"I'm being a bit of a pratt, aren't I?" Nathan said apologetically. "It's just that I was so shocked to see that sword so soon after the mur ..."

Gem could see he was searching for the right words to improve the situation.

She watched as his body language changed and his words grew softer, but still she remained on the other side of the room as he continued, "So soon after the incident; does that sound better? And now knowing it was you ... well, you can't blame me for being angry and with all that about devils and minions; it's all a bit too much for a chap like me to take in, all at once."

She was right, they were a weird mix of frailties and complexities and Nathan was a prime example. Gem relaxed her pose long enough for her to rest the sword on the carpet and lean both hands against it. Nathan stood up and moved over to where she was standing and as he manoeuvred round the settee he said, "That is an awesome looking sword; I'm surprised you can lift it."

She could see he was fascinated by it and she could not help showing off her prowess. Remne would have called it the sin of Pride; *let's hope I'm not in for a fall*, thought Gem.

"If you stay where you are I will show you what I can do with this thing," said Gem, lifting the heavy sword.

"Okay then, boss, fire away," said Nathan, his jovial mood returning. Gem stepped away from the wall, balanced the sword in her firm grip and proceeded to slice the air one way and then another. The sword grew brighter and its song could be heard getting louder and louder. She brought it up to her lips in one fluid motion and in the next she had turned a full circle and sliced the air in front of her. Nathan realised this was not some ordinary girl; she was indeed someone extraordinary and with a special mission to fulfil.

As Gem came to a standstill in front of him he tried to take her in his arms to show that he still loved her and wanted her, but she drew away from him; seeing the hurt at her rebuff deep within his eyes, she said, "No, Nathan, you have reminded me that I must keep my mind on my mission and in loving you I have neglected my duties. I am glad we had this little talk and I am glad you finally see things my way, because there is one more thing I have to tell you ... well, actually two things, but I can't tell you the second until you say yes to the first one."

"How on earth did you manage to make it as a solicitor?" he asked with a laugh as he carried on speaking, "Because you have lost me now. Just ask what you have to ask and I will try with my little policeman's brain to work out what you are going on about."

Oh my God, this is going to be so difficult, thought Gem as she looked into his now merry eyes.

"Do you think you could sit down before I ask you?" said Gem, pushing him with one hand back over to the settee.

"Only if you think it is entirely necessary," replied Nathan, settling himself amongst the cushions.

Gem took a deep breath and leant her sword up against the back of the settee.

She then rested her hands along the settee's back edge and composed herself.

She felt as if the words would burn her tongue, so she said, as quickly as she could, "Now answer me straight away so I know it is coming from your heart: will you go with me to where I have to go and bear witness to the fight? Will you also help Remne and Beth if they need it?"

Gem saw his eyes widen as she spoke, but his answer was there before she had even finished speaking: "You know I will; you did not even have to ask, just point me in the right direction."

Gem would have been extremely relieved if that was the only thing she had to say, but now was the part she had been secretly dreading.

How would he react?

She cleared her head. *Just do it,* she told herself, *don't think about it.*

"Thank you for that, Nathan; now I am going to show you something that might frighten you a bit, but please don't be … well, here goes."

Gem watched from her position behind the settee as Nathan's smile humoured her; she could see he was at a loss to what she could possibly be talking about. He settled himself down amongst the cushions and even crossed his legs in an attitude of peaceful indulgence.

When she saw that he was sitting comfortably, she stepped away from the back of the settee and extended her arms out to the side.

The room had grown slightly chilly, but the small light from the desk cast a soft warm glow around the room. Gem watched Nathan for any reaction and when her wings started to appear, she was not disappointed. She saw his mouth open and shut as she unfolded her beautiful white wings and she could not help running her hand gently up and down their edge, feeling their softness. When her wings were completely extended, she very gently, so as not to shatter too much within the room, beat them in a slow hypnotic rhythm. The smile disappeared from her face when she looked over and saw Nathan practically cowering in the far corner of the settee.

As Gem took a step towards him, she immediately refolded her wings and they disappeared. Hurrying over to him, she practically jumped the side of the settee to sit heavily beside him. "I'm so sorry if it was a shock to you," she said. "Come; let me hold you for a minute."

She gathered him into her arms, all thoughts of putting her love on hold forgotten.

"Say something then, you had enough to say earlier," continued Gem as she stroked the persistently stray lock of hair away from his brow.

Gem heard him release his breath loudly; after a few moments he said shakily, "Well, that's going to take a little bit of getting used to. Never in my wildest dreams did I imagine you would divulge anything like that." He released himself from Gem's embrace and, sitting up a little straighter, turned to her and said, "Does this mean that you are … You know …?"

"What?" replied Gem, suddenly turning impish and finding it quite amusing that he was at a loss at what to call her.

She moved herself a little farther down the settee and tucked her legs under her bottom; with one arm draped along the top, she looked for all the world as though it was the most natural thing to have just shown him her wings. Nathan leant towards her as if seeing her for the first time, but she still was the tall, willowy blonde with a figure like a model; he gave his head a couple of shakes to clear the image of those awe-inspiring wings.

"Does this mean you are an ..." and she laughed as he mouthed the word "angel." "And when this is all over do you think you can ... you know ... when we finally get together?" said Nathan, giving her a salacious wink.

Gem was too amused to be offended, but she leant forward and punched him on the arm all the same, adding, "That's the trouble with you men; you see everything in terms of sex and try to turn everything to your advantage."

"And why not, I would like to know; there has to some advantages of having a beautiful angel as a girlfriend," replied Nathan, rubbing his arm.

"I'm not a fully-fledged one," she said, "because if I was, you wouldn't be able to see me and I wouldn't have been able to enter the realm of man. I have all the attributes, so to speak."

"You can say that again." As he spoke Nathan ran his hand up her thigh.

"No, I don't mean that, I mean I have strength and I have my wings, but I am half human, and that means I can also die."

At her words Nathan stopped his caresses and looked into her eyes, saying, "Then we shall have to see that nothing happens to you, because if anything did, I don't think I would want to carry on."

As Nathan leant forward he kissed her gently on the lips and Gem could feel her own passion rising. Suddenly out of nowhere she heard Remne's voice within her head and pulled away from Nathan, staring vacantly into the middle distance.

"Gem, it's worse than I thought; you have to come quickly."

"Why? What has happened?" replied Gem.

"He is so angry that I fear for our lives before you can get to us," said Remne, and Gem could feel the fear and tension even in Remne's thoughts.

"Have faith, my friend, all is ready this end. I am on my way."

But Gem could not feel a response to her words, and she feared that something had happened to Remne and she would not know she was on her way.

Chapter 29

Gem swung her legs over the side of the settee and pushed herself off the edge. When her feet hit the floor, she went round the back of the adjoining settee and ran her hand over the hilt of her sword, as if reminding herself of its presence. Looking over towards Nathan, she saw that he was watching her curiously and said, "We have to go; I know it sounds strange but I have just heard from Remne and fear for her and Beth's lives."

"Why would it sound strange? After all, it must be an everyday occurrence, you getting messages out of the blue," Nathan replied to her retreating back.

On hearing his words, Gem turned to face him, rounded her lips into a soft pout and blew him a kiss. She then turned and went swiftly out the door and up the stairs two at a time.

Nathan paced up and down, waiting for her to return and tried valiantly to put everything into perspective, but it was all just a little too much to comprehend. He ran his hand through his hair in a nervous gesture and wondered what the night had it store for them both. As he was wishing he was armed, he spied Gem's sword; he looked through the door to see if Gem was anywhere in sight and then he reached down and picked it up.

Or, more to the point, tried to!

He was a big chap and worked out whenever he could, but even so he still had difficulty lifting the sword. As for swinging it about like Gem had … forget it! It had taken two hands just to lift the thing into the air and what a dork he would look if she was to come in and catch him. Could he lift the sword with one hand, as she had? He gave it a go just to see if he could, but the muscles in his arm could not take the extra weight and screamed in agony at being misused. Nathan decided quickly that it wasn't to be and lowered the sword to the ground, placing the tip on the carpet.

The hilt of the sword was very unusual and he leant down to get a closer look.

He saw that it was made up of four angels with interlocking arms. As he leant down closer he saw the four heads turn and look right at him; they all stared back at him! Shaken at what he had seen, he quickly straightened up.

He ran his free hand across his face. A slight film of perspiration covered his brow and he wiped it off. Then he wiped his hand down his trousers. When he looked again at the hilt, all was as it should be and he almost convinced himself he must have imagined it. After all, it had been a rather trying day.

Then Gem burst back through the door. She stood there for a moment, looking at him with the sword and unable to keep the smile from her face, she held out her hand and Nathan had to relinquish it. He was fascinated that she could wield it so effortlessly and inwardly he felt more than a little inadequate.

He looked with interest at the leather contraption she had round her shoulders. His curiosity was satisfied, though, when he watched her place her sword through the loop that was positioned in the middle of her shoulder blades.

After she had settled her sword in place, Gem watched Nathan's face as he looked about the room. Seeing the look of bewilderment cross his features, she was forced to ask what he was looking for.

"Well, you have a bloody great sword, but what do I have? I shall tell you … Nothing. So what in the world am I going to fight with? I haven't even got my gun." Nathan flung his arms wide in a gesture of hopelessness.

Realising he did indeed feel vulnerable, she smiled and went to stand next to him; as plainly as she could she said, "I'm not expecting you to fight. You will be there as a spectator not a protagonist; do I make myself clear?"

Gem had placed both hands back on her hips and watched as her words registered uncomfortably with him, so she grabbed the front of his coat before she continued, "This is a fight you cannot possibly win. So please, if you value all our lives, let me do what I have to do and don't, for the love of all that is holy, do anything stupid. I can't take time out of this battle to keep an eye on you."

Gem could see his face begin to alter at her words and as his eyes started to blaze she knew his natural fighting instincts had rushed to the fore; worse still, she knew she had bruised his ego.

She carried on talking quickly, trying to stave off the inevitable row: "This is getting out of hand. I don't want Him to know that you are there, otherwise your life will be in terrible danger." Gem released his lapels, placed her hands on his arms, and proceeded to stroke them in a declaration of comfort as she added, "What I do need is for you to rescue Beth and Remne, as that is the most important thing. Please, Nathan, can you do that for me?" Before she continued, she bent her head to one side as she looked up at him and said, "He will be too preoccupied with me to take time out to watch them, or at least I'm hoping he will be. So the coast will be clear for you to take them to safety. Will you do that for me? Please, Nathan."

As Gem spoke she moved closer to him and could feel the warmth from his body; she knew that he could feel hers as well and with that small feminine gesture she knew his resolve had weakened. She smiled secretly to herself as he nodded his head in agreement. Who needed angel's wings when she had human feminine wiles?

"Right, let's get to it then, shall we?" he replied, somewhat subdued.

Gem strode over to the curtains and pulled them to one side so that she could look out at the street; Nathan rushed to her side when a sudden string of expletives exploded from her mouth.

"What on earth's the matter?" he asked. "That doesn't sound much like 'angel talk' to me."

Tut-tutting, he leant over her shoulder and cast his eyes up and down the road but could see nothing out of place.

"Seems all right to me," he added, "just a few pedestrians hurrying home and a cat sitting on your neighbour's car."

Gem swung round to face him, her eyes blazing and he could see she had trouble putting into words what she wanted to say, but eventually she spat out, "The bastard took my car! Whoever that charmer is, he is in deep trouble; nobody but nobody takes my car without my permission."

Nathan had trouble trying to keep the grin from his face and thought it better to crease his brow as a sign of solidarity; nodding his head sagely, he said, "Yes, quite right, the bastard doesn't know what's coming to him."

Gem edged closer, peered into his eyes, and murmured, "It's times like these that I think Remne got the better deal," as her eyes scanned his, trying to see if he was joking or not.

Not wanting to antagonise her even more, he turned smartly around and made his way over to the lounge door, saying as he swung the heavy door towards him, "Come on, then, we can go in my car," but Gem had caught the ghost of a smile as he had turned away and replied in a voice full of innocence, "No, that's too conspicuous. I know a better way of getting there; follow me but before you do, turn the lights off."

Smiling sweetly at Nathan, she walked passed his tall frame and was secretly pleased to note the troubled look of uncertainty flash across his features. Nathan hurried to do her bidding and as he followed her into the hall, he was perplexed to see that she had turned left, towards the kitchen and not right, to the front door. He followed her into the kitchen and was amazed that the weight of the sword wasn't giving her any trouble at all. Gem flicked the lights on for a brief second, giving Nathan just enough time to get his bearings and then switched them off again.

He heard her heading over towards the back door and then followed her. Even though she had turned the lights on briefly for him, she heard him stumbling around in the darkness; he whispered, "Sorry ... just 'cause you have eyes like a cat ... it's all right for you ... you live here." Another bump followed his comments and she heard him swear softly.

"Why are you whispering?" Gem asked as she leant up against the side of the door.

"It's force of habit," he explained. "As soon as the lights go out, I go into police raid mode; whispering is second nature to me. All good policemen know how to whisper properly, we take courses in it. As a matter of fact I have a PhD in whispering. Do you know there are many different kinds of whispering? There is the stage whisper and the 'where are you?' whisper that's more like a desperate shout really and there is the ..."

"Please, that's enough, I believe you. Now hurry up and come over here, otherwise we will be here all night."

Nathan could hear the urgency beginning to creep into her voice no matter how much she tried to hide it with the gentle laugh at his humour. "Sorry, I was trying to ease the situation," he explained when he reached her side.

Gem lifted up her hand and stroked his face, feeling his warmth and taking comfort from it.

"I'm sorry too, but we must be serious from now on; one false move could be the end, do you understand me, Nathan?"

"I really don't know how to say this properly, Gem, but if anything happens tonight and it all goes pear shaped, I just want you to know that I ..."

He felt her hand move softly over his mouth, cutting off his words and she said softly, "Nothing is going to happen, do you hear me? This is the last time I want you to speak of this and from now on, I am no longer your Gemini."

Gem raised her face to gaze up at him.

She continued, "I must fulfil my destiny and do what has been chosen for me. I do not rail against what I am or what I am about to do ... I choose it ... I embrace it."

Nathan squeezed her hand as she spoke, wanting to help her, but she placed her free hand on his lips to silence any objections, adding, "This is what I was sent here for. Those that love me know me for what I am, as I know you do. So let's not speak about this anymore." As Gem went to turn away he quickly grabbed her and kissed her with all the love and passion he could muster.

Her lips felt sweet and he felt her respond with equal ardour, their bodies pushing together in an unconscious demand; they became one as he crushed her to him with a demand they both knew could go no further. So with regret they forced their bodies apart and stood there in the shadows, her head for once leaning against his shoulder as if for succour.

She heard his deep voice rumbling in his chest as she pressed her ear against him, all sense of urgency momentarily forgotten. "Now you can be the Gemini you want to be, but that kiss ... you were my Gemini once and nothing will ever change that. No matter what lies ahead, I have to tell you that I think I love you and I always will. There now, it is out in the open, so lead on and let battle commence." He gave her a quick peck on the cheek and said, "For luck," with a half-hearted laugh.

Gemini was a little stunned at his embrace and revelation of love, but she was more worried about his casual attitude about what was going to happen.

She knew he had been in tight situations before, but this was obviously different; she only hoped she was not taking him into a situation that could prove so dangerous that she could not save them all. It was too late now. As she unlocked the back door her fear for her friends' plight returned and she was spurred into action, but she could not keep a small sense of shame creeping into her mind about how much she had dawdled with Nathan.

Nathan followed her into the garden, hard on her footsteps and their bodies crashed together, knocking him to the ground when Gem suddenly stopped.

It was hard to see anything in the darkness and Gem looked around at the neighbouring houses as Nathan scrambled to his feet.

She heard his whisper of annoyance floating towards her: "Why did you have to stop like that? It's hard enough to see as it is without you doing a full stop. I nearly skewered myself on your sword. I thought you were going to go out through the gate; what have you stopped for now?"

She didn't answer him, she just continued scrutinising the houses and surrounding gardens. Her feet made no sound on the earth as she completed a 360 degree turn to end back where he was standing.

Gem could feel the air cool against her skin; after the rain the previous night, everything in the garden felt wet and soggy. She could smell the dampness of the dew as it descended and her ears picked up the night creatures, innocently wandering about their business. How she wished the same could be said for her!

Thinking it best from now on to say nothing, Nathan just stood there as his eyes grew accustomed to the darkness and he watched Gem pace round the garden. He couldn't see her eyes, but he knew they were searching the darkness for anything amiss. When she was satisfied, she pulled Nathan by the arm so that he was standing in front of her; taking a deep breath, she summoned her celestial spirit inside of her.

Nathan felt his lips go dry and the nervous fluttering in his stomach returned as he watched Gem metamorphose into a spiritual avenger.

He involuntarily gasped and took a step backwards as he saw her muscles twitch and once again her wings unfolded.

Gone was the humour of earlier and he felt humbled in her presence; it was hard for him to look upon her without wanting to fall to his knees and ask forgiveness for all his past transgressions. As if she had read his thoughts, Gem stretched out her hand, placed it under his chin and forced him to look at her. As he took in the grandeur of her presence he felt his eyes fill with tears and said, in a stumbling voice, "I had no idea ... you are so beautiful. I realise now ... that ... that was not the real you that you showed me earlier. It's true then ... you are ... you are indeed an avenger!"

"Yes it's true," she confirmed, "and before this night is out you will wish that I am all that you set your eyes upon. Now hurry! We can't dawdle any longer. Get close to me so that I can put my arm around you."

As he drew closer to her so did his feeling of trepidation. What had he let himself in for? It was too late now to change his mind; to lose face in front of Gem would be too shameful to contemplate. No, his destiny was set and it was up to him to bear witness to whatever it was that was trying to destroy the world.

He felt her strong arm encompass his waist and with one bound, he felt himself hurtling skywards towards whatever fate awaited them.

Chapter 30

Remne could feel the car slowing down, but she did not move her eyes or lift her head in case Reynard realised she was not in a deep a sleep, as he thought.

His physical presence was abhorrent to her, but she did not flinch or pull away even when his fumbling hand kept brushing against her knee as he awkwardly changed gears in the powerful car.

Good job Gem is not here to listen to this, thought Remne as she forced herself not to squeeze her eyes tight whenever Reynard crunched the gears. She had felt her energy sapping away from her in the beginning, but as he drove to their destination, she was aware enough to remain in contact Gem when the occasion demanded it. Cold air blew across her face, as he failed to adjust the cooling system and for that she was grateful, as it kept her body and her sanity, in a state of semi awareness. She lay awkwardly in the car but didn't want to move or change her position; she had shut down all that was unnecessary to her and like a comatose patient, she was relying on only what was essential to keep herself alive. She had channelled all her strength into keeping her mind active but had let her body fall into a state of lethargy, so much so that when he stopped he was forced to push her into a more upright position as she slumped against his left shoulder when he applied the brakes too readily.

Remne tried hard to concentrate, but her head felt as though it had been stuffed with cotton. She heard the click of his seat belt being released and his leather seat creak. Her assumption that he was getting out of the car was proved right when she heard the driver's car door open and shut, but still she did not move. He must have walked round the car, because a few seconds later she felt the cool night air as Reynard pulled her door open.

She felt his hands burning her skin when they touched her, but still she remained inert. She offered no resistance when Reynard tried to pull her from the car and she knew by the way he was breathing that his strength was waning. After a great heave he managed to extricate her from the car and she was forced to lean her full weight against him as he moved closer into her body to support her.

Reynard raised her arm and managed to hook it around his shoulder and balance some of her weight on to him. She felt an overwhelming urge to tighten her grip, squeeze the breath from his body and watch his life slip easily away. Instead she opened her eyes slightly; if he had been looking he would have seen them glitter like hard icy emeralds, but she let her head flop to one side and her long hair covered her face once more.

The moment itself had passed, but she knew she had neither the strength nor the ability to extract any kind of vengeance and even more significant it was not her place, nor her destiny. She felt the cold hard wall on her back as Reynard momentarily leant her up against the brickwork as he fumbled to open a door. Her head still felt light and she had no control over her limbs, but her natural instincts were starting to kick in and she could feel her body fighting hard to rid itself of the drug he had forced her to pump into her arm.

Remne could feel herself being half dragged up a small slope and into a building. The inside of the building was unusually cool and she wanted to open her eyes to see where they were, but she could not chance being caught.

Small sounds and smells came to her; by the echo of their feet they were somewhere with very high ceilings. Of course; this had to be the only place they could come to.

The Alpha and the Omega - I am the beginning and the end.

The Great York Minster!

Once more he pulled her towards him and together, like lovers, they entered the Minster; half dragging and half staggering, they walked up the small slope to the top.

Remne knew the layout of the Minster and guessing that Reynard would not want to be seen at the front of the building, she assumed they had come round the back and parked at the north side of the cathedral.

The only door available to them would have to be the one leading from the Lost Property and Minster Police offices.

Remne had to smile at the irony of all, as York Minster was the only cathedral to have its own police force, set up after the fire of 1829 when Jonathan Martin, the brother of painter John Martin, set fire to the wooden choir stalls after his threats were ignored. Since then the Minster Police had kept a watchful eye on all who entered the cathedral, but not tonight, obviously. Remne mused over her situation and wondered if Adam's evil influence had been at work even then.

Reynard suddenly stopped, which forced Remne's attention back to the present. She could feel his chest heaving with the exertion of carrying her, but he had only stopped to prop her onto his shoulder in a better position. They carried on walking straight ahead and as he dragged her up some steps she assumed he was taking her straight into the quire, the highly decorative wooden part of the church where the choir is part of the congregation.

Reynard hesitated after forcibly hauling her up the steps and she guessed he was looking for somewhere to put her. He decided quickly, because in next to no time she felt him dragging her to the right. They were heading for the High Altar.

Her feet stumbled against the steps leading up to the altar. Remne could hear his tut of annoyance at their slowness. Eventually they reached a spot he was happy with, because he suddenly stopped and gave a large sigh as if he had completed his duty.

Then she felt him loosen his grip on her waist and lower her to the floor. She was surprised when he placed his hand under her head so that it did not bang on the floor. This was so out of character that she pondered on it for a while and then she heard him turn away and his footsteps disappeared into the bowels of the cathedral.

Slowly Remne opened her eyes and through the slits she could just make out the lower part of the quire, although everything was at an angle due to the way she was laying.

She saw that the cathedral was in darkness and the only light was the silver moonlight straining to penetrate the stained glass. It was intermittent and weak as it peeked through the high windows to the left and right of the great building. Shadows invaded everywhere and what might have seemed normal during daylight hours now seemed menacingly dark and frightening.

Suddenly through the gloom she could hear voices and for some reason her blood ran cold as she listened to them getting closer. She dared not move and was grateful that her hair hung over her face, obscuring her features.

Remne thought she heard a woman's small cry of pain but it stopped before she could evaluate who it was.

Perhaps it was Beth?

Only time would tell!

As for now, a strong male voice was giving orders for the large candles on the brass stanchions to be lit. She cautiously peeked through the strands of her hair and was amazed at the sight before her. As the candles took hold she could see by their first light that it was indeed Beth; she lay in a curled up position on one of the marble steps leading up to the High Altar.

She saw Reynard going about the task of lighting the candles and in their glow she saw the most handsome man she had ever seen. He uncurled his long legs that had been crossed at the ankles and then he rose sinuously and sensually from the archbishop's throne, where he had been lounging.

Remne could see a mixture of boredom and curiosity cross his face; one finger of his elegant hand traced the woodwork as he descended the stairs and she heard him say in a disinterested voice, "Did you know that the word 'cathedral' is derived from the Greek and Latin word *cathedra*, which means 'seat' or 'throne'?"

"Actually I did," Reynard replied calmly, but he could not keep the excitement out of his voice as he continued, "I've done it. I've found the Book and I've found your prize. Look ... look over there and you will see what I have brought you."

He pointed to where Remne lay sprawled out on the floor near the High Altar. Remne could see him almost jumping up and down in his excitement, like a puppy waiting for his master to pet him.

The soft light from the candles fell across her motionless body as she watched in fascination as the handsome man's look of boredom and curiosity melted, to be replaced with something akin to devotion and the most incredible look of complete hatred she had ever seen, merged into one. The words, when they came, froze her to the core and she was extremely thankful they were directed not towards her, but to Reynard.

"Where did you find her?"

His words were spoken softly and if Reynard had not been so eager to please, he would have seen the danger he was getting into. Instead, he went blindly into the trap the handsome man had set for him.

Remne was reminded of a fly caught in a spider's web and she knew that when he started twisting and turning it was going to be his downfall. As he went from candle to candle, lighting them, she heard the joy in Reynard's voice as he explained to the oddly silent man standing in the warm glow of the candle flames how he came to be there.

"At her own house, I couldn't believe my luck. I travelled up with that policeman on the pretext of looking into affairs up here … and he said he would ask her outright … if I could stay with her and do you know what? The Book was there … just lying on the floor; well, I couldn't believe my eyes, I can tell you. So I brought the Book … and the girl with me. Of course it was hard getting her here … Adam, my friend … her being so tall and … well, I had to manhandle her a bit just to get her in the car."

So this was Adam. She was not surprised. As she looked Remne could see Adam close his eyes at Reynard's words as if he was trying to get himself under some form of control.

When he opened his eyes, they glittered with a terrible light and Remne knew that whatever battle he had waged with himself, he had lost and that something awful now awaited Reynard.

"You actually laid your hands upon her?" Adam replied in a soft silky voice, but now Reynard suddenly became aware that something was wrong and he took a step backwards away from Adam, blowing out the match as he retreated.

At once the fear started to show on Reynard's face and his body language changed again as he rubbed his hands in agitation.

"How was I supposed to get her here for you? I knew you wanted to have her and well …" His voice trailed off and then unexpectedly came back with as much bravado as he could muster.

Remne watched as Reynard tried to get the words out and then she saw him licking his lips as they tumbled into the quiet air of the inner sanctum.

"What was I supposed to do? I've been in the thick of it for months; doing all the things you have asked me to do. I think you ought to show me a little respect too, you wouldn't have her here if it wasn't for me and I might add …"

His words were cut off as Adam suddenly turned, took a step forward, grabbed Reynard by the throat and dangled him in the air like a terrier toying with a rat.

"You have been amply rewarded, you annoying piece of filth. You have been dogging my footsteps for the last seventy-odd years, doing well on the crumbs I have thrown to you, but now I have had enough of your whining.

I told you never to touch her. She is not for the likes of you and the very thought of you touching her makes me want to rip you limb from limb."

In the stillness Adam's words echoed obscenely round the cathedral; not wanting to touch him for longer than necessary, Adam flung Reynard to the ground, where he landed in a bone crunching heap on the unrelenting stone tiles. Remne watched as Adam turned towards her and she could not help but give a small tremor of fear.

Knowing now that her deception was going to be unmasked, she wondered what fate he had in store for her. She tried to swallow but her mouth was dry, leaving only a taste of ash. There was no need to feign sleep now, but still her limbs would not do what she wanted them to do. She wanted to run away and hide, she wanted to get as far away from that evil thing as possible, but she couldn't so the only alternative left was … to be exceedingly brave.

Adam walked over to where she was lying; reaching down, he very gently brushed the hair from Remne's face. She still had her eyes open and watched as a look of utter disbelief crossed his features.

She could feel the anger in him growing as he squatted before her; she felt the icy coldness of his breath as he leant closer, as if his eyes were playing tricks on him.

Remne's green eyes, luminescent in the candlelight, stared back at him, instead of the blue of Gemini's. She saw a small smile tug at the corners of his mouth; whether this was amusement or anger was hard to tell. He held a lock of her hair in his hand and rubbed the silky smoothness between his fingers; Remne heard him say softly, "It is the same hair; it would have fooled even me. No doubt she is coming for Beth and now I have you as well, quite a result really. She will not let her friends die in her place … two bargaining chips are always better than one. You have, my dear, just shortened the odds in my favour."

Adam leant forward and gazed closely at Remne's face, still apparently amazed by the deception, before he continued, in his quiet tone, "It is only a matter of time. I have already waited an eternity to get what is mine; a few more hours will not hurt. You did well in your deception; it was very clever of you. It is a shame I haven't the time to get to know you better like our dear Beth over there."

Seeing Remne's eyes stray to where Beth was laying, Adam said gently, "Fear not, she is not dead; she is just exhausted after our little confrontation."

As he stood up his voice became hard and malice dripped from his every word. He still stood, looking down at Remne, but his words were directed to the heap just visible at the bottom of the steps leading down from the High Altar, where Beth was still curled up.

"I see you have failed once again, my friend; this is getting to be quite a habit with you. So I think I will have to teach you a lesson, one you will never forget."

Adam rose to his feet and nonchalantly placed his hands in his trouser pockets, looking for all the world as though he was in a business meeting talking about stock and shares. The icy tone in his voice made his words resonate round the quire: "I know what the most valuable thing to you is. So I shall take the Book you covet so much; someone else will decipher it and once again its beauty will be denied to you."

Adam half turned away from Remne and she could see a curious mix of reds and greys around his face, making his handsome features turn from bewitching to pagan and back again as the candles flickered across his face.

She was so enthralled by the effect that she was unaware that he had continued speaking until she heard him give a low laugh – a laugh that lacked humour.

"I find it quite amusing that after all those years of searching you have finally found the Book, but before you get the chance to explore it, I am going to take it away just to teach you a lesson. Yes, really, it is quite amusing. Now does that sound like a fair arrangement for all the distress you have caused me?"

Adam turned and smiled as he looked down at Remne, but she was not fooled by his false smile of warm sincerity she knew he was not human. He wore the mantle of a human the way she did, but all she could feel was ice beneath his polished veneer, no compassionate heart below under the surface. Although her gift allowed her to read the hearts of men, she could feel nothing within him at all. Her gift would not allow her to penetrate his inner self.

He was an enigma.

All she could feel was his evil and violence and the only thing she could do was to lie there helplessly and watch the outcome. She felt the urge to draw her knees up like Beth in the foetal position and rock back and forth in an effort to comfort herself. Even though the cold pervaded her body, she was still not in a position to have any command over her limbs; not yet, anyway.

Remne's insides suddenly jumped when, from the dim outer reaches of the High Altar, a maniacal high pitched scream echoed that made the hair on her arms rise rapidly in alarm. She pressed herself as best she could against the altar, trying to distance herself from the figure she could see running up the steps and into the candlelight.

Reynard had a metal chair raised above his head and as he bore down upon Adam he swung it in a menacingly high arcing movement. Remne wanted to close her eyes but she was too fascinated by the outcome. The look on Reynard's face was one of complete lunacy, the look of a man who had reached his limit. Spittle exuded from the corners of his mouth and his breath laboured from his exertion. His eyes had the deranged look of someone being driven completely to the end of his tether; Remne knew it was the loss of the Book that was causing his downfall.

She forced herself to look upon the scene being played out in front of her and with her special gift she forced all her energies into seeing into the heart of this demented man; what she saw stunned her. Adam's protection had finally fallen away, leaving Reynard's true self finally exposed to her and now she could see him for all the vileness he contained.

He was not the wise historian sent from London; he was here to intercept Gem and the Book, his need far outweighing anything else in his miserable, false, unnatural life.

She had thought all along that his name, Reynard Holt, was unusual. Reynard, the red of the fox like the hair of his youth, for who else had owned such red hair and Holt for the false life like a lair he had been hiding in all these years. She had known from her premonition that he was not to be trusted, but she hadn't realised until now that Adam had been protecting him from her.

Now that protection was at an end!

Of course!

The answer came to her in a blinding flash and she wanted to shout her discovery to the very ceiling tops. Caution suddenly prevailed though and as her body lay against the cold stone she watched as the world of Lord Horatio David Penn-Wright, alias Reynard Holt, came crashing down around him. He had not died in that car crash, as the world had assumed. He had been spared to work as one of Adam's minions and she guessed Adam had used his obsession for the Book to keep his hold over him.

A new body, one that never aged, what more could his obsession-fuelled life demand, but all this was being taken away, so what need had he to continue being an obsequious follower?

Adam was still nearby, staring down at her, when he heard the frenetic scream, but he turned and moved forward as the figure hurtled towards him. He did nothing to prevent Davy's thundering passage towards him; he did not step to one side or even try to evade the blow that was about to come crashing down upon him. There was no need. Adam's physical strength far outweighed anything Davy had to offer and with a flick of his wrist, Adam quickly disarmed him. He threw the chair to one side and in a flash he again had Davy by the throat. This time Remne knew that Adam would give no quarter and as she gazed upon Davy's dangling frame she realised Davy suddenly knew this as well.

The first Remne knew she was crying was when she felt the tears scalding her cheeks. She could not pull her eyes away as she witnessed the terrible transmutation of Adam into one of hell's fallen angels.

His tall leathery form filled the area around the High Altar and at first she wondered what the noise was. As she looked at the grotesque form in front of her, she realised to her horror he was drinking the blood of the limp body of David Penn-Wright.

The slurping and gulping noise made her stomach heave and she felt the bile rise in her throat, burning her with its acidity. Remne knew she had to get a message to Gem and as she closed her eyes, blotting out the disgusting scene, she tapped into Gem's mental telepathy.

Suddenly she felt a jolt and quickly stopped talking to Gem. As she opened her eyes carefully, she could see the grimacing face looking over towards her in what she supposed was a semblance of a smile. A hideous one … but still a smile and her blood ran cold as the beast threw Davy's lifeless body onto the altar and then turned his attention towards her. His great leathery wings beat a rapid tattoo as he turned and looked down at Remne.

The candle flames flickered and danced, turning his shadow into the most hideous gargoyle the cathedral had ever seen. Remne could smell the scent of destruction exuding from him.

The blood from Davy's wounds ran thick and wet down his chest and as he stared at her, he reached for the altar cloth and tugged it from under Davy's limp body. One of Davy's arms now dangled over the side of the altar, only inches from Remne's face and she watched as the blood dripped down onto the floor, staining the flagstones.

After he had wiped himself with the altar cloth, the symbol of Christ's shroud, he flung it over Davy's body; this symbolic action was not lost on Remne, even if its significance was lost on the beast.

He again changed back into Adam as he stepped towards Remne and all traces of Davy's brutal butchery had disappeared; in a voice soft and calm he said to Remne, "I can feel her near you, you have spoken to her. Tell her to come to me quickly, for I long to see her."

Adam lifted a lock of her hair again and bending down he raised it to his face and smelt it. Remne could feel the effect of the injection slowly wearing off; she forced herself up into a sitting position as he held onto her hair.

Her body felt cold from lying on the stone floor but not as cold as when that despicable creature in front of her was speaking, numbing her to the very core. She tried to turn her head away from him, but he placed his hand under her chin and forced her to look at him, saying, "You do not smell the same, you look a little alike but you are not her and never will be. So we shall have to do something about you, won't we, because we can't have you running round the place when she arrives?"

Adam looked over his shoulder towards where Beth was lying and Remne could see he was deep in thought. Finally he turned to her and she felt the tears once again on her cheeks as fear for herself and her friends overwhelmed her.

For one brief moment, she had her doubts as to whether Gem could fulfil all of what was expected from her. One brief doubtful moment was all it took for him to read her innermost thoughts. Remne shut her eyes, blotting out the creature in front of her.

What had she done?

"No! No, I didn't mean it!" her mind screamed.

There was no pain he could inflict upon her now that could cause as much distress. She had been disloyal to Gemini and that was unforgivable. Adam leant forward and looked deep into her eyes. His icy breath touched her cheek and fear gripped her insides, turning them to water. His face changed slowly from Adam to Cybil and then back again and she placed her hand over her mouth; she felt herself wanting to scream as he said, "Gemini has no need of friends like you. You are indeed disloyal and so I shall show her what happens to friends that cannot be trusted."

Chapter 31

Large, black, scurrying clouds obscured the moon as Gem and Nathan flew through the night sky, their arms interlocking in a firm embrace. Nathan knew that if it was not for Gem's strength holding him close, he would have plummeted to the ground a long time ago. He was at least being realistic to know this was not a figment of his imagination. At this precise moment he would have been more thankful if it had have been, but he knew that he would not find himself tucked up nice and warm in his own bed.

No matter how he looked at it, it took some explaining. He was really flying through the air, supported by an incredibly good looking woman with two bloody great white wings.

He admitted to himself that he had been terrified when they had first soared into the sky and he had clung to Gem like a frightened child. She had not laughed or ridiculed him; instead she had held him tighter, leant forward and kissed his cheek. Nathan stole a quick look at Gem's face and was amazed at how relaxed she looked, which was totally different from how he was feeling at that moment.

He could feel the sweat break out all over his body and as the adrenalin pumped towards his heart, it found a home and his anxiety grew the longer they flew. Gem stopped flying and silently hovered, which terrified him even more, but as Nathan bravely took a glance downwards he saw they were directly above a large church. The lights around the building were extinguished but he could still make out the formal layout of the building.

The darkness pervaded throughout; it was like looking down into a large black hole; his heart started pumping hard, causing sweat to break out on his forehead.

Nathan looked to Gem for reassurance, but she said nothing and as she continued flying he saw that she was making for the far side of the building, away from the main road and prying eyes, to the small park at the back of the church.

As they neared the ground he heard Gem swear and seeing the look of anger on her face, he feared looking down to see what she was scrutinising. As soon as her feet touched the ground Gem released Nathan and he stumbled and fell to the ground. She folded her wings away and then made her way over to where her car had been hurriedly parked. Gem gave the inside a quick inspection; reaching inside, she removed the car keys and tossed them to Nathan, who was just brushing himself down. She said, "If nothing else guard them with your life."

Seeing the blank look on Nathan's face as he caught her keys, Gem was forced to smile and say, "I'm sorry, am I being too flippant? It's not as it there aren't more important things at the moment." With that, she beckoned Nathan to her side.

As he neared Gem grabbed his arm and together they went towards the small door in the north wall; placing her free hand upon the brickwork, she turned to Nathan and said, "We are not far behind them; I can still feel where Remne has been. Now listen very carefully, Nathan." Taking him in her arms, she planted a kiss upon his lips; releasing him, she said, "As soon as we get inside I want you to go and hide yourself until you know it is safe to come out and watch what is going on. He will be so interested in me that I'm hoping he won't detect you, but if he does … get out, because I'm warning you … hell itself will be on your coat tails. Do you understand me, Nathan?"

"Yes, I understand you, but Gem, please don't do anything stupid or heroic, just do what you have to do to get this over with," Nathan replied, the pain in his voice evident as his nervousness increased.

Gem still gripped Nathan's arm as she tried to impress upon him the importance of the situation.

Seeing him wince, Gem relaxed her grip slightly and said, "Nathan, whatever you see in there, don't make a sound. I can't stress how important that is; also, if you see a chance of rescuing Beth or Remne, then grab it. Don't worry about me, I can fight my own battles; now give me another kiss and let's get going."

Nathan pulled her tightly into his embrace and kissed her passionately on the lips; as he looked into Gem's tightly closed lids he sadly wondered if he would ever be doing this again. Now was the time for action and as she released him, they looked into each other's eyes. There was no need for words now; each knew how desperate the situation was.

Gem took two steps backwards, away from Nathan and raising her hand to silence any questions, she took several deep breaths, closed her eyes and focused her mind totally on the fight to come.

Nathan watched in awe as her muscles tightened and hardened; she even seemed to grow taller. There was nothing of the slim, tender solicitor left; instead, standing before him was a warrior of biblical proportions.

As Gem stood there she heard her sword starting to sing its war song; it was the sweetest music she had ever heard. Turning swiftly away from Nathan, his presence now forgotten, she entered the Minster in her deadly pursuit.

Nathan followed hard on her heels and as they reached the top of the slope Gem suddenly stopped and looked right and left. He watched as she sniffed the air like a hound on the scent of a fox; then, as if by instinct, she made her way stealthily down the aisle on her left to the east end of the church.

Nathan, with no other plan in his head, decided to follow her swiftly disappearing figure. As he ran after Gem he saw her turn right into the part that opened up into the Lady Chapel. He stood for a while in front of a large white statue and realised that this would afford him the perfect hiding place so he forced his large frame into the space behind the statue. At least, he assured himself, he would be able to hear what was going on, even if he couldn't see anything at the present.

Gem walked silently towards the Great East Window that contained the world's largest medieval stained glass in a single window. It depicted the beginning and end of the world, using scenes from the book of Genesis and the book of Revelation, the first and last books of the Bible.

"I am the first and the last, the Alpha and the Omega": the words ran through Gem's head again and again. *Why do I keep coming back to that?* She thought as her eyes roamed around the chapel and then she saw it.

She wondered why she hadn't seen it when she first entered the silent area, but the candles were not bright enough. Someone had lit the small dedication candles on the wooden stand and their meagre light was all she could see by.

It was only when her eyes had grown accustomed to the gloom that she could see it now. Someone had ripped the large cross from the wall in the south transept and placed it in the chapel.

It had taken great strength to do it and whoever it was had leant the head end up onto a chair, elevating it just enough so that Gem could see the person's face; lying along its length, with her arms outstretched along its cross section, was Remne.

Her long blonde hair trailed over the sides of the large metal cross and spilled onto the floor below like pools of molten gold. Gem rushed to Remne's aid and as she approached, she saw her move her head ever so slightly. At least she was not dead, but the ugly spikes in her hands, fixing her to the cross, ignited Gem's anger like lava spurting forth from an active volcano. Gem leant over to try and loosen the iron railings, but along with securing her hands to the cross, they were twisted and curled round Remne's arms.

The person who had done this had shown incredible strength and callousness, because the more she tried to unwind them, the more they pierced Remne's skin. *"Stop, stop now, please Gem. Leave me,"* came Remne's words, thundering into her subconscious.

Gem immediately let go of the metal and stepped away from her tortured body. She looked stealthily about … for once again Remne's words came into her head: *"Take care, He is near."*

As soon as Remne had spoken, she felt him and, turning swiftly round, spied him sitting on the fixed wooden pews at the back of the Lady's Chapel that backed onto the quire.

Gem walked steadily towards him, and she could see the amazement flicker briefly across his face at the sight of her shorn locks. "My, you look so different," Adam said. "No wonder my colleague was so confused, but you will always be beautiful no matter what you do to yourself." He unfolded his legs and stood up to meet her.

"I didn't come here to bandy words with you about your lust for me," replied Gem angrily.

"No? Then what did you come here for?" said Adam, moving down along the wooden kneeling column until he was in the centre of the chapel.

"Your head," responded Gem as she swiftly reached behind her and released her sword. Its light glowed through all the corners of the chapel, and its canticle was high and resonant.

"That is a shame," replied Adam. "I thought we could come to some sort of agreement, but I can see I am mistaken. So be it. It was written so and I shall have my reward at the end of it."

Gem lunged forward, but Adam was too quick for her and laughingly sidestepped her outstretched sword. Still laughing, he stood in the middle of the floor area in the Lady's Chapel and changed his persona from Adam to the beast that lay within him. When his transformation was finished, he stood over seven feet tall, the muscles in his arms bulged and every blood vessel and artery could be seen etched in his leathery flesh.

His chest widened as his ribcage expanded. The same was happening to his legs, making it difficult for him to stand upright and the deformity of his wide chest made it look as if his back was hunched. His great leathery wings unfolded and this forced his shoulders to hunch even more, but what was even more horrific were the long sharp talons emerging from his fingers.

His face had changed from the handsome features of Adam to what could only be described as the most hideous face Gem had ever seen.

The dark leathery skin was pulled back so far that it resembled a death head mask and his now thin leathery lips could not quite cover the long fangs protruding down over his bottom lip. His small pointed ears were raised just above his bald head, giving him a bat-like appearance.

"Now you see me as my true self, Gemini. Am I not still beautiful? Come to me, be one with me and we shall dominate this miserable earth when my Master comes to power." He held out his hand to her as if, in some obscure part of his brain, he thought she would actually accept him.

She swung her sword high but it was not in any attempt to strike him, it was just a reflex action on her part, giving him her answer. As she stalked after him he retreated; with every step she took forward she felt the wrath build within her until she finally screamed, "Do you honestly think I would go with you after what you did to my parents and my friends? No, you are very mistaken if you think I want anything other than your death."

She swung her sword again, making him jump backwards as it cut the air in front of him.

Pleased that he was on the defensive, she continued, saying, "You used to be like my heavenly self until your fall from grace and your Master has kept you falling ever since. Evil has rotted your soul; your lust for power and for me will be your downfall."

Gem twirled her sword violently, indicating her hatred and took pleasure in the fact that he was unarmed.

"Tell me," she cried, "what is your name now that you have changed, so that I can shout it to the heavens when you die?"

"You can still call me Adam," he said. "I like that name, it is the beginning of all things, the Father of mankind."

"And I shall be your Omega, your end!" Gem shouted as she lunged towards him, but he was gone in a flash over towards where Remne was laying.

She saw Adam reach down and pull out his sword from underneath Remne's flowing hair where he had concealed it, her long tresses covering it from Gem's view.

You clever bastard, she thought.

Frightened now that he might do Remne even more harm as he stood beside her, she unfolded her wings and flew quickly to her side.

She needn't have bothered, because once again he was off and with his weapon now in his hand he flew up and round the ceiling and then headed off towards the nave. Gem wanted to race after him but there was something she had to do first; raising her sword high above her head, she brought it crashing down onto the iron railings, just stopping before she reached the tender flesh of Remne's arms.

In the guttering light of the few remaining candles, Gem could just make out the pieces of railing holding Remne to the cross, so she reached over and pulled the black metal, sticky with Remne's blood, out from her ravaged wrists and released her from her bondage.

The small moan of pain was enough to let her know that Remne was still alive and now that she was free, she would leave it to Nathan to help her escape.

As she bent down she planted a kiss on Remne's forehead and as her lips touched her forehead, she was shocked to feel how cold and clammy it was. Gem gently stroked the sweat soaked strands of hair from Remne's forehead, although she had little time to spare and glancing once more down at her friend, she backed away and went in pursuit of her quarry.

Gem rose into the air and followed Adam down to the nave, flying through the quire and out over the organ pipes and through the other end until she came to the nave itself. She had spent many a happy lunch hour in here, gazing up at the high arches, which gave it a feeling of lightness and spirituality. It was the widest Gothic nave in England and in the dark it looked larger than ever. But at the moment it lacked that light, airing feeling. All at once it seemed dark and menacing and the high arches only added more places for Adam to hide.

She did not hear him coming and the blow sent her tumbling down onto the flagstones below; she cursed herself for not paying enough attention.

Gem lifted her right hand and ran it round her left shoulder; as she drew her hand away she felt the wet stickiness of her own blood. It was not deep but was long, trailing nearly down to her elbow. She sat there giving herself time to adjust to the situation, but she knew he would be back for more now that he had drawn his first blood.

Rising on one knee, she saw him coming in for another attack, but this time she was ready for him; bracing her right knee on the floor, she held the sword's edge close to her lips and kissed its sharp edge.

The sword sang out sweet and true as she waited until the last moment to strike. He came in swift and hard, relying on his weight to try and knock her off balance, but she held firm, ducked down at the last minute and then swiftly raised her sword and struck him as he flew over the top of her.

She felt his blood coursing down the sword's shaft onto her hands and as it ran down she saw it crystallise as if a sudden frost had touched it.

She knew she had inflicted some damage, but he had disappeared and as she slowly got to her feet her eyes searched the darkness for him. Realising her best option was to let her sword do the hunting, she pointed it out at arm's length and moved slowly around in a circle; it sang out loud and clear as she pointed it towards the statue of St Peter, York Minster's patron saint.

How ironic that he should be slumped up against St Peter, who was holding the keys to heaven and hell. By the light of her sword Gem could see he was holding his side and she could just make out a large gaping wound, expelling bubbling blood at great speed. It flowed out quickly, but as she watched, fascinated, she saw him breathe upon himself, and his icy breath suddenly staunched the flow.

The feeling of vengeance coursed through her again and she felt no mercy or compassion for the beast. For that was what he was, but as she neared him he seemed to gather fresh energy; she saw his leg muscles bunch and harden and then he jumped high into the air and took off again, leaving her to follow in his wake. Gem saw his ungainly form disappear up into the two-hundred-foot central tower of the cathedral.

She stealthily beat her wings, trying not to make too much noise as she started to rise up the fifteenth-century tower depicting St Peter and

St Paul on the central boss and then she became instantly alert. Gem stopped and strained her ears for anything unusual, because the light was very poor, but she could hear nothing. Thinking she had misjudged his whereabouts, she was on the point of turning to go back down when she felt his presence behind her; his coldness invaded her body, chilling her to the bone, but not as much as when he began to speak; he said, "You were so tender in your dream; it was such a pleasure. Close your eyes again and let yourself succumb. Stop this fighting and come to me. I will give you everything your heart desires, Gemini." She felt his rough hand stroking down her back in a hideous caricature of affection while the other hand started to circle her waist.

Gem slowly turned in his arms and although his disgusting face was only inches from her own, she smiled and with that smile, she could see he thought she had finally capitulated.

She raised her knees in one fast movement and straightened her legs, smashing her heels into his abdomen. She watched as his body went careering back against the wall of the tower, sending down a shower of plaster and brickwork.

She did not wait to see what happened next; realising escaping was better than fighting in such a confined space, Gem decided to fly back through the quire and as she looked down she noticed a small figure, lying lonely and forgotten on the steps. She descended, and as she flew nearer she realised that it was Beth.

What had he done to her? Was she dead? Gem landed and laid her sword to one side; all thoughts of vengeance were momentarily forgotten in her rush to gather Beth into her arms. Her body felt thin and childlike and as she held her close, she could just make out her shallow breathing. Gem brushed the hair from Beth's face and her cry of anguish echoed round the walls when she saw the black and darkened skin around Beth's once beautiful brown eyes.

Beth stirred in Gem's arms, reacting to the noise and once again Gem crushed Beth to her, still unable to take in the extent of her friend's injuries. What had he done to her sweet Beth? Feeling the anger well up inside her, she knew she would not be satisfied until he was finally vanquished.

Out of the corner of her eye Gem saw her sword start to tremble and glow. She gently laid Beth back down on the floor and reached over to grab her sword. As her fingers curled round the shaft she realised this time she was not quick enough; she had broken her own rule and let her friend's agony come between her and the job she had to do.

She felt his sword slip easily though the flesh of her back, but she propelled herself forward before Adam could push home the death blow. She threw herself into a forward roll and as her feet touched the floor at the end of the manoeuvre she hurled herself into the air, away from his slashing sword.

Breathing hard, both opponents came together in the air above the quire in a violent clash of weapons; Gem felt his cold icy breath sting her face as their attack brought them within inches of each other.

Gem saw the anger in his eyes at her rejection and she knew now that he wanted not only to secure the area for his Master, he also wanted to assuage his ego and pride by totally humiliating her.

She was no match for him in close combat fighting, strength wise, but she was nimble where he was slow and cumbersome. Returning back to the ground, Gem took the unprecedented action of folding her wings, giving her more agility to move about.

Her wings were invaluable for getting about quickly, but they hampered her in fighting. Adam descended after her quickly and lashed out. Catching her off balance, he delivered a stunning blow that sent her sword careering out of her hand and sailing out across the flagstones. Suddenly finding she was defenceless, Gemini somersaulted high into the air, landing some distance away from Adam but even farther away from her sword.

She heard his cruel and loathsome laugh and as he bulldozed towards her, he expected her to release her wings and take to the air like before, so he held his sword high and wide. So she did what he least expected and waited till the last moment. Instead of opening her wings and flying upwards, she kept them closed and dove through his legs, towards her sword.

She miscalculated her speed and came to a shuddering full stop when she hit her head against the High Altar; everything went black. She awoke moments later to such a strange sight that she had to shake her head to clear it before she could take in exactly what she was seeing. It looked like a religious tableau straight out of the books of the Bible. There before her, sitting on a high backed chair, was Nathan, and on each side of him, holding on to his knees, were Beth and Remne. Both the girls' heads were bent as if in supplication, but Gem feared it was the combination of fear and pain that was driving their heads down.

As for Nathan the look of sheer panic that was crossing his face was something Gem had hoped not to see. His head was bent at rather a peculiar angle and as the last remaining candle flickered and her vision started to return fully to her, she finally saw the reason why.

Adam, once again in human form, stood behind the chair, with one hand clutched firmly in Nathan's hair and the other one holding a long knife to the base of his throat. "So glad you could join us," Adam said. "Now isn't this nice? I was just getting acquainted with …" Adam bent down towards Nathan's ear and asked, "Nathan isn't it?"

Nathan nodded to the question and looking over towards Gem, he gave the smallest of smiles as if to apologise for getting caught.

Gem could see by the look in his eyes that he knew that his time had come.

Panic suddenly seized her and she looked about for some way out of their situation, but she couldn't find anything. It was like her own personal bad dream where you keep running and running and get nowhere and the baddie is always just two steps behind.

"Time is running out, Gemini," said Adam, breaking into her thoughts. "My Master is on his way, I can feel him moving beneath our feet and you are fortunate enough to have a ringside seat. Now come over here and stand behind this feeble specimen."

As Gem rose to her feet Adam stepped from behind the chair, quickly stooped down and gathered Beth up under his arm. "This, as you know, is just a bargaining chip in case you feel like doing anything stupid. I shall snap her neck as easily as anything; now come behind the chair," commanded Adam as he vacated the area and went to stand in the place where Gem had just left.

As Gem stood in Adam's place, he reached over and handed her the knife that he previously had poised at Nathan's throat and at her look of stunned amazement he continued, saying, "Oh, don't think I have suddenly gone stupid. I know you won't do anything while I have little Beth in my control. Now place the knife back where it was, and when I tell you, I want you to cut his throat."

"Are you mad?" shouted Gem. "What on earth makes you think I will do what you say?"

"You will do what I say because if you don't, I shall kill little Beth and Remne and then I will kill Nathan and anyone else you know or love. I will kill them all." Adam's voice had started to rise as he bellowed his orders, "My Master demands a sacrifice … a token. He needs fresh blood of an innocent to be spilt on the floor of the church … and then he will be able to rise up through ... as the blood will make a passage from this world down to his."

As he spoke Adam could not help walking up and down as he explained to them what was going to happen.

His face had taken on an almost maniacal expression and Gem's heart beat faster as she felt the ground beneath her feet begin to tremble, but still Adam babbled on, "This sacrifice will be laid out before him when he rises through the floor of this Minster ... and it is up to me to tell him the right time to do this ... because it is through me he can communicate his wishes and desires. You cannot defend this church any more ... give up ... you have lost the battle."

As he was speaking Gem thought she saw, through the flickering light of the one remaining candle, some movement just behind where Adam was standing, but she put it down to the poor light and wishful thinking.

Her hand felt sweaty as she tightly held the knife to Nathan's throat; she knew that the time was fast approaching when she felt the earth rumble even more beneath her feet and heard Adam's cry of triumph.

Something had to be done and her mind raced from one scenario after another, but still Adam's words came to her, dripping like poison into her ears: "Give all this up, Gemini; come to me, we can be together." Realising he was starting to lose control, Adam shut his eyes and tried to regain some semblance of composure. He stood again in front of Nathan's chair and held out his hand once again for Gem to take, oblivious to the look of hatred in the policeman's eyes.

Into the small ring of light behind Adam crept a figure unseen by all who were involved in the unholy scene. He crept low hoping his presence would not be discovered. As he came up behind Adam he staggered under the weight of the sword he had picked up. It was too late for anybody to stop him for when Adam heard the man's piecing scream; Gem's sword was already entering his body. Adam howled his anger and his pain to the high vaulted ceiling and turned swiftly round to face his attacker; he opened his arms and dropped Beth to the ground.

Startled by the pain, he forgot about the others and once again he turned himself into the form of the beast.

Gem did not need time to think; she vaulted over Nathan's shoulder and as her feet hit the floor, she was already reaching down for her sword that lay cold and forgotten on the flagstone floor.

The beast had turned to face his attacker and had knocked him to the ground when Gem came up behind him.

The creature heard the sword's war song and knew it was once again in the hands of his nemesis. It was a thought too long in the coming though.

As he looked down he saw the shaft of the sword protrude through his body, sending forth ray after ray of blinding light and as he slumped to his knees he once again returned to the form of Adam.

Gem pushed the sword to its fullest extent right up to the hilt and as Adam slipped to the floor she placed her foot in the small of his back and pulled the sword out as he slowly hit the floor, sending him sprawling on top of his valiant assailant.

Adam's blood seeped from his body and formed into a warm clingy pool of viscous liquid; Gem, fearful of treading in it, stepped gingerly backwards away from the prone figure. As she stared down at Adam, she thought she detected a slight movement underneath the outstretched limbs; rushing forward, she rolled the body of Adam off of the figure beneath and extricated a small, balding figure in dark brown robes.

"Zank you, zank you," said the breathless little voice.

"That's quite all right," replied Gem with a small laugh. "Who are you and what are you doing here?"

"My name is Johan and I come from zee Voodhay Priory. I come to help Remne; she is an angel, you know … also … like yourself … may the heavens protect you. I vurry and vurry und I think, go Johan, go und help dis voman. So I have been here for two nights now, vaiting; I did not know if I vas in de right place but I vait just de same. Then all diz fighting, *mein Gott*, I vas so scared."

"Well, you did very well, thank you, Johan." As Gem leant her hand down to give Johan a hoist up, she thought she saw Adam's body move.

This time Gem wasted no more time; she raised her sword in preparation and holding out her other hand, she hauled the little monk to his feet the moment he clasped it.

Pushing Johan behind her, she gave Adam's body a kick; finding no response, she stepped backwards away from his now dead body and the spreading blood.

Chapter 32

Gem saw that Nathan had gathered the two women to him and was holding them in a warm but firm embrace. The look on his face said it all. He was deathly white and Gem could see his hands trembling slightly as he sat on the cold, hard floor, holding the girls tightly to his body. He refused to look at her.

Johan had disappeared for a moment but he came back into the small circle of light, carrying a large brown satchel, which he threw on the floor. From the bag he extracted bandages and ointments. As Gem bent over him, she watched as he tried to stop the flow of blood from Remne's wrists, but he sadly shook his head when Gem tentatively asked, "Is everything going … to be … all right?"

Gem looked down at Remne and the fear in her uncoiled like a snake waiting to strike. In fear and frustration of having her two friends injured in such a horrific way, Gem wandered off to be on her own to try and gather her thoughts together. She left the comforting circle of light and walked into the deep shadows. She was not afraid now and the near silence surrounded her like a blanket. She could hear Johan softly giving orders to Nathan as he tried to staunch Remne's wounds.

She needed time to think.

She found herself before the High Altar and as she gazed towards the heavens, deep in thought, she rested her hands upon the table before her. She felt the tears spring to her eyes and angrily dashed them away, fearing even this moment of weakness. Her body had not returned to its normal shape, because her mind would not accept it was all over.

Had she actually defeated Adam?

His body lying on the cold stone floor told her she had and the wounds on her own body told her she had fought a good fight. She would concentrate later on her own rehabilitation, but for now she was too worried about Remne and Beth. She wanted to pray but the words would not come; the adrenaline still coursed through her, making her nervous and edgy, so she closed her eyes and willed herself to relax. She was startled out of her revelry by a cold hand encircling her wrist; looking down, she saw the bleeding and broken body of a man.

He had been obscured from view by the blood stained altar cloth. Although he lay on the altar in the shadows, Gem was annoyed with herself for not noticing him earlier. She grew fearful for anything else she might have missed.

She quickly spanned the quire, unconcerned for the moment about the half dead man clinging to her wrist. All seemed as it should; it was only the five of them, seven counting Adam and this man, that had disturbed the beauty and the peace of the building. So returning her attention back to the man in front of her, now that there was no immediate danger, Gem pulled the remainder of the cloth away. She saw that half his chest was open; exposing his ribs and his face looked like it had been clawed by a group of hungry bears. His left eye socket was empty and his cheek held the mark of several slashes, but as Gem looked down she saw that he was trying to talk. She watched as his lacerated lips started to move. Compassion moved within her as she realised who this was and although he was the man who had taken Remne, he had paid a terrible price for his treachery. His grip became stronger as he tried to speak and Gem was forced to bend over his body to have any chance of hearing what he had to say.

"What is it, Holt? What is it you want?" said Gem, close to his ear.

"I want ... you ... to promise ... me something ... first," he replied as the blood frothed and bubbled at the corners of his mouth.

"No, I shall promise you nothing unless I know what it is you want," answered Gem, her anger rising at his audacity.

"I can ... do something for you ... if you ... do ... something ... for me," he whispered.

"What is it? I will not promise but if I can help, I will. There has been enough killing for one night."

Gem moved closer to the altar as his voice faded in and out, but his words got stronger the more he talked; she was shocked to hear what he had to say next: "My ... name is Davy ... I ... think you know who I am.

He took … the Book … away from me and … threatened never to let me see it again … but I … know … something … he did not … know. The Book … has special powers … it can restore … a life to how it was … but only one, that was why … I searched for it … for so long."

Gem was shocked at his revelation and getting closer to his ravaged face she said, "Do you mean you are that Davy, the one that died years ago?" Her mind was racing and as she looked back over her shoulder she saw the beaten and battered bodies of her two friends; her heart felt as if it was breaking.

Davy's words, although softly spoken, dragged her back to face him: "You have to choose; which one is it going to be?"

"You have not asked to save yourself," replied Gem. "Why is that? Is it because you know I would not do it?"

"No, Gemini … there is … something I want … you to do … for me … and that is finish me off."

Gem tried to release herself from his grip, but he suddenly found the energy and strength to hold on to her wrist and as she shook her head at his request, he said, "You must … finish me. He gave me … this life and I served him … but I did not know to what depths … I had to sink … please help me … or I will be forced to be again … something I don't want to be."

"Do you repent? Are you sorry for all you have done? Do you ask God's forgiveness?" said Gem, still bending over him so that her words could be heard by him alone.

Gem could hear the strength returning to his voice as he said, "I do, I do."

And as he released his grip on her wrist she reached down, picked up her sword and nodded. He smiled and as those ragged, torn and bleeding lips were still smiling, the sword of an angel warrior entered his heart and put him to the rest he so desperately craved. She pulled the sword from his body and wiped it on his clothes before she sheathed it between her shoulder blades.

She did not know Nathan was there until he placed his arm around her shoulder and his sweet voice said close to her ear, "It was the right thing to do; you could not let him live and from what I heard you can at least save one of your friends."

Gem turned round to face him and he saw to what extent this choice was having on her, so he gathered her into his arms and offered her the only thing he had … a shoulder to lean on.

Together they went back to the little monk and the two women and as they neared them Gem could see Beth struggling to raise herself from the floor.

Gem rushed over to her and getting down on her bended knees, she held Beth close to her, trying to instil in her some of her own strength. She was a little taken aback when Beth said, "Do not worry about me, Gem; I can see clearer now with no eyes than I ever could with them."

Gem heard the words and put it down to Beth's caring nature; it was so like her to put others first. "But Beth darling, how can I choose between you? It is killing me."

Gem buried her face into Beth's tangled and matted hair as she spoke.

"You are not listening to me, Gem," said Beth, struggling to extricate herself from Gem's embrace.

"Yes I am," said Gem, her feelings suddenly hurt as she heard the rising anger in Beth's voice.

"No you are not. I have lived through things that I will tell you about in time, but for now let me tell you it has made me stronger. My body is weak at the moment but my spirit soars like a bird and I can see all I want to see as soon as someone starts to speak. I learnt that during my incarceration; he was a good teacher although he did not know it."

Gem watched as Beth's face was transformed into something quite ethereal and she was humbled in the face of such humility. Of course Beth was right: the skin around her eyes would heal and she would be as good as new except for the fact that she would never see again. Hugging Beth to her once more, Gem then rose to her feet and went over to the little monk. His fingers worked dexterously but he could not stem the flow of blood from the deep wounds in Remne's wrists; they watched as Remne's life seeped away and her breath became still and silent.

Gem had seen enough. Had they waited too long? Without the Book it would be too late to save her, so turning to Nathan she said, "Go to the car and search for it; see if there is a large book in there and when you find it bring it straight back here."

Nathan raced down the steps of the quire back the way they had come.

As she watched his retreating form Gem was eternally grateful she wasn't put to the test of having to cut his throat. That again was another decision that would have been too horrible to contemplate. Would she have done it, if forced?

She was still standing there deep in thought when Nathan returned with the volume tucked neatly under his arm. He placed the Book into Gem's waiting arms and when her arms encircled it, she went quickly over to Remne's body. She raised Remne's head and placed the Book underneath her long, flowing locks. Then crossed Remne's cooling arms, with the gaping wounds in her wrists, over her chest, she then straightened up and waited. They did not have to wait long.

Stream after stream of long vaporous spirals emitted from the Book. They rose and took on wondrous shapes of all the celestial beings in heaven.

Out of the mist there came a woman of such beauty that it hurt their eyes to look upon her. Her clothes were studded with jewels that glistened and shone and as she neared the place where Remne was laying she said, "I am an old friend of Remne's and I promised I would come for her when her time came." She stopped speaking when she saw Gem's sudden move towards her person and she held up a long elegant hand to halt her progress, saying, "Fear not, Gemini, it is not Remne's turn to join me; you have saved her life by calling on the Book. I just came to give her back the life that was sacrificed in your name. Go to her, go to your sister Remne, go to the person who put your life before hers."

"What do you mean … my sister?" replied Gem, feeling as if her feet had suddenly been rooted to the spot.

"Yes, your twin sister; although you are not identical, you are still twins. She was left with the childless couple on Holy Island, just like you were left with your parents."

"You mean Margaret and Lloyd," interrupted Gem.

"It was too dangerous to let you grow up together and it was always Remne's wish that she be the one to point you in the right direction. She was your messenger and she loves you very much, Gemini. Your work here is nearly finished but this is just a battle, we still have to win the war. Protect what needs to be protected; it will point you in the right direction. Take care, Gemini."

As quickly as she came she went, taking with her the diaphanous beings that had been floating about her and when she went, she left those behind in stunned amazement.

Remne moaned and started to raise herself from the ground, but before she could do so, Gem rushed to her side and threw her arms about her, saying, "Is that why we always fought, because we were so much alike?"

Remne gave a few little coughs, dragging the air into her lungs in huge relieved gasps. Gem took hold of Remne's wrists and inspected the now healed wounds; she marvelled at the smooth, clear skin. Not a trace of the former injury could be found.

Remne propped herself up against the chair and gathered Gem into her arms, and the tears fell from both their eyes in recognition of the part each had played in thwarting Adam.

"What of your injuries, sister dear?" said Remne.

She had waited for so long to call Gemini that, but it was worth the wait and as she spoke, she turned Gem round to look at the wounds that Adam had inflicted on her. Remne could see the blood beginning to soak through Gem's top and was instantly concerned.

"Don't worry about me. I think it's time to go home, don't you?" said Gemini, wiping her hand self-consciously across her face. Turning to look up at Nathan, she added, "I have lost and gained so much tonight; let's head home so that Beth and my sister can regain our strength." She smiled as she said the word "sister," and then holding out her hand to Nathan, who pulled her to her feet, they made their way towards the door in the north wall and home.

As they neared the exit of the quire, Johan suddenly stopped and knocking one of his hands to the side of his head he said, "Vat a silly old fool I am, I have forgotten my bag." Turning, he hurried back towards the now guttering, lone candle.

Gem turned absentmindedly in the quire's doorway to watch Johan's progress in the half-light; she smiled as he waved back when he had retrieved the forgotten bag. She was on the point of turning to join Nathan, who was helping both Beth and Remne out to the car, when Johan's cry of alarm sent shock waves thundering through her body.

She watched in horror as Adam half raised himself from the ground and wrapped a strong arm around the waist of the little monk, dragging him to the ground.

Gem suddenly spurred herself into action and raced across the short distance, but even so she was too late and had to watch in helpless revulsion as Adam's face seemed to cover Johan's as if he were sucking the life out of him. Reaching behind her shoulders for her sword, Gem released its power and drove it down into Adam's back, severing his spinal cord. The pool of blood that had lain beside his body suddenly swirled and moved like molten liquid. As more blood flowed from Adam's body, it started to take on the appearance of silver mercury instead of blood red.

Gem watched as Adam twitched in his death throes and satisfied that he was indeed dead this time, she pushed his body to one side with her foot. Not wanting to touch the liquid that swirled about Adam's body, she released the little monk who had once more found himself trapped underneath Adam's body. Fearful now that the liquid was moving quicker than before, she dragged Johan away from the body; she helped Johan to his feet and they stood together, watching the swirling mass.

The liquid seeped like acid down through the floor into the vault below; what seemed like silver hands, dozens of them, emerged from the liquid and started to pull Adam's dead body down after them.

As the last part of the body disappeared through the large hole in the floor, Gem carefully peered over the edge down into the vault room below.

It did not stop there, though; it went down and down, right into the bowels of the earth. As she leant over she could hear a terrible rumbling below and as she watched, it looked as if she were gazing into hell itself.

Leaning as far over as she could, Gem peered down into the fiery depths and spat her contempt. Her spittle dropped like a single jewel, down onto the writhing bodies that she could see in the flames and as it splattered, the rumbling grew louder.

The ground beneath their feet tilted suddenly as a large jet of fire flew into the air, sending Gem and Johan backwards in alarm. Gem threw out her arm to protect the little monk and in doing so she sent him sprawling onto the floor. Her action saved the monk from the blast, but as she stood there she felt the drops of fire rain down upon her, splattering against her skin.

It was not heat that Gem felt against her skin.

No!

It was damp and clammy and with it came the cold numbing feeling of things left undone. Then it was over and the hole was gone, leaving nothing to mark it had ever been there.

Johan came to stand beside her and as she looked down at the little monk, he said, "His Master is taking him back. You have von zee battle dis time."

Johan's face had taken on a white sickly pallor and fearing he was going to pass out, Gem led him to the chair.

She felt responsible for him; he was not a young man. In fact his years seemed to hang heavily upon him; he looked grey with shock and fatigue and the last thing she wanted was another casualty.

Sitting him down so that he could regain some of his composure, she gently said, "It is over, he is dead. This has been a trying time and you have shown great courage, but we must go. I would take you back to your priory, where you will be safe and at peace, but Nathan's team will want to question you. I am so sorry, Johan."

As she knelt beside his thin frame Gem ran her hand up and down Johan's back in an expression of comfort and compassion. Johan bent his body so that his head fell down upon his knees and Gemini was oblivious to the small vicious twist of a smile and a flash of green deep within his brown eyes.

Raising his head and looking at Gemini, he said, "Silly us, ve nearly forgot zee Book." Reaching down he picked up his discarded bag that was next to the chair and hauled the strap over his head so that the bag lay across his body.

Gem watched as he stood up and then made his way over to where the large tome was still lying, neglected on the floor. As he bent over to pick it up he grunted with exertion, and Gem rushed over to help him. She scooped the Book off the floor with ease, and as she turned away she missed the look of anger that passed across the old monk's face at her interference.

With a hand under the old man's elbow for assistance, Gem started to lead Johan out of the quire but stopped in mid stride as Johan suddenly spoke. Looking down upon his shaved pate, she heard him say, "Ya, Adam is dead and so be it. Zee beginning and zee end. Ya. Dey are all entwined into one."

She wondered at his words as they continued on their way out of the Minster together.

Chapter 33

Why do people have to live in such out-of-the-way, outlandish places? His mind screamed as he drove frantically down through the town, heedless of the natural caution he always maintained and headed for the causeway and back to civilisation. He would be noticed but he was passed caring.

How often did the islanders see a large black car careering down towards the crossing? He was bound to attract some curiosity, but it was late and very dark so perhaps that would be in his favour, because he had no intention of slowing down.

It was not as if the old couple would say anything; they would want it kept quiet as much as he did. Secrets and lies that was what both sides depended on.

Oh yes. He could see it in the old woman's face, she knew her time had come and it would have been over, if that darned cat had not intervened. Even the old man had accepted his fate.

Why, oh why was he foiled in such an easy task?

He thumped the steering wheel in his frustration and could feel the blood trickling down his back at his sudden movement.

He had not checked to see what time the tide came in and what with the pain he was in, he now started to panic that he would be caught by the incoming tide.

Accelerating hard, he ignored all the warning signs about travelling across the causeway when the tide was coming in. He just wanted to be rid of this place; it had brought him nothing but suffering. He ground his teeth in anger as he thought of the cat jumping at him. He could still smell the disgusting thing. He only wished he had been better prepared; he would have sliced the creature in two.

He slowed the large car down by hitting the brakes and dropping the gears straight into second as soon as his wheels reached the water's edge. Easing his way onto the causeway, he realised he was just in time and as he looked out of the car window he saw the incoming tide lapping around the car's wheels, making the crossing doubly nerve racking.

He concentrated hard and his eyes began to ache with the effort but he steadfastly kept the large black car on the quickly disappearing road. He wanted to put his foot to the floor and get the hell out of there, but he fought the impulse, kept the engine revs steady and watched in silence as the great car forged its way across the causeway to firm land.

Small beads of sweat ran down his forehead, which he quickly dabbed with his sleeve and it was not until later that he realised he had been biting down hard on his lower lip.

He had not even tasted his own blood. His eyes had scanned the fast watery emptiness and it was this fear of the water that had nearly overcome him.

His knuckles turned white as he gripped the steering wheel and every so often he scanned the floor of the car. The last thing he needed was water seeping in; hadn't he had enough trouble with the scratches the cat had inflicted on him?

Cats!

He hated them; they should all be exterminated, every last one of them. First cats and now water; would this evening never end?

As the car reached the other side, he heaved a large sigh of relief … at last things were going in his favour. Now that he was safely on his way back to York, he had made up his mind to drive for about an hour; that was about all he could manage, the state he was in. He would have a little rest somewhere out of the way and try and clean his wounds. His arms were beginning to feel stiff and sore and he had trouble steering the heavy car.

Keeping well within the speed limits, he drove past the spot where the police had stopped him the first time. It would not do to have the law stopping him again, for this time he did not have the luxury of his dog collar to protect him and avert suspicion. All would be well when he got to Adam.

He would know what to do.

The longer he drove the more the scratches pained him, so he turned off at the next available junction. As he swung the heavy car into a lane, the headlights caught a dirt road leading off to the right. Wasting no time he turned onto the track and aimed the car into the bushes and into a small clearing, well out of sight from any passing vehicles.

As he turned off the engine the headlights and dashboard lights gave over to the night; darkness enveloped him and all became quite and still. His head sank slowly onto the steering wheel as he gave himself over to self-pity. The scratches on his arms and back were starting to burn once again, now that his mind was no longer occupied with driving.

Struggling with the seat belt, he managed to release the catch and swore softly as the belt rubbed against his shoulder as it sprung back within its bracket.

He could feel his body starting to stiffen as the cat's poison rushed through his body. He tried to clean himself up, but each movement had become an agony. As he opened the car door he gingerly stepped down onto the damp earth and silently made his way round to the boot of the car, running his bony fingers along the side of the car to guide himself. The air smelt cool and damp and he could smell leaf mould and something stronger … sheep. He heard the first of the flock starting to bleat as it caught his scent and one by one he heard them rise to their feet and move away from him, away from something they could not see but were afraid of.

Their instincts told them to remove themselves from danger.

What did he care for the dumb, useless creatures? He had more important things to do. Standing there in the meagre moonlight, he flicked the catch on the large boot lid and balefully watched as it slowly rose.

The small beam of the boot light shone out bravely and he could see his bag as it lay sprawled across the interior. Its contents spread around in total disarray, bearing witness to his hasty departure. His knives glinted ominously, giving credence to their inauspicious use and carefully pushing them to one side, he dragged the heavy bag nearer to him.

Reaching down with both hands, he attempted to undo the zipper on the side of the bag but it snagged and would not move. Frustration and anger bubbled within him, for it seemed even the smallest of things was against him.

That was it!

He was not going to waste any more time; he already felt his injuries taking their toll on him. Little drops of spittle dropped from his lips as he bent over the boot of the car and suddenly he let his anger overcome him.

He needed the anger, needed it like a junky needed a fix. It helped him to summon up the energy to get out what he wanted.

No, not wanted … he needed … craved!

Heedless now of the pain he raked his long nails across the nylon fabric and ripped and shredded the bag until he retrieved what he wanted from inside the pocket. He was careful not to damage what was inside. Even in his anger, he was not that stupid. He held the clear plastic bag to his chest, almost lovingly. It would not do to drop it now, not when he needed it so much.

So with one hand he brought the heavy boot lid down and then carefully retraced his footsteps back to the driver's seat. He was fearful of dropping his package in the dark and the relief he felt upon sitting back in the car was immeasurable.

His hands started to shake as he placed his package gently onto his lap; reaching upwards, he switched on the car's interior light. He was shocked to see his reflection in the rear view mirror. The poison was working quicker than he expected. His skin was like parchment and his eyes were red and bloodshot.

He was dying!

Wasting no more time, he reached for the package; raising it to his lips, he made a small hole in the top of the bag with his teeth and then held it there while the viscous liquid slid continuously down his throat. It was not a cure; it was just a stop-gap until he could get back to Adam. He never went anywhere without a backup and it was in times like these that Adam had said the blood would come in handy.

Things had never gone wrong before and many a time he thought it was an unnecessary precaution, but Adam had insisted. How right Adam was and how wrong he was. That was why he was his Master, after all. He knew everything. This had taught him a big lesson: he would never doubt his Master again. Master had even told him how to get the blood and he happily relived the event as he reclined his seat and drank.

The child would be missed by now, but what did he care? He had covered his tracks. Nobody had seen him take the small boy. He had purposely picked an area to the south of the country, well away from the place they were hiding.

He had stolen a car in Nottingham and then driven to North London, where he had stood and watched as the children played. The child was just one of many playing out in the warm summer's evening. The rain had stopped him snatching on several other occasions, but September had proved sunny until late into the evening.

Fortunately for him all that the children wanted to do was play outside making the most of the end of their school holiday. They would all soon have to get back into the routine of early nights and homework. He knew they returned to school soon after their summer break and this would have been his last opportunity. If he missed, it would have taken a lot more planning and his Master was sending him to the north of the country, so time was of the essence.

He had taken particular notice of the boy's parents, who seemed careless in their attention, believing him safe whilst all the other children were around. He had watched from a distance, checking to see who would be the easiest to take. There was always one who was not quick enough to keep up, or was a bit of a loner and when he had identified his victim, it was so easy to snatch him.

He had timed it to precision, noting when the ice-cream van made its rounds and everyone's attention was taken up with the treats to come. There he was, the one that was always last to get his money, the one a little too trusting of strangers, his thoughts only on the ice cream he was going to get. He had been so easy to take, it was hardly a challenge. The child had taken his hand, looking up at him with wide, trusting eyes as he guided him across the busy road. He had not even struggled when he gathered him into his arms, his little smile still in place as he thought of the ice cream.

The child had wanted to cry out as the realisation dawned on him that they were walking away from the van and the eager clambering children around it, but the strange man silenced him with a withering look. He had spun his little head round, trying to find someone he knew, but there was nobody about and they were heading farther and farther away from all his familiar places. He wanted to cry but was too frightened to make a noise, so he dropped his lower lip in misery and hoped that the strange man would return him to his mummy before too long.

As the man opened the rear door of the car he thought about running away.

Away from the creepy man with the bad breath, but the man's hand held his arm tightly, forcing him to stay close. The child watched as the man reached inside the foot well and dragged towards him a large black bag. With his free hand the man pulled from it a bottle of water and gave it to the boy.

When the child had taken it into his arms the man then lifted the boy into the back of the car and strapped him into the car seat. The man then held out his hand and lying there in the middle of his palm was an inconsequential looking pill. A small circle of white, nothing like the overflowing cornet he had been so looking forward to.

He opened his mouth but the wail did not come; instead the man had pushed the pill into his throat and, snatching the water bottle from his weak grip, had forced him to drink, washing the pill down his young throat.

Careful not to draw attention to himself he had driven slowly out of the area and back up the A1 to York. He had changed cars halfway through the journey, pulling off the busy road down a small country lane to where he had previously left his own car. Before proceeding on his way he had set fire to the stolen car after he had removed all evidence of the young boy. He knew this was not really necessary but he always liked to err on the side of caution.

He had driven his big, black car into the garage and then carried the small sleeping boy into the house. It was so simple to administer the other sedative via a needle while the child still slept. It was imperative that he keep him alive during this process, as he needed his little heart to pump the blood from his own arm. He had then tightened the Velcro strap, which forced the small veins in the arm to rise. He had inserted the needle easily into the child's thin arm and when he had drained the last of the blood, he sat back and watched as the child silently died.

He was glad that he could drain the blood from the body while the child still lived; it always tasted better that way. He had to have young sweet blood, almost like an oral transfusion; it was the only thing that would save him against the cat's poison. His long bony fingers squeezed the last remaining drops from the plastic bag and he gave it one long final suck, his thin lips meeting together with relish.

His head dropped momentarily back onto the head rest as he gathered his strength and his hands lay splayed across his thighs in relaxation.

Heaving a large sigh, he now found he had the strength to go on. The scratches on his left arm still hurt as he explored them with his right hand, but he could cope with them; he would not touch them again, he would leave it to Adam. By the look of them, the blood was starting to congeal and go crusty, but he knew the poison went deep and nothing would save him unless he managed to get back to Adam in time. The blood would buy him some time until Adam was able to heal him. Adam needed him just like he needed Adam and it was that need for each other that might just spare him his life.

He knew he had messed up but there would be other occasions, he just had to make Adam see that. After all, hadn't he been punished enough?

Sitting up straight, he adjusted the seat so that it returned to the upright position. He had things to do and he had to get back and report to Adam.

The moon was now riding high in the sky as he reversed the big car back out into the lane and headed down towards the main road. Looking over his right shoulder, he made sure nothing was coming and then he pulled out and headed south. Now that he was not in so much pain, he pushed his foot down hard on the accelerator and sped towards Middlesbrough and down the A19 towards York.

There were a few cars on the road; their headlight momentarily lit up the inside of his car as they sped passed on the other side of the road. Most of the lorries were holed up in the lay-bys for the night, which made life a little easier for him, as he did not have to keep pulling out and overtaking the great lumbering beasts.

As he neared the great city of York the sun's first rays were starting to peek through the night clouds, bringing a rosy hue to the horizon. He was oblivious to the new day's beauty as his dark eyes sought out the road he needed to take him into the town. He had started to feel agitated the closer he got to the city and now his nerves were jangling like he had drunk a thousand cups of black coffee.

Something was wrong; he was in no doubt now.

Something was very wrong indeed and that something had to do with Adam.

He felt his lips begin to snivel at the thought of Adam not being there. What was he to do?

A pathetic cry of self-pity softly escaped his lips at the thought of being abandoned and his driving started to become erratic.

Where was his Master?

He had always felt Adam there, as if the two of them were joined by some invisible cord, but now that cord was weaker.

Panic seized him.

What about his wounds? Who would heal them? What was worse, he could also die! He pulled the car over to the kerb, fearful of his thoughts and rested his head in his hands. Something was happening to Adam, he felt it in every fibre of his body, but there was no time to think of anything else as agonising pain ... torments of dread and revulsion, then overwhelming grief ... tore through him in wave after shuddering wave.

It tortured his body and set it on fire as if all his joints were being ripped from their sockets. His bony hand gripped the wheel as the pain flowed through his thin frame, forcing his head back in agony, but no sound came from between his thin lips. Then suddenly the pain disappeared and he was left panting for breath. Cold beads of sweat appeared on his forehead and he quickly wiped them away with the sleeve of his jacket.

He lowered his head once again onto the cold, hard steering wheel and tried to gather his thoughts. He envied the human emotion of crying because that is what he felt like doing. He wanted to sob his fear and cry aloud for his Master.

What was he to do? He was cast adrift in a vast world of humanity that was totally alien to him. What did he know about tenderness or philanthropy? Nothing!

It was then the small voice came to him, and he raised his head in remembrance of the voice. His lips slid back away from his teeth in a semblance of a smile.

"Yes Master, I am here," he whispered into the emptiness.

His previously hurt feelings were forgotten in the recognition. He nodded his head as he listened to the small voice, carefully restarted the engine and nosed the big black car back out onto the road towards the city centre. The world was starting to wake up, the opportunist shop owners catering for the early morning worker were starting to open up and delivery vans were starting to clog up the traffic. There were now more cars on the road, even at this early hour.

Cautious as ever, though, he obeyed every speed limit and traffic sign and did as he was directed. The small voice told him to park away from the hideous place of torment but in a position where he could still watch.

When he reached the place that he had been directed to, he turned off the car's engine and made himself comfortable; it would not be long now.

He watched as the cheeky sparrows darted around on the ground, busying themselves with the business of trying to find something to eat. He could hear the lazy call of the black crows as they flew in formation to their early morning feeding grounds, their calls getting louder as they flew overheard.

He craned his neck to get a better look and was so fascinated by them that he all but missed the car as it hurtled round the corner, passing him at high speed.

It was that bitch's car, but he could just make out in the dim light that it was not her driving.

No.

It was a man and he was not hanging about either. He drove the car like a professional, changing gear as soon as his foot hit the clutch. There were two women also with him in the car, one in the front and one he could just see slumped in the back. As the driver sped round the corner the woman in the back was thrown to one side; her face leant briefly against the window but her eyes were closed, so he had no fear of being seen. He could see the cruel burn marks on her face and knew instantly who she was.

He closed his eyes in remembrance, yes, the "Little One." The one with the long black hair, he had enjoyed watching her and he licked his lips at the memory.

Still he waited.

He was beginning to think all was lost when suddenly he saw the small green Morris Minor pulling round the corner. It was not going as fast as the other car, mainly because he suspected she had nothing to fear.

He slid down in the seat as a precaution as the car passed him, making sure he was not seen. He knew the power the woman had and so he took no chances.

At last!

His Master had come!

With the small voice still ringing in his ears he prepared himself to lay eyes on his Master once more.

His happiness knew no bounds!

But what was this? He was confused now. He could see the woman as plain as day sitting in the driver's seat, but the bent and crumpled old man next to her he did not recognise.

Had he got it all wrong?

His Master had told him to wait and follow nothing more. He should have dominance over the bitch; something had gone seriously wrong … and who was this person in the car with her?

No! He had faith in his Master; his Master would not let him down. He had been lost and abandoned an hour ago and his faith had been tested to the limit, but his Master had proved he was there for him and he would not find him wanting again.

When he had thought all was lost his Master's voice had come to him, giving him orders, telling him what to do … and he would do all that he asked, with no questions asked … after all, he was the Master. Perhaps he would forget his own misdemeanours now that he was here to help him.

The thought pleased him immensely and a sly sneer crept across his face.

All he needed now was for the Master to mend his wounds and they would be back on track.

He had been peeping over the top of the driver's door window, keeping an eye on the progress of the car; seeing it getting nearer, he watched in anticipation as it drew level with his own. As the Morris slowly drove past his waiting car all time seemed to stop as he peeped over the top of the door window and looked into those green eyes he recognised so well.

"Master, you are alive!" his mind screamed.

He placed a hand against the window as if touching his Master's face as he passed. In answer the old man placed his own hand against the passenger side window and acknowledged his minion and then he was gone.

He watched stealthily for a while, his heart beating a fast tattoo and then sliding upwards with caution, he kept his eyes glued on the disappearing old car. He had thought he had been abandoned in an unwelcoming world, but now his Master was back and he had to do his bidding.

So like a dog eager to be return to its owner, he started the car, pulled away from the kerb and followed in the wake of the small green car.

Chapter 34

The drive back to Gem's house had not taken long but nobody seemed to want to break the silence. Nathan concentrated on his driving and so was able to justify not talking. They each kept their thoughts to themselves as if they each did not want anyone to invade their private space, for the length of the journey, anyway.

A lot had happened in such a short time and they knew they would eventually have to talk about what exactly had gone on, but for now it was pleasant not to say anything. Nathan's hands still trembled slightly, so he grasped the steering wheel slightly tighter than was necessary; it would not do to fall apart now, but deep down his nervousness persisted.

As they had exited the Minster he saw that the day was breaking and the world was waking up new and fresh. As he assisted the girls into the car he realised nobody but themselves knew what had gone on, what a battle had been raged and won and if he hadn't seen it with his own eyes he would never have believed it either. Was that the reason why Gem wanted him there? He had no doubt it was. Now, though, as the car drew up outside the house, Beth's voice broke into his reverie, saying, "I know this sounds a bit silly, but does anyone have a key? I don't."

It was such an inconsequential thought, but one nobody had given the slightest thought to, that they each found the humour in it and with their laughter a bond was formed and the ice broken.

Nathan checked the keys in the ignition and true enough the house key was missing, so he turned in his seat and said, "No, sorry, I haven't either. I was too busy flying through the air with Gem."

He noticed the change in Beth's ravaged features but was surprised to hear her say, "Oh wow! How was that?" He watched as her hand flapped about before it came to rest on his arm.

"Oh you know, not much to say really, I was too terrified to look."

Sadness filled him when he thought of all the awful things that had happened to this beautiful girl. It must have shown in his voice, because Beth slowly dropped her hand away from his arm and her features became calm again.

Nathan looked at Remne, who slightly shook her head and raised one shoulder as if to say, "Leave her, she'll be all right." They were both taken aback when Beth said, "Please don't feel sorry for me, Nathan; as I told Gem earlier I can see better now than I ever did. Don't ask me how or why, I just can and as for you, Remne, don't patronise me, you of all people should know better."

Remne was the first to speak; leaning over to take Beth's hand in hers, her voice echoed the sadness she felt as she said, "I am so sorry, Beth, you are totally right. I was being patronising, but please forgive me and put it down to tiredness. I know I should have looked deeper but sometimes you forget and just see the surface of things. It is a wise lesson and one I must try never to forget."

"And that goes double for me," said Nathan, putting his own hand over that of the two girls.

"Well, now that is sorted, there just leaves one thing left to do," said Beth, the impish spirit returning to her voice.

"Oh, yes, and what is that, may I ask?" said Nathan, suddenly alert. He had straightened up and sat there watching both girls, who were smiling broadly at him.

"You, my hero, must go round the back of the house and let us in," said Beth jovially, and all they could hear as he exited was him muttering, "I'm going, I'm going," as he clambered out of the car.

Nathan jogged down the street until he came to the service road that was between the two houses; going down it, he turned right and made his way back to Gem's garden gate.

Fortunately he was tall enough to reach over and undo the latch; once more he found himself in the garden he had left only a few hours earlier. His thoughts tumbled over each other and in an attempt to get a grip on reality, he bent over double and took in a couple of deep breaths.

It was no good; he could still feel the cold, hard steel that had been pressed up against his throat. Would Gem have actually gone through with it and sliced through his carotid arteries? He knew she was ruthless when it came to Adam, so he thought to himself, *Keep telling yourself that, Nat ol' boy.* He straightened up and thought, *you're better off not knowing!*

So with his head a bit clearer and his thumping heart more under control, he headed for the kitchen door.

Now that it was lighter than the last time he was there, he made good progress through the house and reached the large front door in next to no time.

As he dragged the heavy door open, he saw the two girls supporting each other; Remne was dangling the house key out in front of her, saying, "It must have fallen off of the fob when you started the car. I was just about to open the door when you arrived, so good timing." She stepped over the doorstep, supporting Beth, flashed Nathan a lopsided grin, and said, "Give me a hand here, Nathan, will you? I'm feeling a bit weak myself."

He immediately offered his hand in support and this time Beth took it without hesitation; she smiled up at him when he said, without thinking, "You did it!" Realising his error, he tried to fumble an apology but Beth stopped him with a squeeze of her hand on his arm, adding, "Yes, I can do it, especially when I concentrate, but Remne was right, we are all tired, so let's get into the lounge where we can all relax before Gem gets back."

Remne leant against the wall in the hallway, supporting Beth while Nathan put the catch on the door, ready for Gem's return. Then when he was ready, he turned and picked Beth up whilst Remne held onto his arm and the three of them, tired, battered, and bruised, entered the lounge. Placing Beth upon one settee, he then turned and assisted Remne onto the other and then left them to make themselves comfortable.

He decided to go into the kitchen and make a cup of tea and try to rustle up something for them all to eat, as the growling in his stomach informed him how famished he was. He was sure the others would be as well, especially Beth, who looked like she hadn't eaten properly for a long time.

The sun had not penetrated the inside of the hallway when Gem entered the house. It felt chilly and a small shiver ran the length of her spine. It seemed a thousand years ago when she had left the house, but reality told her it was a mere seven or eight hours. She had carried the heavy tome in from the car and placed it lovingly upon the hall table, along with the keys from the old car. So much had happened that her mind was unable to dwell on any one event.

She had a sister … but her friend had lost her sight.

At least Beth was alive, thought Gem sadly as she leant against the hall stand.

Johan had followed her up the steps of the house and she felt his presence behind her in the hall. Turning to face him, she started to walk forward but then was hit by a feeling of nausea so strong it nearly overwhelmed her; her head began to spin.

She staggered forward and toppled against the wall, her breathing laboured.

"Thou shalt have no other God but me": these words ran through her brain like a runaway train.

There was nothing she could do to stop them.

She pressed her hands against the side of her temples, trying to ease the pain.

She felt the little monk's strong arm encircling her waist and was grateful to him for his support. She closed her eyes in an effort to get control and felt his soft fingers stroking her face.

She smiled a weak smile; her gratitude to him was endless. After all, hadn't he helped her to vanquish her enemy? The fingers continued to stroke and give her comfort, but the pain in her head was agonising.

She managed to flutter open her eyes for a second and between her long lashes she saw a look on Johan's face that was both unsavoury and unwelcome. She tightly closed her eyes again, convinced she had imagined the whole thing. The pain started to recede and she was able to open her eyes fully. There was Johan with his head cocked to one side with sympathy and compassion written across his features.

How foolish I am, she thought, but the weakness in her body thrust out any thoughts of Johan and she began to slide soundlessly to the floor.

If it was not for her sword, she would have lain prone, but the end of the sword stabbed into the tiles and kept her upright. She thought she heard its soft keening sound and turned her head to listen; it was as if the fight was still in it … but that was impossible: she had fought the fight of her life and although people had died, at least her own loved ones were safe.

She had purposefully not told Nathan the full extent of her injuries, giving in to a foolish act of bravado. There would be plenty of time to rest once they had all gotten home and were safe, she had told herself, but now that the fight was leaving her, the extent of her injuries could now be felt.

She had lost a lot of blood and the poison from Adam's sword would require a lot of healing. Rest was what she needed; she closed her eyes as the pain coursed through her, and still that feeling of unease churned within her stomach.

She heard the soft murmur of voices coming from the lounge and assessed that was where her friends had gathered; as if they had sensed her presence the door was flung open and Nathan strode into the hall. His face, already drained of colour, turned even whiter the moment he saw her slumped on the floor; wasting no time on pleasantries, he rushed to her side.

Gathering Gem into his arms, he hauled her to her feet and leant her tall frame against his and the wall. His hands felt warm against the cold skin of her bare arms.

"And the sinner shall hide his face from me, for my vengeance will be swift."

Again the words came unbidden into her head and she shook her head from side to side, trying to clear it. Her curls bounced around her forehead and Johan watched, totally fascinated by the gesture.

In the strange aftermath of the fight, Johan had forgotten about the rest of group and this error was nearly his downfall once again.

Why did this girl have such a strange influence over him?

He had risked everything to get her, even so, their fight had been honest; he had definitely wanted to kill her.

He could still remember the way his sword had entered body, it was almost sexual and he closed his eyes momentarily to conjure up the image again. It had sliced through muscle and sinew with ease, but she had escaped before he could deliver the death blow, thrusting herself forward and away from his sword and his anger. Now foolishly he had entered her domain.

He had walked straight through her door into the "she-lion's den," without giving it a second thought. He looked about himself in a moment of panic.

What on earth was he thinking about? He must make his escape. He could not afford to come into the presence of that harpy: Remne!

She would guess straight away and as for dear darling Beth, he was sure they would meet again but on his terms. He saw Nathan half turn to him and as Nathan spoke, he composed his features, already formulating a plan.

"Come with us, Johan, come into the lounge and meet the others; we have so much to talk about."

"Yes, come with me, Johan, take my hand," said Gemini, holding out her hand with the long, delicate fingers, a hand that seemed incapable of picking up a sword, let alone wielding it in the way she did.

He wanted to strike Nathan dead; he wanted to drink his blood, dance upon his bones and scatter them to the four winds for the sheer fact he held Gemini in his arms. That could all wait, this was not the time or the place and he was at a disadvantage. He had borrowed the old man's body and it was not up to the exertion he was putting it through. Even now he could feel an irregular heartbeat.

"I vood like nothing better," he replied, a happy smile playing around his old face. "Vood you like me to bring the Book vith me?" he asked, stepping quickly over to where the tome was lying on the hall table.

It was worth a shot, getting my hands on the volume, he thought as his hand caressed the bound Book.

"No, it's all right there for the time being," replied Gem, a frown beginning to appear between her eyes as she concentrated on something.

He could wait no longer, she was getting suspicious and things were starting to get out of hand.

He grabbed hold of the car keys that were lying next to the book and holding them in the air, he said, "Silly old me, I forgot my bag, pleaze excuse me vhile I fetch it."

"Okay, but don't be long, we have a lot of catching up to do," replied Nathan as he eased Gem further up in his arms.

Johan wasted no more time and scooting past Nathan and Gemini, he made for the open door as fast as the little monk's legs would carry him. There was no time left for pleasantries, he had to escape from this house fast; he could feel the safety of his disguise beginning to fade. It was as he passed through the large front door that the lounge door came crashing open and two bodies came rushing through, one blonde, the other dark, but both with panic etched upon their features.

"Stop him!" they both cried out simultaneously, but the effort it had taken to warn Gemini sent them both crashing to the floor, their energy spent.

Johan turned on the doorstep and as the mask completely slipped away, they heard, coming out of the mouth of the little monk, the voice of their enemy ... the voice of Adam, sneering, "Did you honestly think you could get rid of me that easily? I found a conduit, a vessel to hold my essence while I escaped from that place. My work here is not over." As he spoke he held Gem's gaze with his and it was to her alone he spoke. "You might think you are my nemesis, but I am yours also; you can still change your mind and come with me."

The absurdity of the offer made Gem roll out a cold hearty laugh of derision and she staggered in Nathan's arms as Adam continued, "You may have won this battle but there are plenty more to look forward to. Now I must leave you; look for me, Gemini, because I will be coming for you."

As soon as he had finished speaking, he gave Gemini one last look, as if committing her face to memory, turned on his heels and raced down the steps. It was as if Adam's words had changed them into statues, forcing them to listen to him as his evil words dripped into their reluctant ears.

Gem watched in horror as the little monk's voice transposed into that of Adam's. It was as if she could not move, as if she was forced to listen to his utter ravings. She had been so wrong to ignore her sword's song, wrong to ignore the warning words in her head.

Even now as she tried to take in all she was hearing, her sword sang out loud and clear, its crystal notes once again singing its war song. She could only think by way of explanation that Adam had been able to mask his true identity, but Johan's soul was fighting back, making Adam's evilness reappear.

The mask was slipping; there was no telling how much longer Adam could hold onto a body that clearly did not want to be controlled.

Fatigue and pain had numbed her senses, making her fail once again to snare her enemy. Pushing herself out of Nathan's arms, she tried to race after Adam, but it felt as if she was running through molasses. Her movements felt stiff and her legs encumbered, but her mind was clear and so she forced herself to forget the pain and anguish of a few moments ago as her anger took over.

Adrenalin rushed through her body, giving strength to her tired legs. She gave no thought to what she would do once she caught up with him, for to kill Adam was to kill Johan; was she prepared to sacrifice the little monk just to kill Adam?

No matter what happened, there had to be a resolution to this night's work; she owed it to everyone to finish the job.

As she started down the steps a large black car drove at speed past her, towards the fleeing monk.

She thought for a moment the car was aiming for him, but it screeched to a halt just as the brown coated figure rushed into the road. She then saw the little monk yank open the rear passenger door and hurl himself onto the back seat.

Wasting no time, the car accelerated down the road as soon as the door was closed and disappeared from view even before Gem had reached the bottom step. She sank to the ground as weariness overcame her; as she propped herself up against the stone bastion of the gate post, she gazed angrily down the road. She could vaguely hear Nathan calling her name, but her attention was fixed on the spot where the black car had disappeared.

A range of emotions ran through her, not least the one of sadness, which enveloped her at the thought of her failure; she lowered her head onto her raised knee and tried to fight down the bitterness that had risen into her throat. She might have known he would not be so easy to kill. What a fool she had been, she thought, as the tears stung her eyes ... and how arrogant!

Suddenly she felt herself being pulled up off the ground; she was about to tell Nathan to leave her alone, but when she opened her eyes she looked into the brownest eyes she had ever seen. *Like conkers, pools of brown liquid,* she thought.

The handsome man's face was framed with shoulder length black hair, which fell forward as he leant towards her. He looked tired and had a growth of stubble as if he had not had a chance to shave in quite a while.

The stranger smiled down at her and she smiled back at him automatically as if recalling some long lost memory.

"It seems like we arrived just in time; looks like you could use our help."

"Your help?" Gem said, stumbling to her feet as she brushed away her tears and waved off his helping hand. The stranger smiled politely and took a step backwards as he lowered his hand, but a single worry line appeared on his brow as he watched the blood drain from her face. On reaching her feet, Gem was suddenly forced to lean over the stone pillar again and lower her head onto her arms as her head started to spin again. The sudden rise to her feet and the appearance of the stranger had used the last of her strength. She raised her head as he spoke, as if she had momentarily forgotten he was there.

"Let me introduce my friends," the man said. "This is Reese," he began, pointing to a beautiful black woman, "and this is Mahala." The second woman bobbed a little curtsy at the mention of her name. "And last but not least myself," he said, patting himself on the chest. "My name is Joel."

As Gem looked behind to where he was pointing, she saw two tall elegant women, one black and the other white and each one nodded as her name was mentioned. They were both dressed in black clothes, covered by a long flowing coat. They both had their arms folded over their chests as they waited patiently on the pathway, their weight slightly tipped on one hip. Their hair, or what Gem could see of it, was pulled back off their faces, making them look ethereal and serene.

They looked like a couple of Goths on a day out, thought Gem, but she smiled politely, not wanting to hurt their feelings and they politely smiled back, but she could not see if it reached their eyes and was genuine.

To be honest, I don't give a monkey's, she thought to herself.

"What do you want? How can you help me?" enquired Gem as she turned and slowly retraced her steps back up to the house, knowing they would follow.

Nathan was standing in the doorway when she entered and the look of concern that was etched across his face did little to boost her confidence.

She was about to introduce the three strangers she had just met when Remne, who was now standing, rushed forward and embraced Joel and the others, flinging her arms round them in a crushing embrace.

"Oh, I see you already know these people, Remne, so do you mind sharing?" said Gem, practically tapping her toe in annoyance as she leant against the wall, momentarily irritated that Remne once again was in the know before her.

For want of something to do, instead of listening to the happy squeals of the two new women and feeling guilty for having such thoughts about Remne, she decided to take off her sword, as it was hampering her movements.

The leather was biting into her back where her injury was and so to relieve the pressure she brought the sword over her shoulder. As the hilt came down level with her eyes, she noticed that the angels that were embossed around the hilt were moving. Thinking it was a mere trick of the light or due to the lack of blood, she rubbed her eyes with her free hand.

They still moved and then they came together in a joining of hands and swords. She was so fascinated by what she was watching that she was unaware that Joel had moved towards her. As if sensing Gem's withdrawal from them had something to do with her sword, Joel cautiously raised his hand and placed it over Gem's raised hand, forcing her to lower the sword.

"Did you see that? Did you see them moving?" she asked Joel excitedly.

"As a matter of fact, that is the exact reason why we are here," he said as he looked directly into Gem's eyes, his deep dark stare not wavering for a second. "What you see is us – the four of us!"

He patted Gem on the chest and then himself and then he spread his arm out to encompass the other two women.

"We have each had an experience, shall we say, in our own respective parts of the country." Gemini drew in a sharp intake of breath and the stranger held up his hand so he could continue; "Now it is time to join forces."

He placed a hand on either side of her shoulders and held her in a strong grip.

His voice passionate, he said, "We each have a weapon with the same design and we each have someone like you that we would like to kill, but for now we have to be together. We have to join forces."

When he had finished speaking, he let his hands drop to his side and Gemini felt the loss of his touch deep within her soul. To cover her confusion, she raked her brain for something to say, something that was relevant.

"How do you know my sister? Where did you meet?"

The question threw Joel for a minute. Turning his head, he glanced back over his shoulder and smiled at Remne before turning back to Gem and saying, "I haven't. I didn't even know she was your sister."

"Then how ... what ...?" Gem stumbled with her words but could find nothing to say; she looked towards Remne for assistance.

Remne came to where she was standing and placing an arm around her sister's shoulder, she said, "Things became much clearer when I entered the between life."

Remne saw the look of pain sweep over Gem's face as she mentioned her death. So she hugged her before she continued, "When I drifted between this life and the next, I found out there were others like you and me who were fighting their own battles." She glanced over to the three newcomers as she said, "We had to be together and we had to join forces ... to be one. So I called them to me like I called you."

"This means we are not alone, we can defeat this evil thing ... this canker!"

"Yes darling," said Remne as she stroked Gem's face.

"But first we must lick our wounds and get you better. You are no good to us unless you are 100 per cent fit. Do you understand me, Gemini?"

As Gem nodded her head, the blackness folded in upon her. Remne could feel Gem slowly slipping through her grip as she headed for the floor, her own weakness preventing her from holding on to her sister. Gem was unaware that it was the handsome stranger named Joel who scooped her up with ease and carried her up the stairs to lay her tenderly on her own bed.

Remne managed to help Beth return to the lounge, where she tucked a large fluffy blanket around her and ordered her to finish the soup Nathan had heated up. She left the room when she was satisfied everything was ok and then set about issuing orders to the other two women. Reese raided the airing cupboard for sheets, which she tore into strips to use as bandages and Mahala hurried to the kitchen to boil some water for the instruments that would be used later.

In the confusion, they were all unaware of the solitary figure standing at the bottom of the stairs, gazing up in the direction of where Gemini had been taken.

A sad lonely figure stood there and upon his neck he bore the imprint of a deadly knife that had been held at his throat and the tiny beads of blood were still visible caused by the hand of someone he thought he loved; now he was not so sure. Nathan suddenly felt confused and lonely and he was at a loss as to what to do; he lowered his head onto the banister newel post and closed his eyes.

Slowly and gently, he felt a small hand forcing itself into his closed palm that hung by his side.

"Don't be sad, Nathan," said Beth. "Come with me and you can tell me everything you went through."

Even with all the things that had happened to her, he was amazed that Beth had time for him. Never thinking of herself, she offered solace where it was needed and although he knew it was wrong, he was glad she could not see the tears that coursed down his face.

So with one last look up the stairs, he followed the small, slender girl into the lounge.

Chapter 35

When Gem finally opened her eyes, she thought for a moment she had actually dreamt the whole episode and yesterday had been but a bad dream. The pain that shot through her from the injury in her back made lies of the whole assumption. As she lifted her arm to brush the curls from her forehead she noticed the line of very neat thin tapes used instead of stitches to close the long cut down her arm.

"I know you can heal yourself to a certain extent," a disembodied voice said somewhere behind her, "but I saw no reason why we couldn't help you along a bit."

The voice, Gem observed when she suddenly came into view, belonged to the very tall black woman. She had been standing behind her bed, adjusting a long saline drip that Gem now noticed was attached to her other hand.

"Hello," the woman added, "I know we met before but you sparked out so quickly we were not really introduced." As she sat on the edge of Gem's bed, she held out her hand and clasped Gemini's in a warm, friendly grip, saying as she did so, "Hi, I'm Reese, glad to finally meet you." She gently pumped Gem's hand up and down, saying, "He set an awful pace, you know, to get here. I was so glad to have finally arrived, even though we were just too late to get the little weasel!"

"Who set an awful pace?" Gem asked, adding, "I'm sorry, but do you mind?" She tried to extricate her hand from the woman's grip.

Looking down at their hands and realising what she had been doing, Reese's face broke into the most wonderful smile that seemed to light up her whole face. Her lips were full and tinged with a soft redness and the narrow structure of her face indicated her Ethiopian heritage. Gem could see she was tall even by the way she sat on the bed. She had one of her long legs tucked underneath her and the other swung backwards and forwards in a relaxed fashion as she talked.

"It was your sister, you know, that brought us all together. There I was thinking that I was the only kid on the block and I get this message right out of the blue to join up with those other two in London. Well, I didn't have far to go, did I?" she said, laughing again.

"Why's that?" mumbled Gem, suddenly feeling weak again.

"Cause that is where I am from," Reese replied in her singsong voice. "I'm from Brixton. My father is Afro Caribbean and my mother is East African. Well, you know, I thought they were my parents; don't get me wrong, I love them to bits, but I would rather be doing this than hanging around street corners. Get my drift?" She gave Gem a slow conspiratorial wink.

Gem was forced to laugh in spite of the fact that she did not understand half of what the young woman was going on about.

It must have shown on her face, because the next instant Reese leant forward and said in a low voice, "Don't tell me you don't get a kick out of all this power and kicking arse as well. Cause I do."

Reese's full lips came closer as she whispered in Gem's ear, "And it's the biggest turn-on I have ever had." She stopped talking for a moment and looked quickly heavenwards before continuing, "I just have to remember I am doing his work." She nodded towards the ceiling as she spoke and then raised one eyebrow and pursed her full lips as if to say she would remember when it suited her.

This time Gem knew instantly what she was going on about and could not help emitting a snort of laughter as she watched this delightful young woman.

The clap of hands in the doorway put paid to anything else Reese wanted to and with a wave of her hand and a soft "Ciao," she seemed to glide across the room and out through the door that Remne had just entered. Gem held out her hand to her sister and invited her to sit on the bed in the place just vacated by Reese. When she was sitting, they both looked at each other silently for a moment and then Remne placed her hands round Gem's shoulders and pulled her into her arms. Remne and Gem held each other in an embrace that needed no words. They had each thought they would never see each other again, but the bonds that united them were far stronger than any metal that had held Remne a prisoner.

After a while Remne loosened her grip and lowered Gem back down onto the bed, where she brushed the stray curls from Gem's forehead.

"Your hair is starting to grow again," Remne said for want of something to say and she fiddled with the sheets, straightening them as she continued, "Did Reese change your dressing? Don't let her attitude bother you; she is a highly respected surgeon."

"What's with all the other business then?" said Gem, feeling somewhat perplexed. She did not know how to take Reese now, if all she had been saying was a bluff.

"That's just her way of coping; she's just as frightened as the rest of us. Don't worry so much, she's a warm, wonderful person who had to watch as her partner was hacked to death in front of her." Remne smiled to hide the horror of her words. "She is as committed to her new life as you are."

"Oh God," said Gem, covering her face with her hands; her voice was muffled as she continued; "Will this nightmare never end? Is this what we have to expect all the time, our loved ones being systematically killed by these butchers?"

Remne prised Gem's fingers away from her face; emphasising each word, she gently said, "We took on this role knowing the consequences and those that have been killed are standing right beside us in our fight. Don't ever doubt it, Gem."

"I'm sorry, it's just being laid up here, I expect, that's why I am feeling maudlin." Realising she wasn't helping, Gem suddenly said, "When can I get up?"

"Not until later on today, just give yourself a chance," replied Remne. Then as if remembering something, she said as lightly as she could, "There is someone waiting to see you, he has been champing at the bit for ages to get in here, but I kept him out until you were awake."

Looking over her shoulder, she called the person in. He needed no second bidding. Nathan came into the room, eager to see if Gem was indeed feeling better. Remne did not know if it was just her imagination, but she thought she detected the smallest trace of disappointment cross Gem's features. It was there one second and gone the next as if the sun had momentarily dipped behind a cloud on a bright sunny day.

"If you're interested," Remne said, "and I can tell you're not, I'm going to have a laydown in my room, call if you need me." Giving Gem and Nathan one last look, she left them together.

Nathan stood beside the bed, unable to come any closer for fear of disturbing the tubes and sticky tapes that adorned Gem's body. For once she looked like a small helpless child laying there in that big bed, but he knew better than anyone what a lie that was. She was anything but helpless and his thoughts still tumbled around what had happened the night before.

Laying there on the bed looking up at him, Gem wondered why she had that strange fleeting emotion. She did not know who she expected. She loved Nathan, didn't she? Feeling guilty, she called Nathan to her.

"Come here and kiss me," she said. "I've done all the breaking I am going to do for one day."

Stepping closer to the bed, Nathan leant down and planted the softest of kisses on her lips, still wary of hurting her. He watched Gem slowly close her eyes and pull him closer to her, deepening the kiss. Closing his eyes, he tried to push all other thoughts from his mind. He wanted to run his hands all over her body and kiss all her pain away. Never in his life had his emotions felt so raw and exposed. Now that he once again held her in his arms, all thoughts of the knife at his throat receded. He was just so grateful that they had both survived.

He slid down beside the bed so that their faces were on a level; kneeling over Gem, he kissed her forehead affectionately.

Neither of them heard the man enter the room and it wasn't until he spoke that they realised he was standing at the foot of the bed.

"Sorry to disturb you lovebirds, but I'm afraid we have work to do."

His voice had a hint of steel about it and he sounded as if he was irritated about something. Nathan and Gem both looked towards the stranger and for some reason Gem was annoyed by both his tone and his presence.

What was his name? She wondered, trolling her mind trying to remember. Gem saw Nathan rising to his feet and could feel the animosity towards the stranger radiating from him as well. Quickly grasping Nathan's hand, she focused his attention back to her.

"It's okay, Nathan. He is right. There is still work to do and we must not waste a minute. So would you be a darling and leave us alone for a while?" said Gem, smiling fondly up at him.

Gem saw his shoulders relax and she inwardly released a sigh of relief. Nathan leant over and gave her a quick kiss on the lips and as he straightened he said to the man, "Don't tire her, she still needs to recuperate."

As Nathan walked past the man on his way to the door, there was an undeniable bump of shoulders as if Nathan was saying, "I don't give a damn who you are, I'm not frightened of you."

The man looked at Nathan's retreating back as he made his way along the landing, and when he turned back to Gem she was amazed to see he was smiling. "A bit macho isn't he?" he said as he walked towards her.

The afternoon had grown soft and still, as if the world was at peace with itself. The curtains slowly rose and fell as a gentle breeze entered the window. Gem could hear the distant honk of car horns and occasionally the sound of people talking and moving about downstairs.

For some reason, it all didn't matter to her. Her whole being was centred upon the man closing the gap between them. To hide her feelings, she resorted to anger.

"What the hell do you want, coming in here and insulting Nathan? If you have something to say about Adam, all well and good, otherwise get out, whatever your name is."

"Joel."

"What?" Gem replied, her anger flaring.

"Joel, that's my name," he replied in level, even tones but she could sense he was amused, which angered her even more. Sitting up in the bed, she proceeded to pull the saline drip from the back of her hand and when she threw back the covers, she suddenly realised she was stark naked.

"Go ahead, don't let me stop you." Now he was really laughing.

As the blood rushed to her cheeks in embarrassment she was mortified to think he had caught even the merest hint of her nudity. Hastily pulling back the covers, Gem tried to cover her body and her humiliation. As she did so Joel seemed to take pity on her and seeing her cheeks flame crimson, he turned his back and walked towards the window, giving her time to compose herself.

"Are you ready yet? Can I turn back now or do you still need more time?" he enquired as he leant his hands on the window ledge.

"No, I'm ready. What is it you want?"

As he turned to face her, he was not prepared for the vision in front of him.

She had wrapped a silk robe around herself and its figure-hugging material etched every line of her splendid body. The curls on her head looked as if they had been newly washed and shone like a halo around her head. It was the blueness of her eyes that astounded him though. It was as if they could see right through him ... into his very soul.

As he himself did not want to plumb the depths of his own heart he steered his thoughts onto firmer ground. She was tall. Nearly as tall as he was, but there was frailness about her. As if she had seen one too many tragedy.

He now knew why Nathan was so keen to keep him out of her presence. He would do the same. He was unaware he was staring until she spoke again, saying, "Joel! Why have you come here and what is it you want?" Gem demanded an answer and had her hands on her hips to prove it. She had been embarrassed, humiliated and annoyed, all in the space of ten minutes.

She had a right to know!

As he stood before her she could feel the animosity draining away from her.

What is it with him? She thought. *I want to rant and rave at him but I can't. If it had been anyone else, we might even have come to blows.* To cover her confusion, she studied him.

He was taller than her, but not by much. His hair was as black as a raven wing and curled about his shoulders. She could see flecks of grey at the sides, informing her he was no mere lad. The colour of his eyes ranged from brown to black, she realised, depending on his mood. His face was extremely handsome with two deep lines intersecting his cheeks, that seemed to deepen when he smiled and he had shaved since last she saw him. Suddenly realising that he was also studying her, she momentarily dropped her guard and gave a half smile.

"Now that we have assessed each other, are you going to tell me why you have come to my house? I seem to remember Remne saying that she had called us all together and that we must be as one," Gem said, to cover her embarrassment at being caught staring.

The quick movement of getting to her feet and throwing on a robe had taking its toll on Gem and her head felt light. As she sank back down on the bed, Joel felt a bit guilty in being responsible for her sudden weakness.

To cover his own confusion, Joel dragged the only chair on offer in the room over to the bed so that he could converse comfortably with her. Sitting himself down, he indicated to her to resume her place lying down. So flicking her legs up onto the bed, Gem lay on her side, facing him. He wished she was still standing halfway across the room, because now that he was closer to her he could see the soft outline of her breast as it strained against the silky material of her robe. He found his mind wandering away from the subject, so he gave his head a quick shake to clear the image of her nakedness and then he said as naturally as he could, "It is true that Remne drew us together. We had been fighting alone, in our own private battles. Our demons, like Adam, showed us no mercy."

Gem could see him rubbing his arm as if in memory of an old wound.

"We each have suffered loss, but that is private to each of us, as well you know."

She nodded her head in agreement as the bodies of her parents appeared once more before her in her mind.

"We are much stronger if we are united and we have found out, by pooling our knowledge, that this Adam is the key."

Gem could not help but scan his face as he talked. She could not even bring herself to be annoyed that he had seemed to have taken over.

"The trouble is," he said, leaning forward, "we have yet to find out where he will strike next. Things are moving at a rapid pace and it will not be too long before they make their next move."

Gem sagely nodded her head and then felt an almost childlike thrill when he suddenly praised her.

"You hampered him when you killed off his earthly body; it will take a little time before he can reclaim another one; Remne told us that he is just using the little guy's body, Johan is it? As a conduit until he can find a new one, we hope so, anyway." Joel pushed back his chair, rose to his feet and began to pace the floor, still talking as he did so.

Her nearness was too much for him and rather than succumb to his sudden desire of her, he thought it best if he distanced himself from her. Gem could only see the man of action striding the room before her and she liked what she saw.

As he walked he continued, "All this works in our favour and gives us time to formulate some kind of a plan. All we need now is a bit of luck to go our way and we will be set."

Realising suddenly that he expected an answer, Gem hastily replied, "What do you mean we need a bit of luck?"

"I have sent Mahala out and about to see what she can pick up." He smiled briefly as he mentioned Mahala and Gem felt a stab of jealousy that was as acute as any pain.

As she listened she kept her face inscrutable so as not to give anything away.

Who is this woman he is droning on about? She thought to herself, but she was forced to listen as he continued, "She is an expert tracker and her knowledge of all things weird and macabre is quite extensive; don't laugh, but she used to be a librarian."

Gem suddenly didn't feel like laughing. Quite the opposite! Her world was crashing back down on her. What was she doing? What was she thinking about? For one brief moment, she had nothing else to worry about but the attentions of this handsome stranger with the long hair and the dark eyes.

Now that moment was gone and she was back once more in the real world, planning the death of her sworn enemy and all things personal were once again shoved to one side. She was also annoyed with herself for forgetting about Nathan and his love for her. This annoyance manifested itself in the sharpness of her tongue, as she said, "Well, thank you, Joel, is it? Thank you for bringing me up to speed. You can leave me now while I get dressed. I shall be down in a minute and then we can have a proper discussion, with everyone present."

Swinging her feet over the side of the bed, she stood before him but could not meet his eyes. Turning away, she went over to her wardrobe, but she could feel his eyes boring into her back.

"Just go," her mind screamed. *"Give me time to think all this through."*

All Joel could see was her straight back and the tense set of her shoulders; feeling himself suddenly dismissed, he left the room, banging the door as he went. No sooner had he left but the door opened again and with her feelings strangely exposed, she shouted to whoever was coming in, "What now? My room is like Piccadilly Circus with the amount of people coming in and out."

Remne slid round the door and closed it quietly behind her. She leant against the pine door and just stood watching Gem, who still had her back to her.

"You can turn round. I know what is going on. Trust me, I am the only one who knows," Remne whispered.

Gem spun round, walked towards her sister and buried her tear-stained face in Remne's shoulder. Remne wound her arms around Gem and tried to give her what comfort she could.

"Shh, shh now. Everything will work out."

"As if my life is not complicated enough!" replied Gem, giving a little sob.

"That is why you must concentrate on the job in hand first. You will have plenty of time to sort out the other problems, not that it is not all interesting to watch, mind you."

"Oh you! You are incorrigible and highly irritating! You haven't changed a bit and I love you so much," said Gem, squeezing Remne to her.

"Watch the ribs, you don't know your own strength," replied Remne, her voice sounding slightly higher than usual due to the hug.

"Sorry," said Gem, backing off. "Actually I am feeling so much better that I will get dressed and go down and meet everyone else."

Realising she had not spoken about what was uppermost in her mind; she turned to Remne and was about to say something when Remne held up her hand and said, "Beth is perfectly well and is waiting for you downstairs. Reese has put a salve around her eyes and they look a lot better. She has even put stitches in the cut on her face; luckily her cheek was not broken, just badly bruised We have given her a good scrub and done her hair and she looks more like the Beth we know and love."

All Gem could manage on hearing this was "thank you," which she silently mouthed towards her sister. Brushing away her tears, Gem set about gathering her clothes and gave Remne a quick kiss on the cheek as she passed.

Then sailing out through the door with renewed energy, she made her way to the bathroom. Gem was still drying her hair when she heard a commotion downstairs. As she quickly pulled on her clothes, she opened the door slightly so that she could hear what was going on.

There was a clamouring in the hall. Someone had just arrived and it seemed all hell had broken loose. She could hear footsteps on the stairs coming towards her, so pulling the soft cashmere jumper over her head she opened the bathroom door in readiness to meet whoever it was.

"Come quickly," said Reese, showing no sign of being the slightest bit out of breath. "Come on, you must see this."

She was heading back down the stairs as soon as her message was delivered. Gem wasted no more time and raced after the fleeing girl. Her heart had started to pump nervously in her chest.

What on earth was going on? She thought as she took the stairs two at a time. There was nobody in the hall when she reached the bottom, but by the sound of the commotion coming from the lounge; it was obvious that was where everyone had gathered.

As she walked into the room it was as if time stood still. She looked from one person to another, trying to work out what was going on. Remne had Beth in a close embrace by the desk window, away from the fray and Reese was holding Nathan's arm behind his back, trying to stop him from moving.

The strangest thing of all was Joel.

He had his sword drawn and was holding someone down with one arm while he balanced the sword on whomever it was that was concealed by the back of the settee. She could see all their lips moving, but she could not hear the words. It was if the world had turned into slow motion and was gently stopping. She saw Joel shake his head slowly and the veins in his neck protrude with the effort of holding his sword.

She saw the muscles in Reese's arms bunch and bulge as she held Nathan back, but Gem could not understand what she was shouting.

As she turned towards Remne she saw her arms move protectively round Beth as a mother would a child; Beth slowly sank her frightened face into Remne's chest. Slowly, bit by bit, as if she was forcing her body against a wall of water, she turned her head to face Joel. Gem could see his hair dropping in single strands across his face, but that face was contorted with rage as he held his sword high.

What is happening? Her mind screamed. She automatically raised her hand to feel for her sword, but the air felt heavy and dragged at her arm as if it contained everyone's fear and dread. Her mind registered slowly that she was not wearing it and her heart beat faster because of its absence.

She felt rooted to the spot, but as her brain took in the tableaux before her she placed one foot in front of the other and forced herself forward. As she walked across the room, it was as if a spell had been broken.

All hell broke loose.

People were screaming and it felt like she had entered a madhouse. As she neared the settee a young woman who had previously been hidden suddenly stood up. She tried to push Joel away from the person on the cushions, but he remained immoveable. The nearer she got, the more her heart hammered, but she had to see who it was laying there.

She held out her hand and clutched Joel's shoulder and as she pulled at him she said, "That's enough, let me see who it is."

She felt his reluctance by the menacing shrug of his shoulder, but he obeyed and drew away from the prone figure.

As Joel stepped away, the figure lowered his arm. He had it raised in self-defence, masking his face.

There was no doubt about it:

There, to her horror, lying there on the settee, once again in her house, was Johan ... or was it Adam?

Chapter 36

Gem made her way slowly round the settee so that she could come face to face with the old monk. She noticed out of the corner of her eye her sword propped up against the side of the fireplace. It stood there cold and dark, giving her no hint that there was danger about.

As she reached down to touch the cowering man, she heard Nathan's cry behind her: "Be careful, Gem ... he cannot be trusted! He fooled us once before!"

She could hear the strain in his voice as he struggled to get free from Reese's strong grip. She glanced over and gave a little nod to Reese to set him free. As she released him, he stumbled slightly as he rushed to Gem's side. He placed his hands on either side of her shoulders and tried to pull her away, but she shrugged him off.

Gem saw Joel go to raise his sword as Nathan pulled at her. So as not to have the incident get any worse, she suddenly stood up and said, "Nathan, take Beth into the kitchen and get her something to drink; she looks as if she needs something."

Gem watched as Nathan's face registered the dismissal, but it was for the best and the only thing she could do in the circumstances. By the look on Joel's face, it was none too soon.

Looking as if his face was set in stone, Nathan walked across the room, took hold of Beth's hand and led her out into the kitchen. Reese closed the door after him and joined Remne and the others who had gathered round the settee.

Once more Gem knelt in front of the little monk and beckoned Remne to join her. Taking Johan's hand in hers, she said as gently as she could, "How did you manage to escape?"

"Oh, I can tell you that," said a voice behind her right shoulder.

Looking round, Gem saw the other girl ... the wonderful Mahala, she assumed.

"Now, now. Behave," said Remne's voice in her head. *"She is only trying to help."*

Realising before it was too late that the girl had done nothing wrong, Gem urged her to finish her story.

"Well, Joel sent me out to track down those guys that left in such a hurry and I had one hell of a job, I can tell you. I did it in a sort of grid system ..."

As she was just about to explain Joel took a step nearer to her and said forcibly, "Get on with it, M, you are wasting time."

Showing no sign of being intimidated, she smiled sweetly at Joel and continued, though not before Joel had slapped his hand to his side in exasperation as he stepped back.

"As I was saying to Mr Angry here ..."

At this reference to Joel, Gem had to lower her head to hide the smile that had sprung to her lips and she could feel Remne squeezing her hand in agreement.

Mahala carried on as if nothing was amiss, saying, "Well then, along with my superb grid system and my knowledge of where these beasts would likely to hang out ..."

"You found them just like that!" said Reese, her voice full of admiration. She had been hanging over the back of the settee, her eyes fixed on Mahala and the tale she was telling. Mahala clapped her hands together as Reese's infectious pleasure in the narrative took hold. She was just about to answer her when she noticed the stern look that Joel was giving her and so she continued in a more sedate vein.

"I wish it was so, but alas it was a more tried and tested method used only by myself ..."

"How did you do it then?" enquired Gem and she received the full collected force of everyone's stare, informing her to stop interfering in the telling of the tale. Gem opened and closed her mouth but thought it better to say nothing, so with no further interruptions Mahala continued.

"I smelt them out!" Before anyone could throw in a question, she held up her hand as she continued explaining, "Yes, smelt! We all have some little power that is attributed to us alone and mine is an incredible sense of smell. Which doesn't help when you haven't washed for a few days, I can tell you."

Mahala looked round and noticed the others nodding their heads in agreement.

Continuing but feeling slightly put out, she said, "I found the old monk in the back of a dirty old garage. It looked like they were getting ready to dispose of his body. I thought at first he was dead, but I gave him a prod with my foot and lo and behold he stirred. Well, I can tell you I was not going to hang about in there for long, as it looked like they were getting ready to leave. They had that big black car piled up with stuff and it was locked up. So ..."

As she spoke she pulled a small piece of paper out of her pocket and handed it to Gem.

"The only thing I could get my hands on was this ... it was lying on the ground near the monk's feet."

"Carry on," said Gem, wanting to hear the rest of the story.

"I wanted to have a nose round at first but Johan here said it would be better to get away. He wanted me to leave him but I said, 'No way, matey, I have come all this way to find you and I am not leaving without you.' So there you are. I strapped him to me and took the direct route back here and *voila*, here we are."

They all stared at Mahala for a few seconds, unable to register the full extent of the girl's bravery. She had astounded Gem with her simplistic way of explaining the rescue of Johan. Mahala had done, in next to no time, something she had been unable to do. As everyone stood staring at her, Mahala started to feel uneasy and asked, "What is it? Why are you staring at me like that?"

Gem rose to her feet and took the girl's hand in hers as she said, "I am astounded! You went off and just picked him up from under their noses and came back with him. I am truly amazed!"

"What are you talking about? Joel said the old man was necessary to us and told me to find him. He said to be careful but he didn't say anything that would make you feel astounded. I've been gone the whole time since you fainted, trying to track them down. So what have you found out about him?"

This time Gem was truly at a loss for words and turning to face Joel, she said, "You didn't tell her? You didn't tell her what danger she was letting herself in for?"

Before Joel could answer, Mahala grabbed Gem's arm and tried to turn her around but she could not move her.

So shouting at Gem's rigid back, Mahala said, "What are you talking about, what danger? He said it was just a case of tracking and retrieving … Joel?"

Gem could hear the nervous inquiry in Mahala's voice and her anger knew no bounds. She did not wait to hear the explanation that was rising to Joel's lips.

The blow when it came sent him skidding across the front of the fireplace and if he was not so agile, he would have landed on his backside.

As he raised his face to look at her, she hit him again and this time he fell to his knees. If it was not for the intervention of Remne, Gem would have carried on.

"Gem, that's enough," she said softly, but her voice carried a sadness that managed to penetrate Gem's wrath. Even her sword was picking up on her anger and had started to glow, making itself ready for a fight.

"Enough?" she shouted as she bent over him. "Enough? It is a wonder I don't rip your head off. What on earth were you thinking of?"

Although momentarily stunned by the blows, Joel leapt to his feet, his face a mirror image of her own anger.

His dark eyes spat fire at the humiliation of being hit and stepping closer to Gem he shouted, "Don't stand in judgement of me! I did what was best at the time and I was thinking of her best interests. If I did not reveal all the information then, it was because Mahala functions best when she is not stressed out."

"Well, actually that is true!" said Mahala. "Gosh, I don't know what I would have done if I had been told how really scary this was. Who is this chap anyway? You all seem so taken up with him; would you care to let me in on it, seeing as I was the one who brought him back?" Mahala edged over to stand next to Reese, who put a comforting arm around her shoulders.

"This man," said Remne, leaving the two antagonists to cool down, "is the person the demon known as Adam made his escape in." As she watched the blood drain from Mahala's face she continued in a calm steady voice, "Adam is Gem's nemesis and has sworn to enslave her. He took over Johan's body when they were leaving the Minster and came back with her here."

As she talked, Remne knelt before the old man, who was lying prone on the settee. His face was as white as chalk and carefully Remne lifted his hand in hers as she spoke to Mahala and Joel again.

"When you went off in search of this man, you did not know what you were up against; that is why Gem is so angry. We knew Adam could not last long in his body," said Remne, smiling down at the monk, "'cause we saw he was fighting back, but what we did not know was what Adam would do with him once his usefulness was over. He is the kindest, gentlest person I know and his death would have been a big blow to me."

As she finished speaking she held the monk's hand up against her forehead as if asking for his benediction.

"So what you are actually saying is you did not know who I was bringing back, if it was Johan or Adam, am I right?" said Mahala, now grasping the immensity of the situation.

"Yes, you are right and I can only apologise and give thanks that you were not killed in the bargain," said Gem to Mahala, but the anger was still present in her voice.

"Oh rubbish!" replied Joel, rubbing his chin. "Don't apologise on my behalf; I did what I thought was best. I know these women better than you do."

"Don't even go there!" said Remne's voice in Gem's head.

Gem turned back to face him and held out her hand in a gesture of good will and while a hint of a smile was playing at the corners of her mouth, her voice was serious.

"Let me apologise then for thinking ill of you, but you still deserved the punishment for sending Mahala into danger she knew nothing about."

Joel looked at the extended hand and for a minute Gem thought he was going to refuse, but at the last minute he took it and drew her close to his chest.

He whispered so that she alone could hear, "You pack a mean punch, Gemini; it will be interesting to see what else you have to offer." He turned swiftly away and she lost the chance to look into his eyes to see if he was jesting or not.

She turned back to Remne to hide her confusion and knelt beside her. As they studied Johan they could see the bad way he was in. His breathing was shallow and as Remne pulled aside his torn habit they could see several bloody injuries to his torso.

Reese leant over the back of the settee to get a better look and said, "I'll go and get my things and see what I can do to make him a bit easier." Off she went, dragging Mahala with her.

"And as for you, miss, you can get straight up there in that bathroom.

Poo whiff, girl, you do smell," they heard Reese say as they both disappeared out through the lounge door.

Johan tried desperately to sit up, but Remne kept a firm hand on his shoulder, preventing him; brushing flecks of dirt from his face, she said, "Rest now, I will get you something to eat and you can tell us all you know."

Suddenly Joel intervened, "What are you talking about? He will be dead before we get any information out of him." Bending over so that his face was near that of the monk, he said, "Tell us, old man, before it is too late …"

He was unable to finish his sentence because Gem pushed him away, saying as she did so, "Behave, Joel, the man is in shock; let him get his breath, especially after what he has been through."

"No, pleeze, do not argue over me. He is right … I do not haff long … unt there is so much to say."

Johan's soft Austrian accent was punctuated with spasmodic coughing. Remne stood and retrieved the blanket that Beth had used as a cover and placed it over Johan's body. When she had finished her ministration, Johan started talking. His voice was soft at first and then as his fear started to subside it became stronger.

"I haff been touched by so much evil I thought I vood not survive. I found myself in a place dat vas so alien to me that if it vas not for my faith I know I would surely have succumbed."

Johan closed his eyes as he remembered the horror of it all.

"Ve fought a battle, not like you, Gemini … but of wills. A battle just as hard, I think you vill agree. I knew I could not vin, he vas so strong, but at least I let you see if only for a little vhile the true nature of the person you vere dealing wid. I know you were afraid, dear Joel."

He turned his eyes to look over to where Joel was standing near the fireplace.

"And you vere only looking out for everyone … I do not blame you … I don't think it is even necessary to forgive you … no harm has been done."

Gem looked at Joel's face and wondered if he could forgive himself, but her attention was drawn back to Johan as he continued speaking.

"He vas strong like I told you … dis Adam, but he had one failing … I personally call it a blessing …" He turned to look at Gem as he spoke.

"He is obsessed vith you and harbours an all-consuming passion of hatred against anyone who comes in contact vith you. I felt his hatred for

Nathan unt Remne unt as for Beth he now regrets not killing her vhen he had the chance."

Gem lowered her head; her expression was difficult to read, but Johan gently laid his hand on top of her head and said, "Fear not, Gemini, dis passion of his vill be his undoing. Vhen he possessed my body it vas like some diabolical game of chess ve played. I sacrificed something to gain something, as you do in a good game, but unfortunately dis vas no game."

Suddenly Remne was starting to get nervous. She knew to what lengths his devotion to her and the cause went. She was sure that he was quite prepared to martyr himself if he thought that cause was the right one.

"Johan, what have you done? You are frightening me now!" she said, grabbing hold of his hand.

"Oh Remne, you disappoint me, I thought you could see into mine heart," Johan replied, smiling benignly.

"I didn't think I would have to," Remne replied, smiling back.

"Don't upset yourself, Remne. It is a trifle ..."

This time Remne knew her answer as she plumbed the depths of his gentle soul.

"Oh Johan, you must be in so much pain," she said as the tears started to flow down her face.

"What is it? Come on, tell me," Gem said in a voice that demanded to know the truth. She was joined by Joel, who suddenly lost interest in what was on the mantle shelf and turned his full attention back to the monk.

"Yes, tell us what has happened," he said, his tone brooking no nonsense.

Johan looked from one to the other and said, "To be honest ..." but Remne cut in before he could say any more.

"Johan has multiple fractures to both legs and a broken pelvis in two places and the reason he is not rolling about in agony is the fact that his spine is also damaged, paralyzing both legs and dulling any pain he might be suffering." Turning round so that she faced Joel, she said in a voice that Gem had never heard before, "So do you still want to knock him about some more?"

Joel backed away and held up both his hands as he did so; he was about to add some flippant remark when Johan said, "Pleeze, pleeze, *mien kinder*, do not be dis way. Dis vay leads to destruction of our cause. Nobody is to blame, for dat miserable creature he vorks vith, throwing me out of dat first floor vindow like some filthy piece of garbage. My legs are a small price to pay for a little piece of knowledge."

And he held his hand up, showing a gap between his index finger and thumb saying,

"Ya, a little bit of knowledge."

"What knowledge?" said Joel, edging back, but seeing the look in Remne's eye, he stayed where he was.

"I knew zee last part of zee game vas going to be played unt ve vould either die resisting each other or he vould find another body just in time. His vill to live is very strong unt another body vas soon found. It vas vhen he left me dat he vas at his veakest. It vas den a poem sprung into mein mind unt I knew it vas a link to vhatever he was doing next." Johan, as he was telling this last part, tried to reach into the pocket of his habit.

"What are you looking for?" enquired Remne.

"Paper ... a piece of paper. I wrote it down later, vhen they dumped me in the garage. It was on a scrap of paper I found because I vas afraid I vould not remember it. Now vhat have I done vith it ... oh dear, oh dear ..."

He was agitated to such an extent that Remne had to physically hold him down.

"Is this what you are talking about?" said Gem, producing the piece of paper Mahala had given her earlier.

"Ya, dat is it ... Oh thank you, Lord. Thank you. Read it, Gemini ... read it to us all," he said excitedly.

"Okay, here goes. Mind you, your writing is a bit scrawly:

> Came hence he forth across the sea,
> With holy twelve and caskets three,
> They are buried in a place so deep,
> Those precious things that do not sleep.
> For in this place, this tranquil keep,
> Mankind's need alone will weep.
> A lasting epitaph and grave,
> No mortal hand in this was made.
> Buried deep within a glade,
> Two sets of cruets silver laid,
> And yonder forth within dark walls,
> A holy cup of divinity calls.

"What on earth does that mean?" said Gemini when she had finished reading.

"I don't know," Remne said, "but for now we have to get Johan to hospital and I think the best person to arrange that will have to be Nathan. There will be no question asked if he puts the wheels in motion and as for you …"

As Remne leant forward she took Johan's face between her hands and kissed him soundly on the forehead; they were amazed to see the gentle monk blush to the top of his tonsure.

"No more heroics from you. You will not die, I will not allow it," said Remne and with that Gem jumped to her feet and went in search of Nathan, leaving the others to ponder on what she had read.

It took Nathan a little over an hour to secure a safe place for Johan where he could be hospitalised and it took a little over two hours to wipe the smile off his face when he heard that Gem had hit Joel.

They were all gathered in the dining room, this being the only place that could accommodate them all comfortably.

Gem read the poem again now that they were all gathered together.

"Well, any ideas, anyone?" she asked as she looked round the assembly.

There was a general shaking of heads and thoughtful frowns and she could see one or two of them mouthing the lines silently to themselves.

It was Beth's tender voice, still showing the signs of her captivity that broke the silence.

"I think we all need to ponder on this for a while; it's surprising what comes to you when your mind is at rest. We are all still worn out."

So it came as a surprise to everyone when Joel slammed the table with his fist and shouted, "We haven't got time to rest. Adam is out there plotting, and we all know that there is one big event about to take place. We cannot sit about like this."

"As much as it hurts me to agree with him, I think Joel is right," said Gem. "We have to be out there and are seen to be doing something." She saw Joel's eyebrow rise in amusement at her sudden acquiescence.

The air was suddenly filled with the vibrant singing of James Blunt's hit song "Beautiful" from a cell phone and an embarrassed looking Nathan reached into his pocket to retrieve it. All eyes looked at him as he stood up; holding the small phone to his ear he mumbled "yes" and "no" throughout the conversation.

Gem watched his face and was dismayed to see it register first bewilderment, then as he straightened his shoulders, annoyance.

What on earth is he talking about? She wondered and was startled to hear Remne's voice answering back.

"It's his boss; something has happened; I will let him explain."

Gem glanced over at Remne but her face was inscrutable. As soon as he came off of the phone Gem pounced, giving Nathan no time to gather his thoughts.

"Well, what did your boss want? It looked serious. Have you been called away?"

"Do you know I will never get used to you doing that? Yes, I have been called away. I must leave immediately for London."

"Why, what has happened?" replied Gem, jumping to her feet, suddenly guilty for not spending any time with him.

"Apparently they analysed all the information that I phoned through yesterday about what had gone on in the Minster. Then they had a meeting of all the heads of all the religious bodies and in their wisdom they intend to hold a service in Westminster Abbey, showing everyone's solidarity. It is the first multicultural religious meeting of its kind and I am talking every religion. The lot! Every available head of church, sect, denomination, fraction, or schism."

The look on everyone's face was incredulous, but it was Joel who jumped to his feet and rounded on Nathan.

"Don't they see they are falling into his trap? This is it! This is Adam's next move. If he wipes out all the heads of all the major religions … what is left?"

As he spoke he ran both his hands through his dark hair, pushing it from his face in an angry gesture. Then leaning across the table, he spoke to everyone in turn.

"I shall tell you … shall I … it will be something so diabolical, so inhumanly cruel and wicked. It will be the second coming, but that person intends to be Satan himself."

Straightening up, he turned back to Nathan and grabbed his arm. Nathan was in no mood to stand being mauled about and his displeasure showed keenly on his face. They were of a similar height, but Joel's strength far outweighed Nathan's, so he was forced to listen while Joel held onto his arm, but the look of pure venom he shot Joel did not go unnoticed by everyone present.

"You must go down there and convince them they must not gather all in one place."

"There is nothing I can do," Nathan replied angrily. "The service is arranged for Wednesday. The pope is even going to be there."

"God in heaven, preserve us," said Beth as she lowered her head into her hands.

Gem held up her hands for calm. She did not feel like being calm, she wanted to rant and rave at the injustice of it all, but calmness had to prevail. They needed time to think and all this arguing was not helping.

"Please let us try to be calm." Looking directly at Joel, she said, "I know it is hard but we must. Nathan has to go to London and do what he can to try and persuade them to cancel the meeting." Looking round at the other women, she said, "I have faith in you all. We have to figure out a way of stopping Adam and his Master. So please everyone let's put our mind to the task. I am going to give everyone one hour; go where you want, do what you want, the house and garden is yours, but come up with an answer. Now everyone go."

Chairs scraped against the floor as they all started to rise; Joel, who was still standing next to Nathan, remained where he was.

"Leave us alone, will you please, Joel?" said Gem as she joined them. She could see he was reluctant to leave, so Nathan placed an arm around her shoulders. Instantly Gem saw a flash of anger deep within his dark eyes, but then he smiled, making the creases in his cheeks deepen and with a small nod of his head to both of them he walked from the room.

Gem watched Joel's retreating back, but Nathan forced her to look at him.

"We never seem to be alone and once again I am off on my travels. Don't worry; I shall do my best in trying to make them change their minds. Look after Beth, she is still frail; until we meet again this will have to suffice."

Taking her in his arms, he kissed her, but the fire seemed to have gone and all that remained was the flash of metal that still shone deep within the very core of him to, the very corners of his mind.

He released her and she stood for a while gazing up at him, a puzzled look on her face. Fearing that she had noticed something, he gave her a quick kiss on the nose and smiled down at her.

Then he turned on his heels and left.

Chapter 37

After Nathan left, Gem sat down at the table and sprawled her arms out across the polished surface. The wood felt cold on her cheek, but she welcomed its soothing coolness. She felt hot and weary. Nothing ever seemed to go right. She felt lonely and miserable and leaning her head on her outstretched arm, she traced, with her free hand, circles in the fine dust. As her finger went round and round it sent up little specks into the air; she watched in fascination as they danced in the late afternoon sunshine.

She heard a clock chiming in a distant part of the house and hope that someone would sort the rhyme out soon.

She closed her eyes and drifted off in a light slumber. As soon as her eyes were closed, he was there, enfolding her in his arms, keeping her safe. She moaned softly, feeling the strength of his arms, but as she turned her face up to receive his kiss … the hands that held her turned to claws and the face so eagerly anticipated was that of a beast.

She woke with a start, the image still with her, and she was startled further when someone spoke.

"Good dream?"

She shook her head to rid herself of the image and her curls danced in the faded light. Looking along the table, she saw Joel sitting at the far end with his feet propped up on the table top.

She was instantly annoyed to be caught napping and to cover this, she resorted to her best hiding place: anger.

"Do you mind getting your big feet off the table? I would hate it to get scratched!"

"No, I don't mind. It won't matter a toss if we don't find some answers; nothing will. By the way, what were you dreaming about? You were giving out some lovely moans."

"None of your business! It's been long enough; call the girls here and let's see if anyone has come up with anything."

Gem turned abruptly away and walked towards the fireplace as Joel left the room. She could hear him shouting for the others, his tone commanding. Placing her bare foot on the fender, she let her thoughts drift just once, back to her dream. Who was she expecting? Whose kiss would have made her moan? Whose face was she so eagerly expecting?

The door swung open and everyone trouped in; all thoughts of a kiss that was not to be were pushed from her mind when she looked at all their serious faces.

"So has anyone come up with an answer?" Gem asked, leaning on her fists on the table.

"We have all batted some things around," said Reese, "and the nearest we could come up with … was … maybe St Augustine. After all, he was the first saint to arrive in England."

"Go on," Gem urged.

"Well," said Reese, leaning forward on her arms as she looked up and down the table, "he came to England from Rome with a group of monks. He landed in Kent, Thanet to be precise, in 597 and I don't think it's changed since then." Realising her humour was not being well received, she continued, "He was given shelter and then he became a bishop and as Christianity spread he became the first Archbishop of Canterbury."

"And?" asked Gem when she had finished speaking.

"And what?" replied Reese.

"How does this link in with the poem?"

"It doesn't. I just thought I was helping."

Gem wiped her hand across her face and was about to ask if there were any more suggestions when Mahala said, "What about Rosslyn Chapel? It is supposed to contain the Holy Grail deep within its foundations. They say it was put there by the Knights Templar. It was founded in 1446, though, so I don't know if it is relevant or not."

"Thank you, Mahala, that was more helpful," said Gem, looking at Reese, who had decided to pick the remainder of her nail varnish off her long nails.

"Call me M."

"What?" replied Gem, dragging her eyes back from Reese.

"Call me M, everyone does. Mahala is such a mouthful."

"Okay, M, thanks. Now has anyone else got a suggestion, Joel, what about you?"

Joel looked uneasy and fidgeted in his seat. Gem saw his mouth open and close, but in the end he just shrugged his shoulders in a defeated way as if the fight had momentarily left him.

"We need more time," said Remne. "This is no good; we have to dissect the poem. It's a shame you left your laptop at work; we could certainly use it now."

"I don't know if this will help," Beth said quietly. "But I have had a song going round in my head all day and I think it must be relevant."

"What is it, Beth, dear?" said Gem, leaning down the table. She wanted to take up Beth's small white hand in hers to pass on some of her own strength, but she was sitting on the other side of Remne.

"It's an old hymn. We learnt it at school. Everyone knows it ..." Suddenly Beth started singing. Her voice was sweet and pure and as soon as she started, everyone recognised it, but only Reese and Mahala joined in, their voices blending in perfect harmony.

"I know that song, but what in God's name has it got to do with any of this? Please girls! That's enough!" Joel shouted above the singing; fearing that he would not be heard, he banged his fist hard down upon the table.

Gradually, one by one, the girls stopped and as usual it was Mahala who had the last word.

"Oh, you're such a kill-joy. I was enjoying that. It was uplifting ..."

"I'll uplift you in a minute," replied Joel angrily.

"What's that called, Beth?" asked Gem, a smile playing around her mouth; as always she seemed to be amused by Mahala's words.

"'Jerusalem,'" replied Remne. "It's by William Blake."

"Oh my God!" shouted Mahala. "That's it. That is the connection. I knew I had heard it before but you have to take in so many bits of information when you are a librarian."

"What's what?" shouted Joel above the din, now thoroughly confused.

"Okay, let's sit down and work this out. I think we are on to something," said Gem, the excitement evident in her voice.

"Well, the hymn tells us that someone came in ancient times and walked on England's green."

"And ..." prompted Joel.

"Joel, shut up and let her talk," countered Reese.

Gem was taken aback by the seriousness of her tone, having never heard her snap at him before. He seemed to defer to her wishes though and remained quiet.

Well, that's a first! Thought Gem but her attention was soon back with Mahala, who had continued speaking.

"Let me tell you who that someone was, it was Joseph of Arimathea, the wealthy man who took Jesus down from the cross and gave him his own tomb." She looked from one to the other; realising they were relying on her for all the information, she carried on.

"I seem to remember that he came to England and stopped at …"

"Glastonbury," said Beth quietly.

Gem could feel the blood rushing to her brain and her heart pumped furiously. Scraps of information and half-heard discussions came rushing back at her. It was as if a thousand voices spoke to her at the same time, whispering in her ear, telling her what path to go down, warning her of perils, pushing her … pulling her … guiding her and now that one name … Just then her thought went blank.

When she came to, they were standing all around her, but it was Remne who held the glass of water to her lips.

"Have you eaten today?" she asked. "I bet you haven't. You are doing too much, Gem."

As she began to raise herself off the floor, Joel leant forward and offered his hand, which she gratefully accepted.

As she seated herself back at the table, she noticed that Beth had not moved.

"Do you see now?" she said in her same quiet voice.

"You knew," replied Gem, for some reason suddenly hurt by her friend's admission. "You knew all about the poem, didn't you? Why did you not say something earlier, we have wasted enough time on this."

"Okay, okay what's going on now?" said Joel, his voice registering his agitation.

"There are certain things that I know," Beth said, "and they are for you to figure out. Let me put it another way: they are on a need-to-know basis. We each have a job to do and you as celestial half beings have been chosen to fight and protect, except Remne here."

Even though she could not see, Beth placed her hand firmly over Remne's as it lay on the table top.

"My job is a little different but nonetheless perilous. I have been chosen for a reason. I am blind for a reason. Let it go at that, Gem. Now continue with all the information that has been given you."

With that she removed her hand from Remne's and tucked both her hands neatly in her lap; bowing her head, she waited for Gem to speak.

To say that everyone was taken aback by this declaration was an understatement. After a few seconds, Joel went to speak and both Mahala and Reese leant forward as if to say something, but it was Gem, who had been sitting quietly at the end of the table that broke the silence.

A slight sheen of sweat glistened on her forehead as she repeated the words that had been shown to her. She momentarily squeezed her eyes shut as she focused on what she had to say next and with a voice that got stronger the more she talked, Gem warmed to her subject.

"Joseph brought with him twelve followers from the Holy Land, one of them being his own son Josephes. Not only did these men bring Christianity to these shores in AD 37, they also brought with them something so holy that this is what this war is about."

Gem could see the others starting to fidget, wanting to know more. The warrior in three of them starting to rise.

"Joseph brought with him the boy Jesus to these shores and swore to return one day with him, little knowing in what form those promises would take. The poem tells us of 'two sets of cruet, silver laid.' This refers to two small silver containers that hold the blood and sweat of Christ. The other line is 'A holy cup of divinity calls'; this refers to the Holy Chalice, or as we refer to it, the Holy Grail."

Nobody moved and nobody spoke. They just looked at Gem, trusting in her authority over them.

"These objects are buried somewhere in Glastonbury. We have to retrieve them before Adam can lay claim to them. Because, my dear and trusty friends, once his Master drinks what is in those canisters, from that sacred chalice, he will have full and everlasting dominance over this world. He will crush all the other religions and it will be, as Joel said, a 'second coming,' but this time Satan will be our Master."

Gem expected them to remain seated for a while to let all the information sink in, but to her amazement Joel and Reese, who were on opposite sides of the table, suddenly jumped up and smacked each other's open palm in a grand "high five."

"That's more like it," he said excitedly. It was as if he had gotten all his birthday presents at once. "Now we can act and plan. I knew you would come through." He looked at Gem's stunned face.

Gem glanced at Remne, who was sitting next to her and as their eyes met she just shrugged her shoulders as if to say, "Let's get on with it."

Beth remained calm and serene through the whole eruption, but suddenly her voice cut through all the excitement.

"There is just one thing that I must stipulate."

"What's that, sweet cheeks?" said Reese affectionately, humouring her.

"I insist on going to Glastonbury. There will be no arguing about this, my mind is set. I too have my mission to complete. So who will take me?"

Gem felt her heart lurch at the thought of Beth putting herself once more in danger, but she accepted the wisdom of her words and acknowledged her bravery with a hug.

"That can't be," Joel began. "She will be a hind ..." But before he could finish what he was saying he found himself looking into a pair a blazing blue eyes.

"Don't ever question my decisions," hissed Gem. "Beth has more knowledge than anyone about this beast. She has earned the right to go. Now I suggest she go with Mahala, of the famous nose, Reese, and Remne. The four of them are more than equipped to recover the lost items. Unfortunately, I have to recognise the fact that I am in no position to make such an arduous journey."

Having received their orders, the girls rose and started to vacate the room.

"And what of us?" Joel asked. "You and me? What are we going to do?"

Gem realised the two of them were still close together but before she could get past him he placed his hand on the back of a chair and barred her way, demanding an answer.

She looked down at his arm and then up into his eyes, which were now the colour of dark roasted chestnuts with golden flecks that she hadn't noticed before. Pulling her thoughts back to safer ground, she said, "We are going to prepare for church. It is about time you confessed."

"What would you like me to confess to?"

"Oh, I don't know," replied Gem, her angry mood now lifted, "but I am sure we can find something."

His face came nearer and she was sure he was going to kiss her, but just as she started to lower her lashes in expectation, he retrieved his jacket from the chair back behind her; smiling sweetly at her, he then turned and walked out of the room.

Oh bloody hell. I have just made an absolute pratt of myself, Gem thought.

"Warned you, didn't I?" said Remne as she poked her head round the door.

"Oh, go away, you. You are no help."

Remne came into the room and linked arms with her sister.

"Cheer up. It can't be all bad, having all these guys after you."

"Wow. A demon who wants to enslave me, a boyfriend who can't forgive me and now a man whose main ambition in life is to infuriate me. Great!"

"Did Nathan actually say that to you?"

"He didn't have to; I could see it in his eyes," said Gem sadly.

"Trust in yourself, Gem. It will all work out for the best. By the way, I had a call from the hospital and Johan is going to be operated on. I have also informed his fellow monks that he had been doing God's work and has now gone away for a little sabbatical. The less they know at the present, the better."

As they talked the door opened and Mahala popped her head inside.

"Sorry to disturb you two but there is someone at the door for you, Remne."

"For me, who can it be? Nobody knows I am here, unless … Oh my god, unless …"

Remne rushed from the room and Gem followed half a pace behind. If Remne was in danger, then it was up to her to safeguard her.

They both entered the hall and collided with two people standing there.

The woman had in her arms the hugest, most disgruntled cat Gem had ever seen and she instantly recognised it as the cat from Remne's boat.

"Mother, Father! What on earth are you doing here?" Remne exclaimed, sweeping the big moggy into her arms. Gem was amazed to hear the monster start to purr. It was as if someone had started a motor and as Remne rubbed its ears, it seemed to become louder.

"We had a visitor," Lloyd said casually.

Remne let the animal jump to the floor and he purposefully walked into the lounge, his tail erect and waving from side to side like a banner. It was as if he had lived there all his life. Gem could hear the squeals of admiration coming from Reese and Mahala as it entered the room.

She heard Remne and her parents talking softly behind her and thought nothing of it. She intended to say a quick hello and then go up to her room for a laydown, but Remne grabbed her arm.

"Someone was in my parents' house," she said. "He sent someone to kill them. They barely escaped with their lives."

"Actually, that is not strictly true," Lloyd interrupted. "It was your cat that saved us. Without him, then we would surely have died."

"Bless him," Remne said. "I knew he could tell when they were about but I never for one moment expected him to defend you. He kept to the garden when you were up there, Gem, so you didn't see him."

"He was a veritable lion. Did some nasty damage, I can tell you."

Remne could see her father nodding his head as he thought back to the incident; not wishing to be the one to make them go over something so horrible, she quickly changed the subject.

"Now you have a choice," Remne said. "You can either stay here or you can go to my boat; it is moored not far from here. You don't have to go just yet; I am not trying to get rid of you. Stay, have something to eat and rest a while; give yourself time to come to a decision. Is that all right with you, Mum?"

Margaret nodded her head in agreement and smiled wearily. Realising they would be better off with her so the others could talk more freely, Remne took her mother's arm and guided her and her father down the corridor to the kitchen.

Gem gazed after them, fearful now that others were starting to be drawn into the conflict. Turning on her heels, she entered the lounge and could not help smiling when she saw the cat sprawled across Beth's lap.

"Seems like he has adopted you," Gem said with a laugh as she sat herself down next to her.

"Yes and I'm utterly jealous," replied Reese, who was sitting on the floor on the other side of Beth. Her back was propped up against the sofa and her long legs stretched out in front of her. She looked relaxed and at home and the same could be said for Mahala, who was lazing on the other sofa with her head in Joel's lap, much to Gem's chagrin.

"This looks all very cosy, you lot, but when are you going? Because time is of the essence, you know. It might take ages to find what you are looking for and we can't spare it."

As she spoke Gem reached over and stroked the cat, trying not to let the others see her agitation at the delay.

She looked down at Reese's upturned face. Gem could see it was animated and it was only the thought of the impending fight that could make so. Excitement seemed to bubble within her and even though she leant gracefully against the sofa, Gem could see the long lines of her legs and arms were taut with the adrenalin that was pumping even now through her body.

Even her voice was composed, giving Gem reason to doubt her own eyes.

"Fear not, oh noble leader. All is in hand. Mahala, for her laid-back attitude over there, has gathered all the tools of her trade. Not least of these are the Black Death and I have my wonderful Minnie."

"Black Death and Minnie? They are strange names. What exactly are they?" enquired Beth.

"The Black Death," said Reese, sitting up straighter, "is a long black bow made by Mahala herself from seasoned willow. Even I can just about pull the bow down to string it, but its aim is true and steady. In fact I have never seen her miss with it. She has her sword, of course, that she always carries, but I think she prefers the bow. Is this not true, M?"

"This is very true, Reese dear. I love my bow nearly as much as you love dear Minnie."

Mahala had raised her head slightly from out of Joel's lap, but Gem was still annoyed to see she had no intention of moving completely.

"And Minnie?" urged Beth, wanting to hear the rest of the story.

"Ah, Minnie is the name of my sword, which sings in the five and a half octave range, the same as Minnie Riperton."

"Do you mean the singer that died, oh what, ages ago?"

"Yes Gem, I do. Her album 'Perfect Angel' was very apt and I have always been a big fan of hers. She actually died in 1979 at the tender age of thirty-one and is buried in Los Angeles. So how many more coincidences would you like? It just seemed the right thing to do to name it after her."

It was obvious to them all that the naming of the sword was of great significance to Reese, so Gem decided to let the matter drop. She had intended to rib her over it but the look on Reese's face put a stop to it.

Intending to change the subject as an awkward silence had now fallen; Gem was surprised to feel Remne's presence as she stood behind where she was sitting. Remne had entered silently, listening to the conversation. Smiling gently to herself, she looked deep within Reese's soul. She was touched that Reese had a naming ceremony for her sword, something she had omitted to tell the others. Strange that she should do that though.

Then she felt the pain of Reese's loss wash over her as she looked deep within her soul.

"Minnie ... Minnie Mouse ... I see it was also the pet name for your three-year-old daughter that was killed along with your husband. Her small neck broken and her body discarded like a forgotten rag doll."

Remne felt Reese's tears and agony roll over her as she searched. She shut her eyes and withdrew her thoughts away. It was just too painful, but it gave her an insight into why she masked her emotions the way she did.

Remne then turned her attention to Mahala. Like her job, she gave the impression she was an open book, but there was a depth to her that none of the others had picked up on.

What was that expression Mother always used to describe Father? 'Away with the fairies,' that was it, thought Remne, smiling.

That was it; Mahala seemed preoccupied and as she searched her heart she found the reason why.

She was calculating it all. She was turning her mind to her work even as she laid there, the velocity of her arrows, even their speed and angle. Why was she so determined?

An aged woman came into Remne's mind; her face was kind and gentle. Her back was slightly bent and Remne could see a locket gleaming at the woman's neck, a silver locket with engravings on it. Then she was struck down in a frenzied attack by a black-coated figure; cruel hands ripped the locket from her neck. As Remne looked in horror upon the scene in her mind's eye, she felt Mahala's gaze upon her. As their eyes met across the room, Mahala smiled and her voice floated delicately into Remne's head.

"Now you know the reason for my being here, my catalyst. She was my mother, the gentlest person in the world. She meant everything to me."

She was about to ask something when she was stopped in her tracks by Mahala as she continued, *"I too can read the minds of mortal men, although not hearts like you. I gave an oath not to read the minds of my fellow travellers; does that answer your question?"*

Remne gave her a little nod of acknowledgement. They both recognised the other's strengths and a bond was formed between them because of it.

Remne did not have the heart to carry on round the group, so she said into the silence, "Let us take this opportunity to eat and gather our thoughts; nothing can be done until the sun goes down. I take it we are going the direct aerial route. Even though I am a little rusty in the flying stakes, I realise the importance of speed."

Looking over at Beth, she said quickly before Gem could intervene, "Beth can go with Reese; she has the most strength to carry you. Don't argue, Gem, it has all been arranged."

Gem opened and closed her mouth at being forestalled. She was still not in agreement with Beth going, but she knew the consensus of opinion seriously outnumbered her and that included Beth herself.

Slapping her hands onto her knees, Gem then stood up and faced the group, looking round at the one man and four women around her; she smiled openly and genuinely before she said, "Although some of us have only just met, I look upon you all as I do Beth and Remne. We are one; we will fight to the end or lay down our lives in the process. Our little band has been nominated to save the world and it is with pride that I say to you now that it is an honour to know you all."

Everyone had their eyes turned to look at Gem as she stood in the centre of the room. The silence that followed after her speech was very profound.

Reese looked across at Mahala, who had risen up onto her elbow as Gem was talking, although she was still draped across Joel's lap. When Gem had finished speaking Reese got up to her feet and as she did so she said, "Yer fine, that's all well and good, but when do we eat?"

Chapter 38

They waited until night had fallen. It descended like a thick blanket, dragging in the mist and cloaking the town like a veil. As they all stood in the garden, sound was muffled by the encroaching weather. The overhanging trees protected them once again from any late night prying eyes.

Gem knew they were safe; she had previously stood alone under the trees and watched for any movement from her neighbours. Fortunately they were old and hopefully safely tucked up in their beds. It would be unlucky if a bout of incontinence suddenly struck them. She felt the coldness of the night caress her skin and an involuntary shiver travelled the length of her spine.

She wanted to go with them.

It was not right that they should go without her. She craned her neck backwards and gazed upwards; her mind floated above the mist and reached for the stars. Up there things were clearer; she could think properly and put things into perspective. It was only when she was back on the ground that things got so complicated.

A soft whistle brought her back.

Suddenly spurring into action, she ran towards the back door and jumped up the steps, nearly landing on top of Joel, who was just turning away after summoning her.

"I wish you would stop throwing yourself at me," he quipped, "it's very embarrassing."

"Oh, you conceited thing. If you didn't keep getting in my way, I wouldn't have to keep falling over you."

"Shh, you two." Remne's voice floated towards them in the darkness and duly chastened, they lapsed into silence.

As her eyes adjusted to the dim interior of the kitchen Gem could now make out Remne as she hugged her parents good-bye. Mahala and Reese were helping each other with their equipment; Gem could almost feel their excitement. It was palpable and contagious and she wanted to go even more because of it. As Gem went to voice her objection at staying, she heard Remne's voice calmly whisper inside her head *"Don't even think about it, Gem."*

"But ..."

Then a voice Gem recognised as Mahala came floating in as well, as if it was some paranormal party line, *"You are not well enough yet, we need you 100 per cent."*

"Oh great! Now there are two of you invading my head."

"Give it up, Gem. Accept what you cannot change. You are not coming and that is final."

"Okay! Okay, you win," said Gem out loud.

Joel, who had his back to her, turned and looked at her as if she had suddenly lost her mind, all she could manage in reply to his stare was a slight shrug of her shoulders and an embarrassed laugh.

Now here they were, standing under the trees.

The grass was damp with the moisture from the fog and beaded itself on cobwebs round the garden. As night descended the air had started to feel chilly, but as the clock had ticked away the temperature had plummeted. Gem could see their breath as everyone breathed in and out.

Winter is only just around the corner, she thought wistfully, *In more ways than one.*

They had all said their good-byes and Remne had ushered her parents back inside the house, fearing that seeing her true self might have a detrimental effect on them. They had nodded in understanding and with his arm around a tearful Margaret; Lloyd had taken his wife back to the lounge.

Reese leant down so that Beth could put her arm around her shoulders and as she straightened up Beth's feet dangled in mid-air.

Everyone was ready.

Gem watched as all three women took slow, deep breaths. Her eyes grew round in amazement as she watched them change. She had not been able to view herself when the changes happened to her. This was what it must have been like for Nathan, to stand with a mixture of awe and reverence and a little bit of dread thrown in for good measure.

Mahala's and Reese's muscles stretched and expanded, but Remne, who was not a warrior, only grew taller; Beth's body looked small and forlorn as she clung to Reese's neck.

Then with no warning they hurled through the mist and were lost from view even before a final farewell had reached Gem's lips.

She stood there with Joel under the trees, staring as the swirls and eddies in the thick mist hid their sudden departure. Not a word was spoken between them, but they drew involuntarily a little closer to each other, both of them wondering what this night would bring.

It took the flyers a little over an hour to reach their destination. The weather had drawn in to such a degree that trying to make out any distinguishable landmarks was proving quite difficult.

Remne pointed to the town that they could just see through the dark, menacing clouds. Those same clouds seemed to be getting lower to the ground with each passing minute. The twinkling of street lights that shone out spasmodically through the darkness helped point them towards the Glastonbury Abbey.

The wind had started to pick up and buffeted them around like some invisible hand. Reese adjusted her hold on Beth, fearful now that she might drop her as the wind picked up, but Beth clung to her as if she was the last life raft on a sinking boat. There was no way Beth was going to let go and the thought brought a smile to Reese's face. For one so small and delicate, Beth had certainly shown a lot of grit and determination.

Dragging her attention back to the job in hand, Reese slowly lowered herself to the ground and despite the high winds she managed to stay upright. After folding away her wings she dropped her shoulders to enable Beth to reach the ground and they waited in the shadows for the others to make their way over to them.

"This night is turning nasty, I have never seen anything like this before," said Reese, looking around at the sky.

"It's strange, isn't it?" Mahala said.

Reese who was being buffeted by the strong winds shouted across to her, "What is, M?"

"Well, to have such a high wind and yet the clouds are not moving; they seem to be gathering. Look over there at those big black clouds around the hills. Weird!"

"This is no ordinary night, we must be on our guard," said Remne as she joined them. She was breathing heavy; she was not used to the physical side of flying such a long distance.

Mahala and Reese exchanged glances and a hint of a smile played around both their lips.

Pushing her bow higher up on her shoulder, Mahala led the way across to the ruins of the abbey. Remne grabbed Beth's hand and held tight as she guided her across the open area. A streak of lightning split the air, illuminating everything around. Immediately all four of them dipped to the ground, trying to make themselves as inconspicuous as possible.

Mahala was the first to rise and running swiftly, she made her way over to what remained of the outer walls. Another flash rent the sky and they could see the walls rising like dead fingers, each one pointing upwards to the sky and the imminent storm.

They took shelter against the cold stone walls as the thunder rolled down upon them and keeping Beth inside the group, they huddled together, trying to get their bearings.

"Something's wrong!" shouted Mahala over the storm. They could see her concern written all over her face, with every flash of lightning.

"I don't feel anything and neither does Minnie," responded Reese, tapping the sword that was strapped diagonally across her back.

"We're in the wrong place!" shouted Beth as another roll of thunder echoed around their heads. Her voice sounded calm and calculated as she continued, "We have two shots at this and if we choose wrong then we have wasted time. So what is it going to be, Wearyall Hill or the Tor?"

Mahala and Reece exchanged glances, but it was Remne who broke the silence.

"The Tor I think. The other places that are nearby, including the Challis Well, are all too obvious. We do know that the layout of the land was different in the time of Joseph of Arimathea. There was water up to the base of the Tor. Everything emanates from the Tor, the spring for the well, the view of the abbey and Wearyall Hill. It is like a triangle of history versus legend."

"Well, that's it then, don't let's hang about. Come on, you lot, let's be off, time's a marching."

Pushing herself out away from the walls, Mahala unfolded her wings and took to the air before the others could reply. Reese once more gathered Beth into her arms and followed her comrade. Remne, although somewhat slower, was not far behind, but she was fuming that Mahala had acted so irresponsibly and without caution.

It was only a matter of minutes before they were all reunited. Mahala was crouched on the ground by a clump of trees in a small glade, staring up the hill that was rising majestically in front of her.

"What's wrong?" whispered Reese when she got to her.

"Shh."

Mahala held a finger up to her lips and pointed. The screen of vegetation shielded them from some men who were moving about on the upper terrace. Even though the angle was quite acute they could still see the lights that danced at the entrance of a small tunnel.

"They're here! They have found what we came for! Damn them!" hissed Reese.

Beth grabbed her arm and whispered, "All is not lost. They haven't found it yet. They still seek it. If we are quiet we may yet get what we came for."

Reese searched Beth's face, half convinced that she could really see, but the eyes that looked at her were lifeless and glazed. No spark twinkled deep within them, no sign of recognition or expression lay within those twin pools of ruined brown.

Mahala, who was laid out flat upon the damp grass, whispered back as she sat up, "What do you suggest? I can take a few of them out from here." She slipped the bow from her shoulder and notched an arrow onto the string.

Beth sat with her back to the hill, looking small and frail in the darkness. It was only her face, pale and white, that they could see. The rest of her was huddled within a large dark ski coat that Gem had given her to keep warm.

"Give it a few minute and the time will be right," Beth said. "If they leave someone outside, then take him. If they don't, then we shall enter the tunnel."

All three of them turned to stare at Beth, bewilderment clearly showing on each of their features. They wondered how she knew there was even a tunnel, let alone men around it.

Beth's smile was enigmatic as she sat and twiddled with the toggles of her jacket. As the minutes ticked away they could feel the storm's first soft droplets beginning to fall. The rain gently patted onto their clothing, darkening the colour wherever it hit. Then it grew stronger and with it the power of the storm started to increase. By the time they turned to climb the hill, the rain was lashing at them with ferocity. The strength of the wind lashed the rain into their faces, causing them to constantly wipe it from their eyes.

As they inched their way forward they realised that whoever was left on guard must have retreated to the safety and warmth of the inner tunnel, as Beth predicted.

Remne watched Beth through the teeming rain, slipping and sliding on the wet grass, unable to get her footing. The other two had forged on ahead, eager now for battle and leaving them to make their own way. Stepping over to her, Remne gently put her arm around Beth's waist and Beth immediately clung to her.

"Thank you, Remne."

Remne did not bother to answer but concentrated on climbing. Beth felt small and light within her arms; carrying her was not a burden. She had no weapons like the other two to hinder her progress and as Mahala and Reese were needed to guard against attack, Remne felt she had to do her part ... and that was safeguarding Beth.

It looked as if Beth had more of a part to play in all this than any of them suspected. Gathering the frail young woman into her arms, Remne forced her way upwards towards the entrance of the tunnel.

When they reached the terrace, the rain had plastered their hair to their heads and ran in rivulets down their clothes.

Both Reese and Mahala stopped to unleash their weapons; Reese's sword flashed as the lightning bounced off it, they could hear it starting its war song and Reese lovingly put her lips to the lethal blade and kissed it. They heard her muttering something, but none of them had the heart to enquire what she was saying.

Mahala tested her sword, making sure that it cleared the strapping as it dangled at her side. She looped the strap of her quiver over her shoulder and pinged the string of her bow a couple of time, testing its strength.

Finally they were ready and leaving the violence of the storm, they entered the tunnel, fully aware of the different violence that lay within.

"Will you sit down? You are driving me crazy."

Joel had watched Gem stride up and down for an hour now and it was seriously getting on his nerves.

"What? Oh shut up, you are getting on mine. How can you sit there and just do nothing?"

"What exactly are you achieving, striding up and down, may I ask, except wearing a hole in your carpet."

"You're right, of course. I am achieving nothing," Gem said, sitting down heavily on the vacant sofa opposite Joel. "I wish I could sleep like Margaret and Lloyd," she added, "but still, they don't know the half of what is going on, bless them."

Suddenly she jumped to her feet again, as the need to be doing something washed over her. Her nerve endings felt raw and exposed; she needed to do something … anything.

Joel, whose body was stretched out along the sofa in a vision of effortless relaxation, swept a hand across his face when he saw her on the move again.

"Where are you going now?"

"To get the Book, I'm going to see if it sheds any light on what is happening."

As she left the room Joel swung his legs back down to the floor; shoving the magazines to one side, he made a bit of space on the coffee table.

Gem entered the lounge carrying the heavy tome and Joel patted the space next to him. Raising an eyebrow at him, Gem thought it was prudent not to say anything; placing the heavy book down on the table, she settled herself on the seat next to him.

Joel was intrigued and fascinated by the Book. Never before had he seen anything like it. He ran his fingers over the leather bindings and gold tool work on the cover, but it was when Gem opened it and turned the first page that he involuntary took a quick intake of breath.

"It's so beautiful. Where did you get it? I've never seen anything like it in my life. Can it really tell you things?"

"Slow down," Gem said with a smile. "It belonged to my grandfather, then Beth's uncle. They both had a go at deciphering it. They wrote a lot of the deciphering on paper that they slipped in between the pages. It was their life's work and both paid a price for hiding it."

As Gem flicked the pages she took a sneaky look at Joel's face and was pleased to see his eyes gleaming in the soft lighting. Suddenly his whole demeanour changed and his eyes took on brilliance like jet and he grabbed her hand to stop her flicking over any more pages.

Annoyed at being grabbed, she tried to pull her hand away from his grip, but she was powerless. His fingers dug deep into her wrist as he involuntarily summoned up his inner power.

If I was fully fit you would not be doing this, she thought savagely.

Joel had not moved, his eyes were riveted on one of the loose pages tucked neatly inside the book. Gem forced herself to look at where he was staring and as he slowly released his grip upon her wrist, her face registered, like Joel, the shock of what she was seeing. At one point in their joint career, her grandfather, or maybe Beth's uncle, had deciphered something that they were unaware of, or of its significance.

Years before, they had sat at their desks and tried to unravel a mystery they were not privy to, little knowing what those actions would bring.

Her hand shook slightly as she reached for the page. With the passing of time the paper had turned yellow, but the writing was remarkably legible and that was the reason why it had caught Joel's eye.

The writing itself was bold, with a curling to each character. Gem recognised it immediately; it was Beth's uncle's writing. Would tears have splashed the page if he had known what danger his niece was putting herself in?

Would his old heart have given out before he had finished writing, if he had known beforehand that it was his beloved niece he was writing about?

As Gem read the words a big lump came into her throat and she handed the paper to Joel as she said, "You read it … I can't," and he watched as large tear spilled over her lower lashes and coursed down her face.

> Came hence he forth across the sea,
> With holy twelve and caskets three,
> They are buried in a place so deep,
> Those precious things that do not sleep.
> For in this place, this tranquil keep,
> Mankind's need alone will weep.
> A lasting epitaph and grave,
> No mortal hand in this was made.
> Buried deep within a glade,
> Two sets of cruets silver laid,
> And yonder hence within dark walls,
> A holy cup of divinity calls.

As he finished reading the first part he looked at Gem but all she could do was nod for him to finish reading.

But warning strong to those four that follow,
A danger lies within that hollow.
Wickedness lurks within the glade,
Of mortal men and evil shade.
Your holy quest alone will falter,
And gather to ourselves a daughter.
Oh brave and lustrous one of gold,
Into our presence now behold.

Laying the paper back inside the book, he turned to Gem and gathered her gently into his arms as she sobbed broken heartedly. If the verses were right then one of them was not going to return and suddenly to Joel, the night seemed to stretch endlessly in front of him.

Chapter 39

Whoever had been standing guard had left a small lantern burning just inside the entrance to the tunnel. By its soft beam they could just make out that the floor of the path gradually sloped downwards.

"We don't need the lantern, I know where to go," whispered Mahala as she crouched near the entrance. She had one hand resting in the dirt and as she knelt, she lifted her nose and smelt the air like a bloodhound on the scent.

Rees was finding it difficult to stand still and her feet shuffled about, sending up little eddies of dust as she bounced about. Her drawn sword flashed in the lamplight and Remne could see she was only waiting to be let off the leash.

It was easy to see that Reese wanted retribution and satisfaction for what had happened to her family. That was her human heart talking and was only to be expected, but Remne also knew that Reese would not jeopardise one quest for the other.

"Come on, come on," Reese urged as she passed her heavy sword from one hand to the other. "Let's go, we can't hang about here, the guard might return."

The light from the small lamp spilled over the group and each of them looked as if they had just come from a shower and forgotten to dry themselves.

Instead of looking bedraggled and exhausted, the light bounced off bronze and white muscles, taut with tension. Both Reese and Mahala were dressed in their usual fighting gear. Their sleeveless t-shirts did not restrict their movements and the tight trousers tucked inside soft leather boots protected their legs. They did not feel the cold like Remne, who shivered involuntarily in her thick jumper; Beth, who had been standing to one side, came over and slipped her warm hand into hers. Remne squeezed it gently to say thank you.

Mahala looked up at Reese and her smile broadened; quickly rising to her feet, she slapped Reese on the arm and the pair of them rushed off into the darkness.

That's it, thought Remne, *they're off the leash. God help those they find.*

Grabbing hold of Beth's hand, Remne hurried as best she could down the long tunnel. Suddenly the pathway opened out and forked off in four different directions; Remne thought she heard noises coming from the left hand section and made towards it.

"We have to go to the right, Remne," Beth said. "After all, Jesus sat on the right hand of God."

"But I thought the others …"

"Let them do what they have to do. We must go this way; hurry, we don't have a lot of time."

Remne had to duck her head as she entered the smallest of the four tunnels. Beth was in front of her and her pace quickened as if she knew where she was going. No light penetrated along the dark damp tunnel and the storm was far behind them like a dim distant memory.

Nothing seemed to hamper Beth's progress, but Remne found herself having to place her hand against the cold, hard stone of the tunnel, in an effort to stop herself from stumbling.

Remne noticed the change immediately; they were no longer in the close confines of the tunnel, because she could now stand to her full height. It seemed they had entered a chamber of some sort. It was not until she heard the striking of a match did she think about bringing some.

At least someone is prepared, she thought and then another thought struck her: *Why matches and not a torch?*

The tiny flame bravely tried to illuminate their surroundings, but shadows crowded in and out at them as the flame flickered.

Beth made her way over to the edge of the chamber, her hand out before her as if judging the distance to the wall. Remne watched as she bent down, but Beth's back was to her, so she was unable to see what Beth was doing.

Suddenly the chamber glowed with light that emanated from an ancient oil lamp.

How long it had been sitting there, waiting for someone to bring it back to life, was anybody's guess. Remne realised that Beth had no use for the lamp, so she must have known in advance that the two of them would be together … alone.

Beth held the lamp high so that Remne could see the tunnel where they came through. As she turned she saw another three tunnels going off of the chamber and she started to have doubts about their eventual success.

"What one do we choose now?" said Remne as her voice bounced off the walls and disappeared down all the tunnels, as if it was trying to wake the Tor from its slumber.

Realising her mistake, Remne clamped a hand over her mouth. Beth turned to face her. Her face glowed with an inner radiance and she smiled broadly but she lowered her voice so that it would not carry, "What is the Trinity?"

"The Father, Son, and Holy Ghost," replied Remne in a whisper but still slightly perplexed.

"Exactly and who would you say was the greatest of these three?"

"The Father, of course! All things emanate from him."

"That is why we must go down the middle tunnel; the others lead to certain death."

Without another word Beth handed her the lamp, turned and disappeared down the tunnel; all Remne could do was follow.

They travelled for what seemed like ages but Remne knew it was only a few minutes; it was the darkness that gave all things a different perspective. Beth came to a halt and indicated for Remne to stay where she was.

"Do not come any closer. It is too dangerous for you. Promise me you will stay exactly where you are. Do not move."

The urgency and hardness that had suddenly appeared in Beth's voice forced Remne to nod her head in affirmation but on impulse she said, "What about you? Won't you be in danger?"

"Me? No … I suffered my dangers a long time back. This is what I am meant to do." Her voice changed dramatically as she said, emphasising each word, "And I must do it alone!"

Remne watched as Beth turned away and headed on up the tunnel. She hunkered down on her heels and placed the lamp on the ground in front of her. The air felt dank and rancid like a room closed from sunlight for far too long. She longed to fill her lungs with good clean air. She longed to go on her boat with her cat and just sail the canals in peace. Peace always came at a price though. She had long ago figured that out and lowering her head to her folded arms, she patiently awaited the outcome of Beth's search.

She did not have long to wait; the blinding light that came from farther up the tunnel in Beth's direction was like the light from an exploding star.

It forced Remne to shield her eyes and she pressed her head further into her arms to protect them. Then a passing of what seemed like a million bats flew around her, forcing her into a foetal position. As she lay in the dirt and grit, small pieces of stone pressed into the side of her face and she could taste the passage of years in the tunnel's dust.

Not trusting to move, she lay there until a small hand shook her shoulder and tentatively raising her head, she saw Beth standing beside her.

"Don't be afraid," Beth said. "I have what we came for." Lowering herself to the ground, she sat next to Remne. "For you to look upon the face of God would have meant your death. He showed me the way when I was a prisoner. He told me that the cruets and the cup were kept together, placed here in secret by Joseph and his followers. They knew how to carve tunnels out of rock; after all, that was where they laid the body of Christ, in a tomb hewn from rock. They worked in secret until they found the exact stop to leave their holy treasures. Then they sealed the entrance to the tunnel and it has lain undisturbed until now. Adam took my sight away, little knowing to what ends he was fulfilling. I paid a small price." Then suddenly holding a box out so that Remne could see it, she said, "And I have retrieved what we so desperately need. So rise up, Remne and let's leave this place as quickly as possible."

Remne could see in the glow of the lamp that the wooden box she was holding had carving round the sides and on the lid. It was nothing out of the ordinary, but it carried within its wooden heart the hope of the world.

This time Remne led the way. She was more than eager to vacate the underground workings. She was never happy in enclosed spaces, so the thought of finally getting out into the open was all the spur she needed.

They re-entered the chamber and Remne blew out the lamp and left it on the floor. They did not need it now; soon they would be out into the night air and homeward bound.

They made their way back up the tunnel to where the four tunnels merged and Remne could just make out the small entrance in the distance.

She was in the process of turning round to face Beth, to offer words of encouragement, when a blow smashed into the side of her face, sending her reeling backwards to fall at Beth's feet.

It was not powerful enough to knock her out, but still she shook her head to clear the fuzziness the blow had inflicted. When she started to get to her knees, someone grasped her hair, pulled her up and then delivered a vigorous knee thrust into her abdomen, completely knocking the air from her lungs.

She was no fighter and was not a match for the giant of a man that held her. She had no weapons, only an agile mind and that was of little use up against the man who now held her in his iron grip.

Blood trickled down the side of her face into her eye and she had difficulty focusing in the darkness.

Then a light blazoned out, filling the small chamber with its radiance and for a moment she wished it was still dark and she did not have to view the terrible scene before her.

Two men had hold of Reese, their muscles bulging with the effort. They were big men, as tall as Reese herself and another had hold of Mahala's hair as she lay unconscious on the ground.

In the centre of the group stood the most odious man Remne had ever looked upon. He would have been of average height if he stood upright, but his shoulders were hunched, making his arms look like they were too long for his body. What was worse was the grin that had spread across his face now that they were all his to command. He licked his lips continuously as if imagining what he was going to do to each of them, but he suddenly became serious and looking over towards Remne, he said, "Don't hide in the background, Beth darling. Come closer and give me what you are holding."

Bravely Beth stepped out into the full light, leaving the comfort of the shadows behind her and when she reached him, she offered the box to him.

Both Remne and Reese struggled in the arms of their captors, but it was of little use.

He held the box with trepidation, fearing its contents, but his Master had given him this commission to vindicate himself for all his wrongdoings and he was not going to fail. Turning to the men holding the girls, he said, almost regretfully, "I must leave now. I have to get this back to the Master.

You know what you have to do; don't forget to reseal the entrance with their bodies inside."

After he had finished speaking, he looked at each one of the women and sadly shook his head.

"What a waste. What a feast I could have had. Never mind, look on the bright side. I shall have something to look forward to. When this is all over I shall return and have that feast as a reward for doing so well."

Then he turned, scurried off down the tunnel to the entrance and disappeared from sight in next to no time. As soon as he had gone it seemed to spur the men into action; Remne could hear the man who was holding her draw his dagger from its sheath. She remained slumped in his arms, pretending to be weaker than she was, hoping to put him off guard.

Reese was putting up one hell of a fight and the two men had difficulty holding her.

The man who had hold of Mahala's hair suddenly let go of her and her unconscious body slumped to the floor of the tunnel with a soft thud. He paid her little attention now that she was out cold and rushed over to aid his fellow comrades that were trying to hold Reese.

Nobody heeded Beth, assuming since she was blind that she did not need watching. She edged over to the light and in a split second she had extinguished it. That was all Mahala needed, she jumped to her feet, unleashed her sword and drove it through her captor even before he could raise his weapon.

Then all hell seemed to break loose. Remne delivered a stunning kick to her captor's leg and she heard it break as he crashed to the floor in the darkness. As he rolled in agony she dropped to her knees and desperately searched for his dagger. Her fingers scrabbled about in the dirt and she could feel some of her nails ripping off in her frantic forage. Her long hair hampered her movements and it was only now that she could appreciate why Gem had shorn all hers off.

She knew roughly where he had dropped it and when her fingers closed round the hard handle, she lifted it quickly and plunged it into his heart. She heard the soft gurgle as blood filled his lungs and after a few twitches he lay silent. The fight continued around her and then all was silent. Reese's breathless but jubilant voice broke the silence:

"Will someone please turn that light back on so we can assess the damage? I've definitely been hurt; how about you, M?"

Before she could answer, Beth relit the little lamp, flooding the area with light.

"Oh, well done, Remne, you got one," beamed a triumphant Reese; turning to Mahala, who was sitting on the floor with her back up against the wall, she said, "That was a darn close call, I thought we had it there for a minute, M."

When she did not reply, Reese wandered over to her, stepping over the bodies of the men as she went. She wiped the blade of her sword across the back of one of the fallen and sheathed it in its holder that was located across her back.

Then extending her hand down to Mahala to help her to her feet, she was surprised to see the girl shake her head in refusal.

"Come on, M, get to your feet; what's up with you? I want to compare injuries before they fade."

Reese's happy demeanour turned to one of horror when Mahala lifted her hands away from her stomach, exposing the extent of her injury.

It was not an ordinary gash; it was ragged and long and covered the full width of her stomach.

Blood had soaked the area around her and if she had stood upright, then the contents of her body would have spilt out onto the floor. Reese dropped to her knees beside the stricken girl and gently assessed the damage. The surgeon in her was unable to mask the full extent of her terrible injury. Tears welled in her eyes and she could not bring herself to look Mahala in the face as she spoke.

"You will be okay. Let's just get you home where I can work on you. You'll see, I shall have you up and about in no time."

"You always were a bad liar." Raising her hand, she stroked the side of Reese's face as she spoke.

"One thing is true, though: get me home. Fly like the wind, Reese, make sure I am home before I die. There is something I must do. Now bind me up as best you can and let's get the hell out of this place."

Remne tore the shirts from the dead men into strips and passed them to Reese, who quickly and efficiently bound them around Mahala's wrecked body.

Finally, together they made their way out into the open. The rain had stopped but the night still carried an air of menace about it. The clouds were black and heavy, as if they were full of tears waiting to be shed.

Remne finally put her finger on what was different. The wind had stopped, but a strange stillness enveloped the whole area. When they had entered the tunnel, the noise of the wind and the storm had been so loud and so strong, but now it felt as if God himself was holding his breath.

Reese gently laid Mahala on the ground and turning back to the entrance; she lifted her sword from its sheath and brought it crashing down upon the ground. As her sword hit the dirt and grass surrounding the entrance, a loud rending sound could be heard and slowly the tunnel started to close. After a few seconds it was impossible to tell that it had ever been there.

Turning back to the others, Reese lifted Mahala into her arms and, after giving Remne one last sorrowful look, she released her wings. Holding Mahala tightly to her chest, she was airborne and out of sight in seconds.

Remne's heart felt like lead as she gathered Beth to her. She was unaware that their tears mingled with each other's as they flew off in pursuit of Reese and her sad burden.

As Beth lay in Remne's tight embrace she blamed herself for the outcome of the venture. She should have known that they would be lying in wait for them somewhere along the line.

Her heart felt like breaking as she thought of having to tell Gem about the outcome. She had not predicted this turn of events. They needed four warriors to complete the prophesy and if one of them was on the point of dying, what were they supposed to do?

As the wind whipped around her, Beth pulled the hood of her coat up around her head and fastened it more securely. When this was done she offered up a small prayer:

"Oh Lord, you have shown me what to do up till now. Show me the way forward so that we can defeat this evil."

All that was left to her was to wait and she was used to doing that. Now only time would tell what path they must now take.

Chapter 40

By the time Remne and Beth had arrived back in the garden of Gem's house, all the lights in the back of the house were blazing. Remne lowered Beth to the ground and watched as she made her way tentatively inside, her hand stretched out before her as she negotiated the steps. Remne took a minute to gather her thoughts. Never before had she flown so far or so fast. She filled her lungs with the cold clean air, quietly folded her wings away and gradually returned to normal.

There was something missing though.

She felt cheated that they had lost the box, but there was more; she was angry that there had been nothing she could do about it. These feelings of anger were alien to her, but if she was honest with herself, she was not a bit jealous when she saw Reese and Mahala running off down the passage to confront who knows what.

She was a messenger!

That was her purpose. Or did the purpose suit the person, not the other way round? She didn't see Gem until her sister pulled her into her arms for a crushing embrace.

"I prayed all night that you all would come back safe, but it was not to be, was it?"

"No. They put up a brave fight but in the end it was not to be. I'm so sorry, Gem, we had it in our hands, only to lose it at the final hurdle."

"Don't worry about it for the moment. You are not to blame; come inside. Mahala is asking for you."

Remne sadly raised her head and replied, "For me?"

"Yes, Reese has made her as comfortable as she can, but her time is nearly up and she wants to speak to you privately."

Remne nodded her head, accepting the fact that there was a bond between herself and Mahala that none of the others knew about.

"Where is she?"

"She's in my room. Hurry now, Remne, she hasn't got a lot of time. Do you want me to come with you?"

"No," replied Remne "it's okay, I'll go on my own."

When they reached the stairs in the hallway, Remne hurried upwards and Gem watched her till she reached the top. Then turning around, she went and joined Joel and Beth.

Margaret and Lloyd, who had been awakened by the noise of their arrival, were also in the lounge; smiling, Gem reassured them that nothing had happened to their beloved daughter.

Remne did not bother to knock but pushed the door gently open and when she entered, she saw Reese cradling Mahala in her arms in one last loving embrace.

Mahala's face was deathly white as if all her blood had drained away from her on the flight home. There was a slight tinge of blue round her lips, heralding her death. When Reese saw her standing behind her she gently laid Mahala back down on the pillows, leant forward, and kissed her on the forehead.

"Don't you worry now," Reese said. "We will get this job done, one way or the other. I have always loved you M; you were the sister I never had. Wait for me and then we can be together again. All of us."

Remne stood there patiently, fighting back the tears as she listened to Reese.

"Say hello to Christopher for me and give Minnie a big kiss, tell her Mummy loves her."

Remne watched as Mahala lifted her arm and dragged her friend into a weak embrace. Reese started to sob into her friend's shoulder; fearing that she would die before they had a chance to talk, Remne stepped forward and pulled Reese away from the bed. The suffering on the black woman's face was evident to see, but she knew Mahala had something important to say to Remne, so blowing a final kiss to her friend, she swiftly left the room.

Remne sat in the place just vacated by Reese and leant forward to catch what Mahala was saying. She looked weak and helpless lying there, so Remne was amazed to see her suddenly smile. She opened her parched lips and in a weak voice she managed to say, "Look."

Remne looked at her closed hand that was rising off the bed.

Again she said, "Look."

Remne held out her open hand and Mahala dropped something into it.

The locket lay there in her palm, the light picking up its fragile beauty.

Tears fell from Remne's eyes in great huge droplets as she recognised the locket belonging to Mahala's mother. Although weak her voice gathered strength as she talked and she raised her head off the bed to emphasise her words.

"I told you I would get it back. The pig had it round his own neck as a trophy. He did not wear it for long. I knew he was there as soon as we entered the tunnel. I could smell him. I want to wear it when you bury me; not only that, I have a gift for you."

As if the sudden exertion had drained her strength, her head flopped back down on the pillows.

"Me, why me?"

"You are the only one who can accept it. It is given with love so do not be afraid of it. I will be with you in spirit to guide you."

Her voice had grown weaker and Remne had to bend over her to hear what she was saying.

"Come closer," Mahala insisted. "Come closer."

Remne leant over so far that her ear was practically touching Mahala's lips. As soon as she was near enough Mahala grabbed Remne's head in a fierce grip and turned her head so that their lips were practically touching.

Her voice was weak and scratchy, but she had summoned up from deep inside her soul the strength to do what she had to do.

"Forgive me, Remne, but I can take no chances. I have to pass on what I am to someone and I have chosen you."

Remne watched as Mahala's eyes rolled back inside her head and all her life force drained from her open mouth into Remne's.

It was like a funnel of pure light and Remne's eyes watered at the sheer brilliance of it, forcing her to shut her eyelids. When it was over, Mahala slumped farther into the bed, as if she was crumbling away. No longer the warrior, she became once again the young librarian.

"That is it, I can go now. There is nothing to keep me here. You are now four again and can fulfil the prophesy."

Remne felt the changes starting within her and realising Mahala's time was very near, she decided to help her final moments.

"Because you have given me a gift, then I shall give you one."

"I have no need of gifts. My end comes swiftly."

Remne summoned the angel to her.

"You are too early, Remne," the angel said. "Her time is not quite over."

"Forgive me but I ask for just one favour. Bring her guide to her now so that it makes her passing easier. She is suffering greatly, although she does not complain. It is such a small request."

"I can't see why not," the angel said. "Come closer, guide."

As the woman came within the circle of light, she looked upon her daughter's face with love and affection and taking hold of her hand, she helped her from the bed. Together, arm in arm, they followed Death.

An hour later, Remne entered the lounge. Fortunately Margaret and Lloyd had returned to bed. Gem had assured them that nothing more could be done.

They would see to the body in the morning, phoning the people on the list that Nathan had left those people in authority who had been primed to keep secrets and anyway it would have frightened them half to death to see her as she was dressed now.

She was in the same kind of outfit that Mahala had worn; dangling by her side was her sword and over her shoulder was Mahala's bow and quiver.

She did not have to tell them Mahala was gone, but she would have to do some explaining as to why she was standing in the middle of the lounge with Mahala's weapons strapped to her.

It was Joel surprisingly who spoke first; she had expected it to be Reese.

"What in God's name are you dressed up like that for?" he said. "You are a messenger, not a warrior. Take it off; you offend the memory of a great fighter."

"She is no longer a messenger," Beth said quietly from the corner of the room.

Gem, who had been too stunned to speak, suddenly shouted, "Hold on a minute! You don't just suddenly become a warrior."

"Quite right," chipped in Joel.

"You do if that warrior passes on her life essence to someone deserving of it and Mahala obviously thought Remne deserved it," said Beth.

"So what you are saying is that Remne is now a fully-fledged warrior and we are four again."

"Yes Gem, I am saying exactly that."

Gem needed no second bidding; she vaulted over the back of the sofa, grabbed Remne and hugged her to her chest.

"Now we are truly sisters."

Remne looked over towards Reese, who had remained quiet throughout the whole noisy proceedings. Gem took the hint and let her sister go, watching sadly as Remne walked over to Reese.

"Well, what do you say, Reese? Is everything okay with you?"

Reese lifted her large brown eyes and searched Remne's face before she gently nodded her head.

"It's fine with me. She trusted you and so do I. I just wish it did not have to come to this. I miss her so much already."

Remne rubbed her hand up and down Reese's arm in commiseration before she turned to face Joel.

"Are you still against me or do I have to prove myself?"

"No, I go along with the popular vote. I cannot afford to stand alone; besides that, time is running out and we have plans to make."

"Oh, you are so condescending," said Gem, jumping back over the sofa.

"And you are annoying and aggravating."

"Children please, behave!" said Beth with the first smile she had made since returning home. "Gem, may I make a suggestion? Can you phone Nathan and confirm what arrangements have been made for tomorrow's gathering?"

"Of course, Beth, I will do it straight away and as for the rest of you, I think it is time to check your weapons. We will be leaving just before daybreak."

Gem gave them all a swift glance before she left the room but added to Remne, "And that goes double for you."

Smiling at her sister, Gem left the room and Remne realised for the first time in her life what had been truly missing from it: comradeship.

This was it, she thought. *To be brothers in arms, Mahala had recognised the need in me even though I could not see it myself. Now I am truly a warrior. We are four again and it was always meant to be me; the four of us … the Guardians.*

It was so blindingly obvious that she wondered why she had not seen the truth of it before.

Taking the bow from her shoulder, she glanced over to where Joel was laying back on the sofa. He seemed to be quietly assessing her and when he caught her staring back, he just smiled an indulgent smile as if humouring her. Then he closed his eyes and went to sleep.

Gem went into the dining room to phone Nathan. She already felt emotionally drained and was not looking forward to having to tell him the outcome of tonight's little foray.

The phone rang four times before he answered and when he heard it was Gem she could hear the stress in his voice.

"Thank God you've rung. I was getting really worried. What has been happening up there with you? If it is anything like down here it's murder, I can tell you."

"Speaking of which," she began.

She thought the line had gone dead and was about to say something but after a while he spoke. His voice sounded gruff, as if his words were hard for him to get out or he could not trust himself to speak.

"Who was it … what happened?"

"They went to Glastonbury: Mahala, Reese, Remne … and Beth."

It was as she said the last name that she heard him take a sharp intake of breath.

"And?"

"They found a box, what they went for, but there was a fight and the box was taken away from them and in the process someone got seriously hurt."

Gem could hear the raw emotion in his voice as he said just one word: "Who?"

A little part of her heart died that moment, but she accepted the truth of the situation. Here were two people that she loved, both wanting to be together, but because of their love of her they would sacrifice that love.

She could not cling to something that was not meant to be, when she did not even know where her own heart lay.

It was up to her to say something, so putting him out of his misery, she said softly, as the tears ran down her cheeks, "It was Mahala. She died about half an hour ago."

Again there was silence at the other end of the phone and she could hear him wiping his cheeks as his hand rasped over his whiskers. It was obvious he was crying; he kept his voice even, but it was too late. She had heard the sigh of relief he had given when she had said Mahala's name.

"I'm sorry, Nathan."

"What for? Because they failed?"

"No, because of us."

"Oh, it's that obvious is it? I tried not to let it happen. I'm so sorry, Gem, but we were meant not to be. Beth needs me and I need her, you can see that, can't you?"

"Of course I can, silly. I wish you all the best in the world, you are a lucky guy. Just don't leave it too long to tell her how you feel. After all, there may not be many tomorrows to come, if it all goes pear shaped tomorrow and speaking of which, what is the setup down there?"

Gem brushed the last of the tears from her face as she listened to Nathan explain what was happening. It had been a difficult phone call, but now that they understood each other, she felt her mood lift.

Nathan could never forget the image of her holding that knife at his throat; it would have destroyed them eventually. It was better like this: a clean, honest break.

Rising from the chair, Gem left the dining room and entered the lounge. She popped her head around the corner of the door and called Beth over to her. When Beth reached her, she placed a hand on Gem's arm and gently asked, "Are you all right?"

"Yes of course, it's just that Nathan wants to have a word with you and what he has to say can't wait."

"Yes, I know, but are you all right?"

Finally catching her meaning, Gem leant down and kissed her friend on the cheek.

"Yes, I'm perfectly fine and I wish you all the luck in the world, both of you. Now go on with you, get in there and take that phone call."

Her face alight with smiles, Beth gave Gem a quick squeeze and made her way over to the dining room, where Gem had left her mobile; all she heard was, "Hello darling," as Beth closed the door.

"You are not taking that cat."

"Why not, he wants to come. He wants to be with me."

Joel felt he had been banging his head against a brick wall for the last ten minutes. Arguing with a blind person was not what he was used to.

"Oh what's the use?" he said, giving up. "You will probably sneak him into your bag the moment my back is turned."

"Thank you, Joel. It is not for my sake; he told me, in fact he insisted on coming. He said he had some unfinished business to attend to."

Joel leant down and studied Beth's face, wondering if she was taking the mickey, but her face registered nothing but seriousness. Two lines had appeared between her eyes as she fought the cat's cause and as he leant nearer she suddenly smiled, catching him off guard.

Lowering his voice so that the others could not hear him, he asked, "Did he really tell you that?"

Dropping her voice to a whisper, Beth answered in the same manner, "Yes, he really did."

"Ummm!"

Straightening up, he clapped his hands together to draw everyone's attention and then leaning his arm along the top of the fireplace he said, "I have made a decision: Beth is taking the cat and I want no arguments from anyone about it. Is that okay?"

Reese leant over towards Remne when Joel was not looking, laughed and whispered into her ear, "I see Beth got her way then."

"I could have told him that at the start," Remne whispered back, "but it was just such fun to watch."

"What's that, Remne?" Joel asked. "Did you say something?"

"I was just saying, that's good, the cat can watch our backs."

"Ummm," he replied suspiciously.

Joel stared at them, causing them to find something really important to do with their gear. Remne could see Reese biting down hard on her lip to stop herself from laughing out loud and she coughed loudly to cover the giggle that finally escaped.

Fortunately Gem burst into the room at that moment, every inch the warrior. She had returned to full health and was impatient to be on her way, but her eager face suddenly became touched with sadness.

"Has everybody said their good-byes to Mahala?" she asked.

When everyone nodded, she continued, "Margaret and Lloyd have decided to stay here, where it will be safer for them. They will be easier to contact if we have to reach them quickly."

Gem looked over at Remne, who nodded, fully understanding the implication of her words.

"Right then, if we are all set, let's be on our way."

As she turned to go, Joel suddenly said, "By the way, I decided Beth could bring her cat."

"The only person who didn't know that was you," she said. "I thought you would have learnt by now not to argue with her."

Gem did not even break her stride as she headed for the door and disappeared through it before Joel could think of a suitable answer.

Reese was unable to contain her mirth any longer and let forth a bellow of a laugh. Remne was pleased that the grief of Mahala's death had been accepted by them all; they would mourn her at a later date, but for now the laughter was bonding them together.

Joel strode across the room and picked up the leather strap that held his sword. Looping it across his back, he then rigorously attacked the buckles that fastened it across his broad chest, annoyance showing in his every gesture. He then reached down and picked up his sword and slid it into place and it was as he did this that all the tension left him.

Standing there … a warrior, he looked across the room at Beth and smiled.

Beth was sitting in the same position on the sofa, still stroking the monster of a cat and slowly she turned her head to face him and smiled back.

Chapter 41

Gem carried Beth, only too pleased to have her friend close to her, where she could keep an eye on her. Remne had the dubious pleasure of carrying her cat, whose allegiance now had been switched to Beth; at first he objected at being separated from her but remained quiet throughout the journey, much to Remne's relief.

They flew swift, high and fast in close formation. Remne heart raced with the exhilaration of it all. No longer was she struggling to keep up. Her physique changed from slim girl to warrior, just as the others had and she revelled in its strength and potency.

The skies over London mirrored the skies over Glastonbury: heavy and menacing. They could feel the static in the air and occasionally it would spit forth forked lightning, illuminating the underbelly of the black clouds.

Gem had informed them just before they left that they would head directly for Westminster Abbey, the garden of St Catherine's Chapel to be precise. Nathan, as instructed, had turned off the outside lighting to the abbey so they were able to arrive in some semblance of anonymity.

It would not have mattered if the lights had been blazing; because the clouds when they arrived hung so low they swirled around the bell towers.

The wind raged, causing mini whirlwinds round the perimeter of the abbey and it seemed its power was increasing with every passing minute. Leaves were being stripped from the trees, leaving the branches bare, as if winter had suddenly arrived; several plants in the garden had been uprooted and more were leaning over dangerously, their stems bent double, nearly touching the earth.

As soon as their feet touched the ground they raced towards the entrance to the Little Cloister as the heavens opened. Gem didn't bother to release Beth but kept her close to her body as she ran, but as soon as they were inside the cloister, Gem lowered her to the ground.

As Beth brushed her abundant dark hair from her face, Gem could see that her skin was flushed with excitement. Two rosy spots of colour stood out against the whiteness of her face. The dark smudges around her eyes had started to fade, thanks to the administration of Reese. The marks of where she had been hit stood out red in contrast to her white skin; these would also eventually fade but they would leave a scar. It just needed time for her to start looking young and beautiful again.

"You need feeding up," Gem said and she watched as Beth opened her large coat and ran her hands over her stomach.

"In time, Gem. My stomach has shrunk and I have not felt like eating since my release."

Gem placed a comforting hand on her shoulder, but she suddenly pushed Beth behind her when she heard footsteps quickly approaching.

All four stood shoulder to shoulder, their swords drawn and ready, listening to whomever it was that was fast approaching. Gem released her breath as she saw Nathan burst from the shadows; she lowered her sword to welcome him.

She would have felt insulted if she did not love Beth so much, because as he approached his eyes were scanning the area for Beth's presence.

As Gem stepped to one side he finally saw what he sought and without any further ado he swept Beth up in his arms and kissed her soundly on the lips.

Gem turned away at the sudden impulsive gesture, not wanting to look upon their obvious happiness and found herself face to face with Joel. The look of amazement on his face spurred her into words as she said, "What?"

"Nothing, nothing."

Holding his hands up in front of him, Joel slowly backed away and then thinking better of it, he came forward again. She could see he was itching to ask a question.

"What?"

"Are you and lover boy not together then?"

"Mind your own business!"

"Okay, don't get upset, I was only curious."

"I'm not upset. It's just you, not only are you annoying, but now you're nosy."

Joel once more lifted his hands and backed away, this time a grin spread across his face from ear to ear. Fuming, Gem turned her back on him.

Nathan walked up to Gem, who was now standing slightly apart from the others.

"You okay?" he asked.

"Yes, I'm fine," she snapped.

Then realising her mood had nothing to do with him, she smiled gently at him.

"I'm sorry, Nathan. I'm not upset with you and Beth, I couldn't be more happy for you both. Don't mind me, it's probably the tension. Now what is happening? Have all the dignitaries arrived?"

"I could not alter the minds of any of the heads of religion, but they have agreed to exchange their lesser officials with trained soldiers. Their argument was their faces are too well known and it would immediately cause suspicion."

"Have they any idea what they are letting themselves in for?"

"Yes, I am afraid they do, but don't forget, they are men of such religious conviction and they feel that their faith will keep them safe."

"I remember not so long ago the pope getting shot and it was not his faith that saved him, it was his bulletproof car."

"Now Gem, don't be cynical. They want to prove themselves; this is their way of testing their own faith. I don't have it in me to deny them."

"You've changed your tune?"

"That's because I've been cooped up with them all day and all night. It's mighty hard to question someone's right to be here when they all think they are God's chosen."

"Do you think this will bring the faiths closer together?"

"For a while, maybe, if it all turns out all right, but it is human nature to create divisions, no matter what the cause. No Gem, I think the real hope is with the people. A new faith may rise out of this, bringing all people closer together."

"And you're just the man to do it."

"Do you know what, Gem? I truly think I am. I've decided to leave the police force and work to create harmony between the different faiths; Beth is going to help me.

"There is one piece of good news; after they sat down and discussed everything, they decided to pour a load more money in keeping up the restorations on all the different churches. York is going to have about $50 million spent on it and the same with Canterbury. The pope has agreed to loosen a few purse strings as well, so for now it looks like the churches are safe from satanic invasion but ..."

Nathan's frown deepened as he looked back up the corridor.

"But what?" urged Gem.

"That's if things all go well today. What if ..."

"Well, if it doesn't ... we've certainly got our work cut out for us."

"Sorry to interrupt this tête-à-tête," Joel said, "but I think we should get moving."

Nathan had to laugh when he saw the look on Gem's face at Joel's words and patting her on the arm, he ventured a suggestion.

"He's not a bad bloke really; in fact, I like him, you could do a lot worse."

Gem looked at him as if he had gone suddenly off his head.

"You must be absolutely mad, if you think for one minute ..."

"I think the lady doth protest too much," said Nathan and turning his back he walked back over to where Beth was waiting for him.

Gem wanted to stamp her foot like a petulant child but resisted the urge to do so; instead she called for their attention.

"As you know, it's a new day, but you wouldn't believe it looking at the weather. The heads of all the religions have now gathered in the main body of the abbey. I don't have to tell you that the logistics of this are tremendous; we have to protect these religious leaders whilst defeating Adam and his Master. To make matters worse we do not know what Adam looks like now, so be on your guard. They also hold the sacred cup and cruets and we now know this is going to be their way of giving life to their Master for all eternity.

"Come close to me now, fellow Guardians and put your swords with mine and pledge."

Joel, Reese and Remne came at Gem's bidding; standing in a circle, they intertwined their swords to form a star and together they said,

"Oh Lord,
Give me patience to seek out my foe,
And strengthen my arm to wield my sword,
Give mercy and clemency to those enemies who plead for it,

Forgiveness and a swift end to those that don't.
We offer up this pledge to you along with our lives.
Thy will be done.
Amen."

After they withdrew their swords, they stood for a moment with their heads bowed. Reese let out a whoop of delight and leapt forward; with the adrenaline pumping through their bodies they all raced after her towards the main part of the church, all eager for the fight to begin.

Nathan grabbed hold of Beth's hand as they were left briefly on their own and with the cat bounding in front of them, they followed as fast as they could down the Little Cloister, then turning right they made their way along the long corridor past the museum and Pyx Chamber.

The high vaulted ceiling echoed sharply to the sound of hurrying feet, as Gem and the other raced over the large flagstones. Beth and Nathan heard their steps suddenly cease, as all the religious representatives raised their voices as one to start the Service of Salvation.

The air outside crackled with lightning and as it flashed, it lit their way as they hurried along the cloister. The windows rattled to the boom of thunder, which rolled repeatedly onwards. They couldn't tell when one boom started and another finished, so close was the thundering.

Rain lashed against the windows as if a thousand hands were scratching at them, trying to get in. Never before had Nathan seen a storm of such intensity, the noise of which seemed to vibrate round the very heavens and then crashed down upon the abbey as if it wanted to smash it into the ground.

Beth had to slow down, as her breathing had become laboured; Nathan wanted to tell her she shouldn't have come, but he knew the rebuke was useless and why did she bring that cat? It was just another thing to worry about!

Nathan watched the huge animal bound in front of them, but whenever it got too far in front, he sat upon his haunches and waited for them, his tail flicking backwards and forwards. His yellow eyes were round and bright, as if he too knew the reason for being there this day and revelled in it.

It did not move when they finally reached him but sat patiently … waiting.

That cat is acting mighty strange, Nathan thought as he stopped for Beth again and as he looked down the corridor to his right, he saw the Chapter House. Nathan hesitated and then, leaving Beth momentarily alone, he walked down towards the far room. He suddenly came to a decision and hurrying back to her side, he said, "I am going to leave you in the Chapter House with the cat. You will be safe there. It will be away from any fighting and I would feel better knowing you are out of harm's way."

Nathan was surprised that Beth did not offer any arguments, but thinking no more about it, he guided her along the corridor and into the Chamber House. He scoured the area until he found a chair for her to sit on. Beth was insistent that he place it so that she was facing the door with her back to the window and having no time to argue, he reluctantly agreed.

Thomas the cat jumped up and made himself at home on Beth's lap, immediately starting to purr as he washed himself.

Nathan's lips lingered longer than necessary upon Beth's, but he was torn between wanting to stay and protect her and his need to fulfil his commitment to his job. Beth gave him a swift kiss and pushed him from her, adding softly, "Go ... go, you are needed elsewhere. I'm fine here, don't worry about me."

Nathan gazed down at her, but he knew she was right, so turning swiftly; he exited the room at a run and headed off to meet up with the others.

He was unaware that Thomas had jumped down from Beth's lap and was silently following him along the corridor, on a quest of his own.

Gem had never seen anything so beautiful as the architecture of the building. There were apses with radiating chapels and characteristic Gothic features of pointed arches, ribbed vaulting, a rose window like her lovely Minster in York, and flying buttresses.

She had a love of ancient buildings and it showed in her face as she looked about her.

They had entered the main body of the abbey just as prayers were being offered and so as not to offend the gathering of holy men, the four blended into the shadows at the sides of the church.

Waiting.

Even Joel's voice behind her did not interrupt her scrutiny of the designs.

"The design of the abbey was based on a continental system of geometrical proportions."

"How do you know that?" she asked.

"1 was an architect in my former life."

"Really?"

"Yes, really. See over there?" he said, pointing to the middle of the church. "Those features are purely English, it has only a single rather than a double aisle and way down there," he said, pointing back down the church, "it has a long nave with wide projecting transepts. And did you know it has the highest Gothic vault in England? It's 120 feet but it was made to seem higher by making the aisles narrower."

Gem interrupted his speech by silencing him with a quick flick of her hand. She had just noticed Remne emerge from the shadows, her drawn sword in her hand. Reese had seen her movement as well and was instantly alert. She watched as Remne tested the air like a gun dog on a scent, a gesture so reminiscent of her lost friend that her hand involuntarily squeezed the handle of her sword with anger at her loss.

They could hear one of the Canon's standing on the High Altar, offering up his thanks and praise to God, but something jogged within Remne's mind. As she stared, an old and bent bishop tottered up to receive communion, his long robes swaying about his legs.

Remne gradually edged down towards the front. She had started to pass the chairs that had been placed before the High Altar for the dignitaries, each one holding a member of one faith or the other, each one praying as their religion took them.

She slowly walked past Poet's Corner, situated on her right and Gem and Joel, over to the left, kept pace with her. As they neared the front of the congregation they were alarmed to see the old bishop take from underneath his robes a wooden box with carving on the side and lid and offer it up.

Remne and Gem converged at the same time, both running forward to stop the old bishop from delivering the box.

Hearing the advancing warriors, the old bishop nimbly jumped to his feet.

He had undone his tunic to remove the box and when his raiment flapped open, Remne recognised the odious man from the tunnel.

Suddenly fearing the worst, the congregation rose to their feet in alarm at seeing two women rushing towards their clergy with drawn swords. The men Nathan had planted in the congregation drew round the holy dignitaries, trying to protect them. Even as they stood shoulder to shoulder, they allowed the fleeing bishop to pass between them, ignorant of his identity.

They had each been issued a short sword that had previously been sprinkled with holy water and blessed by all the holy men. Guns and bullets would have been useless against this kind of foe, so they had to be ready for hand-to-hand combat.

With the dignitary within their allotted circle, they unsheathed their swords and waited.

The young canon backed away up the steps, still holding the box. Fear was written all over his face and for an instant Gem was confused. Taking advantage of this, the young man turned and raced towards the altar, stripping his vestments as he went.

Reese, Joel, Remne and Gem advanced towards him, their swords drawn and ready. When he saw them coming towards him he started laughing.

"Do you think it would be that easy? Gem, you've come back to me."

Joel heard the "shades" coming up behind him and turning swiftly, he met them sword on sword, their demonic faces half hidden by their black hooded cloaks. Then suddenly there were more of them emerging from the shadows and Reese, giving a howl of delight, threw herself into the battle.

Remne notched the arrows to her bow and as if Mahala were guiding her hand, her arrows flew straight and true. When the arrows entered the shades, they disappeared back to where they came from, but it seemed there was always more to take their place.

Gem left them to fight and turning quickly to the men protecting the dignitaries, she shouted, "If you truly value their lives, get them out of here!"

She could see that the soldiers, some with shock etched upon their face, were fighting valiantly against the black hordes from hell. If the soldiers managed to get them out or not, she could not waste any more time; the young Canon had placed the box on the High Altar ... and was preparing to open it!

Gem threw herself up the steps towards the man, with every intention of thrusting her sword straight through him. She had her sword raised high above her head, but when she brought it down and thrust it forwards, he was no longer there.

Searching around her, she suddenly spied him high above her, his wings stretched out beside him, his chest bare.

"Do you prefer me like this, Gem? Do you like my new body? No? Don't tell me you preferred the old me."

As she looked up, she recognised Adam's voice and smiled. She knew deep within her heart that this was going to be their last meeting. By the end of the day one of them would be dead and she prayed it would not be her.

She watched as the Canon's body melted away, to be replaced by the hideous beast she thought she had killed once before. He changed fast and before she knew it, he was,

hurtling towards her, his leathery wings beating strongly, the talons on his feet splayed, ready to impale her.

She thought she heard cries coming from the congregation when they finally saw what they were up against, but any lapse of concentration now would be her death.

Aware that for the present he was unarmed, Gem dived towards the altar, her main concern being the retrieval of the box. Her fingers closed around the smooth olive wood and she dragged it towards her. It was surprisingly light, or perhaps it was just her imagination.

Adam's cry of anger at seeing her with the box spurred him on and kneeling down behind the shrine of Edward the Confessor, he retrieved his sword.

He slashed the air as he advanced and Gem realised she could not fight and hold the box at the same time. Racing down the steps, she slid it across the floor towards the entrance of the Great Cloister, where it finally came to rest after bouncing against the wall.

Adam sliced down towards her head, but she lifted her sword horizontally and parried the blow. He had the advantage in height as he loomed over her from the top of the steps, but she was nimble and managed to get round him. She had to turn him away from his prize and make him follow her back towards the High Altar.

Blow after blow rained down upon her and each time she parried his strokes and then counterattacked when he least expected it.

He raised his arm and the blow came down heavily, making her lose her footing; she stumbled back against the High Altar. As he came in close their swords clashed together between them, leaving no room for either to manoeuvre.

Gem felt his breath upon her cheek, but it was his words that cut like knives into her soul, making her want to vomit.

"There is still time," he said. "Fighting is futile, you know I want you … come with me, Gemini … be mine."

When he had finished speaking, he slowly opened his mouth and as the saliva dripped from his lips, he deliberately sloughed his tongue along the length of her cheek. Gem closed her eyes tightly; it was worse than being injured and she pushed with all her might, trying to break the contact.

For an instant she felt the length of him against her body and the touch of his body made her mind scream, spurring her into action.

She threw her head back and then brought it forward with such venom that it smashed into his face before he could avoid the blow.

Momentarily stunned, she then pushed with all her might and managed to squeeze out from under him and run to the end of the altar. She checked to see how the others were doing and quickly glancing over to Joel, she saw the look of rage and hatred marring his handsome features.

He had obviously seen what Adam had done to her but was powerless to do anything to help her. So he fought with ferocity against those that he could reach and Gem had to smile at his determination.

There would always be more than enough for him to fight, so long as Adam lived and called them to him.

Suddenly the earth started to move under her feet and she momentarily lost her balance again.

Adam's Master was getting impatient.

As he came in again with sword raised Gem heard a soft whistling noise and the shaft of an arrow protruded through Adam's chest. He howled in pain and anger and turning to see who had fired the shot, he suddenly stood still for a minute as he pulled it from his body. Gem saw that Remne had notched up her last arrow and was making ready to fire it. As she released the arrow, he soared into the air and Gem, who had just regained her feet, had to duck quickly as the arrow whistled past her ear.

He did not make for the high vaulted ceilings as she expected him to; instead he flew over Remne's head. Although nearly exhausted, Gem knew instantly that he had spied the box lying against the far wall and gave chase.

Remne, now with drawn sword, was once again surrounded by dark shades. Battling ceaselessly, Gem heard her offering down a benediction as her sword entered one after the other.

As the beast swept past what remained of the congregation, she heard voices raised in prayer and song as the soldiers battled to keep them safe.

Their numbers were depleting rapidly, but they fought bravely and with conviction. She could hear the different languages mixed with different religions, but they were all asking for the same thing.

Deliverance.

Men were dying around her as she ran down the steps and followed Adam.

She kept her thoughts only on Adam as she stepped over fallen bodies, but she was too late to intercede. She watched helplessly as he picked up the box and raced off; she was powerless to stop him.

Knowing that he would have to come back to the altar to fulfil his covenant to his Master, Gem called across to Joel and Reese as she turned and helped Remne with her attackers.

"He has gone down the Great Cloister; can you manage here?"

"Don't worry about us, we're fine," Reese said.

Standing back to back, Reese and Joel looked as if they had their work cut out for them as more and more shades started to appear.

"I'm fine too. Get going," Remne ordered, throwing herself with gusto into the fight.

Gem raced down to where she had seen the beast disappear and when she turned the corner, there he was.

He had not gone far. He was standing about halfway down the Great Cloister, facing her. He had reverted to the body of the young Canon, and Gem could see he still held the box in his hands, but blood ran freely down his chest where Remne's arrow had pierced him.

He lifted the lid off the box and a look of such perplexity sculptured his beautiful features that Gem found her steps faltering as if she were walking through deep water.

Her sword trailed along the ground as if it was too heavy for her to lift it, but she forced her body forward. His words were carried softly to her: "This is not how it was meant to be."

Lightning and thunder crashed with such ferocity outside that Gem was worried that the windows would shatter. Still she walked towards him. The space between them seemed to stretch out into infinity and she heard her own voice, asking calmly, "Ask forgiveness and I will spare you."

"You know I cannot do that."

The beauty of the young Canon's face brought tears to her eyes, but like everything about him, it was just a mask. Adam had inhabited his body too long to be able to save it and Gem's heart grieved for the young life.

"Give me the box."

"That's just it, Gemini, I can't," he said, holding the empty box out towards her. "You have finally found a way to thwart me. I did not expect you to be so devious. When my man came back, he said your friends had all been killed. How wrong I was to take his word for anything."

"Ask for forgiveness, then. Come back to where you belong, before you fell from grace."

"That was so long ago. I loved you then and it was that love that made me fall. There is nothing you can do for me now, Gemini."

As he stared down at the empty box, he suddenly lifted his head as if a voice that only he could hear had called him. As the shadows plucked at his features Gem thought she saw traces of tears upon his cheeks, but she could not be sure in the dim light.

The young Canon then turned to look down towards the Chapter House and the look of perplexity was replaced by one of fury and indignation.

What had he seen? thought Gem, fighting against her inability to move.

Turning back to face Gemini, he shouted at her as his anger exploded, forcing him to change back into the beast.

"You thought to trick me, bitch! But I can still release my Master."

Gem watched as he stamped off, his talons tearing at the flagstones, not towards her as she had expected but along the corridor that had suddenly taken up all his attention.

She was unsure what had led to this sudden turn of events, but she had to find out and quickly. Finding herself no longer walking as if in slow motion, things had suddenly and dramatically reverted to real time.

She finally reached the spot where he had been standing and it felt as if a cold hand had clutched her heart as she saw him making his way towards where a slim young girl was sitting, facing the door.

Cradled in her lap was a small olive box with carving on the side and lid, identical to the one that the beast had thrown to the floor in his rage.

Her dark, sightless eyes held no fear within their lifeless depths, but as Gem raced towards her, she was amazed to see a smile forming on her beloved friend's lips.

"Beth!" she cried. "Run! The Beast is nearly upon you ..."

Her warning seemed to go unheeded and as the beast entered the Chapter House the great doors banged shut behind him and Gem was powerless to open them.

She tried to prise them apart with her sword, but they would not move. She heaved her shoulder against them but to no avail. Knowing that her efforts were futile and ineffectual, she resorted to banging her fists upon the sturdy door for want for something to do.

"Don't hurt her ... please don't hurt her."

Her pleas turned to sobs as she slowly sank to the floor. Her fists still beat ineffectually against the door, but she knew all was lost and her heart felt like breaking because of it.

Then suddenly, through all the cracks and crevices, there came a blinding white light. The light was so strong that as Gem banged on the door a violent heat radiated through and seared her hands.

Thousands of voices seemed to ring in her head and the beating of wings surrounded her as she slumped to the floor. She managed to cover her ears with her hands and curled herself up into a foetal position to protect herself.

As swiftly as it came, it went and as she staggered to her knees, the doors suddenly opened and there before her was Beth, still sitting upon the chair as if nothing had happened but standing before her ... was the beast.

Blood ran from his eyes and ears and he shook his great head as he tried to clear his vision.

A strange light still clung to Beth; it spiralled around her like a living entity ... protecting her. Then it slowly became absorbed into her body, until nothing remained.

Gem grabbed her sword and moving swiftly around his slumped frame, she positioned herself between Beth and the beast. There was no time to evaluate the situation; she extended her wings and stood majestically before him and plunged her sword deep within his cold and evil heart.

As the beast fell to his knees, Joel and Reese bounded together through the door, followed closely on their heels by Remne.

The four of them finally stood together, each one representing the angel on the hilt of their swords. Now the true meaning of their work became apparent and through this unity they stood as the Guardians.

They stood in a circle round the kneeling form and each unfolded their wings, then thrusting together as one, their swords entered into the prone figure.

A mighty howl tore from the beast's lips as it slumped to the ground.

This time Gem was not going to take any more chances and as she raised her sword high above her head. The beast's face turned once again to the young Canon and his beauty momentarily stayed her hand. His lips formed her name and as the blood frothed at his mouth she heard him whisper, "I thought it was the Book ... they were protecting ... I did not contemplate ... for one minute it was Beth and to think I had her in my grasp the whole time ..." As he coughed a large well of blood gushed from between his lips. "Time will tell if ... you have won, Gemini ..."

The young Canon's back arched suddenly and his legs flayed around as he summoned up the great beast within him. They watched as the Canon's face was replaced with the vile and hideous features of its host. Now that it was back to its unnatural appearance it turned its large head in her direction. She saw the slash of a mouth start to smile as his lips formed her name and then without waiting for the words to reach her ears, she brought her sword down with such force that the head rolled cleanly from his body.

Blood gushed from the neck and spread wetly across the floor. It pooled around the torso in large viscous puddles. This time, though, there were no silver hands to drag it down to safety and as they all stood round in a circle they watched as the body twitched in its last death throes. Then before their eyes they saw diaphanous spirals of mist swirl around the fallen body and lift it into the air. They each stepped back in stunned amazement when the overpowering smell of sulphur assailed their nostrils. Gem could hear the others gasping for breath as the monstrous body disintegrated before them, each piece and particle gathered up into the gossamer-like haze. As Gem looked closely she could just make out shapes and figures flying amongst the swirls. Faces and hands were momentarily shown to her as the Death Angels gathered up all the remains.

Turning to Reese, she saw that she was smiling and talking to someone that she alone could see. Then just as suddenly as it appeared the mist was gone ... and so was the body of the beast.

"I take it the rest of the shades are gone," Gem said.

"Yep," said Joel, wiping his sword across his knee. "They disappeared as soon as that light appeared. Scared the hell out of me as well, I can tell you."

They all seemed a little shaken by what had occurred and Gem did not want to dwell on Adam's parting words. She felt the wrath and hatred draining out of her and as she watched the others starting to relax she turned and knelt down in front of Beth.

Streams of golden light glittered through the stained glass window as the sun tore through the disappearing clouds. It sparkled and danced off Gem's sword as she placed it on the floor beside her. Quiet now ... its war song finally over.

The room then became awash with luminous, brilliant light, its healing beams shining into every window of the abbey. Gem placed her hands on Beth's knees.

"Is this what I think it is?" she said, tapping the top of the box.

"Yes it is and I'm sorry I lied to you all. I couldn't tell you what I was doing, because you might have stopped me. I couldn't chance not being in the right place at the right time. There were two boxes when we went to Glastonbury. One held the cup and the other the cruets, so I just placed them in the one box. When I handed the empty box over to that odious person in the tunnel, I knew he would not look inside. He would not dare."

"But why this place, how did you know he would find you here?"

"Look around, Gem. Look at the walls. He had to come here; the Book said so. It was the combination of me, this room and the relics that gave off the power to defeat him."

As Gem looked around, there upon the wall were paintings from the book of Revelations, the same pictures that decorated the Book.

"He would not have been affected if he opened the box in the abbey; he could easily have called his Master to him."

As Gem listened to all what Beth was saying, everything that had happened finally fell into place.

It was Beth who was the centre of all this, she was the chosen one; they were her Guardians, banded together through fate to protect her in this final battle.

No wonder she had not told anyone, who could she trust? They all could have stopped her one way or the other, if out of love, if nothing else.

She had guided them to do the right thing and as she looked at her friend she realised that if Beth had not been abducted, she would not have been blinded. Then she would not have been able to sit here and expose the holy relics with no ill effect.

God indeed works in mysterious ways.

All along she had thought it was all to do with herself and that she had to protect the Book, but she had been so very wrong. It was Beth who was the most important person in this room. It was she who had forgone protection to fulfil her own destiny. Beth placed the box on the ground next to her and Gem rested her head in her lap and said, "Can you forgive me?"

Beth's hand stroked the top of Gem's head, but before she could answer, a pale-looking Nathan rushed into the room. Gem straightened up out of the way, as he pulled Beth to her feet. Then he gathered her into his arms.

Tears coursed down his face and it was obvious to all that he thought he had lost her again.

Remne tapped him on the shoulder and as he turned to face her, he pulled Beth close to his body as if she still needed protection.

"How are things out there?"

"Not bad. Catholic is talking to Protestant and Jew is talking to Muslim and they are all helping the fallen. So perhaps some good will come out of all this."

"Let's hope so."

As she turned away from Nathan her gaze fell on the little olive box with carvings on the side and lid and the furrow between her eyes deepened.

Joel extended his hand to help Gem to her feet, but the sadness that overwhelmed her made her shun his outstretched hand.

Not taking no for an answer, he reached down, placed a hand under her arm and then forced her to her feet. He could feel her body shake with emotion.

"There was nothing else you could do," he said, "everyone's path was written for them. You could not save Beth any more than you could save Mahala."

Gem heard Beth's voice as Nathan went to carry her from the room.

"Gem, darling, there is nothing to forgive. Trust me; I love you too much to want you to think any of this was your fault. I welcomed my fate."

The tears when they came washed down Gem's face in great healing streaks. Joel crushed her body to his and swore to himself that he would never let her go again.

Finally he could let her see how much she meant to him. He had nearly died himself when he had seen her in the clutches of that beast. It rankled with him still that he had been unable to help her, so he knew how she was feeling towards Beth.

As her sobs started to subside she raised her face and Joel covered it with kisses. Finally he got a small smile from her and as she tightened her grip around his waist, she said, suddenly serious, "Is it all over?"

Just at that moment, Thomas, the big yellow cat, came bounding into the room.

Beth wriggled in Nathan's arms so that he eventually had to lower her to the floor. As soon as her feet touched the ground, the large cat came and sat next to her and proceeded to wash the blood from his fur.

As Beth rested a hand on his big yellow head she smiled up at them and said, "It is now."

Chapter 42

The wedding of Nathan and Beth took place that Christmas. All his friends in the police force formed the guard of honour when they exited the old church. Although he had left the force in early December like he promised, he was still held in high esteem and affection.

Beth, to the amazement of her doctors, had regained some sight back in one of her eyes, but they did not hold out any hope for a complete recovery.

"Who knows?" she said to Gem when they came out of the hospital together after the visit, "Stranger things have happened."

Gem still worried and fussed over Beth's health and although she had gained some weight she was still not back to full fitness; she worried that all the arrangements for her forthcoming wedding were taking their toll on her.

Now as Gem stood and watched the happiness dance around on Beth's face as she accepted the congratulations from their friends, she could not have been happier for them both.

After the last few months of tying up all the loose ends, they all deserved to relax.

She'd had enough of government officials and religious officials asking awkward questions.

At least one question had been answered though and she found herself thinking about that day once again.

After the battle in the abbey, the mystery of how the cat was covered in blood was solved when the army did a sweep of the church. At first they thought it was one of the Catholic clergy who had taken shelter in a side chapel at the end of the nave.

The look on the dead man's face forced a couple of the battle-hardened veterans to turn away in horror. Long deep scratches ran the length of the old bishop's torso and they found bite marks on his hands where he had obviously tried, in vain, to defend himself. The soldiers had called Gem and the others to help identify the body and Reese gave her usual whoop of delight when she saw it was the odious man from the tunnel.

They had each patted the contented cat in turn and praised him for his bravery and resolution in finding his quarry.

As for the little olive box, it was just too powerful an item to be given to any one particular religion. It was only their group and Nathan, who knew the relics even existed. Gem had seen the worried look on Remne's face as they contemplated what would happen if it fell into the wrong hands.

The others did not want to know what Gem was doing with the box and wisely Reese pointed out that the fewer people who knew the better.

So one cold December morning, Remne and she travelled to a cold and deserted heath land, situated near a lake that looked like glass.

Two wild rose bushes were growing in the cold and brittle soil, their delicate branches straining upwards to catch the early morning sunshine. Their growth was intertwined, covering the ground with prickly stems.

Gem parted the frozen soil with her sword, making it as deep as possible.

Then carefully she lowered the small olive box down into the ground. She had tied a thin line around it so that it went far into the earth and when she was satisfied that it was deep enough, she let go of the string.

As she smote the ground once more to close it up, Remne heard her gently say, "Take good care of it, Mum and Dad. I leave it in your hands. God bless you and I love you."

They walked away arm in arm, happy in the knowledge that the covenant that Gem had put on the land meant it would never be disturbed or go out of the family.

"Do you think the Guardians will ever be needed again?" Gem asked as they strolled back towards the ruined house.

"Who knows, Gem? The only thing I can tell you is that if we are ever called again, I for one will be more than ready."

"You really surprised me. I thought you would not take to the warrior life at all. Just goes to show, you can't always tell about people. As for Beth, we can take it in turns to look out for her and protect her. She is such a special person and now that she has teamed up with Nathan, there will be no stopping the pair of them. I've given them my house in York as a wedding present and they are going to turn it into a place of religious learning. I wish them well; a lot of tolerance and understanding is going to be needed to bring all the religious factions together, but if anyone can do it, they can."

As they walked through the garden they saw Joel through what was left of the upright beams of the derelict house. He had a sketch pad in one hand and was deeply engrossed in what he was doing.

Gem had decided to build a new house where the old one had stood finally giving in to the love of the land and her memories of the place. Joel had agreed to design it and even here she had to smile because she had finally found the love she had been searching for. There was no need for secrets with Joel, he knew all there was to know about her. Her identity, like his, was not a burden between them. She loved him with all her heart, as she did her sister, but he was so preoccupied lately that sometimes she felt the overwhelming need to jump in her car and slam the gas pedal to the floor in frustration.

They had both talked about their life together and had agreed that they wanted Remne to come and live with them when the house was finished; she had thanked them for the offer but declined.

She preferred her boat and besides, Thomas, who with feline diplomacy had once more switched his allegiance back to Remne, had never lived in a house for too long. He liked to hunt along the river bank and was getting too old to change. Remne would visit as often as possible, but she liked the gently leisurely pace on the water.

Now a month had passed and here they all were together. As Gem looked about her at everyone enjoying themselves at the wedding, her heart grew heavy as she remembered that she had not seen or spoken to Joel for nearly a week. She had expected to see him at the wedding, but as she looked around she could not see his tall muscular frame.

Reese was there, though, bubbling enthusiasm as usual. The hospital had offered her old job back, but she had refused. She had seen too much of death and destruction, she wanted peace. Now was the time for something new and it was with great pride that she told them as they sat round the table at the reception that she was going to work in Africa for three years.

"I am going to help build an orphanage in memory of my husband and daughter. It is where I can give all this love I have," she said, patting her chest to indicate her heart; her voice cracked slightly with emotion as she concluded, "to all the unwanted little children. I have all this love inside of me that is just bursting to get out and it needed an outlet and at last I have found it. I am going to call it Hope Orphanage and all contributions for work or donations will be greatly appreciated."

Remne got up and walked round the table and hugged her.

"I knew you would find the right path to follow. You just had to give yourself time. Speaking of which, where is Joel, Gem?"

"I don't know. In fact if you must know, he proposed to me last week and I rejected him. I told him he was the most unromantic person I had ever met and I haven't seen him since."

"Why on earth did you do a stupid thing like that?" asked Reese.

"I don't know, okay? I was annoyed and I panicked. I did not expect him to ask, especially as we haven't … you know … done anything."

"Oh come here," said Remne, giving her a squeeze. "You are such an idiot, the most stubborn and pig-headed person I know. Good job. I'm your sister and love you."

"Do you think I frightened him off?"

"How should we know?" chipped in Reese, delighted now that the party was starting to get more interesting. Beth and Nathan came over and sat at the table and Nathan was finding it hard to keep a straight face.

Then the lights in the hall dimmed and the band started to play. A lone spotlight twirled around the floor and a baritone voice started to sing, it was deep and sexy; very different from the singer who was on before. Reese jumped up and down in her seat, clapping her hand with excitement. Remne, who had been standing next to Gem's chair when the music started suddenly pulled at Gem's arm, forcing her to stand up.

The spotlight centred on Gem as she moved forward and still the words of the song came floating down to her pulling her towards the middle of the dance floor.

She started to hesitate and looked over her shoulder throwing Remne a look of bewilderment. Remne strode towards her and gave her a little shove and sent her sister in the direction of the band.

The stage was plunged in darkness as the spotlight stayed upon her so she was unaware of the singer jumping down from the stage and was making his way towards her. She looked once more over her shoulder and when she turned back round Joel was standing in front of her singing the last bars of the love song. Tears started to run down her face as Joel got down on one knee and said, "Gemini Hawker will you marry me, because it has taken me a week to learn this song and I am not getting off my knee's until you say yes.

Gem grazed lovingly down at him and nodded her head. "Is that a yes?" said Joel jumping to his feet.

"Yes, yes." Whispered Gem through her tears her chin wobbling so much she found it difficult to get the words out.

"That's all I wanted to hear." He said as he enveloped his in his arms.

About the Author

Jacqueline Bell was born in the county of Kent in the UK but now lives on the beautiful island of Gozo in the Mediterranean. She lives there with her husband, their Pekingese a Shih Tzu puppy and a rescued cat. Although she writes continuously, this is her debut novel.

Lightning Source UK Ltd.
Milton Keynes UK
UKOW051210180713

214012UK00001B/62/P